Some Day My Prince Will .com

Some Day My Prince Will .com

By Dianne Purdie with David Purdie

Order this book online at www.trafford.com
or email orders@trafford.com

Most Trafford titles are also available at major online book retailers.

Note for Librarians: A cataloguing record for this book is available from Library
and Archives Canada at www.collectionscanada.ca/amicus/index-e.html

Printed in Victoria, BC, Canada.

ISBN: 978-1-4269-1550-5 (Soft)

Library of Congress Control Number: 2009934820

*We at Trafford believe that it is the responsibility of us all, as both individuals
and corporations, to make choices that are environmentally and socially sound.
You, in turn, are supporting this responsible conduct each time you purchase a
Trafford book, or make use of our publishing services. To find out how you are
helping, please visit www.trafford.com/responsiblepublishing.html*

*Our mission is to efficiently provide the world's finest, most comprehensive
book publishing service, enabling every author to experience success.
To find out how to publish your book, your way, and have it available
worldwide, visit us online at www.trafford.com*

Trafford rev. 9/25/2009

 www.trafford.com

North America & international
toll-free: 1 888 232 4444 (USA & Canada)
phone: 250 383 6864 ♦ fax: 812 355 4082 ♦ email: info@trafford.com

For David – my soul mate and twin flame

And to everybody who is looking for theirs

Acknowledgments and Important Notes

This book has been a very long time coming as it has been over ten years since David's first email to me. So who has made this book possible? Well, first would be my soul mate and co-author David Purdie (he wrote half the emails). Without him this would be a very different story. I've always had a book in me but it would not have been this one. Thank you my love for finding me.

I started this book and put it down countless times. There were always other things that needed to be done or my mood wasn't right. I needed to be "in the flow" to do this. The eccentric woman you will read about is actually a mild mannered legal secretary now and I have my law firm, asb law, to thank for allowing me to work all of my full time hours in four days so I can stay home and write on Fridays. This has allowed me to finally finish this book that is so important to me. Thank you asb law. (There is a second book so I still need Fridays off.)

Janet Cunningham of Heritage Authors has been my editor and her help has been invaluable to me. Janet has been a speaker on my cruises that you will read about and she knows me very well. She has also cruised with David and knows him quite well. Because of her intimate knowledge of us she has seen things that other editors wouldn't see and her gentle suggestions of how to make it better have been so appreciated. I have really loved working with Janet and thank her so much for all she has done both in her overall review and in her line editing as well as in her friendship.

Janet and I have laughed about the subtle differences in US and UK English. I have made it a point to write in US English, as ten years ago I was very much American. All of David's writing in the book is in UK English. So I must ask my American readers to not think he is illiterate or my editor has not edited. I must also ask my British readers, particularly my friends and colleagues who think I have come so far in speaking and writing in English to allow me my American spelling and talking for purposes of this book. The truth is, having been here for so many years (can't tell you how many or I'll give away the next book), the British way sounds and looks correct to me and Janet has had to edit out all my British spellings, most noticeably the word "realise" in England which is "realize" in America.

The British sense of humor is also a difficult one for Americans who aren't used to it. It is very dry and understated. For example, there is one place where David says "Why would I want a green card? I'm British." I say that you really have to understand the British people to understand what he is saying. As he used to explain to me when I first moved there, Britain used to rule the world (most of the map was pink). There is a bit of soft spoken and not necessarily serious superiority in their attitude that America was their colony until we threw their tea into the water in Boston. British people don't think of themselves as foreign wherever they are; everybody else is foreign. I have probably done a poor job of explaining that but it is my feeble attempt to explain one aspect of the British sense of humor. I hope my American readers will enjoy David's writing even if they don't understand it all. I was obviously charmed by it.

The very talented artist of "The Enchanted Frog" on the front cover is Jaime' Christina Wren. The way I met her is an example of synchronicity in action. I was supposed to be having a night out with three of my work colleagues/friends to have dinner and see the play "Menopause The Musical." Two of my friends couldn't make it at the last minute so I suggested to Jacqui that she bring her daughter as I had enjoyed seeing that play in Florida with my own daughter, and I would bring my husband. It turned out that both David and Jaime' are artists. Jaime' wants to be an illustrator and David was short on time to do the cover picture himself so I told Jaime' the concept and she said she would do some sketches for me. The result speaks for itself. Thank you Jaime' "The Enchanted Frog" is perfect and you have a great future ahead of you.

Two close friends, Paula Tiara and Addie Bambridge have read the entire book and given me feedback on everything from misspelled words to content that they thought might have been better said a bit differently. They have also encouraged me, laughed with me and kept me going. Another close friend, Beth Hunter has read a lot of the chapters and has been such an inspiration to me to keep telling my story. She has been my own personal fan club about my writing style, honesty and the depth of the story. Her own story has in many ways paralleled mine although she lived in England with her first husband. Beth has a book in her too that I hope one day she will write and I can encourage her. A big thank you to Paula, Addie and Beth.

This book is all true but I have changed some names (most specifically ex-husbands) and because I've done that to protect privacy I have also changed my daughters' names and my parents' names again to protect privacy. Their pictures are in the book though with my first ex-husband's permission. You will read about my wonderful daughters in the book and a letter my younger daughter Nicki wrote to me is in the conclusion. I printed out an unedited version for each of them a few months ago and they have both helped with very valuable feedback. Nicki was busy finishing her masters degree, so more of the recent help came from Marley who provided valuable input that my editor Janet agreed with. Thank you girls for all you have done and still do for me. You aren't just daughters you are my best friends.

My step-daughters Vickie and Rachel have been helpful and supportive as well (their names are unchanged). Rachel even gave me the great idea when I thought I would never finish this book to end it at the turn of the millennium and start the second book where this one leaves off. Thanks for that Rachel.

My parents have helped to make me the person I am today, with my unique personality. Their support and encouragement have been a constant in my life. I have described them as challenges in the book but want them to know I love them and am grateful for their great love for me, and my daughters.

I am grateful for my "cast of characters", most, but not all of them talked about in chapter eight. You are all unique and do make this quite a story.

I am grateful to you, my readers, and hope you find value in my life lessons to move on in spite of deep pain. Life is about change, growing, and not being afraid to live and love even if you have been hurt in the past. My story is like a fairy tale, hence my enchanted frog on the cover. Your story can be the same. Just stay optimistic and happy and open to the infinite possibilities that exist for you.

Please note that the email addresses in this book are no longer in use but we can be contacted through our web site www.somedaymyprincewill.com. We do offer coaching services for writing your profile online and for envisioning and nurturing the right relationship for you.

Endorsements

"In Some Day My Prince Will .com, Dianne Purdie has written her true story of "kissing a lot of frogs" before finding her prince. After two failed marriages and with young children, Dianne enters the arena of internet dating where she begins writing to a man by the name of David in England. E-mail communication gives the opportunity for deep discussions about metaphysical concepts as well as sharing the humdrum activities of life with someone who listens and cares. Readers will discover the blatant honesty that both Dianne and David express before they meet... preparing the way for truth that few couples attain. A delightful and magical story."

Janet Cunningham, Ph.D., internationally-known specialist in regression therapy and author of 10 books, including *Caution: Soul Mate Ahead!* and *The Upward Spiral: Breakthroughs to Joy*. www.JanetCunningham.com and www.HeritageAuthors.com

"Everyone who knows Dianne and David know they belong together and everyone who has loved knows how challenging finding your divine right partner can be. Despite living on two different continents, the technologies of internet and intuition brought them together. A beauty-filled story that restores your faith in true love."

Shola Arewa, Author of Opening to Spirit and Energy 4 Life, Spiritual Coach and International Speaker. www.shola.co.uk

"I met Dianne many years ago when she booked me as a guest speaker on a Dreamtime Cruise. She was charismatic, dynamic and spiritual ....an impressive combination. But it wasn't until she met David that I watched her step into her power and her completeness of being. Their love story is one of courage, persistence and proof that true love conquers all obstacles. This book will make you a believer in the power of love and Spirit and how they can unite us all."

Kathryn Harwig is an internationally known speaker and author who has written seven books and travels the world teaching intuitive development. You can learn more or contact her at www. harwig.com

"I have been on two cruises with Dianne and David when Dianne booked me as a guest speaker on Dreamtime Cruises. Dianne's love story of meeting her twin soul David shows that anything is possible, that dreams really do come true no matter where you live and how far away you are. Dianne's book is an inspiration to us all to dream our dreams and bring them into reality. She shows us that love is the most powerful force there is."

Carmel Greenwood is an internationally known speaker and author who has written three books, Letting Go & Loving Life, Soul Energy and Wake Up Mum – drugs are stealing our children. www.carmelconcepts.com

"Dianne gently and movingly reminds us of how we have a choice in approaching life's lessons. Her style of writing carries us with her on her quest for love and how David and Dianne found each other – again. In this technological age, it seems only fitting for this true fairy tale to be .com. I highly recommend this book and look forward to the second one which takes Dianne to England."

Amantha Murphy is a shamanic healer and teacher who follows the path of the Goddess. She facilitates workshops worldwide and leads sacred pilgrimages in Ireland. www.celticsouljourneys.com

Table of Contents

Introduction

Do you believe in synchronicity and destiny, mixed in with some well deserved good karma? Well I do.

It was 1999. I was a single mother of two wonderful teenage girls and I owned my own business, Dreamtime Cruises & Tours, which created, sold and marketed new age spiritual, personal development and holistic seminars at sea on cruise ships. I had actually created a very nice life for myself if you didn't look too far beneath the surface and see my debt and other business problems, my problems with men, my challenges with my parents accepting me for who I am, etc.

My life was very busy and I had no time or interest in meeting men through the bar scene or any other scene for that matter. The very best way for me as I enjoy both writing and reading was getting to know people through their emails on match.com. In 1999 internet dating was still relatively new and not as high tech as it is now. You couldn't wink at people or anything fancy like that but you could search under certain parameters for somebody to email. I had actually been dating somebody for the past year whom I met on match.com but for various reasons that I discuss in the book, he was not "the one" and I was ready to find somebody else. I had learned so many lessons in dating (and marriage) and really felt ready to attract to myself my highest and best mate. That was my affirmation and I did believe it would happen. I thought I would dip my toes in the water again and see who would bite so I signed on to match.com again, this time for only a 7-day trial membership.

Well David wrote to me and there was an instant interest on both of our parts and a knowing that we had a lot in common and would enjoy writing to each other. Before the 7 days expired David and I had exchanged personal email addresses and that would be my last time on match.com. I didn't know on June 29th 1999 that I had just "met" my husband to be (who by the way lived in England) but I had a very, very good feeling about him.

This is a multifaceted book. On the one hand it is a story of an internet romance that caused me to follow my heart to England, get married for the third time and create a whole new life. This book also flashes back to my life before meeting David. Chapters 2, 4, 6, 8 and 10 are all flashback chapters.

This is also a book about finding the right career, following my passion in business and creating the life of my dreams. It is an honest book that follows me as I flash back through two marriages and divorces, being a single mother of two girls and my unique relationship with them, my financial challenges and my struggles with my parents to understand and accept me for who I am. But above all, it is a spiritual book full of lessons learned and still being learned about unconditional love, giving and receiving, trusting, not resisting, co-creating with the universe or God, forgiving, overcoming guilt, healing our wounds so we don't keep repeating the same mistakes over and over again, accepting ourselves and loving ourselves, and connecting with others on a soul level. It is about synchronicity and destiny and how much of a difference one person can make.

David's story is here too and interwoven into the book. We created this book to help raise the consciousness of humanity to the possibility that anything is possible, that dreams really do come true, that our challenges are our greatest stepping stones and teachers and that we are all worthy and capable of creating heaven on earth. Imagine if we all did that.........

We live in challenging times for many reasons and we are currently in the midst of a global recession that is affecting many relationships. People are turning to alternative sources of income and many don't have the time or the money for traditional dating. I truly believe that internet dating is the answer and that it can work as well for you as it did for us.

David and I each sent approximately 200 emails to each other before we met in person (almost 5 months after the 1st email). We told each other our stories of our past and present and our hopes for the future. You can read all of that in this book.

Why not read this, be inspired and try it yourself. If you believe, like we do, that anything is possible, then someday your prince (or princess) will also .com.

The story behind the story

I remember being a little girl in the 50s and playing with my Barbie and Ken dolls. They would kiss, say nice things to each other, get married and live happily ever after, as people did in the 50s. I had a Barbie house and a Barbie car, Barbie's friend Midge and her little sister Skipper. Life was so simple then. Mothers didn't work, there were no computers, fathers worked in the same steady jobs and life was predictable. I remember my mother reading to me a lot. I used to love the fairy tales where a frog turned into a handsome prince, a prince woke a sleeping beauty or a fairy godmother waved her magic wand and rags turned into a beautiful ball gown. The best bit was that everybody lived happily ever after........

Well, I'm happy to report that my parents did, and still are, living happily ever after. They have been married 63 years so far and although they watch TV in separate rooms and bicker a bit over this and that, it is evident that they are as in love as the day they met.

Me, well, it wasn't as easy for me, or for many people in my generation of baby boomers. People younger than me weren't finding it easy either. Sure, we were liberated as women, which our mothers weren't. We had it all – husbands, careers, babies. We were exhausted! The 80s brought in greed, and the baby boomers became the "me" generation, entitled to it all, but very often at the expense of one's husband or wife as all of us felt entitled to having the perfect life and we blamed our lack of it and our unhappiness on somebody outside of ourselves. Divorce was rampant. The term "work life balance" had not yet been invented, or if it had, I hadn't heard of it. I worked very hard as you will read, trying to have it all. The truth both then and today is it is a very difficult balance and very often one of the three loses out. It is more often the marriage than it is the children or the career.

The 80s brought my first divorce and the 90s brought my second one. I was a single mother for most of my daughters' growing up years.

I have always been a positive thinker and a believer in the law of attraction and the fact that our beliefs create our reality. This made me see most challenges as growth and learning opportunities and something I must have drawn to myself for my further development. Although, I must admit, sometimes I did get stuck in the present moment heartbreak or problem and I had to keep reminding myself that when one door closes another one opens and that I was exactly where I needed to be to allow that new beginning to occur. This book looks back on these times and relives them with the goal always in mind of letting go, forgiving and knowing that something really good is going to happen soon.

David and I are true twin flame soul mates and we seem to have the same life lessons. Of all the achievements I have had in my life, I have to say that succeeding in a loving relationship is the biggest one. I wish this success for everybody. If I can do it so can you!

Chapter One
A Memorable Email

It was both the 29th of June and the 30th, 1999, when a letter arrived in my email box from match.com, forwarding to me a message from forposta. It was sent from England on the 30th and arrived in Florida still the 29th. I had just rejoined match. com after dating through it and other internet dating services for the past year and a half. I certainly had plenty to do with a business and being a single mother of two teenage girls but this was my diversion. I would happily tell the girls in the office when a "boy" wrote to me. I hadn't been on the site for almost a year and I was hungry for the opportunity to take my mind off of business problems, teenage girl problems and the mini-sadness I was feeling. Nothing major, just a bit of a cloud over my head; some say the upcoming eclipse in the summer of 99 was affecting all Aquarians like this. This was a free 7-day trial membership, just to see if anybody who could be meant for me was out there. I didn't spend a lot of time on this profile as I had on profiles in the past as I wasn't sure I'd go beyond the trial membership this time; I didn't really know if I was in the mood this summer. My name before was SeaGoddess but I couldn't go back with the same name (some silly rule) so I had to change it slightly. If I met somebody in this little 7 day period I'd be surprised.

My profile: aquarianCgoddess
Creative, Passionate and Soulful 45 year old female, located in Central Florida, seeking 39 to 59 year old male.

I'm not an average woman and you wouldn't be an average man. I'm self employed in a creative career and live life in a passionate way. I'm a single mother of two really cool teenage girls. My interests include reading, writing, travel (especially cruises) and spiritual and metaphysical learning and seeking. I have long dark hair (kind of a witch/goddess look). You would be an intelligent, passionate man, also on a spiritual path. You are successful (in your own eyes) in all aspects of your life, sensitive and intuitive. I would find you handsome. Our personal chemistry is good. I eagerly await your arrival.

*   *   *   *

In previous versions I had added that I'm now happy and complete within myself but the right man would be the icing on the cake. I wasn't all that happy at this moment and couldn't honestly say that, so I didn't. One thing was clear with me and internet dating, and that was that I would always be completely honest and would use my intuition to tell that I was writing to somebody who also had that desire. I felt that once you are in your 40's, have been married at least once (twice in my case), and on a spiritual path, you can really get to know somebody on a soul level by writing to them – as long as both people are clear in their desire for complete honesty.

In the evening on the 29th of June, 1999, (I think 2 days after I had posted my profile), I received from forposta@match.com:

*   *   *   *

Hi Goddess
You sound wonderful….

I have no idea whether I am your man or not, maybe my profile will help.

I have a successful and unique business on the other side of the Atlantic (England).

I have an interest in the spiritual and have total faith in our ability to succeed at anything we want enough.

I have a large feminine side to my masculine nature, in my artistic/creative and caring nature. I have often been told that I am a good listener with a good ability to analyse situations, and feedback good and effective solutions to personal problems (except my own).

I too have 2 girls, however mine are 20 and 22, probably older than yours....but just as important to me.

Hoping you find this interesting enough to read the profile and contact me.

Very best wishes

David

* * * *

Wow! Very interesting to say the least. I was only searching in Florida, this man was obviously searching a bit further from his home base. Just the few words he said here spoke to me in a very good way. Owns a unique business, good, so do I. Interest in the spiritual, positive and success oriented, very good. I'd found that so many men who were spiritual tended to be airy fairy and not have any real connection to the business world which is definitely something I need in a man (head in the clouds but feet planted firmly on the ground). Husband number one for me had his feet on the ground (a bit too firmly) and husband number two was all in the clouds! I knew that now I wanted a man who had both. So far so good. Strong feminine side, artistic, creative and caring. Excellent! Admits he isn't as good with his own problems. Honest! Two daughters, great gives us a bit more of a common ground. Good thing they are grown! Important to him, very good. Yes! This man has definitely inspired my interest to read his profile!

*   *   *   *

His profile: forposta
David is looking for a lovely woman with Intelligence, Sense of
Humour and Sensuality
45 year-old male located in West Sussex, England, seeking 30 to
49 year-old female.

I am a very happy, hard working and positive person, who
is looking for a desirable woman to start by being an e-friend,
and hopefully progress into a long term relationship. Adventure
is the key….a voyage into the unknown. I am looking for an
equal relationship, I love giving and have no limits, I don't look
for short term returns, but I do expect a fair amount of affection
(this doesn't necessarily mean sex). I do things in a different
way to most people and that's how I have managed to create
a unique company in the Electronics Industry that performs
special services that are not available anywhere else in the world.
I am creative, designing and making stained glass windows and
3D objects as a hobby with a view to a second business. I   drive
a Jaguar and have a Kawasaki 550GT motorcycle and love the
freedom of travel. I enjoy food, both cooking and eating, whether
a romantic dinner in, or a top class establishment. I also like
renovating the flat, gardening, cooking special meals for two and
any other creative activity. I am not happy sitting doing nothing,
unless it is with someone very special where doing nothing is
actually doing loads under the surface. Additionally I have passed
my Advanced Driving test and will be aiming at doing the same
with the motorcycle. Long distance visiting is not a big problem
to me. I look forward to hearing from an attractive woman who
wants a man that is not a dictator but more of a supporter and
good friend. Please contact me if this is you!

*   *   *   *

*His physical description was 5 ft. 7 in., a few extra pounds
(cuddly) and his picture showed a nice man, warm smile, with short*

*brown hair and a bit of a belly. My first husband was only 5 ft. 5 ½
inches and I'm only 5 ft 2 inches so height isn't a problem. The type
of man I'm usually attracted to is dark hair and eyes, a Spanish or
Italian look. From picture alone, in the past I wouldn't have selected
him. However, besides the fact that all the good looking men leave me,
I was now open to looking with my heart and my intuition and seeing
way beyond what the person's initial physical appearance would have
said. I actually did find him attractive. He had a gentle loving energy
about him and looked like a huggable teddy bear. Besides, I have a
belly too! Who am I to make that a criterion for selection? I looked
at his picture with his words in mind; looking for an equal partner,
happy, hard working and positive, gives and receives affection (so
many men can't receive real affection), likes to cuddle, likes to cook!
Bingo! I hate to cook. I looked at him and asked his picture would you
honor both the sensual me and the businesswoman me. His picture
and his smile said yes.*

I responded to him immediately:

*   *   *   *

Hi David

I absolutely find your profile and your note interesting enough
to read and to contact you! You sound wonderful too! Tell me
about your unique company that performs special services that
are not available anywhere else in the world. You have me very
curious! My company is Dreamtime Cruises & Tours and I do
spiritual, metaphysical, holistic and personal growth seminars and
conferences on cruise ships. The next one is August 22nd sailing
from Los Angeles to the Mexican Riviera. Want to come? I still
have one man needing a roommate or there are still a few cabins
left if you want your own. My cruises are 70% single women so
you'd be very popular although I might not want to share you. I'm
very affectionate and giving. I like that about you (that you like
to both give and receive it). Congratulations on having 2 girls 20
and 22. You survived the teen years. I'll bet you are a wonderful

father. Mine are at an interesting age, 13 and 15. For the most part I really enjoy them, but I do enjoy my quiet times when they are with their dad on the weekends.

I'm glad you wrote David, I'm looking forward to knowing you more.

Warm hugs

Dianne

*   *   *   *

Eeek! I was trying to sell him a cruise! How crazy is that! I guess I was proud of what I do, the business I had created and I wanted to tell him about it. Plus, coming on one of my cruises would be a great way for us to meet. This man definitely touched me in a special way. Could this be why I had a desire to sign back on match.com for 7 days only? Is this a very strong example of synchronicity that I so strongly believe in? There are no coincidences or mistakes. But he lives in England! He is geographically challenged. I do love England though. I've felt an affinity, sort of like a past life connection to the British Isles ever since going there for the first time on one of my cruises in the summer of 1997. But I can't move to England, I have two very American teenagers. Is it worth pursuing this? ....

*   *   *   *

Chapter Two

Who Am I Anyway
The End of My First Dream

Born February 9th 1954, I'm from the generation that has, at least in the US, had the longest adolescence in the history of mankind. My generation has found it acceptable to "find ourselves." Our parents stayed married to the same person, and the husband worked for the same company for 50 years. The wife stayed home until the children were for the most part grown before finding work outside of the home. They saved and bought things when they could afford it. We find it acceptable to decide one day that we aren't happy and honor ourselves while dishonoring all previous commitments. At least that is what we did in the 80's and 90's which is when most of my story that I'm sharing in this book took place. Most of my generation, and I'm certainly no exception, wouldn't dream of waiting to buy a washing machine, an outfit, a car or a trip until we had the money saved up. We thought nothing of buying on credit as long as our happiness was assured. Many of us have come full circle now and realize that things do not necessarily cause happiness; however, lack of things doesn't either.

We certainly created "self help" in its many forms. Our parents didn't even know they needed help, and maybe they didn't; the system worked for them. We did therapy, body work, inner child work, re-birthing, personal growth seminars and retreats, past life regressions, experiential personal growth intensive workshops, avatar, course in miracles, meditation, dance therapy, women's groups, men's groups, psychic counselling, hands on healing, full moon ceremonies, etc. etc. Ok, well I did all that (except men's groups) and I know I wasn't there alone. I think I finally do know who I am but more on that later.

I was forced to grow when my first husband Stan, who was my high-school sweetheart, told me he wasn't happy. He was a dentist. He's still a dentist actually. I don't think he's very happy as a dentist but that was his choice when his mother said he could be a doctor, dentist or lawyer. We attended a week-long program in Santa Barbara, California that was designed mostly for doctors and dentists and their spouses. It was a very expensive combination of practice management, financial management and life philosophy. It was 1987.

I liked most of the things we were learning. I wasn't just his wife; I also worked in the practice as business manager so everything we learned was equally relevant to me. We learned how the dentist is the "source" of the business and must proclaim his vision and make sure that he has a team of "10's" around him. In fact whether it is in his practice, his financial affairs or his home, everything in his life must either be a 10 or add meaning to his life. I, it turned out, was neither. He realized much later that happiness comes from within and you can't expect another person to make you happy. We both learned much later that relationships must be constantly nourished to survive. Meanwhile one of his dental hygienists, who happened to be my cousin's wife, was apparently a 10. I saw it coming; my cousin didn't. To make a very long story short, one day he told me he had found an apartment to move to and a few weeks later on a Friday he asked me to give him the keys to the office and that would be my last day.

This was December 1988. Our daughters, Nicole (we sometimes called her Nicki) and Marlene (we always called her Marley) were 2 and 4 years old. My life was our two daughters and his dental business. His life was his dental business, watching football on TV (which didn't interest me at all) and apparently Lisa. Lisa was 14 years younger and obviously enchanted by this older man dentist. She showed him the attention that I guess I didn't. He wasn't showing me any either. Much later I realized that if you want somebody to be nice to you, be nice to them. If you want somebody to worship you, worship them. Stan and I just weren't doing that for each other. He wasn't all that into babies although he was a good enough father considering it was really me who wanted children, particularly a second one.

I was really enjoying motherhood. We had waited until he had finished dental school and his two years in the Navy as a dentist and had started a practice before even trying to get pregnant. He was the type where everything had to be perfect first and the time just wasn't right. When we were both ready it took much longer to get pregnant than I thought it would. So, although we married when I was 21, my first child, Marlene, was born two weeks after my 30th birthday. She turned 25 in February, 2009 and I turned 55. My how time flies. It really seems like only yesterday I was giving birth to Marley. Two years later I had Nicole. I was thrilled to have 2 girls. I only wish I could have spent more time with them.

I worked in the dental office all day from the time Marley was about 2 months old. Stan required that. He didn't want a wife who just stayed home. I didn't want to just stay home either but part time would have been nice. As it was I was more than full time. Stan did the dentistry and I did everything else. We were both very ambitious and tried many alternate ways to increase our income including Amway and investing in real estate. I did most of the work (bookkeeping, dealing with the tenants and people fixing up the houses, working with people we sponsored in Amway, etc.). I think we were done with both of those side businesses by the time Marley was born, certainly by the time Nicole was. By the way, we didn't make any money; we lost it. Just building the dental practice to the level where it was one of the top practices in the country was more than a full time job for both of us. Stan couldn't do anything in a less-than-excellent fashion. I highly recommend him as a dentist. As a husband, I don't know; you'll have to ask Lisa. In his spare time Stan relaxed with sports, in my spare time I took care of our two little ones.

We had a full time housekeeper, Millie, who took care of the house and my babies while I worked. She was a practical nurse and very good with them, good to the extent that I felt left out sometimes even though I did come home everyday at lunch time to nurse them both until they were 8 months old. I really enjoyed nursing my babies. It was a form of inner peace for me. One memory that still hurts is one day I took off work and took Nicki to her toddler tumbling class. It's a mom and baby kind of fun place where you help your toddler do all sorts of things. When I got there with her the other mothers said "Where is Nicki's mother?" Millie had told the other mothers that she was the mother. No, I didn't fire her, nor did I say anything, I just buried the hurt and felt angry with both Millie and Stan.

I had my parents keep the girls for the weekend when my husband moved out in December 1988. I couldn't really cope with motherhood at that moment. During the two hours it took him to actually move his possessions (I kept the furniture) out of the house into a small van he had rented, I took a long walk. I basically just kept walking for two hours. My throat had an incredible lump in it that was holding back excessive sobbing. I cried a little but stayed presentable in case I saw anybody or anybody talked to me. What had happened? This was my high school sweetheart, the first man I had ever had sex with. The man whom I knew was destined to be mine even though we had times of dating other people. I put him through dental school! I helped him establish a very profitable dental practice. I worked my ass off so that we could get rich and have it all. I let another woman raise my babies so that I could work in his practice! I didn't go to graduate school so that he could go to dental school. I was Mrs. Dr. Stanley Silver. Now who the hell am I going to be?

My parents were a God-send in that they lived locally and offered themselves to me for babysitting as often as I needed them. They were overpowering, very critical of me, and made it clear they were doing this for their darling grandchildren, not for me. I was obviously bad or why else would my husband have left me. I stuffed my resentment and hurt because it was obvious I needed help.

The first thing I needed was a new career. I was the office manager of Stan's dental practice. Could I do that for another dentist? Maybe, and that was one of the things I tried doing. However, owning your own business and being somebody's employee are quite different. It wasn't for me. I tried going back into real estate, something I had done for a few years in the early 80s. But being a single mother and real estate don't really work well together, not if you want to be successful anyway; and I did have a strong success drive. I thought about getting a masters degree in business and went to the local college part time to take business law, accounting and marketing. It all seemed so theoretical though. I really wanted to be an entrepreneur and the coursework just didn't seem necessary.

All this happened in the first five months of 1989. Oh, and did I mention I probably read 10 or 15 self help books at this time. One of them had in it a technique for releasing painful feelings and moving on called the love letter technique. You write a letter to somebody that has 5 different sections in it. It starts with anger and goes to grief and guilt and then progresses to hope and love. It is meant to clear feelings, express feelings and move on. I wrote one of those to Stan. He answered me briefly two years later and did express love and regret for what went wrong. I do believe that it helped me to write that letter.

The company that Stan and I had spent a lot of money with for practice, financial and life management did have some very good philosophies and tools for personal growth. I must say I had mixed feelings about them because their insistence that everything in Stan's life be a 10, must have contributed to the end of our marriage. However, he wasn't the only one whose life wasn't a 10. Mine wasn't feeling all that magical either; so in a way he took the role of the bad guy but he freed both of us to really find happiness. One of the philosophies that still repeats in my head now is "Why would you choose to be unhappy about that?" Basically this means something may have happened, whether it is some jerk on the road passing you, your boss is totally unreasonable and you therefore hate your job, or your husband leaves you. Each of these is a situation that has happened. To some degree you have experienced a loss. However, you can lose once or you can lose many times depending on how you react to this experience. How you react and experience the situation is always a choice. The first question should always be "Can I change the situation?" If you can't change it, can you live with it? Can you accept the unacceptable? That is also a choice. If you can change it (peacefully) do so, if you can't and choose to live with it, then why would you choose to lose twice by being in emotional turmoil about it. Choosing peace and letting go always seems like the best answer for continued happiness.

It was time for me to choose peace and let go and this company was having an in-depth experiential personal growth week in Mendicino California in May of 1989. I paid the fee and registered for the course and travelled, for the first time by myself, to California, for a week that would change my life.

Chapter Three

A Slow but Sure Beginning

Warm hugs

Hi Dianne

You sound wonderful too. Especially as I am just about wakening to the spiritual side of life, and only one of my current friends are even vaguely interested.

The cruises sound great – but I would rather not share unless it was with someone I thought was truly special. (Maybe one day that could be you.)

I would like to continue learning about spirituality, but have no mental barriers to any kind of learning – which I always had during my marriage. Divorce is giving me a new freedom to travel both with my mind and body.

I do feel your affection even in your first communication, and you don't appear to be held back from saying/showing it. I find that very attractive, and would love to know more about you – yourself. I do enjoy hugs and feeling wanted – not only for moral or financial support.

My two daughters are like chalk and cheese. Vickie, the oldest is a nurse in a hospital about 60 miles from here. She is a determined and strong willed young lady who will do very well in her career. But I have worries that she will not do so well personally.

Rachel, my youngest (since I lost my son), on the other hand, is very loving, creative, artistic and without direction, so my worries are reversed.

I do love them both deeply and do as much as I can to support them morally.

Do tell me a little about your girls. Mine battled at the ages yours are and I never thought it would end. There was no way of getting reason into their heads – thank goodness they now both appreciate each other.

It was really great to receive your message and I hope to hear again soon. Do you have a photo or some special way of letting me see you before the day we meet – as I feel sure we must.
Long slow warm hugs
David

*   *   *   *

I really like this man. He feels real to me, and honest and affectionate. I don't really have a lot of time to devote to this online stuff right now, so I think I'll tell him to write to me at my real email address and I'll get off match.com before somebody else writes to me.

*   *   *   *

Re Warm Hugs
Hi David

The way you describe your daughters is similar to how I'd describe mine. My oldest, Marley, is determined and strong willed, just like your Vickie. My youngest, Nicole, is loving, creative sensitive and even psychic, sounds like your Rachel. Mine are both honor students and cheerleaders. Their main interests are boys, telephone and AOL. It's fun and challenging being their mother. Yes, they fight and are very competitive with each other.

14

I'm so sorry you lost your son. Tell me how that happened if you are okay talking about it. I can't imagine. I'm glad divorce is giving you a new freedom in body mind and spirit. That's good. I've been divorced twice and grew a lot both times. I don't want to be divorced again though.

I don't have a whole lot of time to write right now but I really look forward to continuing to communicate with you. You seem gentle and special. Attached is my picture. Can you send me one of you? Also, write back to me at my real email address which is Goddess254@aol.com, [email address no longer in use] and don't forget to tell me about your business.

Long slow warm hugs and soft kisses   :)
Dianne

Re Warm Hugs
Hi Dianne

I love the message and the photo. Must be ultra brief as I am at work and just going off for two days – should be able to write Wednesday or Thursday evening. Love the soft kisses – maybe one day.
Thinking of you
David

*   *   *   *

Well, that wasn't much of a reply considering I sent my picture. Maybe he really was on his way out on a business trip. Only time will tell.......

*   *   *   *

A few days later......
Today's chat from a Virgo
Hi Dianne

Our daughter's similarity was terrific until you mentioned "both honour students and cheerleaders...." Vickie either is very good at keeping things quiet, or has little interest in boys (of any age). This could be that she doesn't have the confidence in that area. Or she is still very much a   boy and sees boys as people who share common interests like military aircraft, U2 pop group – and not as sex toys or future husbands. However, it was said to me on more than one occasion that she and I have such a strong relationship that she is measuring them (boys) by me, and therefore isn't likely to find one of her own age group, who is a knowledgeable listener, and would be supportive. I don't necessarily agree with this theory, but do understand where it has come from…..

When she lived at home, and her mother and I lived together, she and her mother would not get along no matter what happened. My wife would not forgive Vickie any action that was normal in adolescent girls (moods, bad temper, and a wish to get out and do things, not be stuck indoors…etc). This used to cause bad feelings between them, and as Vickie's father I used to discuss the situation with both her and my wife to try to get a reconciliation between them, but I was obviously no Kissinger. Although they would both agree to act better when talking to me, my wife would not behave well or forgive Vickie and so the wars would start again. This may have left Vickie with no-one else to confide in, and so rather than see her alone and hurt, I would be there for her. This was used by my wife as politics in telling people that Vickie and I would gang up on her – which was not true. I appear to be rambling, so I will move on to Rachel.

Rachel is the daughter that gets called "the lovely one" by those who don't remember names. It is true she is easy going, witty and (dare I say it) more girlie to look at. But for every plus there is a minus, and her weakness is that she is preoccupied with her life and generally will contact me only when she needs something – just as well I'm always pleased to help. (Vickie will be the first to offer help.) Rachel is very much like my side of the family in both looks and temperament. She is placid, easy going, creative, and unfortunately very little awareness of her potential for creation – but I am working on it. She used to compensate for my support of Vickie by siding with her mother. Thank goodness that side of my life is over.

My son – well he died in February 1997, after a road accident when he was hit by a van on a pedestrian crossing. He was 13 years old, and although I say it myself – a wonderful boy. Always cheerful, very creative, adventurous and always showed gratitude for attention. He was not frightened to show his affection. I have to say I liked him as a person, and miss him so much. Every day I think of him and wish he was here. I find this very difficult to type with tears in my eyes but do like to talk about him. His 16th birthday would have been three days ago, 5th July. I do wonder whether he would have changed into some teenage monster, or would have just matured into a caring nice adult. I hope the latter.

My wife did spend almost two years writing to me telling me how much I must be hating her and everything to leave her and set up on my own. But despite her regular attacks (up to only about 6 months ago), I hate no one, not even her, with her lack of thought for others, least of all me. I believe very strongly that hate is the sort of evil that kills creativity, love and everything worth having in you, but she has no comprehension of my views of the power of positive thought. The divorce has given me peace, and eventually I will be able to regard it all as history….that which has happened and can be learned from.

My interest in spiritual things has come from realising that there are powers like telepathy that we possess, and most people have no concept of. I know so little and would love to know and do more. In my search (only just started), I have been hearing about dreams and the different levels, and the power that is there for the taking, in problem solving, designing and general life solutions.

Until very recently I didn't dream at all. I suffer from a problem called "sleep apnea", which kept me from going into a deep sleep (where the dreams are). However, since I started learning about this, I have been able to sort out designs for my flat and garden, plus solve personnel problems at work, all by using some very simple techniques I have heard. This is probably child's play to you. I find it fascinating, but not surprising, that we can do much more than the man in the street might think. The friend I was talking about in a previous message, the only one who has any interest in the spiritual side of things, has some very unusual views and I am not sure what to think of them. One is that she calls me a God Man (only one o). She is generally not a fan of men, who she feels always put women down. I think she is not really looking at all of me, I think she is only looking at the feminine side of me, which is larger than most men.

In a way I hope she is right, because the best type of woman for a God Man is a Goddess. You say some wonderful things that make me want to meet you – well not just meet you.
Thinking of you and looking forward to your reply.
David

p.s. – I hope this message was not too depressing – I am normally a very positive person.

*   *   *   *

Wow, I really do like his style of writing and thinking. I printed this out at work and shared it with the girls in the office. My new "boy" is a British Virgo. Maybe he isn't stereotypically British or Virgo for that matter, as I wouldn't have thought that an independent, free thinking Aquarian like me would go for a proper, detail-oriented chap. Maybe he is stretching my preconceived notions and encouraging me to look further beneath the surface.

The only other "boy" I was writing to at this time was Teresa's brother in Mexico. Teresa works for me and is a really lovely woman who moved here (actually California first) from Mexico, got married, had two girls (her oldest is the same age as my youngest), and became a single mother about the same time I was becoming one for the second time. Teresa is my friend, and I tend to hire friends to work at

Dreamtime. On one of the cruises, when we were in Mexico I met her brother Manuel. Manuel is extremely spiritual, kind-hearted, good looking and with the Latin lover persona that has always captured my attention. Hmmmm, Latin lover or British Virgo. Well, for the time being I'd continue to write to both of them and see which one lasted. I sent David back a very quick note from the office that day.

*   *   *   *

Re Today's chat from a Virgo
Hi David
   I'm at work, I'll write to you tonight. Can't wait to read your long letter better tonight and respond.
Dianne

3rd of the day from 11:25GMT
Hi Dianne
   Your note has cheered up an otherwise dull evening. Do you have any other pictures of you? I would like to see more. (If I am allowed.)
   Have you been working on your trip business, or do you have another occupation as well?
   Thanks for the note, that way I know you are there before I go to bed, and it is so good to know you want to read and reply; that is how I feel, but you must say if I become boring or dull, I don't want you to lose interest.
Good night from me, thinking of those soft kisses…..
Yours David

*   *   *   *

Very interesting. It's almost like he picked up intuitively on the fact that I was wondering if a British Virgo could be as interesting as a Latin lover in Mexico. "If I am allowed to see more pictures", how funny! The Mexican sure wouldn't ask permission. Brits are funny! But I'm not losing interest. Maybe part of the intrigue is the cultural difference. I do love the British accent. That short little note of mine written from the office made him happy, wow. I'm actually not going to be able to do any better now though because time has really gotten away from me tonight. Marley actually wanted to be with me to watch the movie "Stepmom" and I thought it was a good idea to just chill with her hence the following short message to David.

*   *   *   *

Re 3rd of the day from 11:25GMT
Hi David

Sorry this is just another quick note to say I'll do better tomorrow. I was watching the movie "Stepmom" with my older daughter. It was a bit of a tear jerker. Did you see it? Then I got online and a friend that needed to talk instant messaged me and that lasted an hour. Now it's 12:30 and I can't do our conversation justice. I loved your letter, not depressing, simply soulful. I want to write a good one, not when I'm exhausted though. Until tomorrow....

Warm hugs and soft kisses.....

Dianne

2 days later......

Finally have a few minutes
Dear David

I had my mother as a houseguest last night so I couldn't get online as the computer is in the guest room/office. Her air-conditioner broke and she can't stand to be hot.

You really sound like a good father. My daughters never experienced conflict between me and their father because they were two and four when we separated. They did experience some conflict with me and my second husband. They were 10 and 12 when we separated. Now, I should probably stay away from marriage (or living together) until they are in college (3 and 5 more years). I'd like to think that the next time will be forever and wonderful, but change seems to be a big part of my life.

I feel for you so much about the death of your son. I can't even begin to imagine what it is like to lose a child. I lost a good friend. Suzin was my business partner and best friend. She had been in a car accident the year prior and her foot was almost completely severed. She had to have several surgeries to try to get the nerves and blood flow and everything working again. On the last surgery, a blood clot or clots from her foot went to her heart and lungs and brain, and put her in a coma. When she was in the coma, I knew she would die and I wrote her a poem that her daughter read to her and said she seemed to move in response to it. She did die and I miss her quite a bit. I do think that some of the things I've manifested since she's been gone have been gifts from her in spirit though. I know I'll see her again.

I agree with you about hate and anger. I try to keep it out of my life. I'm a very positive and love-filled person. I take risks and wear my heart on my sleeve. I'm glad to meet you David, we are definitely kindred spirits. Take care and have a nice weekend. By the way, you never told me what kind of business you have.
Love
Dianne

$$* \quad * \quad * \quad *$$

Looks like I'm the first one to use the "L" word. However, I'm really using it in a friendly way, like I would write to a friend, and I feel a very strong friend energy with David. Of course I felt that friend energy with Randall too who I still emailed and saw occasionally. But he's another chapter.

$$* \quad * \quad * \quad *$$

David and Dianne's first pictures to each other

Chapter Four

A Week of Intense Personal Growth

At the end of chapter two I was on my way to Mendocino California for a week that would change my life. This was May 1989.

It was truly beautiful in Mendocino; a rugged north western coast beauty that I was unfamiliar with being from Florida. My group had about 20 people in it; from memory I'd say it was half men and half women. Usually this type of thing attracts more women but since this was an offspring of the company I mentioned previously there were a lot of doctors and dentists as part of the group. A large part of the group was also their wives or ex-wives. There was a lot of sadness in a group of people who by ordinary reality standards "had it all." The truth was none of us really knew how to be happy. We had spent so long searching for it outside of ourselves, using the different roles that we play (mother / father, daughter / son, dentist's wife / dentist, friend, girlfriend / boyfriend, sister / brother, teacher / student rich person / poor person, etc) to define who we are and whether we should be happy or not. Few of us had truly gotten it that happiness, like success, is an inside job and that our beliefs and our choices totally create our reality.

The week consisted of talks by Rick, experiential group exercises and journaling while we sat in our spot. Our spot was a location that we each intuitively found somewhere on the cliff overlooking the Pacific Ocean. A good part of our week was spent in silent contemplation at our spot.

The first spot exercise: Write a page starting with "I am" and pick a metaphor (seagull, ocean, rock, etc) and describe how you want your life to be.

What I wrote:

"I am the ocean. I am everywhere and I will travel the world. I take many forms and many colors. I go on and on with no beginning and no end. I have no fears. All of the universe is contained within me. The secrets of life are in my depths. All I need to do is be still and listen. God is within me. Love is within me and an immense power and universal energy are within me. Salt water heals and I have the power to heal, nurture and make whole myself and others.

"Some parts of me beat up against rugged and strong rocks. I am stronger because of that. Some parts of me wash ashore on warm tropical sunlit beaches. I am warmer because of that. My vastness and openness leave me exposed to the elements and to sea monsters, pirates and white knights dressed as illustrious cruise ships. I am vulnerable because of that. I choose to be vulnerable. My life will never be led in fear of hurt, rejection or pain because that to me would not be life and I would dry up and cease to exist. I welcome my life and future with open arms and an open heart. I am deep and I am intense, I am also loose and carefree; I am the ocean and I am eternal and excellent."

It is very interesting that I mention cruise ships here as I later created a career around cruise ships....but that's another chapter. The main point in what I wrote is my desire to be vulnerable. Many sane people would have advised me to not be vulnerable, that I need to protect myself from being hurt again. But intuitively I knew that the only way to experience life was to remain totally open to all possibilities and to risk living and loving and to learn from each experience. Didn't somebody famous say "it is better to have loved and lost than never to have loved at all." I intuitively felt I would love and lose a lot in my lifetime. Perhaps that is part of my life's lessons. I truly want to live my life with passion and purpose and when I die know that I have really lived. So, all considered, the little story I wrote comparing myself to the ocean is a quite good metaphor.

The second spot exercise: Make a list of things resented or not forgiven or forgotten.

My list:

- My parents treated me and still do treat me like a baby.
- My parents over-protected me to such an extent that I rushed into marriage to create my own life.
- My parents don't choose to understand me.
- My parents try to make me feel guilty about going someplace or doing something for me. They feel my life should be dedicated to my children as theirs was and still is dedicated to me and my children.
- Stan abandoned me both physically and mentally.
- Stan walked away from our relationship without even trying to save it.
- I was not important enough for Stan to have unconditional commitment to me.
- Jim (a new person I started dating) did not call me last week.
- Lisa destroyed my marriage.
- My cousin had no understanding of what happened between Stan and Lisa.

Make a list of things that cause stress and things that cause emotional pain.

My lists:

Stress:

- Not having time for me
- When the girls act up
- When my parents try to make me feel guilty
- Bugs
- Bumper to bumper traffic
- Getting the girls to school and me to work on time

- Getting the girls to bed

Emotional Pain:
- Lack of love
- Lack of affection
- Lack of physical contact
- Lack of communication
- When my daughters think I don't love them
- Rejection

Make a list of the things in life I'm trying to control.
My list:
- My parents
- My daughters
- My ex-husband
- My new relationship
- Time
- Knowledge of future
- My friends
- My growth
- My feelings
- Controlling not being a controller

Regarding the last one, Rick had told me that although I deny being a controller I was just trying to control not being a controller. Wow! So am I a horrible person? No, these are all just what Rick called memes (ideas), things that exist outside of ourselves and in our mind and controlling would be such an easy one to let go in order to have inner peace….or would it.

If I let go of control, I would probably feel a sense of relief, particularly regarding control over time, knowledge of the future, my parents, my ex husband etc. In my new relationship, I would feel helpless and at the mercy of his control, but if I don't let go I'll lose him for sure. That may be okay too. The world around me would do just fine if I let go of control. Everything would probably work better.

Another exercise was to write a page or so about why I am here and what will my breakthrough likely be. Here is what I wrote:

"I am here because there is a way that I want to live the rest of my life and I intend to find that way this week. I have recently been totally rejected by the person I thought I would be spending my life with. I am already well on the way but I would like to experience really letting go and realizing that now more than ever there is a whole world and life out there for me. I would like to understand if at all possible what happened so I don't repeat past mistakes in future relationships. I want to learn how to love myself, and others, unconditionally.

"Love is probably my need if I had to pick a need. I believe in love and commitment and I want to experience it in my life again. Of course I don't want it to be an addiction and I don't want to be dependent on it. I also hope to get clear on what I want to do with my life career wise. I'm intelligent and don't want to waste that but I also don't want to depend on my career for my identity and self worth. I want a life too, and I want to be a good mother to my two small children.

"Regarding my children, being a single mother is difficult. I want to approach that with a sense of fun rather than fear or dread. I want them to not suffer from the divorce and I want to be a facilitator in their growth and happiness. I want to be able to maintain my inner peace when things get tough as they can with a three and five year old. Things also get tough with my parents and their acceptance and understanding of me. I have to find a way to mentally let the hurt go.

"I am here because I am basically an independent free spirit but I've been married forever and I have never been free to do my own thing. This is my first trip alone in my life. It certainly won't be the last but it's the perfect launching point for my new life. I expect a lot from this week. Mostly, I guess I want to experience that there are unlimited possibilities for me and that I am the recipient of the gift of life and I can make it wonderful.

"My breakthrough will be really letting go of Stan and not being dependent on love so I don't go quickly back into the same thing again."

The week was intense, these notes really only represent the first day or two. I got very close with people in my group, which was nice. I learned a lot, including how easy it could be to let go. This was demonstrated by holding and then dropping a pencil. I became an individual that week. I found that there was a "me" in there after dropping all of my roles in life and that I was actually a very nice person with a lot to offer myself and others. With tears, but a much lighter heart, I threw my wedding ring into the Pacific Ocean and I left feeling relaxed, revitalized and peaceful.

Chapter Five

We are Becoming a Relationship

Feeling So Close

Dear Dianne

You may think me daft, but I missed not hearing from you, even though it was only a few hours since your short message.

I do very definitely want to meet you. I have the feeling that we are very close even though we have never met or said more than a few pages of chat. I feel very open to you, which is not really the me that I recognise after such a long time of pain. Hitting a special date in October may be difficult as we have two exhibitions, one in September, and the other in October. However, the idea I have, if you agree to our meeting, is to take a fly/drive holiday to the States, and maybe visit potential customers while you are busy.

I was so worried that my photo would be a problem, but your comment gave me a wonderfully warm feeling. I hope that we can be good friends until that vital five years are over. My business plan has a sale in seven years to create my pension fund.

*   *   *   *

It is obvious from this email that there was at least one from me that I didn't save that came before this. At the time I didn't think I needed to save my emails although I did save most of his. He was not yet saving all of mine so a few are missing. I can fill in the blanks by saying that I remember telling him that I thought he was adorable.

29

I believe I must have also said that we can be friends but I can't see progressing the relationship until my youngest daughter is in college, hence the vital five years he mentions.

*   *   * . *

The business is very different from yours, as we are in electronics. What we do is unique in that we say that we will save anyone from having to throw away any PCB (printed circuit board). We will modify, repair or manufacture parts to keep the electronics going for another 20 to 30 years. This is not a cheap service, but it can save a company tens/hundreds of thousands of dollars a year by using the service. Our very poor website is www. prsl.co.uk, but it was created by an ex-employee without proper consultation, so it doesn't portray the company's total quality approach to work, customers, staff and premises. (It will improve by the end of the year.)

I occasionally have my mother stay with me. She has been unhappily married to my step-father since I was 3 years old. She believes that at 67 it is too late for her to start again. I am torn as to how hard to push her into thinking about the situation rationally. She is not an affectionate person, no hugs, kisses or even little touches or sentiment, which I put down to the same problem I had and resolved by locking myself up mentally, and blanking all personal pain. So my visits from her are more geared to giving her a break.

I am sorry that you have lost your business partner, I would hate to lose mine. Your partner died of something quite like my son. He had a broken pelvis from his accident, and the local hospital said that all would be well, the pelvis only needed pinning. However, the London hospital lost him when he had fat embolism coming from that break. It only goes to show how vulnerable we all are in this world.

I look forward to reading your poem. I also turned to poetry, but not my own. In the film "4 Weddings and a Funeral" (my favourite of all time) there is a poem, read by the gay lover of the funeral star. It contains the lines "He was my life, my north, my south, my east, my west…." I don't actually have the words; you have to hear it said in a Scottish accent, very emotive, and so appropriate, as I too loved Scott.

I was talking to one of the many interviewees for our latest vacancies at work. He was saying how he used to lose his temper, through frustration, failure, etc. He now has changed to a style similar to mine. No matter what the problem, there is something good to come out of it, and I don't lose my temper or raise my voice more than about once a year, and that is only if someone is throwing away their talent, and have not listened to any guidance.

It has been very hot (for the UK) while I was at work today. Luckily, I like it hot and not cold. (So it's Florida, not Alaska for me.) It's nearly 8:00pm and I ought to start preparing my tea. Tomorrow I hope to work in my garden, if it will be as nice as today. If not I have now ordered the last door for my kitchen, and finishing the kitchen renovation will take over. I love creating meals and look forward to one day cooking for you. What are your likes/dislikes in food?

Looking forward to any message from you, you are very special.

Warm thoughts, soft kisses, and gentle caresses

Lots of love

David

*   *   *   *

What a beautiful ending. He has used the "L" word too and sent warm thoughts, soft kisses and gentle caresses as well. I would very much like to be the beneficiary of those things as well as the giver of them with somebody like him. He is somebody I want to take the physical slowly with and really get to know him first. Well, that is certainly the beauty of a long distance email relationship.

31

He seems to be a truly kind person with the way he helps his mother; and he seems to have a good insight into her psyche as well as his own. I find it incredible that his son died in a sort of similar way to my friend Suzin, and both of them in 1997. I do believe in help from the spirit world and strongly feel that Scott and Suzin brought me and David together. The poem that moves him sounds incredible. I'd love to watch that movie with him. I suspect he is the kind of sensitive man who cries at movies. I really do feel love for this person and closeness too. He shares my philosophy that everything has a reason and something good comes from every challenge. These are all really good things to build a relationship on. I guess tea means dinner in England. I would love for him to prepare dinner for me.

It's hard to describe what I'm feeling right now. In a way a sense of peace that I've never felt before. I could relax with David I think. The relationship feels nice and even easy. I've never had it easy with a man. There has always been something wrong, or something that kept my energy hyper and gave me a sense of drama. I always wanted to see a psychic to see what was going on. I have none of those feelings with David. I just want to let it unfold in the easy way it is without any drama. Or maybe I'm just out of energy and am projecting ease onto the situation because I can't deal with anything but ease right now.

I'm only 6 weeks away from The Summer Wellness Cruise sailing from Los Angeles to the Mexican Riviera so all the last minute craziness of selling to and escorting a large group are upon me. Plus the total eclipse of the sun is also only a few weeks away and that is affecting me a lot with a low grade depression as my chart predicted it would. So how can one properly evaluate a relationship in the midst of these two thing?. All I can say at this point is I'm glad David entered my life and I do feel love for him. I just think perhaps it's not the best timing for me right now.

The next letter I have is from David, so again I haven't been saving my emails at this point. However, I must have sent him my poem written to Suzin when she was in a coma, as he mentions it, so here it is:

*   *   *   *

My Friend

We met thousands of years ago when goddesses first appeared
Your light shines so bright, my sister you are here.
Through time and space and illusions many
We lived we learned we loved together.

On ships tall and grand we set sail many times
Seeking our soul's grand purpose.
We are a pair you and I with our dark hair and eyes
The SeaWitch and the SeaGoddess.

SeaWitch you are wise, you are kind you're alive
You're a succulent wild woman!
You're as deep as the ocean as strong as the wind
You're a woman, wife, mother, daughter and friend.

You cry with me, laugh with me, take on my pain
Help me through life again and again.
You're my strength, you're my pillow, you've eased all my falls
Men, children, business, friends, you've helped me with it all.

I can't say goodbye to a friend such as you.
I know you'll never leave me, it isn't what you do.
I'll see your eyes everywhere, your smile and purple hair
I'll remember the love you gave me.

Goodnight for now Dreamtime's rose
Our vision now you'll inspire
Dear God heal her soul, light her spirit, let her soar
Suzin….my friend….my sister.

You Wow

Hi Dianne

Is there no end to the number of ways you amaze me, you appear to have talent at everything you do. I can't wait to meet you one day. That poem was so moving, lovely and special. I feel closer to you every time you show me more of the real you. I am so sorry about your partner, you sound like you were really close. I don't know what I would do if my business partner Shirley should go. She is the opposite side of me – she slows me down when I go into overdrive. She builds me up when I am down – like the divorce and losing Scott. Luckily for her, she gets her support from her husband Steve.

Last November I was in Cuba, only 90 miles from your coast line, but didn't know you were there. What a shame.

If you agree to us meeting, what is the weather like in November/December?

I spent today working in the garden. I was planting two grape vines, one white, one black, clearing up after the last day in the labours of the court yard, then lastly, the most skilled part….. positioning the furniture so that the ice bucket is in the shade and the lounge chair isn't. The temperatures over here this year are improving so it's just as well I have started making it liveable out there, summerhouse, etc.

At last I have found the necessary parts to complete my kitchen – they have discontinued the kitchen so I was not able to buy the doors for the last cupboard, but now I have ordered a glass door, which will go well with the rest and allow me to show off some of my things. (If I'm careful to keep it tidy.)

I am travelling this week, and should be back on Thursday evening, so I will write again then. I'll be training a company in basic repair techniques and then going selling in that area (north of London, Hertfordshire).

Have you ever been to England? I have been to the states only once, when I was 14 years old, to see relatives in Boston and Montreal Canada.

Anyway, time I checked my chicken – my tea.
Lots of love and soft kisses
David

*   *   *   *

*Again no saved email reply from me. If I remember correctly I
was writing very short ones that in my opinion were horrible replies,
but they were apparently enough to keep him interested. I know I
would have replied and told him about my Magical Mystical Britain
cruise that I took in the summer of 1997. It was one of my last cruises
with Suzin. The very last one was Bermuda from Boston and she died
the week she got back from that. This cruise around the British Isles
(including Ireland, Paris and Amsterdam as well as England, Wales
and Scotland) was an incredible experience for me. First of all, it was
my first trip to Europe. I was 43 that summer and had never been to
Europe! I was completely enchanted by what I saw. Such a contrast to
the cement block flat Florida I'm used to. I remember being amazed
at how green the grass was and that it was everywhere, with beautiful
rolling hills and with cows and sheep grazing very close to the road.
I was truly in another world. I remember feeling like I was home. I
resonated so much with that countryside. I feel like I've had at least
one good lifetime in that land.*

*So, yes, I had fallen in love with his land before even knowing
about him and I'm sure I had expressed that to him. I find it very
interesting how destiny and free will seem to interact to bring us our
life. Destiny and free will mixed with attracting to us what it is we
either need or want or feel at some level we deserve. I really believe
that I am truly ready to attract my highest and best mate and that I
now deserve him. It is quite possible that I have found him.*

*The other thing I really liked about David from that last email
was that he worked in his garden and in his flat. I've never had a
husband or a boyfriend who enjoyed doing that. I come from a "hire
somebody" mentality and this was new and different and interesting
to me. Don't get me wrong, I'd still personally hire somebody rather
than do this kind of work myself, but I found it very nice that he
did it.*

*   *   *   *

Virgo Knight Returns to Castle

Hi Dianne

I have returned from my trip away, at full speed, only to find that the wonder of the age (my laptop) has decided that this international chat is too much for it. So I have driven to work so that I can write to you from here.

Please don't feel that you have to write long replies to my letters to you. Some of your shorter ones have been seductive, moving, lovely enough, and I would rather keep hearing from you than put you off by expecting more than you feel comfortable giving.

I have now made up my mind to have my holiday in the US, so now there is lots of research to do as to the best way of doing it and exactly when (are there any times that are out for you). I really do want to meet you – but I am just a little nervous that you may find me less interesting than my emails – but I hope not.

The training course I was running this week set off to a very poor start as they had not done the very simple tasks that were agreed between us, i.e. setting out of tables, tools, white board, etc. Still, they were fast learners and we soon caught up the slow start. Shirley, my co-director, is the demonstrator at our training sessions (I do all the talking – which may sound like me, but I just act the part really). She is very critical of our company (in an attempt to always improve things) and so she felt the day was a complete disaster. The next day was then spent trying to convince her that these issues are not as important as achieving the goal of having six people able to do the work that previously they either thought was impossible or didn't know could be done at all. (They are probably used to their own level of inefficiency and didn't notice it.) In case I haven't made it clear, she lacks self confidence in front of others, (and doesn't like the spotlight being on her), and is always wondering – what do they think about us? Very useful thoughts from a QA (Quality Assurance) Director.

Tiredness looms over me like a large tidal wave that is just waiting to rush over me and send me to sleep, so I will end for tonight.
Warmest of thoughts – to you especially – but not forgetting your family.
David

*   *   *   *

No email from me to share but I'm sure I wrote him a quick one encouraging him to come anytime to visit me and assuring him that I would find him wonderful in person. I must have apologized for not writing much because the title of his next email is "I understand."

*   *   *   *

I understand
Hi Dianne
I always want to call you Goddess, it seems so appropriate. I do understand the pressures of home, family and business, so there is no pressure to write me long replies, as I love all you have written, and long every day to hear more about you, your world, family, business. Don't be pressured by me, I just have a very unusual amount of energy when it comes to you. Normally I suffer a lot from exhaustion caused mainly by my Sleep Apnea.

I have just spent all the time since my last email creating a set of charts for each department at work, showing the overall responsibilities of the department/team, showing who is in it, what their position is etc.

I really can't wait to meet you; maybe you would be able to have a day off when I come? The temperature sounds fine. Lucky I am not bothered about C or F, I work in both. It's very silly over here, for nearly 20 years we have not made up our minds what to do about metrification.

I didn't think much of Paris either. I prefer Ireland to any other part of Europe; it's so varied and beautiful.

Did you go to Tintagel where Arthur's castle is? That is really magical, even though there is not much left now. Arthur's dog has a grave in North Wales. I camped near it 35 years ago. It was a wonderful time in our history/mythology.

Although I am interested, I know very little about spiritual matters, and am really looking forward to growing in this area, maybe with your help. I am receptive to most things now. It has taken a lot of problems before the sceptical barriers have dropped.

Lots of love and caresses

David

*　　*　　*　　*

I'm embarrassed to say that the next email is also from David. I am thankful today that I was able to hold his interest in my time of relative silence. Each letter from him made me more and more attracted to everything about him. Maybe I had a self destruct mechanism built within my psyche that refused to believe that somebody this wonderful could be attracted to me and I subconsciously tried to repel him. I remember being very depressed, when I shouldn't have been. In looking back though at the things I mentioned in the last chapter, I can fast forward to this point in time and say that the financial pressures had increased as had the problems with Dreamtime. Randall (who I was still talking to) was telling me I had no choice but to go bankrupt and I refused to do that. I wasn't telling David how bad things were for me business wise and financially. I thought maybe he was attracted to me because of my business and it was too soon to tell him how I was struggling. Maybe that is the reason for my silence. I'm not good at putting on a happy face and not acknowledging the stress. It turns out David was going through pure hell at this time in his life as it was the ending bits of his divorce that got finalized in September. So really both of us were not 100% honest, or might it be better to just say we didn't reveal all at this point. I actually think we both were very honest in everything we did reveal.

The next email from David is dated the 16th of July 1999. So when you think that all of this so far only represents a little over two weeks, we have gotten very close very quickly and actually have told each other quite a bit!

*   *   *   *

Weekend With Friends

Hi Dianne

Hope you have a good time this weekend, it's always good to see friends, so don't worry about not writing. I will look forward to next week even more.

Today has been very hectic – more interviews with prospective employees. How are you supposed to do interviews with people that you know are not suitable before they even speak? I go very much by body language and general aura around the person. The interview only sorts the suitable ones into a priority – but we still have to go through a half hour sham with candidates only suitable on paper.

After them we had a meeting with the Managing Director (CEO) of HSBC (Factoring), who presented us with a unique vase for being valuable customers for 10 years. This was followed by two hours of in-depth conversations relating to the state of the economy, and that PRS was doing so well to be moving forward when all of manufacturing was suffering from the strength of the pound – thus slowing down our exports. Yawn.......

That meeting went on until nearly 5.00. I had planned to leave at 4.00 because I was having friends over for dinner at 7.00. When the HSBC people left I had not planned a menu or done any shopping.....ooops!

So racing along to the shop, I planned a meal – decided on the ingredients to buy....then the finger of fate moved again. Two of the main ingredients of this special dish were not available. Time to re-think the menu. All bought and got home by 6:15 to find the flat just as I had left it....oh no.

Still, they arrived at about 7:30 and Mr Cool had it all prepared, flat tidy and drinks chilled…..I surprise myself sometimes! One day I will make someone a wonderful wife or butler!

All this was after coming home from work last night (having emailed you) and working until 1:00am to get the laptop functional again. It's now much faster than previously and fully working again.

Do have a wonderful weekend.
Long slow kisses
David
xxxxx

*   *   *   *

Wow, he does sound like superman! I must be superwoman though as my little tiny email is entitled "really really busy."

*   *   *   *

Really really busy
Hi David

I'll write to you this weekend. Business has been really busy and my houseguest of last weekend went away for a few days and then just came back, so I can't get online until Friday night or Saturday.
Love
Dianne

The end of a tiring week
Hi Dianne

This week is (hopefully) the last of interviews. The positions have been filled mentally – just offers and hopefully acceptances to go.

Last night I rang and spoke to the girlfriend of one of the applicants to say we would like him to ring in and discuss the job offer. He told our receptionist that he was so excited that he got up at 6:00am and watched the clock until 9:00 before ringing in to talk to us. I hope they all feel so keen (as long as they make it through the probationary period). It might be difficult to tell someone so keen that they hadn't made it.

Looking forward to having you back soon.

Lots of love

David

Looking forward to your safe return

Hi Dianne

I thought I might have lost you, deep into cyberspace. That's one of the problems of no personal contact, just computer to computer.

It was really wonderful to get the message, and I am very happy to wait for you. I know what busy is like, and hope all is well with you and the family.

Tomorrow Vickie is due for another of her short stays – one night. Just to check that I have cleaned and tidied up I expect.

On Sunday I am hoping to take Rachel to either "As You Like It" or "Romeo and Juliet", for our annual pilgrimage to Arundel Castle for the open air theatre.

At work we have just offered the role of Workshop Manager to the best qualified and most experienced candidate. Unfortunately, some interviewees are rejected as they leave the reception area, and yet we still go through a half hour interview with them – just in case! We must work on the idea of having a fire drill, just as they are about to leave reception.

Last night I got home from work at dusk (9pm ish) and there was a fox in the driveway, the first I have seen in the two years I have lived here. I hope he wasn't just passing through. I will put some food out and see if he returns.

It is now 9:30pm and I am due back here at 8:30am. I will sign off for now and look forward to hearing from you again – no matter how short. I always have an excited feeling seeing your email waiting to be read.

Love and warm wishes
David

*   *   *   *

I really think that Scott and Suzin must be working some kind of magic for him to remain interested in me with my relative silence. Again I don't have the email that prompted this one but as it is entitled "friends sounds an excellent foundation", I can remember that at about that point I told him perhaps we should just be friends. I think I was feeling very tied down and committed to my business and children and wondering if I could do a relationship at this point in my life

*   *   *   *

Friends sounds an excellent foundation

Hi Dianne

Hope you got the first stage of the sleep you needed so much.

I have just got up and am running my bath, before going shopping for the picnic at the end of today's walk with the walking club. We end at a village where they have a Medieval Fayre with Ram Roast and all sorts of entertainment by the village people. (No cowboys or construction workers – just people who live in the village).

After another long lay in tomorrow, I am due to drive to Vickie's to assist in her selection of a flat to buy. She has made up her mind that Southampton is where she is staying for the foreseeable future. Then it is back to pick up Rachel and her boyfriend to see an open air theatre production of "As You Like It" – also with picnic.

I feel exhausted just thinking of what's ahead – but life might be boring if it were not so busy!

Don't worry, if I visited you – the first time would be short – just enough to see if we got along face to face as well as I feel we could. My visit would be used for work and sightseeing also. One thing I would love to see would be a space launch, probably something that is old hat to you. The September exhibition may well generate interest in the US, hopefully anyway, let's see what happens.

Must go and have that bath.

Lots of love and good wishes

David

Re: Friends sounds an excellent foundation

Dear David

The things you do sound so interesting!! We don't have anything nearly as interesting here in Orlando, just Disney, Epcot, Universal etc. It was funny, when I was planning my British Isles Cruise with my speaker who lives in England, Celtic Shaman and Arthurian expert, John Matthews, we were planning which castles to go to and he made the comment "It's just another bloody medieval castle". I said that the only castle I had ever seen is the one here at Disney World that belongs to Mickey and Minnie Mouse! That certainly changed his perspective. What is everyday to some is awe inspiring to others.

I'd go to Disney with you in November, it's cool enough then. I wouldn't go near it in the summer! I have to get going here and get something accomplished. Talk to you later.

Love

Dianne

From my castle to Mickey and Minnie's

Hi Dianne

As a British man, I don't understand the concept of Disney Land from an adult's point of view. I have looked on it as a place to take children. So many people have said it is for adults as well, but I have never yet asked…how? I look forward to being shown your area, as I will one day look forward to showing you mine.

Today's fayre was great, weather brilliant. Ram roast was tasty, atmosphere out of this world, town band playing brass instruments, including a local tune – Sussex by the Sea. To top it off they flew five hot air balloons from the site.

I ought to say it is a tiring life going everywhere, doing everything, maybe I ought to have a holiday doing nothing. But I feel I would be wasting valuable time that could be so short.

Anyway, I will go and put Vickie's tea on. She is due back from the air display soon.

Lots of love and kisses
David

Re: From my castle to Mickey and Minnie's
Hi David

You do have a busy life! I did close to nothing this weekend and it was really enjoyable. Yes, Disney, Epcot, MGM and Universal Studios are all for adults. I don't really have words right now for why that is so, but it is, trust me. I'll look forward to taking you there. Tomorrow I'll mail you some of my brochures so you can see what I do. Gotta run, I need to go over a week's worth of mail before going to bed. I didn't touch anything while I had a houseguest here. Until later......

Love
Dianne

Doing nothing over a weekend!
Hi Dianne

Yes, my life is incredibly hectic. My business partner says I will burn myself out if I'm not careful. Well I am a man, so listening to that type of good advice falls on both of my deaf ears.

Tonight I am off to Rachel's. She has said that she wants to cook a meal for me. This will be the first she has done, since she moved out of the family home where she lived with her mother.

Don't worry – if you tell me they are for adults, I trust you, and look forward very much to having the opportunities to see you and them together. By the way, you won't need to worry about the houseguest part of my visit. I wouldn't suggest that I stay; it will be wonderful to see you without disrupting your whole life. That sounds very cheeky – it wasn't meant to be. I was just saying I am not expecting anything. If you are busy I would be just as happy to take you out in the evening.

I feel that last paragraph sounds dreadful – but the words are not clear to me so heaven knows what it sounds like to you.

Good luck with your post, I hope there was nothing too urgent.

We have never discussed spiritual things have we?

There never seems to be any time on either side of the pond.

I ought to go or Rachel will think I got lost.

Lots of love and warm thoughts
David

Re: Doing nothing over a weekend!

Hi David

Your words sound wonderful to me. Actually you always have something good and interesting to say, and you are very honest in your thoughts and feelings. I like that in a man. I'm going to be really busy for the next few weeks now before the cruise, so if my letters are short please don't take it personally. Tomorrow I'll mail the cruise brochure to you so at least you'll see what is keeping me so busy.

Gotta go pick up Nicki from cheerleading practice. I realized that you may not have cheerleaders there like we do here, and may not realize that it is an athletic sport with gymnastics and stunting as well as dancing. She competes all over the country. Both of my daughters do it. It's a nice clean-cut sport for them that keeps them hanging around with nice people. Till later.....

Hugs and kisses
Dianne

More and more to learn

Hi Dianne

Even though I am not a negative or down type of person, your emails always give my spirits a good lift.

I do try to be as open and honest about feelings and situations as I can. However, I feel more at ease with you, and it is therefore easier. It is always a worry when talking to people you have never met, to know how they will react. We do seem to be getting along fine – don't we?

I am aware of the presence of Cheerleaders, but although they are now over here too – I have never seen one, other than on US TV or films. (It makes it sound like we are in the back woods somewhere!) I did think that they just chanted supporting slogans, bobbed up and down a bit, and kept the opposite team's eye off the ball. I learn more every day, and am pleased it is a clean-cut sport. There appear to be so many "bad people" out there whose intentions are to ruin children's lives with drugs, violence, etc. It is so nice to see that you are looking after Nicki and Marley so well. It is obviously difficult with the business, home, children, visitors, and me writing to you. But you appear to have it all under control, and without moaning either.

A small coincidence – one of my staff is taking himself and his wife to Orlando in November; but I don't expect our paths to cross. He is taking his wife away to many nice places – before it is too late – she is suffering from MS and won't have many trips like that left. (Makes you grateful for what you have.)

Ought to go, but don't worry about short notes, they always make me feel good – only unexplained silence is painful.

Lots of love and hugs

David

*   *   *   *

This was the last email in July so at this point we are one month since first "meeting". I feel good about this relationship. Just wish I felt better myself.

*   *   *   *

Chapter Six

Tony and the Start of Dreamtime

I met Tony eight months after Stan left me. My life during those eight months was a whirlwind some of which I have mentioned earlier.

I went back to college to take business classes in consideration of an MBA. I was taking accounting, business law and marketing. I tried to go back into real estate but found it wasn't the right job for a single mother being mostly evenings and weekends. I tried to work for another dentist but that didn't work out. After several short-lived jobs I was in a high pressure job as executive assistant to a developer. I moved with my young daughters from the large home on a golf course that Stan and I lived in together to a small 2-bedroom apartment in Altamonte Springs. I had a short-term boyfriend (two months) and a one-night lover.

Add to all of this the pressures of being a single mother and you can imagine my life. I think I kept doing so much because if I stopped I might feel the pain and not be able to get up again. I kept going to avoid just sleeping. I also kept going to prove to my parents that I was capable and not have them come and simply take my daughters away or take over to a degree that left me a non-entity.

When I write about this today, I am amazed at how time flies. I do believe it moves a lot faster as we get older. This time in my life was 20 years ago! How can 1989 be so long ago? It went in the blink of an eye. They say that in the spirit world they look at our brief visits to earth as just that, a blink of an eye, a brief moment in time. Looking at my life from a human in a body perspective I have to agree with the spirit world that it is really all over in an instant. While this gives reassurance to "this too shall pass", it also is a call to live in the present and enjoy it as it is so soon gone. But I digress. Putting myself mentally back into 1989 I was wishing it would pass very quickly.

Toward the end of this eight-month period I went to the intense personal growth course that I wrote about in chapter 4. Shortly after that course I met Tony in the office of the developer I was working for. He had been called in as the computer consultant to train staff on some computer applications. In fact I was the one who was given his phone number and called him.

There was an instant attraction when we saw each other. Physically he was very different from Stan and other men I have been attracted to who are normally short and dark (Italian, Spanish or Jewish types). He was tall and blond with long hair, blue eyes and very slim. There was a look of recognition in both of our eyes when we first saw each other, like we knew each other from another lifetime. Whenever he was in the office we would gaze at each other and smile. We became friends and I found out that he had also just taken part in an experiential personal growth course. I invited him over one weekend when Stan had the girls so we could compare notes about our courses.

Tony was a very good listener and even though I had completed this personal growth course my world was stressful and I was greatly in need of love. He was very loving. I asked him if he had ever been married and he surprised me with the response "I'm married now." Apparently it was an open marriage and she knew that he did whatever he wanted to do. She didn't want to do anything other than be with him so that was a bit one-sided but he told me he was free to be his own person. I didn't really approve of that or like it, but his wife wasn't who I was thinking about that day. We talked for hours, listened to music and held hands and kissed once or twice. Then I remember him saying to me "I will honor you either way but would you like me to make love to you?" My head nodded yes and I took him by the hand to my bedroom.

The lovemaking was good; it was loving and tender and I was able to completely remove his wife from my mind. Tony was a contradiction in that in some ways he was very spiritually aware and advanced in his thinking and in other ways he was lost and had a deep sadness. We fed some sort of need in each other and couldn't get enough of each other. On the nights Stan had the girls, Tony stayed with me. Yet I soon wanted more of him than I was getting. I didn't like him going home to his wife. So, this evolved into his spending half of his time with me and being part of my life with my daughters.

One thing I remember vividly and I wonder if Nicki also still carries this memory was when she was playing in the back of the apartment at age three sat in the grass and happened to sit on the home of some very mean red ants. She screamed. Tony was there and had the presence of mind to grab her up and take her inside directly to the shower where the water poured down on her taking the ants down the drain. He and Nicki bonded. Marley was a bit harder on him, being older, not as trusting and she was her daddy's girl.

Tony wasn't consistent, but when he was good he was very good. He even joined the parent's group at the elementary school, not just the PTA but the level above that which was even more involved. I can't remember what that was called. He was very much into A Course In Miracles. We actually both attended a weekly group for that. His interest went beyond that though into Attitudinal Healing which to simplify it briefly is about inner peace and healing through forgiveness and love of self and others. He spent a lot of time at these groups and doing one-on-one work with people. The people were most often women; again easy to see from my comfortable happily married spot now, but not something I chose to see back in 1990. Or perhaps I was also one of those women he was helping when I didn't have the strength to help myself.

He was the opposite of Stan in that Stan was seemingly all about the business and the money and our relationship was always about acquiring more. Of course that was the greedy 80s that we had lived through together. The decade where everybody was looking at themselves and how their life could be better, but looking for it largely outside of themselves rather than as happiness being an inside job that didn't necessarily have to do with having a lot of money. Again, looking at my relationship with Stan with the hindsight of all I know now, we really just needed to nurture our relationship and it might have lasted. However, I do believe that my soul's purpose in this lifetime included so many other things that I could not have done had I stayed married to Stan. So as painful as it was at the time, change had to happen. It was absolutely in my higher good.

I thought Tony was perfect. He didn't care at all about money. (He didn't need to he had mine!) I was completely blind to the fact that all the money I was getting from the divorce was supporting all four of us including Tony as he simply could not get around to billing people for work he did for them. I didn't want to constantly nag; it was easier to just throw money at the problem. Tony was spiritual like I was and into all of the things I was. We went to full moon ceremonies together and through that had a network of likeminded friends. Tony had long hair and was a rebel, like me, but even more so. One memory I have is on Halloween. He wrapped himself up in ace bandages to be a mummy. I was a witch, which is something I have always resonated with. Some trick or treaters came to the door and one of them said to him "are you a dead hippy?" You had to be there but that really is what he looked like with his long hair coming out of the ace bandages! Nicki thought he was cool, Marley wasn't as impressed.

This was the early 90s and living together wasn't as accepted as it is now. Now people have "partners" and see no need to marry. Even people my parents' age are doing that. At the time though my parents were very judgemental about the married man that was living with me almost full time. Tony saw no need to get divorced as he still felt love for his wife and she had done nothing wrong. Their relationship wasn't even sexual anymore although the nights he stayed with her were in her bed and he does sleep naked. He would take his pillow from our bed and travel with it to her bed. What was I thinking? I don't know, I only know that for whatever reason I must have needed him in my life. It does give me an understanding of how women can stay with alcoholic or abusive spouses or partners.

At a breaking point that I eventually reached, this was no longer acceptable to me so I gave him an ultimatum. While he felt there was no real need to divorce her and marry me, I felt like there was no reason not to and he couldn't argue with that either. He didn't want to lose me and agreed that he would divorce her and we would marry. This took a couple of years and there was constant drama and intensity in our relationship. Looking at it now, that marriage never should have happened. From the spiritual point of view that everything is as it is meant to be and it is all a way for the soul to learn and evolve and that everything happens for a reason, then absolutely it all should have happened.

In addition to meeting my physical and spiritual needs (albeit not full time) he helped me determine my best career. I had already stopped working for the developer and had taken a job as a teaching assistant for learning disabled children at a local elementary school. This didn't pay very much and I missed the business world to some degree. Through a process of elimination we decided I would like being a travel agent as I liked working with people and I liked travelling. I also wasn't too bad at selling and at treating people like a guest in my home, which was the philosophy acquired back at Stan's dental practice. I quit work when that school year ended and enrolled in a three-month full time travel academy. I enjoyed travel very much and after getting that diploma I got a job at a travel agency selling vacation packages, flights, cruises, tours and some foreign travel as well. I loved cruises myself and saw that the most money was made in cruises and that it was a good value for the client. Tony supported my ideas about creating seminars at sea on cruise ships for groups of like-minded people who were interested in the metaphysical/ spiritual topics that we were interested in. These cruises would be well-being and personal growth oriented and designed to help people (turned out mostly women) who were facing challenges in life like divorce and health issues. The idea of Dreamtime Cruises was born.

I started out doing this from another travel agency as an independent contractor paid on commission only. I soon realized how easy it is to set up your own travel business particularly for selling cruises and I did all of the necessary registrations, licenses and memberships, created a corporation and started my business from home with only Tony and I working in it. Luckily I was getting enough money from Stan with temporary alimony, division of assets and child support that I could afford to work a business and not draw any income, at least for the first couple of years. The business was my passion and more of a full time hobby than something that got treated like a business as far as actually making money.

Tony was essential with his computer skills as he did the desk top publishing of brochures and onboard programs and he set up my spreadsheets so I could monitor all of the cruises I sold and determine what I owed the cruise lines and what my seminar mark-up and commission was bringing in on each sale. This was the early 1990s. Now there are incredible computer programs for doing all of this and email and e-brochures and websites and online registration have taken over. It is amazing the differences in technology and ease of doing certain things. I joined AOL and had the screen name dreamtime. If somebody tried getting that screen name today it would have multiple numbers after it. I was in the beginning of email! I was also in the beginning of the popularity in seminars at sea in general and certainly in metaphysical, holistic and mind body spirit ones; so I was a trendsetter. Now there are a multitude of these cruises but I do feel that I started it all. It became all encompassing and who I was. My name for myself was seagoddess.

Tony set up my spreadsheets and did my brochure and onboard programs for me but I did everything else. I seem to remember a similar theme in my relationship with Stan; however, this business really was mine and was who I was. No more Mrs Dr Silver, I was the seagoddess. In writing this today and knowing what I know now, it sounds almost as silly but let's keep the story in a proper order (at least within the chapters).

My first body mind spirit cruise sailed in May 1991 and had four speakers; a Course in Miracles teacher, a past life regression therapist talking about past lives, a psychic teaching intuition and an astrologer teaching astrology. The group had approximately 30 people and we sailed the Western Caribbean to Jamaica, Grand Cayman, Mexico and Key West with 2 and a half days at sea to have seminars. The group bonded in an incredible fashion which was what my vision saw would happen. In Mexico we took a group excursion to the Mayan ruins of Chichen Itza and the regression therapist did a group regression on the top of one of the pyramids. I'm not sure how we kept others away. Maybe we had chosen an out of the way location or maybe we looked so strange that nobody living in ordinary reality wanted to come near us. In this regression we all experienced a life as Mayans in this area. Perhaps we had all been there together at that time in a past life and this cruise had truly brought an old tribe together again. One person broke out in blisters on her back, others felt very uneasy at locations there that the guide said people had been pushed or jumped to their deaths. One explanation the guide gave was that it was where they had sacrificed virgins. I never felt that sense of unease so perhaps was never a virgin! I did feel a headache and a sense of my head in a vice and that was attributed to a memory of being a baby when they shaped their heads from birth by putting them in a vice. In any event Mexico has always been a place I have resonated with and I do feel I have had at least one past life there. This was an incredible group bonding experience.

The astrology was very psycho-spiritually presented and all about how our worldview and our destinies are so linked to our astrological aspects. One very interesting person in our group had experienced an accident that led to a near death experience about 10 years prior. She never felt like the same person after that time and had a complete personality change. The medical profession had attributed it to the trauma and stress and of course tried mood swing drugs, antidepressants and other typical medical answers to make her normal again. When we explored the date of her accident and the astrologer did her chart for that date, it became clear that when she had died for a short time on that day and came back to life, she was essentially born again and had a new astrological chart with a completely different personality attached to it. This felt right to her and I would like to believe changed her life.

While not a financial success (I had worked 9 months from planning this cruise to it actually sailing and a group of 30 didn't really compensate that amount of work), that cruise was a spiritual success and convinced me that I was now living my passion and that this was the work I was supposed to be doing. I did two more small cruises like this one that I simply called body mind spirit cruises and then a very auspicious meeting occurred between myself and Peter Einstein which changed the business and took it to a different level. To be continued in a later chapter....

Chapter Seven

I Survive the Eclipse and the Cruise

A strange day
Hi Dianne
   I have missed your e-mails. I look each day and have that horrible sinking feeling when the box is empty or has junk in it. However I don't feel that there is a problem. Like you I am very busy and so understand that it is not possible to spend all the time at the keys – anyway it makes it so much nicer when you do send a message to me. I will look forward to something spiritual from you. I trust that the signs will be improving from the 22nd and I don't want any tragedy at sea.
   We are planning to allow the staff to witness the eclipse on the 11th and they should be able to see 98% unlike the people going to Cornwall in the Southwest of the country, who will get a full 100%.

$$* \quad * \quad * \quad *$$

(England had a very good viewing of this total eclipse of the sun. The US didn't see it at all if I remember correctly.)

$$* \quad * \quad * \quad *$$

Business is getting extremely hectic – which is good – but Shirley, my co-director is away on jury service. Just as well I thrive on being the ball in the pin-ball machine.

Today was a very mixed one for me.

THE BAD (and good):

Two boys aged about 9 and 11 stole the valve caps from the tyres of my Jaguar – value $10 - $15 – not much..... except they were given to me by Scott, and so couldn't be replaced. Some of my staff had tried to stop them, but they got away. So one of the witnesses said lets drive around and try to find them. We couldn't see them anywhere, so stopped and asked a friend of mine who lives near the factory if the description of the boys meant anything to her. She thought it did. Just at that moment they walked around the corner – she went straight up to them and told them my problem... I got two of the four back and an apology – and they sounded like they meant it. I couldn't even talk; I was so choked up to get them back. The police would have done nothing – this system worked so well. A good solution.

THE GOOD (and bad):

I went home early from work 4:45 instead of 8 – 9pm, and played golf with Graham, a friend I went to school with. He always wins – (thank goodness it's not competitive). Unfortunately his wife had just been diagnosed as having breast cancer, with a good prognosis they are told. It was good to have a chat and a pint. On the way home the heavens opened, floods, broken down cars all over the place, but I had to get home hell or high water to see if there was a message! I shall look forward to the weekend – no pressure (wink).

Lots of love

David

*   *   *   *

Again there must have been a small letter or two written by me that I didn't save. How can you not love a man like this? I don't know what I could have said to match his depth but he is obviously still with me.

*　　*　　*　　*

Inner Strength

Hi Dianne

I do think you are right about the level of protection, but I feel guidance comes that way too. I misread your message – I thought you were saying you were there to watch over me too – I was very disappointed when I re-read it. The explanation is much harder to come up with. I have believed in a type of telepathy, which is either us sending a message, or receiving one, or a premonition. My business partner and I can make the statement – we haven't heard from a person for a long time, and within a day, sometimes minutes – they ring up! This happens to both of us. Any explanation?

Faith is a difficult one for me. I don't know what to have faith in. I have previously believed in making everything work for me (but never at other people's expense). I am changing to feeling we have tremendous powers that are mostly dormant, like the telepathy. I want to learn more about using them, or developing them.

Is your chaos due to the eclipse? If so will it affect everyone that way, or is it positive for some?

We will be allowing everyone a chance to see the eclipse, then I am off on another sales trip. We decided not to leave until after it was over. We should get a 98% complete view – in Cornwall where I play golf once a year, they will get 100%. But like the New Year this year, the hotels in that area have escalated their prices.

I wish I wasn't so busy and could come on the cruise with you, not just to limit your losses! Like you I do create my own world. This is actually working much better recently – the last 3 months.

Your battles with the magazine are so negative aren't they? Is there a truly spiritual magazine you could replace them with? Things shouldn't be controlled; they should be run in the spirit of partnership. It sounds like they are very short of money – or desperately greedy. None of us need that. You must never give up and go out of business. You are obviously doing it for an important reason.

* * * *

This will make much more sense after reading chapter 8 which talks about where Dreamtime goes business wise when Peter Einstein starts to work with me. He brought in a magazine as a partner with him which created a difficult working situation for me.

* * * *

Don't worry about saying what is on your mind, it adds to your big picture in my head, but I hope you feel more spiritual soon for your own sake, the battle sounds out of character.

I have heard of Thanksgiving, but know nothing about it. Can you tell me more when you have time? What is it, how long is it, does everything stop for it? If I visit then I might try to visit potential customers if I get some US enquiries from the two exhibitions coming up.

I am in the middle of decorating the castle (my bedroom) but physical energy ran low, moving the heavy oak furniture. Now I am feeling it's time for tea.

I think I will send you (mentally) some of my inner strength to beat your problems of the eclipse. I feel that I have enough to share currently, and I can't bear to think of you suffering at the hands of greed. I have always detested that, but have never been able to beat it, only bypass it.

Lots of love and a hug for strength
David

* * * *

I can only imagine what I might have written to him to get this very diverse topic response. I know I was depressed and my business wasn't doing very well and the business partners in this cruise were greedy and using me and my staff and not paying us enough. I really appreciated his point of view as a fellow entrepreneur, as opposed to Randall the accountant who only saw the dollars and cents of it all rather than seeing it as my calling and that I was making a difference in the world. The next chapter will be about my business and the people involved, so I won't say too much about it here. David was a good person to talk to about it. But I didn't tell him it was failing as my identity was just too tied up in it and I wasn't ready to admit defeat or change again who I was. I was worried that I attracted him based on being the owner of Dreamtime Cruises & Tours and I needed to stay this person at least for now.

I'm intrigued by the cultural differences – him not knowing what Thanksgiving is and calling dinner "tea".

Again, I didn't save my own email in between but certainly saved his next one that very eloquently describes the eclipse.

*   *   *   *

From out of the darkness came the light ....
Hi Dianne

Thank you for your kind words, that I am nice. Those words seem almost a curse to me. At work, it is seen as a weakness, in that I am happy to give employees the benefit of the doubt, or be understanding at their troublesome times, giving them time to recover etc. Then people take advantage. It's enough to make anyone else become cynical – it just makes me doubt the whole philosophy of my life – do unto others etc.

In my personal life it made me a soft target for manipulative female friends, that I see as friends and they see as a suitable mate. I see relationships as moving through various stages by mutual consent, friend to soul mate to lover etc. I see the mutual as being vital and keeping those destined to be friends as friends, rather than spurned potential lovers is not easy. I am destined to lose more than a few along the way. Please don't misunderstand what

I am trying to say. When the right person comes along (and she may have just done so), I will be willing to move boundaries, with mutual consent. If however one of the people has a doubt, they don't move until both agree.

I appear to have digressed again. Thank you for the thought but it was a bad word in UK English.

Please don't worry too much. I do miss you, but am incredibly busy and have no problem in working instead of opening the soul.

Don't worry about your mood – Vickie is also an Aquarius and I am very used to the fixed bit…. but I do sense you fighting against it. I don't even mind if you are stubborn, as long as you care, and you really seem to me that you do.

I am a Virgo (30 August) – but I didn't note your birthday so it's your turn to reciprocate.

The eclipse was a weird day for me. The weather people had said it was going to have an 80% chance of cloud cover. This was the case at 8:00am on my way to work. By 10:00 it was clear and hot. The first stage started then. The local shops were selling special sun glasses for the day and I bought 20 pairs and gave them out to the staff. At about 10:30 I decided to video the event so I used a pair of glasses taped to the front of the camera and recorded from then until 11:30 when it was all over.

There was no sign of anything happening until 11:05 when through the glasses it looked like a new moon. The temperature was still hot and the light was still bright. However, then it turned very cool, and the light went very eerie, and the hairs on the back of my neck reacted as this bright sunny day stopped. The seagulls went mad, through the same sensations that were troubling me (I expect), the automatic lights came on …..no words can explain fully the sensations. It did not get totally dark for us as we had 98.8% eclipse.

I don't expect you will have picked up the feeling of the moment, they are difficult to explain; but I do understand why these events have such an effect on you, and any sensitive person.

Please forgive my total ignorance, but whose idea was the pumpkin pie – the pilgrims or the Indians? Is there a period this is associated with? We are not taught much about the States, other than silly things like grain production, Wall Street, 1492 and the War of Independence where you threw away our tea and had a party in Boston. It sounds terrible doesn't it, considering our two countries are supposed to have a "special relationship".

Thanksgiving does sound good for two reasons. The first being yours, which sounds good, having you to myself. The second that there is a shuttle launch due on the 2nd of December. I did get your cruise brochures and wish we could meet that way, under the Caribbean skies, but I hope that Florida can be as good. I have a certain nervousness about it even now, because you see me through the keyboard where you are not physically there. I am no oil painting, or great wit. It worries me that you could be very disappointed in the real me.

I can associate closely with businesses that have uneven cash flow. Ours is currently in the low season. We have two low seasons, now and Christmas, both related to people having their holidays and not being motivated before or after. I am sorry about the problems with your Italian trip. One day we should go there. You can show me the magic of it and I would love to show you the history.

It was great to hear from you again…thanks!
Love and hugs
David

*   *   *   *

More from him – I must have had some sort of reaction to his reaction about "nice". I also must have said that I could be a bitch sometimes hence his mention of the B word.

*　　*　　*　　*

Feelings

Hi Dianne

Before I say anything else, I am so sorry for my tirade on the word "nice" when it was very obvious that you were holding out a hand of friendship – and one I dearly wish to take. You are so right; it is my judgement of people that is wrong and not necessarily my way of acting with them. It will be so good to meet face to face with someone who is as different from the "normal" world as I feel. My view is we will either have a wonderful relationship face to face, or we will know on the first meeting that we will not. Already I know which way I feel it will be. I don't profess to understand you yet, and maybe I never will. Sometimes it is better not to know everything; it takes out the mystique, and you have plenty of that. So if anything were to turn you into the B word, it would have to be very serious, especially as you have been very tolerant of me and my little ways.

I do hope your business problems are on their way out, I know what a drag that can be. I'm glad the eclipse description came out ok. As for the feelings part of it, it was just me, and I am so glad you appreciated it. I am not as good with anyone else; maybe it's just the anonymity of the keyboard! However it is real, and can only really happen through trust. I am sorry that your last relationship didn't have male feelings disclosed. I guess testosterone rules. Who knows, I may have too many female hormones, I do cry through sad films!

Today I had a call from Vickie. She has done some research in the area of my true father, who left mum when I was three. She has found that there is an organisation that assists with the location of ex-military personnel. So I have given her his army number, regiment, an old address and will see how she gets on. She too is an Aquarius (31st of January). She has always been the one to write and get things actioned. She has written to Maggie Thatcher, The

Queen, and anyone that she could express an opinion to who may help the cause she was fighting for that day.

Rachel and her boyfriend (live in lover – but I am supposed to assume they are just friends) have decided to take me out for a meal, in repayment for the Shakespeare and other things, this Friday. Matthew is thinking of starting a business, but I feel he is a little young, and he has got to have some guidance in the general thought processes related to start up.

Talk again soon....warmest of thoughts
With hugs and kisses
David

*   *   *   *

I saved an ecard I sent him on the 19th of August 1999 in advance of his birthday as I would be on the cruise during his birthday.

*   *   *   *

Happy Birthday to My Prince

To my Prince from the land of dragons and castles ..... from your Goddess in the land of Disney and Cruise ships ....I can't wait to give you a birthday kiss in person.
xoxoxox
Love
Dianne

Bon voyage
Dear Dianne

Thank you for your birthday message. I too wish you could be with me. Do have a wonderful time. I hope the stress headache goes away before you walk up the gang plank. I hope you are reading this before you go. I wanted to thank you for keeping my spirits up over the last few weeks. Do have a wonderful time.

Lots of hugs (not from the other sailors)
Thinking of you
David x

*   *   *   *

The Inner Voyage Summer Wellness Cruise was good. We sailed from Los Angeles to the Mexican Riviera and had three days just at sea for our seminars. I put myself at a good table for dinner and had many interesting conversations with people, my favorite of which was Dr Gladys Taylor McGarey, a holistic doctor in her 70s who has a very special holistic clinic in Scottsdale Arizona and uses Edgar Cayce remedies and encourages people to listen to their own inner physician. This woman radiated love and true spirituality and was a very calming influence on me. My friend Merrifran (my fairy godmother) who I will talk about in a later chapter was there as well. She was in her 80s. These two women are the epitome of "wise women" and I hope I will age as gracefully and model my future years with them as an example.

This cruise group was less than 200 people, small compared to the big winter cruise we had with 700 people but still a lot of people to play hostess to. As a big part of the philosophy of my business was to treat people like a guest in my home and to show them that spirituality can be fun, particularly on a cruise ship, I was always "on" and looking after people's needs. Being with Gladys and Merrifran at dinner and feeling David in my heart really did help me make this week a good one for myself and many other people. I told Gladys and Merrifran about David and how something inside of me was telling me that he is the one, the person who balances all of the aspects of me and mirrors me in so many ways. The logistics of how this would work, being 4000 miles apart, remained to be seen, but the warm knowing feeling was good for now.

David wrote to me on the 28th of August in anticipation of my return home. It is hard to believe it has only been two months (almost) since his first email to me on the 29th of June.

*   *   *   *

Welcome home sailor
Dear Dianne

It's good to have you back and away from that 30% of the ship that are male and after their holiday romance.

I hope that you were not too stressed by the organisational part of the pre leaving work and you soon unwound and had a great time. I look forward to the 1st of September when you are back, taking into account the UK/US time difference.

Last weekend I had my development manager Daniel and his wife Sue around for dinner. It was the first time they had been to the castle, but I had been to their place for dinner three times so it was time to rectify the balance. When they arrived they had brought me a special bottle of wine. It was from Daniel's village in Romania and is from the year he was born (1962). I feel so honoured by the gift. I don't quite know what to do with it! I dare not drink it, it is obviously of great significance to him, so now like a character in a Tolkien novel, I have become the keeper of the bottle, to guard it for eternity.

Another employee is definitely working his ticket out of the company. He even challenged me for spending $20 more than he had asked for on the purchase rec (I am doing the buying while one of my staff is on holiday). He wouldn't even stop the challenge after being told the logical reasoning, or when I told him I owned the company and felt I had the right to make executive decisions without consulting him….. a bad move! I am actually very placid and easy going, but he is far too slow to pick up the vibes that I was not going to waste my breath over such a small deal, and he was wrong to buy only the exact number of items needed. I had to just walk away.

Well I will sign off for now and look forward to our first face to face meeting

David

xxxxx

*　　*　　*　　*

There must have been a short email from me acknowledging being home and tired and telling him how well I felt the cruise went, especially spending time with Merrifran and Dr Gladys.

*　　*　　*　　*

Re: Welcome home sailor

Dear Dianne

I am so pleased that the cruise went well. It always helps, doesn't it. I am very selfish, I am pleased that you didn't have a shipboard romance and you were kept out of mischief by your fairy godmother. She sounds wonderful and a good friend who obviously knows a winner when she sees one.

I would love to cook for you. I feel it is a very special kind of giving to create something very special for someone who then eats it. Not much else like it. Here's a suggestion for you, I cook, you demonstrate the accuracy of your fridge magnet.

*　　*　　*　　*

I had told him I have a magnet that says "I kiss better than I cook".

*　　*　　*　　*

Now that the eclipse is over are you feeling better? I do hope so. It's heading on past 12:30am so the four poster calls.

Warm wishes with love

David

xxxxxx

Chapter Eight

The Rise of Dreamtime, the Fall of Tony and the Cast of Characters Along the Way

At the end of chapter six I mentioned Peter Einstein. When most people hear the name Einstein they think of the famous genius. Well Peter Einstein is a genius of sorts; he is a creative genius. In projecting my mind back to 1993 to write this, I have to say he was a mixed blessing in my life, but I so strongly believe that everybody we meet and everything that we do is meant to be and is something our soul is meant to experience. Peter took Dreamtime to a whole new level but I lost Dreamtime and my dream; it became Peter and his. Similar to what happened to me when I was Mrs Dr Silver. As human beings on a growth path we do tend to repeat the same lessons until we learn them.

I'll start from the beginning. I had three mind body spirit cruises under my belt in 1993 when I received a phone call from Peter Einstein. He was promoting his wife's "total intuition system" and somebody who bought it told him about my cruise that she had been on. The coincidence was that he had just had a flash of inspiration while taking a shower. He believed that in the shower, with the water hitting his crown chakra he was put in a natural intuitive and creative state and he got some of his very best ideas in the shower. In this shower produced vision he saw people learning about intuition while having the time of their lives on a cruise ship, sailing to beautiful islands in the Caribbean while learning and sharing with like-minded people on the days between islands when the ship was at sea. What a great idea. I guess great minds think alike and I was a great mind before Einstein was! As I was a travel agent and knew how to do what is necessary to conference at sea he saw me as the ideal partner for his idea. So I received a phone call from Peter Einstein. He talked a lot, but so did I; he was very enthusiastic, a quick witted New Yorker. The business woman in me wanted to take Dreamtime Cruises & Tours to the next level and Peter Einstein the Madison Avenue marketing genius who happens to have a psychic wife and a spiritual mindset seemed like a good vehicle....so I said yes to the partnership.

Peter handled our marketing, our selection of presenters, negotiations with the presenters (free cruise or half free cruise, flight included or not, how much they would get per referral, etc etc). With Tony's help in desktop publishing and Peter's writing of the copy, I would get the brochure produced and be the one who would mail it to our mailing list and the mailing lists of speakers. I would sell the cruise, match single people with roommates, create all of the post sale documents, negotiate with the cruise line for group price, free spaces, rooms for meetings, etc. If you think perhaps I did more than Peter did for my half of the partnership you would be correct. Like I said though it was very similar to my marriage to Stan and probably a lot of women will see themselves in this very same scenario.

Tony was my desktop publisher and my spreadsheet creator and provided some help with mailings as well. However, I was ambitious and a bit of a workaholic and he wasn't (to say the least). He wanted to just sit and watch films in the evening and I wanted and needed to keep working. I was about either my business or my children and could see no need to waste any of my precious time watching TV. My strength grew and Tony's power over me weakened. I no longer felt like he was rescuing me. I no longer needed to be rescued.

I hired my first employee just a few months before the first Intuition Cruise sailed in February 1994. Katie was a seasoned cruise seller, a good friend and very open and interested in the spiritual, intuition, personal growth and natural healing topics our cruises were about. She also happened to be the wife of the brother of my cousin's new wife. Follow the plot now. This is my cousin whose first wife married my first husband, Stan. (This is not fiction.) I guess my selected cast of characters in this life liked to keep it all in the family!

Katie loved selling, making friends with the clients and spending a long time on the phone with them. She is from Ireland and certainly had the gift of gab! Of course this saw my phone bill rise quite a bit but she was making sales so I ignored the expense. The other problem was she and Tony didn't get along at all. This business was still in my home at this stage and Tony was out of the house working close to 50% of the time so they didn't have to clash too much. She thought he was lazy and bossy and he resented her coming in and acting like my partner in the business when he saw himself in that role. After all, he had started it with me. I saw both points of view and frankly neither of them were ideal for what I needed to make this a success and neither alone had the potential to be a full partner. Tony was of course also very suspicious of Peter. Tony didn't draw a salary but of course he had free room and board with me. Katie drew an enormous salary that was hard on Dreamtime from the very beginning. My daughters saw us all as quite funny. They were 7 and 9 at the time, the golden age for children really, not yet pre-teens. They shared a bedroom in this house so that the third bedroom could be an office. At this age it was still okay and they liked having Katie and I there when they got home from school without a need for day care after school. Katie loved them and they loved her and she had a son a year younger than Nicole whom they got to see often as well.

Tony and I got married in January 1994, about a month before the 1st Intuition Cruise sailed. We had lived together for four years and I saw no reason why we shouldn't get married. He had finally divorced his first wife and although things between us weren't ideal, we did meet a large percentage of each other's needs. It seemed we were supposed to be together. My parents were judgemental about our living together and I thought they'd accept him more if we were married. It turned out that they just didn't like him. We had a small wedding at our friend Kelly's house. She was a spiritual minister and half Cherokee and performed a beautiful Native American wedding. Our only guests were both sets of parents, Nicole and Marley and Tony's nieces and nephews whom his parents were babysitting. Tony and I both wore black. It was a far cry from my first wedding which was a large Jewish wedding with me in a traditional long white bridal gown. Our working honeymoon was the Intuition Cruise one month later.

The Intuition Cruise took place on the now retired SS Norway which in 1994 was the largest ship afloat. The theme was "go with the flow" on the first ever Intuition Cruise. We sailed from Miami to the Eastern Caribbean with about 20 presenters and 120 guests. We followed the philosophy that I learned back in Stan's dental practice of treating people like a guest in our home. Katie, Tony and I bent over backwards to make sure everybody was having a wonderful time. You know, sometimes even spiritual people can be downright mean and some people did not exactly meet my vision, which was to travel with like-minded loving people. Although we made every effort to match people with roommates they would love, there were the inevitable few who didn't and who complained.

I had one phone call at about midnight after being sound asleep from one person who was in a triple with two friends but who couldn't believe that the triple bedding meant that one was sleeping in a rollaway bed. This no longer happens on the new modern cruise ships but it apparently did happen on this ship and there was nothing I could do to change that situation. Funny though, this person who called me late at night turned out to be Suzin Bailey who became my close friend and business partner and who died in 1997. This cruise produced another guest who is still a good friend today, Lynn Monson who is now Lynn Hayes and married to her third husband Rich who is also absolutely perfect for her. Lynn is a realtor and an astrologer and has her own Astrodynamics website. We now take a cruise every couple of years with Lynn and Rich. I knew that on this cruise I was meeting people who I was meant to meet and the connections made on this and future cruises among guests was enormous.

But back to this first cruise. One of the comments from it that Peter and I continued to use in marketing for years was from Ruby Yeh who said "People weren't just relating person to person they were connecting soul to soul" and that was very true. It was an incredible experience and 120 people was a wonderful sized group. It could be handled by me, Katie and Tony with a little help from Peter who saw himself as the cruise director. Tony was the audio-visual person who made sure microphones worked, meditation tapes were playing when needed etc. He was also Tony, the person who liked to rescue women and he spent a lot of time talking to women who were in distress and needed to talk to someone. These cruises attracted a lot of women who were seeking their own inner peace and may have just been divorced. I didn't really trust Tony that all he did was talk as he was often gone very late at night; a bad scenario considering that this was our honeymoon.

This first cruise was an enormous success and Peter and I immediately started planning the next one. Suzin and I became very close friends. She lived in Virginia outside of Washington DC and owned a Native American, Celtic and New Age shop called Yesterday's Memories. She was a past life regression therapist and a very interesting woman. Other than the fact that she had very large breasts and I didn't we looked very similar with both of us having long black hair and wearing a lot of purple. She was very much my protector and didn't like the way Tony treated me or the way Peter treated me either for that matter. She had money and wanted to invest it in doing Past Life Cruises so that I would have another specialized niche away from the Intuition Cruise. So very quickly Suzin and I became business partners. We were very close and some people even mistook the business partner relationship and thought we were gay partners. We told people that no, we like men, but our relationship was in many ways a soul mate relationship and when taking an astrological compatibility test we actually scored higher together than we did with any man!

Suzin and I planned our first Past Lives Cruise for 1995. Janet Cunningham, Linda Adler and Henry Bolduc were the speakers and I still consider them friends today. Janet was one of the three in the triple on that first cruise! Henry Reed joined those three speakers later in a Past Lives and Dreaming Cruise. These cruises were special for Suzin and I, but not financially profitable. Still it seemed like we were doing what we were meant to be doing, and having fun doing it. All of the participants loved our cruises.

I also partnered another body mind spirit cruise with my good friend, holistic physician Dr Roy Kupsinel. This was on a Russian ship, which meant a lot to us as we both have Russian descent. This cruise took us to the Mayan sites in Mexico, Guatemala and Honduras. Spiritually it was a big success. The group size was less than 20 people though so Roy and I made no money. Roy was a presenter on one or two more of my cruises and our friendship continued until his "refolding" (as Roy describes death) from cancer quite recently. Roy was a magician and a photographer in addition to being a holistic physician. I am now very good friends with his third wife Beth, so the soul family connection continues. Our friendship started in an email about Roy's untimely death.

In the summer of 1994 Katie and I knew we needed more help so we brought on Paloma who had just graduated from the University of Central Florida in finance. She had been Katie's son's babysitter for many years and Katie highly recommended her as a person and an employee. Katie wasn't wrong and Paloma turned out to be a very special person who I still consider one of my best friends. She was business minded and able to do all of the spreadsheets and other financial things. She wasn't hired to sell but was able to do that as well and she was welcomed into the inner circle at my home where my children came home from school and gave Paloma a big hug as well. She and Katie also felt very close to Suzin. This wasn't a typical business; this was a reunion of a soul family. Nobody was particularly happy with Tony, myself included. He had a hard time saying "we" when speaking of us. It seemed like a temporary visit he was making in my life. The Cat Stevens song kept playing in my head "you know someday you're going to leave her but for now you will stay….."

Suzin and I took a cruise together in October of 1994 to check out a Holland America ship as a possible venue for the Past Lives Cruise. As Holland America is more the line for older people we watched in fascination as older couples danced together, held hands and really seemed pleased to be with each other. I had the foreboding sense that this would never be me and Tony. Something really deep inside of me longed for this though, but not necessarily with him. I really wanted to find my other half whom I would grow old and content with. Content, not meaning settling for something but meaning full out happy and really comfortable with who I am and who my life partner is. I had a sense of knowing that this is possible and that I wanted it for myself. Tony picked us up from the cruise when it returned to Tampa and was very distant. This was not what I wanted for myself.

The first Past Lives cruise sailed in the winter of 1995 and so did another Intuition Cruise. The Past Lives cruise was my and Suzin's style and we were the hostesses and it was us rather than Peter so nobody was overshadowing me. Tony was not onboard this one and I made a heart connection with one of the passengers named Mark. I probably would have slept with him but he didn't want to rush into that as I was married. He played the guitar and sang for me and it was a very healing and uplifting situation. On that cruise I met another person who I called my fairy godmother or my angel. Her name was Merrifran. She was about 80 and a very spiritual loving woman. She was a protector of me and felt I was doing God's work in these cruises that were helping so many people. Our friendship grew after the cruise and she ended up loaning me $20,000 a couple of years later to try to keep the business going. I am today still paying that loan back to her children as she has passed to the spirit world. I miss her unconditional love and acceptance. She provided what my parents couldn't as their love to me seemed conditional on my behaving a certain way.

I think with the help of Katie, Paloma, Suzin and Merrifran my strength and confidence slowly grew. Tony was leaving me alone a lot and doing "attitudinal healing" with other women. Attitudinal healing in itself was a good thing, based on the principles from A Course In Miracles but I think that the bottom line was Tony was a womanizer and used this as a way to meet and grow close to women. Our relationship was failing. It was so evident to my friends but took me a little longer to accept. I was like an abused wife in that I kept forgiving him and coming back for more. He left in December 1995. It took me a year of therapy to get over him. Looking back now I have to ask "what was I thinking!" All I can say is that perhaps this second bad marriage was necessary because it taught me more lessons and brought me closer to being the person who was ready for a really good relationship.

One thing I have to say I learned is that you have to love yourself enough to allow a loving relationship in. You have to romance yourself (flowers, candle lit bath, me time, etc) and be as good to yourself as you want another person to be good to you. This is a simple formula but not easy for most women who tend to be givers but not good receivers. The principles of the law of attraction, which are much more in the forefront today than they were in the mid 90s, are very simple. Give out the right energy or vibration into the universe to attract what you want, not what you don't want. Your beliefs and way of being and thinking create your reality. We are meant to be happy and joyful and we serve ourselves and others much better when coming from a place of joy, inner peace and well-being. If everybody had that how could there possibly be wars. This paragraph is probably one of the most important ones in the book. I wish I had read it myself in 1995; I might have saved myself a lot of grief. Don't be afraid of change and know that there is something better for you out there if you just believe and know you are worth it. (Think of me as the good witch Glenda telling Dorothy that all she has to do is click her heels together and believe and think to herself that there is no place like home). That is the law of attraction and belief in action.

One other thing that is important to remember is the concept that the universe abhors a vacuum. In other words create the space to allow a new and good relationship in. If you are in a relationship just because you don't want to be alone, the universe is less likely to bring the right relationship to you as it doesn't know that you desire one.

Back to the story and the cast of characters. 1995 and 1996 brought several Intuition Cruises and Past Lives Cruises. On one of them I met my friend Paula Tiara who is still my good friend today. She has created and is living her dream in that she has built a mountain retreat on top of a mountain with separate cottages that she rents out. It is in Virginia and called Serenity's Edge. She and I have helped each other through many relationship and business challenges.

In 1996 Peter made the decision to take the Intuition Cruise to a whole new level and he partnered with a new age magazine to create The Inner Voyage Cruise. This cruise brought in more famous presenters like Joan Borysenko, Dr Larry Dossey and Dannion Brinkley. The magazine gave it a full page ad in all of their issues and hundreds of people signed up. I believe 1997 contained our biggest ever cruise with 700 guests! I had to get over my fear of public speaking when I took the microphone and welcomed everybody onboard that cruise. I had expressed to a friend who is a neuro-linguistic programming (NLP) therapist that I couldn't do it and he said to me four simple words "what if you could?" It sort of scrambled my brain to think, oh, what if I could? Maybe I can. This is an excellent tool for many things.

I knew if I looked at the audience as people with egos I would have freaked out. Instead I looked at them as if I were looking only at their heart and soul and I wasn't nervous at all. I smiled and used the line from "Field of Dreams" that said if you build it they will come and I said something like "We dreamed this and you came and for that I am grateful and I welcome you."

On the first Inner Voyage Cruise I met another dear friend, Katie Toomey. She and I have spent many hours talking and helping each other through relationship issues. She is a single mother with four children and is certainly a person to be admired for all she does. She is a nurse who welcomes newborns into the world and whispers to them that they are incredible spiritual beings. She tells them that they must remember that no matter what anybody says to make them less than that. It would be interesting to trace some of these newborns into later life to see what a difference such an affirmation and knowing makes. She is also a hypnotherapist and healer and is working on her first book.

Three other people I met through the Inner Voyage cruises that are my friends and who will be discussed more in a future book were Tianna Conte who sailed with her soul mate William Dubs, Louise Hauck and Kathryn Harwig. Tianna's soul mate passed to the spirit world shortly after that cruise and Tianna tells an incredible story of their communication during his death and beyond it. Louise is a medium who communicates with the spirit world and talks about the continuity of life. She has been on quite a few of my cruises since meeting her on an Inner Voyage. Kathryn is a psychic and spiritual advisor and a palm reader who has also been on many of my cruises. All three of these women have incredible insight into how much of the world there is beyond the world that meets the eye.

I am certainly blessed with really warm and talented friends and I have my creation, Dreamtime, to thank for this opportunity in my life. My daughters sailed on at least a half dozen of these cruises and although they were young their eyes were opened to a whole new world of interesting albeit eccentric people.

My part onboard The Inner Voyage cruises was minor really, as was my company in the promotion of the entire thing. It was a joint venture between Peter and the magazine and Dreamtime was only the travel agent. We made a 10% commission only. I, of course had to staff up to handle all the sales, mailings, roommate matchings, dining table assignments etc. I also moved the office from my home to a 500 square foot office in a professional office building.

In keeping with my previous style of hiring friends we hired two people before the 1997 cruise. The first was Gloria who was Katie's mother in law and the second was Teresa who was and still is a good friend of mine. She became a single mother at the same time I was becoming a single mother for the second time. Nicole was in the same class as her older daughter Melissa. Teresa is now a successful businesswoman owning Alkemy Skincare Day Spa. Both Teresa and Gloria turned out to be very good sales people although as commission was involved in the sales we started to get a bit of competition in the office that wasn't always pleasant. Gloria never thought of herself as a sales person but was a real natural as was Teresa. I think it was the product that inspired all of us.

I felt we still needed more help and hired another friend, Janet. Janet was also very good at sales, but she and Katie had conflicts and it started to not be much fun anymore at work. All of these women were very good at what they did albeit they did stay on the phone a bit too long and my overhead really grew beyond what I could afford. I was in the situation of needing a large staff for several months each year leading up to the big winter cruise but I found myself overstaffed at other times. Paloma pointed out to me that we were borrowing too much money and had too many staff but I buried my head in the sand pretty much like I did about Tony for so long. I think maybe that when you are in the midst of a life lesson you need to stay in it until you are ready to leave it and I wasn't ready to leave it or let any of my friends go.

Suzin and I planned a Magical Mystical Britain Cruise for the summer of 1997. It had Celtic Arthurian expert and shaman John Matthews as the only speaker and the cruise visited ports in England, Scotland and Ireland as well as Paris and Amsterdam. Because this was 12 nights and a bit more expensive that a 7 night Caribbean cruise it didn't sell very well. We ended up a group of only 12 and that included me, Katie, Suzin, the presenter John and his son. Suzin and I paid for 5 out of 12 of the passengers. You don't need to be a business person to realize we took a significant loss on that one. That was my first trip to Europe though and I felt a very strong affinity to England, Scotland and Ireland, very much of a déjà vu past life knowing. I felt like I was home there. Katie of course was home in Ireland and her parents greeted us from the port in Dublin.

Katie and I pushed Suzin in a wheelchair around the ports. To backtrack a bit, the previous Christmas Marley, Nicole and I visited Suzin in Virginia. The night before we arrived she was in a car on very icy roads going food shopping. She was the passenger and had her feet on the dashboard. The car skidded and crashed and one of her feet went through the windshield leaving her foot hanging by very little. It was almost completely severed. Her husband called me and told me not to come but we came anyway as we had to see her. Nicole and Marley loved Suzin as well. Suzin never really healed properly and never fully regained feeling in that foot.

Still, a month after returning from the British Isles cruise, Suzin came with me on an Inner Voyage that sailed from Boston to Bermuda. She wanted to support me in standing up for my rights and for more money and was my cheerleader when I left after that cruise to meet with the magazine in Boston. We were in the same taxi after the cruise, me going to the rental car place to get a car and her going to the airport. She squeezed my hand and said "Take good care of yourself; don't let anybody take advantage of you." I felt weird saying goodbye to her that day, a strong sense of foreboding. She was going into the hospital in a few days for reconstructive surgery to her foot that would hopefully re-join nerve endings and let her walk again.

I never saw her again. After the surgery a blood clot from her leg travelled to her heart and lungs and put her in a coma that she never came out of. It was while she was in the coma that I wrote the poem that I shared with David called "My Friend." Her daughter read it to her while she was in a coma and told me that Suzin visibly moved. Katie and Paloma and I were at work together when we got the phone call that Suzin had died and we held each other and cried for a long time. Suzin made a difference in my life even though she was only in it for three and a half years. My daughter Nicole, very intuitively climbed on my lap at home that night and cried with me. She also wrote a poem for Suzin. Janet Cunningham was with me by e-mail processing Suzin's untimely death in 1997, as she was a close friend of Suzin and talks about a past life they share in her book "A Tribe Returned."

1997 was also the year that David's son died and the year that he left his wife. On a global scale it was the year that Mother Teresa and Princess Diana died. It was the year that I saw England, which would soon be my home. If somebody said to me then when I visited England that in a few short years I would be living there with my third husband I would have asked what they had been smoking! It is funny how fast life changes......

Marley, Dianne & Nicole
Greek Isles Cruise 1998

Dianne with Peter Einstein (The Captain)

Katie, Dianne & Suzin – playing bingo

Suzin & Dianne hosting the Past Lives Cruise

Chapter Nine

We Instant Message, Talk on the Phone, and Grow Very Close

*   *   *   *   *

I must have sent him an upbeat and provocative email before this.
I am obviously feeling better now and more ready to really get close.

*   *   *   *

An Officer and a Gentleman – Maybe?
Dear Dianne

I very much look forward to living dangerously and finding
out you are an improper wild American Girl. (Within reason
– as I am fun loving but quite reserved until I know the rules.)
It's sad you feel the Queen would not accept you. As an ex-
British commissioned officer (ex being the commission and not
the British) she has to give her personal permission before I can
have any form of foreign relationship.

I very much look forward to meeting the SeaGoddess – and
only you can find out if I am a British gent or not! But you are
correct about laughing at each country's silly ways.

I found your comments about sex refreshing. I have never
found it very important, because I never felt close to my wife. I
long for the time when two souls can lay close together and merge,

giving and only feeling for the other. My past was not like that, maybe the future will be.

I do not see myself as possessive, but I would like to visit you, not you and a new friend. Unless that is possessive, I am very much in favour of your independence and strength and would like those to remain while the souls developed a closeness that would remove any need for possession due to the loyalty that would create.

If fish isn't your number one food, what is? I can cook many other things, but keep it simple if you are in a kissing mood while I have the apron on. I too look forward to cooking for you!

I am pleased you are feeling so much better now the eclipse is over. It comes out in your writing too, lots more energy and vitality.

I am glad you like my unusual sense of humour. It is generally wasted on people over here; they just think I am insane. It is true I am on a totally different wavelength to most people and that has actually been a big advantage in business!

I am so sorry about my delays in writing. I have been having a bad time still sorting out my final finances for the divorce. I have a rare face-to-face meeting to try to reach an out of court settlement on Thursday evening so wish me luck. I must say I am not very optimistic, but it will be vital to avoid a court hearing and extra aggravation.

It's getting quite late 8:00pm and I am going home now. I will be thinking of you.
Love and hugs and gentle kisses
David
xxxxx

*   *   *   *

Again I didn't save my emails but they must have been improving, flirty and talkative based on his responses.

*   *   *   *

Sleeping Beauty needed for tired Scot
Hi Dianne – I am back again

I too look forward to meeting the mysterious Sea Goddess from over the ocean with the poetic phrases to charm any poor innocent boy to his unsuspecting peril …like the Cyrans of the ancient mariner.

The Kennedy Space Centre sounds favourite. On the 2nd of December there is a shuttle launch and watching it live could be so exciting to a poor sad chap like me.

To sort of clarify the finances, after our divorce and before we can receive the final certificate the finances need to be agreed. Up to now all my calculations and offers have been rejected out of hand and it has been very stressful and frustrating. My normal negotiations at work start with both parties having a goal in mind and you meet somewhere in the middle. This time I arranged a meeting with her and our old friend Graham (to witness). I went along with a proposal, and had it refused. A small reminder that if we went to court it would cost us both a lot more money and the deal was underway. I had to change everything, but we have now got a signed agreement and my solicitor (lawyer) has the details, but I am still cynical about its outcome, having been disappointed so often before. Thank you so much for your positive thoughts, they have moved me so far in the right direction…we are so close to the end….fingers crossed.

I now will not have my new PC until I return from the exhibition next weekend at the earliest, then I will sign on to AOL. Alternatively we could always have short calls on the very old fashioned but more sensitive tool – the telephone. What do you think? It would be nice to have a voice that can be used to read the email messages out loud to me. Currently your messages are read in my voice and you lose most of your charm consequently.

I loved the picture, you have wonderful eyes – they were revealed line by line to me as I opened you up. I will send you another when I return after Saturday.

Sleep well – lots of love

David

xxxxxx

*   *   *   *

Yikes, talk on the phone?! Why did I find that thought so frightening? I think because I had not yet told Randall it was over and in fact I agreed to let him visit me this next weekend. I can't really talk to David or go full force into this relationship until I end that one.

*   *   *   *

Survived the Hurricane

Hi

I survived the hurricane. It went ashore in North Carolina so Florida didn't get the worst of it. I did get to miss one and a half days of work as hurricane days as schools, banks and even the post office closed down so Dreamtime did too. I'm really busy right now, will write again in a few days.

Love

Dianne

Re: Survived the Hurricane

Dear Dianne

Well, I am so glad you survived Floyd. Like you it's been very hectic here. The problems of settlement are now over, as is the exhibition. Next week I will be in Scotland until Friday night then Saturday going to Southampton to help Vickie move into her new flat. Back for that week then the following week another exhibition and selling for the week, then it's time to consider my holiday.

How have things been with you? I have received the literature on your cruises. It looks very tempting, especially with your little note. How about you tell me about it when I see you, assuming we are still on....

I have made enquiries about fly drive holidays to the US and they are very expensive. However, doing the same thing through scheduled airline, hiring a car there and booking accommodation all separately appears to give the very best of all situations, including total freedom.

Your latest photo taken on that last voyage was truly wonderful, you look really great.

If you read this before Saturday night I would really appreciate a line or two from you. It's very poor when both of us are so busy. I have now got the new computer home today, signed up with AOL and looking forward to instant message chatting soon.

Warmest thoughts

David

xxxx

*   *   *   *

It is almost as if he could tell I wasn't 100% with him yet. Notice how he says "assuming we are still on". Well, Randall came to visit this weekend so I couldn't answer David before Saturday night. The romance was definitely gone. I told him I thought we both wanted different things and I saw no point in continuing this just for friendship and sex. Randall was off in a week or so to see the country as a truck driver and he still wanted to be able to drop in when in Florida and have me as a girlfriend. He still spent the night on Saturday but Sunday morning we both knew it was over and he left. David was the one who intrigued me. I no longer had anything in common with Randall. He was a boyfriend though and another chapter for me to close in my life. Looking back on my relationships, he probably lasted longer than any boyfriend who didn't become a husband.

*   *   *   *

Knight to Goddess
Dear Dianne

I have now loaded AOL (my screen name is DavidHPurdie) so tell me when and we'll give this instant message thing a try.

Since I removed the financial dealings from everyday worries my life has started again – no depression – less stress, and now I can see how she was dragging me down into the depths of despair – but now I am free, and I wish to have a great holiday.
Lots of love
David
xxxxxx

24th September 1999 – We Instant Message [please note these email addresses are no longer in use]

Goddess254:	there, now I have you on my buddy list
Goddess254:	it's nice to "talk" with you!!
DavidHPurdie:	and you
Goddess254:	now I can hear your British accent…how sexy
DavidHPurdie:	not as sexy as yours I'm sure
DavidHPurdie:	this is a very hectic time as you may have read and tomorrow is my last day home before a week away
Goddess254:	I'll miss you, you won't be online I take it?
DavidHPurdie:	that's right
Goddess254:	I'm getting a temporary roommate next week – my friend and hairdresser Terri who is getting divorced – she'll be staying in the office here

DavidHPurdie:	how many offices do you have?
Goddess254:	I only have one real office – I mean the home office/4th bedroom
Goddess254:	it will be weird with a roommate, I'm an only child and used to privacy
DavidHPurdie:	me too
Goddess254:	you are an only child too?
DavidHPurdie:	yes
Goddess254:	did we talk about being only children?
DavidHPurdie:	not that I recollect
Goddess254:	my parents overprotected me
DavidHPurdie:	mine were just the opposite
Goddess254:	that's why I had 2, didn't want a child to go through what I did
Goddess254:	let you do what you wanted?
DavidHPurdie:	I had 3 but it wasn't all my doing
Goddess254:	sounds like your wife was quite controlling
Goddess254:	I'm independent but not controlling
DavidHPurdie:	no – but not protective (parents) slow down please
DavidHPurdie:	yes, wife was
DavidHPurdie:	I'm glad you aren't
DavidHPurdie:	ok now
Goddess254:	sorry...oh no, I'm too fast for you...slow enough now
DavidHPurdie:	that's much better, remember I'm a novice
Goddess254:	yes, an aol instant message virgin – thanks for getting on aol for me
DavidHPurdie:	I couldn't wait – like most virgins
Goddess254:	an eager learner I see
DavidHPurdie:	yes please
Goddess254:	you are funny
DavidHPurdie:	don't laugh at me – I might cry
Goddess254:	I was going to say you were nice but that got me in trouble once

Goddess254:	I love a sensitive man
DavidHPurdie:	I am so sorry – that was stress – and you can call me anything – anytime
DavidHPurdie:	I'm very sensitive – hopefully to you more than about myself
Goddess254:	I'm kind of stressed myself right now, business isn't as good as it should be
DavidHPurdie:	I am sorry – what do you feel is causing it?
Goddess254:	people don't book cruises for March in September
DavidHPurdie:	I do a small amount of business advisory work over here
Goddess254:	even with our early booking incentive
Goddess254:	it will be fun for you to look at my business when you come here
Goddess254:	basically I need more business!
DavidHPurdie:	I would have thought the niche is growing
Goddess254:	it's not fast enough or the advertising needs to be elsewhere
Goddess254:	anyway sensitive boy I'm really looking forward to discovering all of your sensitivity in person
DavidHPurdie:	do you think it is the sort of job you could cope with?
Goddess254:	well we won't know for sure until I try…..
DavidHPurdie:	how would you tackle such a large task?
Goddess254:	one step at a time with great care….lots of listening and quiet time too
Goddess254:	I communicate better with my heart than with my head
DavidHPurdie:	I like the sound of your approach
Goddess254:	me too actually, don't get the wrong idea about me…I'm not fast..
Goddess254:	although with the right man anything could happen

DavidHPurdie:	that sounds nice....I hope you meet him this year
Goddess254:	I hope I do too! I love silence actually....just holding hands and cuddling, looking at the moon and the sky, sitting in the hot tub
DavidHPurdie:	you make me smile...that's a great start
Goddess254:	you make me smile too...only 2 more months till we meet
Goddess254:	how long are you staying and where else are you going?
DavidHPurdie:	I have no booking yet but the plan is about 2 weeks travelling down the coast to you
DavidHPurdie:	I hope you feel the same when we meet
Goddess254:	down the coast from where?
Goddess254:	I will
DavidHPurdie:	I thought I might start at Boston (I have an Aunty there who has written after 32 years)
Goddess254:	and you could have a tea party there hehehe
DavidHPurdie:	that was one of the sadder days in US history
Goddess254:	long drive from Boston but you would get to see NY and Washington DC if you drive
DavidHPurdie:	but a party with you sounds very good
Goddess254:	but if you are only spending 2 weeks in the US you would run out of time
Goddess254:	it would take you 2 weeks to get to me with those stops
Goddess254:	you'll spend a week here won't you?
DavidHPurdie:	would it, I haven't planned it properly yet
Goddess254:	aren't you tired...it is late in the land of dragons and castles
DavidHPurdie:	a little, but excited about having a 1 2 1 with you
Goddess254:	you make me laugh!
DavidHPurdie:	I need to get to know who you are

Goddess254:	I need to get to know who I am also
DavidHPurdie:	making you laugh is exciting too
Goddess254:	no kidding, sometimes I really don't know
DavidHPurdie:	feel free to get to know me
Goddess254:	I want to do that David
DavidHPurdie:	this is making a good start
Goddess254:	aren't you glad you got aol?!
DavidHPurdie:	YES
Goddess254:	so next week is Scotland? I remember liking it there
DavidHPurdie:	lots of travelling and a very little time for me – staying in Edinburgh for hopefully 4 nights
Goddess254:	do you travel alone?
DavidHPurdie:	no my business partner Shirley travels with me
Goddess254:	Shirley travels with you!
DavidHPurdie:	yes – in her own hotel room of course
Goddess254:	very interesting, I'm looking forward to knowing more about your business and all about you
Goddess254:	Oh wow, I'm going to have to say goodbye quickly because I have to pick up the girls from cheerleading….
DavidHPurdie:	and I should really go to bed…but I've really enjoyed this
Goddess254:	me too….a lot of kisses from me to you…. bye…..
DavidHPurdie:	xoxoxoxo bye……

*   *   *   *

That was really nice….I am feeling ready to talk to him on the phone now. A bit nervous but ready…..

*   *   *   *

Good morning Goddess of my (K)night
Good morning

As I slipped out of bed to run my bath this morning – I noticed that you were still fast asleep. I couldn't resist giving you a little peck on the neck – I hope it didn't disturb you.

I felt that our time on AOL was really great and I hope we can do more soon. I find it sad that without a printer I couldn't keep the message to read today (to prove it was not a dream).

Busy day today – off to work – final preparations for the trip and finishing off some of last week's unfinished jobs from all that negative distraction. Then over to mum and dad's – they are a story on their own – too long for now and not much more positive than the marriage – but I must not be negative or mum will lose out. Back to clear up – do the washing ready to pack and leave early Sunday.

Bath is now run, I see you still asleep (3am in US) so I will slip away in your night. Hoping to catch you before going to bed tonight.
Big gentle hug and warm kiss
David
xxxxx

We are so good together
Dearest Dianne

I am so glad that you didn't feel differently about me in the morning. I like writing to you and I love your responses. I feel that we will get on very well, which always has been a worry, that meeting you for the first time could be a problem. But always a sense of humour will oil the slideways of a relationship, allowing awkward situations to be negotiated without problems – and I feel the number of awkward situations with you will be minimal.

I have just got in from work 8:00pm and all I have done since I ended work was pick up my suit from the cleaners, go to my parents for a cup of tea, which I left half of saying I wasn't going to stay there listening to anymore bickering. It's been a hard enough week without all of that. My energy is low this evening and a big hug, or failing that a nice hot bath is the order of the day...so as you are not here, I will have a hot bath and relax, with you on my mind.

As a goddess you have all the power you need to vest a kingdom on me (and you do by your presence in my life). So it is with great pleasure and a humble heart that I graciously accept this honour. xxxxx

I had no idea you were in the own your own pool area of society...just as well I own a castle! It turns out talking to mum that I also have an aunt near Orlando, that I also saw 32 years ago, who used to live in Boston too...but I don't remember her.

So pleased you liked our AOL time and I look forward to more (or talking on the phone) on my return a week from tomorrow. Lots of love and kisses
King David of Castletown
xxxxxxxxxxxxxxxxx

*   *   *   *

I must have explained to him in my next email that half the houses in Florida have pools that it is no big deal. But what kind of castle did he live in?

*   *   *   *

King of the Castle asks what's a hot tub?
Hi my Goddess

Regardless if others have a pool, you are very special to me anyway. But what is a hot tub?

Theoretically all Englishmen live in castles – but I am a Scot. I live in a 2 bedroom flat; it's my sense of humour that makes it a castle – it's the theme of my bedroom (Scottish castle, four poster

bed, carved oak furniture, armour, etc). One day it might be a castle, but not now.
Talk again soon.
Lots of love
David
xxxxxxx

*   *   *   *

I am really finding the differences in our cultures intriguing and I longed to hear his voice now with his British accent. We agreed to speak on the phone when he returned from this business trip. I sent him my phone number along with an explanation of what a hot tub is.

*   *   *   *

Here's to bubbles!
To my dearest Goddess
   Well a Jacuzzi – that sounds wonderful! I have seen them at ideal home shows and films – I think you are right that I will love it.
   I suspect that some of my mail has gone missing. I sent a batch of pictures showing all rooms (including the bedroom), so if it has gone missing then remind me on my return and I will be very pleased to resend them.
   My birth date and time is 30th August 1953 (18:30 Glasgow time). My middle name is Hugh.
   I couldn't leave without seeing if you had replied, then I couldn't leave without replying. I love reading your wonderful messages; they have such warmth and feeling. Wishing you many sales of cruises.
Lots of love and another hug for the road.
Your silly king
David
xxxxxxx

* * * *

I love that he is a King and I am a Goddess. This is a bit of a fairy tale, hence the title of this book being Someday My Prince Will .com. He is more than a prince though he really is a King among men. He is so different from any man I have ever known. If he really is what he seems to be he is the perfect man for me in that he is both a hardworking businessman and also a sensitive spiritual man. This means he has the best qualities of my ex-husbands without having their faults. I do believe that I had to believe with all my heart that I was ready and worthy to meet such a man in order for him to arrive. He is exactly what I asked the universe for but due to our geographical distance he probably arrived too soon in the grand scheme of things as neither of us could move to the other just yet. But what am I saying? At this point we have not even talked on the phone, much less met! Why do I feel so strongly that he is my soul mate?! I do feel I love him and I feel very connected to him on a soul level.

He called me on October 4th 1999, just a little over three months since our first email but it seemed we had known each other forever. His accent is incredibly sexy and he felt that way about mine as well. That very first "hello Goddess" was really special. It was a feeling of yes, hello, I remember you. We both felt like we had been together before in other lives and that made it all the more exciting to now be connecting again and finally to hear each other's voice. It was a peaceful feeling. Our song became "You can relax now" from the Sprit of Love CD because we both felt that way. With Tony there was only drama. With David I felt an overwhelming sense of peace. Nice.

* * * *

You are a wonderful kisser
Good evening Goddess

I feel that our phone call was warm and wonderful, and there is something so special about your voice, full of warmth and sensuality, and wow you are so special!

96

That was a truly wonderful kiss (with your eyes open). Were you waiting for me to turn into a frog – or is this something that is done over there? Over here we are supposed to close our eyes (maybe so we can't see what the other person is thinking).

I don't mind personal questions either. How else will we get to know each other? I am sorry if I concentrated on your body. I have no expectations or even desires for a specific type, only I am not keen on the idea of having ribs showing. I do prefer the thought of a woman being curvy and feminine, not like the super models (boys with breasts). I accept that I do need to lose weight, but luckily mine is dropping off slowly, and hopefully will stay off. This weight was due to my ex-wife insisting on me eating everything she cooked – and that was always to excess.

The thought of us in the hot tub sounds great, and skinny dipping sounds too brave for me just yet (especially with your neighbours watching).

I am so glad that we have spoken and that has reinforced my feelings for you and hopefully yours for me.

Lots of love and a slow kiss…

David

xxxxx

*   *   *   *

I feel peace and comfort with him. Probably enough to actually tell him that my business wasn't going as well as it could. In fact it was doing very badly. I was at first afraid to tell him because I think part of what attracted him to me was the fact that I owned a business just like him and in fact it was a spiritual business that he finds very interesting. So it was a big step to tell him things were not very good and in fact to ask him for business advice. But I did, starting with the contract with The Inner Voyage. Turns out he was also experiencing business stress and we can be soundboards for each other. He must be stressed; he calls me Dianne instead of Goddess!

*   *   *   *

I am safe (just stressed)

Dear Dianne

I am safe – thank you for asking and caring. I didn't write last night as I wasn't feeling very well. I had a headache and was tense with stress. So will you be in later for a phone call? About 12:00 UK time, 7:00 US time? Then I will talk to you about your contract. I too have been thinking a lot about you.

Love

David

Strong determined Sea Goddess – assistance is available

Dear Dianne

I will keep this ultra brief – don't worry about your situation. I want to help spiritually not financially. I will see how I feel in the wee small hours and ring if I can. The stress is not related to your problems, much more related to Shirley's mother's recent death.

Do take care and I hope to talk very soon.

Love

David

xxxxxx

Energy transfer transatlantic style

My dearest Goddess

I have so enjoyed your chats and discussions; you have never been far from my thoughts. I have spent lots of time thinking about both your problems and meeting the real you. I see both a very strong and spiritual woman mixed with the soft tender and loving person who needs moral support in the business day to make sure that the future is as rosy as she would like it to be.

I hope I can be the things you need. But you must not put your faith in me but in yourself. You can do this with or without me. I just hope it may be easier with me.

I am suffering from a lack of knowledge of the market and the product, but I will always be here to talk to, and soon I will be there to give you a nice friendly warm and supportive hug and kiss and to say "you can do this." xxxxx

Do take care – lots of love and best wishes.

Your Scottish King

David

xxxxxxx

*   *   *   *

Very nice and very different than Tony who specialized in rescuing women, myself included. This is also a testament to how far I have come in my own personal growth to have attracted a man like him who wants to help but not rescue me.

*   *   *   *

Chapter Ten

Randall, Denial, and the Escape to Winter Springs

I haven't really said much about Randall yet other than to say it was now over. I met Randall on match.com about a year prior to meeting David there (summer 1998). Talk about being on a rebound, my goodness. He said he wasn't on a rebound but his wife had just left him for a man she had met on the internet. She actually hadn't physically left yet but was in another bedroom in their home preparing to take the children and move from Florida to Pennsylvania to move in with her new relationship. Randall wasn't very happy with her anyway but being left is bad for anybody's ego and the big thing was his children, whom he was compulsively close with. He really didn't want them leaving with her. He had a lot of anger that he was trying to diffuse with his new found spirituality. He found me knowledgeable and open and he created a relationship with me quickly and passionately.

And where was I in the summer of 1998? Well, let's see. It was 2.5 years since Tony had left me and I had looked for love and acceptance in many ways, including through my body, for probably close to two of those years. I had kissed (well not just kissed) about a dozen toads in search for my prince, the man who would find me worthy of staying with and loving till death do us part. In the summer of 1998 I was ready to be in a relationship with somebody who could both give and receive love. Love of the heart, soul, emotions, spirit and mind variety. Yes, and body too, but not just body.

In the summer of 1998 Marley was 14 and Nicole was 12. The past year had been really hard for me in the single mother department. Damn Tony for not being able to stay and be a family with me. Damn Stan for his judgmental ways with his perfect wife, money and mother, who all thought I should be much stricter and keep control of the situation. Regarding my parents, well I might have well have been a teenager myself, the way they treated me. So, three teenage girls, with no man (other than my father) to help us, and lots of people judging us.

They were all correct that I wasn't strict, or overprotective. I wanted to be different than my parents were to me. I was an only child and very overprotected and I resented that. It wasn't until much later, as I learned to see things from other people's point of view that I really understood my parents. Miraculously, once I understood and forgave them, they started to understand and forgive me. I mention this here to show that I was trying to do the opposite in raising my own daughters. From a very early age, I taught them to be their own people, not to be afraid, to take risks and live with an open heart.

Of course, pre-teens and teens don't really need a lot of lessons in being their own people and having no fear. I felt a bit of compassion for my parents at this point in my life with my daughters, but I didn't let on. The neighborhood we lived in had a few "less than desirable as role model" young teenagers in it. A girl named Kristina became friendly with both of my daughters but primarily Marley since they were the same age. Kristina lived with her father. Her mother lived in Tampa and was not deemed an appropriate parent for Kristina due to drugs, sleeping around, etc. Her father was more financially stable and not on drugs but he certainly was a bit of a playboy and Kristina was left alone quite a bit from age 12. I felt sorry for her, not really having a mother she could talk to and I tried to take her under my wings a bit. She called me mom and spent the night at our house a lot. Of course my parents did not approve of this girl at all and were constantly telling me to not let her in my house or let my daughters go near her. I didn't really feel that was the way to handle the situation and in fact, I felt that anything you forbid a teenager from doing, they will surely do just to rebel. A big part of me really wanted to make a difference in Kristina's life, but another big part of me wanted to leave that neighborhood and get Nicole and Marley into a completely different school system.

Marley went through a "gothic" phase with Kristina, wearing black clothes, black eyeliner and lipstick and not smiling. Okay, I could live with that. She was still a straight A honor student and she had no interest in drugs or cigarettes and not really even in drinking so as far as I was concerned this was still a good kid. My parents, Stan and Lisa, and Stan's mother were very concerned and very judgemental of me. Randall came into my life at a time when I really needed somebody to agree with me and be on my side and thankfully he did. He strongly agreed with me that Marley was a very good kid, just going through a phase of growing up.

Two things happened though which made me decide I had to leave that neighborhood. One was that one of Marley's "friends" broke into the house and stole from me. The other incident happened in the middle of the night. Apparently Marley and Kristina would sneak out of Marley's upstairs bedroom window and walk around the neighborhood in the middle of the night. One night at about 3am, Kristina walked into my bedroom and woke me with "Sorry mom, you need to get up, there is a policeman in your living room." This was not cool at all. A police officer had found them walking the streets, thankfully doing nothing else wrong and not in any dangerous situations, and had brought them back here. I thanked him and told him I'd keep my eyes open in the future (sure I'll just sleep with my eyes open from now on!) He did not file a police report. When he left my patience and liberalism were extended beyond breaking point and

I started shouting at Marley. She said some nasty things back to me and I did something I had never done before, I slapped her in the face. I regretted that the second I did it and even more when she slapped me back. Neither of us had hit each other very hard but both of us had our pride shattered and didn't really know what to do or say. I said "Just go back to bed and stay there, I'm going back to sleep!" I don't think I did sleep any more that night though. By the morning I had made the decision to move to Winter Springs.

My business, Dreamtime Cruises & Tours, was suffering a bit at the time, but my eternal optimism and feeling that it was my life purpose, caused me to throw more money at it (received from investors) and continue to draw the salary I had been drawing in order to qualify for a mortgage on a more expensive house. Yes, common sense told me not to do that, and Randall represented common sense in this case as he is an accountant, but my very strong desire to make a really good life for my daughters won and I applied for and received, a higher mortgage in order to build a much nicer house in a much nicer neighborhood. It was a four bedroom two bath home backing up to a pond. I went an extra $20,000 and had a pool built as well. I thought that would be a good thing for me and my daughters. Randall advised against it and, needless to say, so did my parents, but I did it anyway.

The house was finished in December 1998 but based on construction having begun already Marley started 9th grade at the brand new Winter Springs High School and Nicole started 7th grade at Indian Trails Middle School. When you think about how everything in life has a purpose and every person met and every decision made leads to something else it was the right thing to do. There is really no wrong thing to do as everything will lead to a lesson and growth opportunity. Ironically, the boy who robbed from us in the old neighbourhood showed up at Winter Springs High School as well, as his father wanted to give him a fresh start with different people and convinced the school system to let him in that school. The moral of that story is the old adage "You can run but you can't hide". For the most part, it was a better place for both of them to be. Kristina was too young to have transportation to this house and by the time she was able to drive there, she had calmed down and so had Marley.

Randall lived a 4 hour drive away from me. He visited me one weekend out of five, on a weekend that Stan had the girls. When we were together we were very much a couple and when we were apart he emailed me daily and called about once a week. Our emails were long and philosophical. We were both going through our stuff and were sort of mirrors and sounding boards for each other. His stuff had to do mostly with what happened to his marriage and his daughters leaving. He insisted on keeping his house and living there because that way they have their home to come back to if they decide they are unhappy with their mother.

I asked him how long he intended to keep the house and live with that expectation and he said until they were grown which was basically another eight years. So although he had a job that he could get anywhere, as opposed to a business, he had no intention of moving to the Orlando area for our relationship. In fact, he quite liked it the way it was because it was all romance and no day-to-day real life when we were together. He had a belief that staying in the romance stage is the only way to make a relationship work. I, on the other hand, believed otherwise. I truly wanted a 24/7 relationship and I chose to stay awhile with Randall to see if he would change as I did feel deeply for him. I'm not sure I felt love for him, other than in a friend sort of way. We were very good friends for each other and once every 5 weekends I was his goddess. He brought me girlie gifts (earrings, perfume, flowers, etc.) and really enjoyed romancing me. He enjoyed making love as well and did it in a very intense, passionate manner. He didn't have the receiving problem that many men have and he had no problems giving either unless you consider the fact that he was completely unable to do either 24/7. I didn't want to go back to casual dating and sex though and Randall knew all about me and my cast of characters. It would be a lot of work bringing somebody else up to speed. We had much in common in our family backgrounds and were both Jewish by birth although not religious.

Randall stayed compartmentalized though. He didn't want to meet my parents or do much with my children. He didn't even want to come on my cruises as he couldn't afford to and wouldn't accept my offer of my business paying for him. I ended up taking a single cabin on the cruises and didn't even play my prior game of seduce a handsome waiter. Perhaps I had outgrown that or no longer needed it for my self worth. Or maybe I was just honoring my mutual agreement with Randall that our relationship would be monogamous.

As it became evident that Randall was not going to enter into a real relationship with me, I began to stop looking forward to his visits. Although I was in denial about Dreamtime which was failing, I used the status of being owner of my own business to live the life I wanted to live. I got my nails done, had massages, took my kids to their cheerleading, gymnastics, dance etc. and enjoyed swimming laps in my pool and sitting in the Jacuzzi and relaxing. Randall started becoming bossy about what I should be doing with Dreamtime, (downsizing, living in a tight budget, and perhaps even going bankrupt). I didn't want to hear that possibility as I believe strongly in karma and feel that money borrowed or spent must be paid back. I did go to consumer credit counselling though and got on a debt management plan. I wouldn't admit this failure to my parents or my children yet. Thinking back on it now, what a tremendous amount of stress that represented. I lived one life and every time reality tried to intervene I did an excellent job of ignoring it. I continued to borrow from investors, credit cards and loans. My credit was excellent at the time, I had defaulted on no one and my payments were all on time. I disappointed nobody, not my staff who relied on me, my daughters who relied on me nor myself. At least I didn't know I was disappointing myself. When I get bodywork and healing even now, practitioners wonder where all the pain came from that I pushed so well into places like my solar plexus (belly) charka. I think a lot of it is the hurt, fear and disappointment that I did such a good job of denying.

Randall got a tenant to rent a room in his house and was looking for another one to help make ends meet in that big house he was saving for his children's return. At the same time he was looking for another career as he was no longer happy being an accountant. He came to the conclusion that he didn't want to be tied down to anybody or anyplace for the time being and he went to school to be a truck driver. That's right, a truck driver! In the summer of 1999 he graduated and set off across America in a truck. He still called me and felt like we still had a relationship but I was over him. I had already started writing to David and just didn't have the energy to relate to him as well. I barely had the energy to relate to David as astrologically the summer of 99 was just doing me in. Add to that the financial stress that I was pretending I didn't have and you have a down kind of summer. But David was keeping me interested and happy. Randall did ask to visit one more time in September. I didn't have the heart to say don't come but I made sure that David and I didn't talk on the phone until after I had truly told Randall in person that it was over.

Chapter Eleven

The L Word, the S Word and Anticipation of Meeting

Hotel is good

Good morning my Goddess

Just the shortest of notes to keep in touch. I am just leaving now for a week – the last long trip before I can look you in the eye and see if voices, messages, and e-feelings translate as perfectly as we both hope.

I totally agree, staying at a hotel – both of us need time and space to assess the situation properly.

Lots of love and long thoughtful kisses

Your king

David

"Brilliant" day here

Dear David

Thank you for sending me a little note before you left. It means a lot to me that you do that even though I know you are really busy.

I'm going to mail the "Juicy" book so that you have it when you return from this trip. I'm also going to send with it a few pictures of me since I know my 2 pictures confused you.

When making your plane reservations try to get here at least one day before Thanksgiving so we can get acquainted and then still have plenty of time to enjoy the energy of my home. I'll have an empty house the entire time Thursday through Sunday (my roommate and my kids will be gone). I'm looking forward to relaxing with you besides wearing you out at the theme parks! We could go to Epcot the day before Thanksgiving. We can visit Kennedy Space Center even if the launch is cancelled.

This morning after reading your email, I went for a swim and sat out by the pool for about an hour. The sky was the most brilliant blue you can imagine, not a cloud in the sky. I wish that kind of weather for you when you are here. I thought of you when I enjoyed the energy of my surroundings.

I know I won't hear from you for a week, but I was thinking of you and wanted to tell your email. Have a wonderful week my King. I send you warm, juicy long kisses and hugs.
Love
Dianne

Lovely thoughts from me to you
My dearest Goddess

I have raced back today with you never far from my thoughts this week. This weekend is very busy, but I will be contacting you either tomorrow night or Sunday, as I can't wait to hear your wonderfully uplifting and lively voice again…it means a lot to know I can do that.

As yet no "Juicy Book". I look forward with anticipation to your photos until the real person can entrance me. I hope to be making my reservations in the next week or so, otherwise I will be buying the tickets on my way to you. I will keep you informed of my itinerary.

I am so glad you had written to me while I was away, it is so wonderful to read it in your voice. I have to go now (unfortunately) but I will contact you again very soon.
Lots of love and kisses (with a massive gentle hug)
Your returning King
David

*   *   *   *

I don't have my next email but from David's it appears I told him about the alligator that was found in my neighborhood and there also must have been some discussion about the differences in UK and US English.

*   *   *   *

Watch out for the gators!
My dearest Goddess

Please do not regard the language of words as significant… we will have a new language soon. The Prime Minister of Britain in the 2nd World War made the most significant of comments about communications between the US and the UK when he said "We are two nations separated by a common language." Our strength is in being able to discuss any communication difficulty and resolving them satisfactorily. But very soon we will move way beyond words…..

I do hope that your Mr Right is going to meet you very soon indeed, and that he may have this address.

Garden in the UK is a plot of land belonging to the property, and in the north of England they call this a backyard. Never worry about asking me to explain anything – when I am tired, I am not at my best, but I will always do my best, even if that means explaining that I was wrong in my approach or comments – as I was the day I said not to use a term of endearment… (sorry). Thank you for such a good description of Florida. I will definitely be watching out for alligators.

I have just woken up. I had nodded off for about an hour. It is now 12.30 and I'm exhausted after yesterday which was my first day back after my trip away with lots of catching up and data collection.

I will contact you again tomorrow.

Lots of love

David

xxxxx

109

Re: Watch out for gators

Dear David

Thank you for writing to me after waking up from your nap. That means a lot to me and your emails put a big smile on my face. My morning started out poorly with an argument with my mother. I have tons of work to do today so I better sign off and do it. I may be buying Marley her car today. There are good deals on 99 models right now and she'll be 16 in 4 months. Is 16 the driving age over there? Here it is, with 15 being the age to drive with an adult over 21 in the car. My daughters inherited some money which gives them each $20,000 for a car when they are 16. That's a long story too and I don't remember whether I told you that one or not. We are looking at a Mercury Couger. Do they sell American cars there? You may not know what this car is. Anyway, it's a sports car. Write soon, I love hearing from you.

Much love

Dianne

A shortage of hugs?

Dear Goddess

I will do my writing now and working after so that I fall asleep working and do not disturb our chat.

You have reminded me that I have not contacted my mum recently; you are getting most of my calls. I am rarely here, and until just before I went away last week I found it very difficult to ring her due to my stepfather (of 43 years) always hogging the phone and not wanting to put her on. Much the same as when I pop in to see her, he will not leave us alone to talk; he has to be there to correct "those little mistakes" she makes in every sentence. It's so wearing that the bickering caused me to walk out last time I was there.

My mum is not an affectionate person, not a huggy mum, which I have always regretted, but I put this down to her living the last 43 years with a man she does not like, and so she retracts deep within herself to protect against the agonies of the reality.

When Scott died, and I was having problems with my ex-wife, I decided I would visit a counsellor. I did this once and during this visit she asked loads of questions about almost everything, and I mentioned my mum and her non-hugging. She said...had I thought that my mum didn't love me, and I did feel a sense of relief at the possibility. There could well be an element of that as she has suffered the last 43 years as her way of giving me a good start. However, when my Canadian cousin came over and both her and her mother gave me a hug on arrival and departure (and mum didn't) it seemed very odd. Next time I saw her, when I left she touched me on the arm (small but significant). So who knows....the ice may melt. Dad is a much longer and more fraught story...for some other time.

Answers

Driving age for cars is 17 over here (with no lower age except for mopeds), motorcycles are also 17 (was 16 when I started on motorcycles).

We have very limited sales of US cars; they are regarded as more of a special market for enthusiasts and are mainly older classics.

By coincidence, I am taking Rachel to test drive a new car on Saturday before she comes here for my next dinner with Doug and Eileen. However, she will be buying that herself on finance if she likes it enough.

How do you stop the alligators from swimming in your pool? I would not care to share you with one of them, I can't swim that well!

Must dash – talk again soon.

Lots of love and hugs

David

xxxx

Re: A shortage of hugs?

Darling David

I will find it quite easy to make up for your deficit in hugs. I am a hugger if I'm with a man I love. Was your wife also a non-hugger? We sometimes do try to heal our wounds from our primary family by finding a spouse who hits the same raw spots, kind of a way to heal it with a different face. I went to a therapist (our word for counsellor) for two years. In my case my father started out really touchy feely and warm and loving. Once I started to look like a woman he really backed away. So I started a pattern of me finding men who were initially very warm and tender and then quickly went cold on me. Interesting that you may finally be the opposite of that. Maybe I'm healed! Hopefully I will be a healing for you as well. We can talk about this more I'm sure in person and on the phone.

I checked my email last night and got your letter. I wanted to respond right away but couldn't because my roommate was home and the computer is in her room. I can write longer letters during the day on Saturday when she's at work or on the weekends when she is visiting her boyfriend in Virginia. Lots of what you said we can talk about on the phone too.

The alligators don't just walk the streets here. You don't have to worry. They do have a law in this state though that swimming pools be either fenced in or screen enclosed and part of the reason is bugs and animals as well as kids drowning. My pool is screen enclosed and the lake that is behind me is fence enclosed so even if there were an alligator in it, he couldn't get in my yard.

Well, I'm at work so I'll sign off. I'm feeling closer to you by the minute. It's a strange but nice sensation.
Much love and many hugs
Dianne

Fighting 4 Dragons!
To my dearest Goddess
How could you be so perceptive? I have definitely been out fighting dragons (4 in fact).

Dragon No 1…The internet. It wouldn't let me in to write to you last night; no amount of retrying would get me in.

Dragon No 2…. Tiredness. I had an early(ish) night 11:00, and so slept for a full 7.5 hours.

Dragon No 3…. Work. Shirley has felt unable to stay at work and has now gone home for a week's compassionate leave, which I totally endorse, but do feel rather alone, to fight the cash flow and general business issues.

Dragon No 4….. Fear. I have made my reservation and have a real fear that you will be upset that I will not make it for Thanksgiving. I do know the personal effort you have put in to keep the time clear for me. I feel very bad but I will miss that date, and hope very much you will have it in your heart to forgive me.

My plan is to arrive on Monday 29th November. I have missed you desperately too, and this is exhausting me, so I will await your reply before saying anymore.

Lots of love

David

xxxxx

Re: Fighting 4 Dragons!

To my dearest King

Dragon No 1: Did you try AOL? Don't worry though, I have no expectations of an email every night. It just makes my day when I do get one.

Dragon No 2: I've been tired too. In fact I have a cold. I hate having a cold. I took my zinc, vitamin C and Echinacea to make the duration shorter. I also went to bed early last night. Sleeping for a full 7.5 hours is a good thing, you might want to try it more often!

Dragon No 3: I can relate. When I have more time or if we talk on the phone I'll tell you the latest with my business. I'd be lost without Paloma there so I'm sure it's hard for you without Shirley.

Dragon No 4: Forgiveness granted silly. Remember, I'm not a bitch. Thanksgiving weekend would have been better since I'm off for four days anyway but hey, I'm the boss, I can take off whenever I want to. However, my house won't be empty so we'll create our energy elsewhere and you'll just have to meet my kids and my roommate when you come over to use the hot tub. How long are you staying?

I miss you sweetheart (is sweetheart okay or is that a bad word?). I have to run now and take Marley to her football game and then pick Nicki up from the mall and take her to her sleepover. I'll definitely be home by 7.30 in case you are awake and want to call. Be gentle with yourself. Did you get my juicy book yet?
Much love
Dianne

*   *   *   *

We spoke that night and grew even closer. I had been the first to say "I love you" to him and I asked him if he loves me since he didn't really respond instantly. He said that he loved me but perhaps not on the same terms that I am saying just yet. I asked him on which terms does he love me. His reply was "Those that I have said all the time since I put it at the bottom of the letters....not in the biggest of ways....but in a higher level than friend.....and someone I long to meet....and to kiss....and to look deeply into the eyes of.....so we can be sure in person that what we are feeling is real." It sounded more like a protection from being hurt. I felt like he did love me but he was holding something back. There was still a month at this point before we would meet......

I also opened up a bit more about the problems with my business. Randall thought I should go bankrupt. I knew David, as a positive thinking risk-taking entrepreneur like myself, would be more open to positive solutions and to hanging in there and keeping the business going. It seemed we were both mirrors for each other in business and our conversations were very helpful to each other. Although looking back on 1999 as I write this now, both of us know so much more than

114

we did then, which would have been helpful to both of us. I have to believe that every lesson learned was meant to be learned and that perhaps now we can be good teachers to others regarding business.

We also talked about what he doesn't like about himself physically and how he was afraid I wouldn't like him. I was beginning to lose patience with this insecurity because I felt that we had connected on such a heart and soul level that his physical appearance (as long as he was clean and smelled good) was not important. I feel physical attraction is a chemical thing, almost like we do explore a potential partner with all of our senses including smell. I'm looking for my soul mate, my best friend, and his earth suit in this lifetime is almost irrelevant. This concept is something I want to share with all people out there looking for love and is one big reason I wanted to share our story in a book. So many people are looking for "tall, dark and handsome" and may skip over the perfect person for themselves by appearance being a top criteria. I believe that like attracts like and that for so many reasons David was likely to be my perfect match that I finally really did deserve.

*   *   *   *

Love talking with you

Dear David

I really enjoyed talking with you as I have from the first time. Your energy seems to merge nicely with mine. I'm really looking forward to your visit. I'll work hard so my business is doing really well sales wise before you get here. I may have to go into the office a couple of times but for the most part I'll be free. Maybe it would be a good idea for you to stay in the airport Hyatt the first night. Then we don't have to drive anywhere before we can just sit and be together. They have a nice restaurant so don't eat the yucky airplane food and wait for me. I'll get a price for the night of the 29th and let you know it on Monday.

Love

Dianne

Your strength, caring, compassion and love xxxxxx
Dear Goddess

Your name says it all; you are everything, and understanding too.

Some of my problem is I never wanted to put on weight. I fought the whole time I was married against the size and content of the meals. But when served, a mix of childhood training ("finish everything on your plate or it will be back for the next meal"), guilt trips caused by my ex-wife, and general self weakness, made me finish them. This has left me with a big belly (now slowly reducing – thank goodness) and a pair of breasts that would look much nicer on a girl.

Lastly and nothing to do with the weight is my teeth. They are twisted and gappy like a troll. I have looked into dealing with them, but was advised that while I have sleep apnea and have to sleep with a machine it will not be worth doing. Sleep apnea is a condition where I stop breathing whilst asleep, which reduces the blood oxygen levels, causing the body to struggle for air and so wake up. This happens all night resulting in the body not ever going into a deep sleep. Without the machine I'm a zombie by comparison to normal. The machine pumps air at a pressure into me and so keeps the airways open and keeps all well through the night. The slightly better news is that it appears to affect people with collar size 17 and over. Mine was 18.5 and it has now dropped to 17.5 and I hope it will continue well below that and then this dreadful machine will be a thing of the past.

You said something so wonderful last night and I do feel that I slapped it down rather hard – I didn't mean to do that. I too feel very strongly drawn to you, but will not allow myself to go down that road until we have met (maybe because I don't wish to get hurt on our first date). I don't have a name for this feeling, as I have not been in this position (of being so attracted to anyone) for over 25 years – maybe ever. I long to meet you face to face, and have long meaningful conversations, and to look deeply into your eyes and kiss you and hold you and experience your world.

Take care, have a good night
Lots of love to my Goddess
David
xxxxx

      *   *   *   *

So my perceptions were correct that he was feeling insecure and didn't want to be hurt. I don't particularly want to be hurt either but I think that the personal growth courses I took did open my heart and make me want to live from my heart even if that made me vulnerable as closing my heart and living in fear was not a good alternative. So I guess you could say I wore my heart on my sleeves.

      *   *   *   *

Re: Your strength, caring, compassion and love
Darling David

Thank you for really sharing your feelings. If you'd like a little advice from somebody who has been through probably $10,000 worth of personal growth classes and read hundreds of self-help books, what you really need to do is accept yourself exactly the way you are. Love the creation that is you. Accept, honor and love the weight as it did serve a purpose, even if that purpose was one of protection from a relationship and pain. My weight has a lot of emotional factors that I've explored with a therapist. I think Americans are much more therapy oriented than British people. You probably see it as a weakness. I don't see anything about you as weak. In fact I see you as noble. When you can fully accept the way you are the universe can make the changes for you easier. Self love is really important. I find you easy to love, be gentle with yourself. Regarding your teeth, as long as you brush and floss and your teeth are clean and your breath is good it doesn't matter to me if they aren't perfect.

I don't know what you are so worried about. We get along so well! I have seen your picture you know and I find you very attractive so stop acting like I'm beauty and you're the beast! Just be yourself, like you told me.

I have to run, I'm late to pick up Marley, just didn't want to keep you waiting since I know it was scary for you to send this to me.

Lots of love to my king

Dianne

ps – I don't mind if your weight means you have breasts just as long as you have a penis (size doesn't matter). I know, I'm a naughty American girl......when you finish blushing please write back. I'm really not a slut......

Re: Your strength, caring, compassion and love

Dear sexy Goddess

Just a quick note as I'm at work but I wanted to say that listening to you I have no ideas of you being anything other than a lot more forward than me (but very lovely anyway) and I do hope I'm not too slow for you. I'm not a slut either and never imagined you were. I would be far too slow for anyone like that, unless they were starting a collection of sexual conquests by racial stereotypes (The reserved British King).

Don't worry I may be slow – I am still with you! xxxxxxxx

Lots of love, hugs and long passionate kisses

David

xxxxxx

You naughty girl xxxxx

My wonderful Goddess

Thank you for being so understanding, warm and YOU! I did find it difficult, as I could see there was a better than average chance you may discover for yourself. I do feel so much better that we have discussed it. I am really not too bad about myself, I have reasonable confidence in my day to day life, but what may happen soon is not usual for me – it is special and I want you not to get shocks, as this may lose my confidence and ruin everything. You are really special and I wouldn't wish that to happen.

On your worry that I may be short of something – I have just checked …… and one present and correct ….. (and yes you did embarrass me, but in a wonderful way). I have never met someone so American before! As long as your embarrassing always remains private, I will be happy to be warmed by your charm and loveliness.

Lots of love and kisses

David

xxxxxxx

Re: You naughty girl

To my wonderful King

I'm so glad I didn't scare you away with my openness. I've never met anyone so British before. I told you the queen would not approve of me. I'm actually looking forward to the more reserved approach to courting a woman. Men here are too grabby. I'm tired of it.

Speaking of sex, please don't get the wrong idea about me. Okay, so I'm a little more experienced and quite a bit less reserved than you. I am a succulent wild woman like the book I sent you. I hope you'll find that a good thing. In the past 1 ½ years I've only been with one man. It's been a few months since I've been with him. He had a vasectomy so we didn't need a condom for birth control. We both had HIV and other tests before we got together and maintained a monogamous relationship. He is a blood donor and his blood is tested regularly for HIV so I know he was safe besides the fact that I completely trust that I was the only woman he was with (and I was his only after a 20 year marriage). So, if we should decide to be intimate (not until at least the 5th date), I am safe.

Write back and let me know you are still with me….

Love you

Dianne

Chapter Twelve
The British Queen and our own Kingdom of Florsex

*   *   *   *

As the last emails showed that I was a bit more outspoken than the typical British woman David's humor came through and so did mine as we wrote a few to and from the Queen emails. I love his sense of humor and the differences in the British and American ways that we are laughing about here.

*   *   *   *

Unworthy use of the internet
(This came from an email address that David created for the purpose Elizabeth@hotmail.com)
For the attention of Dianne AKA Sea Goddess

It is my sad duty to inform you that your behaviour to one of my most loyal and honourable subjects is regarded by my government and myself as totally unacceptable!

You stand accused of corruption of an innocent, witchcraft and general lewd behaviour.

As one girly to another, I find him rather dishy (but he doesn't know it) and I therefore hold first claim to his body – if he ever wakes up to the idea he has one! You know men fall into 2 types – those who know too much and those who don't!

I feel sure that as a businesswoman, you can see the priority I have over you and so offer you in compensation free use (for 5 years) of my old ship "Brittania" and feel sure you would be able to make good use of it.

If you refuse to accept this very generous offer, it could become necessary to re-colonise the area known as the USA in the name of the United Kingdom of Great Britain and Ireland. However, I feel sure this will not be necessary.

I await your reply and will mobilise my yeomen at dawn if no reply is forthcoming.

Yours etc

Elizabeth R – Queen of England, Scotland, Ireland and the Commonwealth Empress of India – and generally hard nut who is about to lose Australia to the Republicans

Re: Unworthy use of the Internet

Hey Liz!

Guilty as charged girlfriend…corruption of an innocent, witchcraft and general lewd behavior. I am proud to say you are correct! I have this great spell that enchants British innocent men and puts them uncontrollably under my power to ultimately do with as I wish. The tantric sex techniques I will practice on him will make him mine forever, so you shall have to look elsewhere for your fun. Yes, I do believe he is a dish (who doesn't know it) and I intend to wake this poor slumbering lad up.

Keep your Brittainia queeny; it is too old for my use. Cunard line did have a nice ship that is my namesake "Sea Goddess". I may consider letting you do lunch with him in exchange for that ship, but his body/mind and spirit/soul remain under my enchantment. Re-colonize the USA if you must. It probably wouldn't be much worse than our current political system.

Can I sell you a cruise? You'd be a lot of fun on the Inner Voyage. I believe I could arrange a royalty discount and a very nice stateroom.

That's my final concession to you. You can take my cruise (if you pay me) and I shall keep David. He will be found in my stateroom doing all the things he will enjoy doing once he realizes (with my help) that he has a body.

Very truly yours

Dianne (aka Sea Goddess with an attitude)

A message from the Queen

To an amazing Goddess

I have just got in from work and have read both of your messages ..... and the one from the Queen. (BTW she sends her regards.)

Her message (or as much of it as I am permitted to tell you without having to shoot you after) is as follows:

My loyal Officer King David of Littlehampton

It has come to my attention through the security services that you may be considering a liaison with a colonial subject from the region once patrolled by my namesake (QE1) loyal subject Sir Frances Drake of Plymouth.

You must be warned of the evils of such fraternisation, and any entry so mentioned could be regarded by my courts as treason! Please do not think that a few thousand miles will impede my knowledge of your activities; we have eyes everywhere and you are being watched now and now and still now.

So Goddess, I have a real dilemma, what should I do? Do I go where my heart leads, or do I follow the old queen's instructions? Luckily, her mother Elizabeth Bowes-Lyons, has also written upon hearing of my plight and she has said:

I understand my little girl has written to you forbidding any further friendship with the Sea Goddess from Florida. As a red blooded British Lass, I could not stand by and watch you suffer in such a cruel way. Therefore I give you permission to kiss this wonderful lady (provided you do not grope or in any other way cause her offence) the condition is such that you may only be allowed back in to the Kingdom of Castles if you possess a letter of total satisfaction with the services rendered by yourself to the said Goddess. (Silence from yourself will in itself be considered an agreement to this permission), plus one bottle of the best Gin.

Well, what do you make of that then Goddess – should I listen to QE2 or QETQM? I will let you decide my fate ...... Please choose wisely.

Love and kisses

King David of Littlehampton

xoxox

Re: A message from the Queen

Dear King David of Littlehampton

You are so funny!!! How could I not be absolutely crazy about somebody as special as you. You leave me absolutely speechless. I'm so glad the queen mother approves and I'm sure Diana would smile down from heaven on us. If the queen doesn't like me I guess I won't be welcome in the mother country and we'll have to live in Florida. I suspect you can get used to alligators and bugs as long as I'm keeping you warm at night. You are such a noble king to risk it all for me.

Love

Your Goddess

Eddy and Wally 1999 style

Good evening my sweet Goddess

Apparently her majesty has taken a shine to your colonial brashness, and concedes that you may have me on loan until a suitable fee/exchange can be made.

Living in Florida sounds fabulous – except for those pesky insects and dinosaurs you live with (the alligators, not the politicians).

I am making good headway through the juicy book and am enjoying it.

This British King would not be the first to give up everything for a beautiful divorced American woman. It is probably one of those possibilities that could be looked at in the future, but I don't feel it will rock the world like the last one did. (Do you want to be called Wallace?)

Tiredness still rules, especially on driving and selling days, but I have lots of work to get on with. Can I look forward to talking to you on Saturday night?

Lots of love – longing for your succulence

David

xxxxx

Our Kingdom

Dear David

I'm so glad the queen has "taken a shine" to me (whatever that means). I'll assume that's a good thing. Your queen is quite funny, and to think she has a hotmail account too! I'll accept borrowing you until we can find a suitable exchange.

Tell me more about your military background. In fact, tell me everything you have been doing the past 25 years. I want to know everything about you. Did I tell you that my parents met through corresponding? It was during World War II. My mother was actually writing to my father's brother who was a marine. He was badly injured and couldn't write to her anymore and so he gave his brother (my father) her address. My father was in the army (I believe in France). They wrote for I think about a year. He came home (they both lived in New Jersey), they met and they decided to marry pretty much at their first meeting. They obviously got to know each other quite well by writing and had a feeling they would like each other in person as well. Whenever they tell me it is dangerous to meet men on the internet I ask them why it is so different than what they did. They had World War II.com! Everybody got married right away then; it was the way to ensure the woman was a virgin bride. Then of course there was the baby boom. I assume the same baby boom took place in your part of the world. My parents actually waited 8 years to have me. My mother had a hole in her heart and was told she'd die in childbirth by four out of five doctors. So I was a "miracle baby". That's another long story.

We shall create our own kingdom you and I. It will have the best of both worlds (you and me) and we will design it in a way that feels good for both of us. That can be created and recreated day by day. I really honor and respect (and love) the person that you are. I'm liking you more every day.

Well sweetheart, I have to get ready to pick up the girls from cheerleading practice. They do have competition the Saturday you are here. I hope you don't mind doing that, it's really fun. This Saturday night will be great to call me; I'll be home by 6pm.
Love and succulent kisses
Dianne

Our special Kingdom

Dear Great Goddess of the Sea

A kingdom of our own sounds like heaven – why don't we have a little heaven in our lives – we both deserve it.

A shine (as in someone taking a shine to another) means that they have a soft spot for you, or really like you. (Philip says he doesn't have a soft spot for you, quite the reverse – but then he has never known when to keep quiet!)

The Queen – God bless her – has had to make a few changes to her image since the very unfortunate death of your namesake. She now has a website, has opened up her houses (castles and palaces) to the public for money, and generally has had to move into the nineteenth century. I sound like a republican (too much time with Doug). He is, I am not.

My Military background:

I was an officer in the Royal Airforce VRT, which means that Her Majesty has indeed made me a commissioned officer in her armed forces, but I only ever had to train cadets. But I was uniformed, and when regular airmen saw me in uniform they had to salute. I found this very odd, and I had to salute higher ranking officers too. I have pictures of my visits to air bases for summer camps, but none of me in uniform.

It is too late tonight to explain the last 25 years, (why 25 years?).

You hadn't mentioned about your parents meeting through letters in WW2. How does your uncle feel about his loss?

Lucky for you that 20% of doctors were right about childbirth; that explains about you being the only one. Well, if it's a miracle baby who writes to me – even better.

You don't have to put (and love) in brackets. I can tell how you feel. You will just have to understand I have a very high definition for that, and have to clarify its meaning in my own mind before I say it. It is an area that may not have been trod by me before. I think it has….a long time ago.

You say some really wonderful things to me and make me feel really good, both about me and us. I will not mind if you have things to do with your daughters on that Saturday – are you inviting me?

Looks like we have a date this Saturday. xxxxx

It's late again and I am quite tired – no, very tired. I have been selling and travelling today. Plus, I have spoken to my aunt from Kissimmee. She asked me to stay there. I don't think so! She is 84, and I last saw her 32 years ago. So I will visit, and that way I will be able to see a lot more of you – I would like to get past 5 dates.

The very warmest of thoughts

David – King of (un-named kingdom)

How about Florsex (a blend of Florida and Sussex). That's more juicy than Susida, don't you think? Or do you have some ideas of your own?

For now I will sign off as King David of Atlantis (the gap between us Sea Goddess).

Re: Our special Kingdom
Dear King David of Florsex

I do believe I have corrupted you! Florsex is great! I can tell you've been reading your juicy book. You are a very good student. Just don't get too American on me. Your British charm is a large part of what I adore about you. I've been enchanted with the British accent ever since falling in love with Peter Noone in the 6th grade. Remember him, Herman of Herman's Hermits. You can sing to my mother "Mrs Kemp you've got a lovely daughter..." and I will swoon at your feet.

Of course I was inviting you to the cheerleading competition on December 4th. We won't stay for the whole thing, just to watch Marley's team and Nicki's team. I have so many places I want to take you. Definitely do not stay with Aunty! You can visit her once or twice; maybe the second time I can go with you. I'll turn on my proper personality for her benefit. Does she have children? Do you have cousins here?

What you were in the Royal Airforce was probably similar to what my first husband, Stan, was in the US Navy. He signed up in dental school hoping to get a scholarship. He didn't get a scholarship but he still owed them two years as a Navy dentist. He was a Lieutenant, so I do know what you mean about saluting. The sticker was on both of our cars so if I went on the Navy base they saluted me! I agree that was odd.

Why 25 years? I don't know, I guess because that is your adult life. I want to know about every year of your life actually but we have plenty of time for that in our week together of getting to know each other.

My uncle didn't lose because he never had my mother. With my father it was instant connection. They are very much in love, always have been. Speaking of love, it's an interesting concept. Since you do sign your letters love you obviously feel love for me.

That is a human emotion when you feel a heartfelt warmth toward somebody. I know you feel that. Being "in love", the romantic concept is another type of love, not necessarily higher and better because the warm heart-to-heart human love must always be there even at times when passion and romance are at a low point (as they can be occasionally in a long term relationship). Regardless, I like your reserved approach and your "high definition" because when you look into my eyes and tell me you love me I'll know that you really mean it. It isn't just a word and you aren't just saying it because you want sex. I already know that about you.

I think I better get to work. I do take liberties since I'm the boss but I have tons of work to do. I always check my email around 4:00 my time so if you happen to be around and want to get on AOL then we can chat for a few minutes.
Love and kisses from your Goddess
Dianne

Re: Our special Kingdom
Dear King David of Florsex

I am amazed daily by your creativity, wit and just you in general. I feel so bad that the long letter you were writing about yourself for me got taken by the evil gremlins in hotmail. To the best that you can reconstruct it please do because I want to know everything about your life. Maybe so you won't get tired and also so hotmail will send it you can write just a little bit every day. Then by the time we meet I will know you really well.

Are you familiar with the men are from Mars and women are from Venus guides to dealing with the opposite sex? I gotta tell you (in case you hadn't noticed), I don't follow the rules real well. The woman is supposed to let the man do all the pursuing. The fact that I told you how I feel about you is a big no no. The man likes to catch the woman just like he used to hunt and catch the animals that would be the family's dinner back when we lived in caves. So if I let you chase me around the room a few times, will that make you feel like you hunted and caught me? I could play hard to get but that would be so not me. I just want to lie down next to you, hold you really tight and receive your energy and give you mine. I feel like I felt it come in over the computer today. So you won't have to chase me very far to cuddle with me even on our first date. Don't tell the other Martians and I won't tell the other Venusians.

I think we've come a long way this week. More than most people do in four dates. Our kingdom awaits you.
With warm and tender kisses and much love
Dianne

Coming soon – at a screen year YOU
To the wonder Goddess of Florsex

I will keep this ultra short, I am about to have my bath (no peeking) and I am going to be later to work than I ought to be today. Will restart the story (his-story) tonight in little bites as last time the computer ate what I had started!

I love you, you are so special – don't worry about Mars/Venus, I am not a hunter. My feminine side says it has to be mutual, and chasing says one sided so gentle touches and cuddles are best.
A long slow kiss – especially for the effect you have on me....
King David of Florsex

PS – We better develop this kingdom or we will need a grant from the UN and be treated very 3rd world.

Chapter Thirteen

Our Histories
(His-story and Her-story)

My personal history – hope the computer doesn't eat it again!

To the Goddess of Florsex – the most special person I know

You asked about my history so I will have another go. I have not started at age zero, my memory is very poor.

Unknown name – Age 2ish, whilst living in a Glasgow tenement, the girl in the corner shop, we used to play together. So I am told.

Forgotten name – Age 8ish, whilst living in Essex (a lot of British counties end in sex – strange, isn't it?). The girl next door, she was about 16 and lovely, no other memories.

Angela – we were both age 13ish. Tall leggy blonde (her, not me) – well what a waste, at 13 I had no idea how to behave (things haven't changed) but we did kiss very well in her hay loft, very well indeed when I think back. We went out for about a year. It ended when I went into hospital to have my appendix and tonsils out within a few months. It was a natural break and we were too young to be where we may well have been just a few months later.

Sue at age 17 ½ (she was 16). A curvy little redhead – this time we were never destined for much, but it had potential in that we got on great, went out for about a year prior to any activity, but there were two things that stopped it from working out. Class (she had it and I didn't) and she kept calling me stupid when I made her laugh (this was affectionate but I just couldn't handle the truth). I was a poor engineering apprentice and she was the village doctor's daughter who spent her long summers in France. I got the cold long winters, but it meant lots of close cuddles, even walking was very close. However, I was unable to cope with her family disliking the motorcycling poor boy that didn't go to private school, etc. I have often wondered what she and they would make of me now.

Mary Ann Peters (in my calendar as MAP – I was a Venture Scout so it looked appropriate if read by someone else) at age 18 ½ ish. She was 40, divorced and looking for someone to show her that her husband was wrong to leave her and that she was still attractive. She was very thin due to not eating after him leaving for a younger woman. A very passionate affair, but she didn't teach me anything about women so I left that relationship satisfied but no wiser. We went out (stayed in mostly) for about 18 months and I think I loved her. Her friends told her to break it off. Eventually she told me that she had been seeing someone else who had got very ill and was going to die soon. I wanted to stay and offer her support, but she threw me out. I cried, but got over it within a few weeks.

Chris at age 20 (she 21). I wasn't going out with her, or anyone, but wanted to go out with a work colleague of hers, and Chris was going out with a colleague of mine who it turns out was going out with several women simultaneously, and as you may have guessed he was married as well. As I wanted to get messages to Rosemary and this guy wanted to get messages to Chris, I took them both and resented taking his (even though I had no idea about him). When he let her down and I still wanted to get through to Rosemary, I kept talking to Chris. Rosemary, it turns out, was going out with a policeman, but Chris never told me that, I found that out much later. She eventually told me I was going to get nowhere. We met a few times for drinks and nothing happened; there was no reason for it to, no sparks, only friends.

A while later, Graham my best friend who had been going out with Moira for the same amount of time as Chris and I, announced that he was going to get married. We discussed the situation and I said I wasn't likely to get married in the near future as I didn't have anyone in mind. He said that Chris would have me if I wanted to get married too. That made me think and the conclusion was that sex wasn't that important (well it wouldn't have been I had not had true passion where two people want to please and be pleased for love of each other) and being able to talk was all that was necessary. So I got engaged. She was very experienced (used would be more appropriate as it turns out she slept with lots of guys so she would get taken out). She had low self esteem because of her weight problems.

We got married and almost as soon as we did, she stopped trying and started using guilt as a weapon. During my time of being married there was always pain and suffering and after 10 years we had a long talk and I told her I had reached the end of my tether and would leave if I couldn't see any improvement.

I had always prided myself on being totally faithful to the marriage, but I went away on a training course for a week and met a lovely Irish girl who said she too was having marriage problems. We went out for dinners, picture and finally had an evening in. We sat and talked in my hotel room, and although I was desperate to hold her, etc I was totally unable to make the first move. Now I am very pleased because I remained faithful in body if not in mind.

As for women friends, apart from Shirley, business partner, friend, supporter, defender, and now person to be defended, and happily married for 20 years, there is Dorothy. Dorothy is a very spiritual older lady about 60, who is very like you (except she is a celibate vegan – not virgin, she only eats vegetables, no animal or fish extracts). Very unusual, odd some might say, as she has some very unusual ideas about life, the universe and everything. She believes we live on many planes simultaneously. The celibacy and veganism is to raise her to higher levels when she chooses. She is great fun to be with, hates men, keeps telling me how awful they are (like I was a girl) and asking me to confirm it – but what do I know. Anyway, she can only see my feminine side. It's a little like a gay relationship without the sex!

You now have my total sexual (and not so sexual) history, up to the point when I signed on to match.com.

There have been many answers to my profile, some sounded very good. One I met for lunch, looked good, curvy blond (I have always had blondes as a fantasy along with redheads, brunettes or any woman with life in her), but in hindsight she never told me much about herself. Her messages were just short questions, and I would write back loads hoping to open her up....nothing. So during the meeting I thought face to face she would open up – no, just silences, no spark at all. I realise now that this is because her son was a drug addict and she was not looking for a husband, more of a father for her son.

There are two others whom I communicate with, neither romantically, one general chit-chat, one chat and business advice. All the others have gone silent, and I have not bothered. Nobody told me about themselves, until now.

But there is one who comes so close to being perfect. That relationship is very special to me. I am able to ring her and have long wonderful conversations that are full of life and vitality (sometimes very vital). She has tolerated my depressions, listened to my worries, and just recently awakened feelings previously not experienced by me. I think she is wonderful but I have never met her. Now every time I see a picture of her she changes, and I can't wait to take her by the hand and see if the reality is anywhere near as good as my imagination is painting. I do hope so. I don't know if she is going to be the ONE, but I do want to find out. She has little idea what an inexperienced lover I am. I think she expects a stud in shy man's clothing. She had better be a fast teacher!

Well that's the story so far....

Lots of love

David

xxxxx

*   *   *   *

How funny....... and honest! But actually I was asking about his entire history, not just his sexual and relationship history. I will encourage him to tell me more than this. I guess he is quite inexperienced as he's been with one woman for 23 years and very few other than her. My own sexual history had me marrying the first man I slept with but I did make up for that lack of experience after that relationship ended and even more after my relationship with Tony ended. I'm not proud of that but it was what I needed to do at the time I guess to feel good about myself and feel wanted. David doesn't know that entire history yet. I probably do feel comfortable telling him. Not just yet though.

*   *   *   *

Re: My Personal History – Again

Dear wonderful King David

Thank you for sharing with me the relationships in your life. I feel I know you even better. Every relationship leaves its impression on our psyche. I believe, like Dorothy, that we exist on many planes simultaneously. I've spoken through mediums to people in the spirit world. What is to say they haven't already reincarnated? The mediums and others believe that they may have. Only that one aspect of them that is speaking with me is in the spirit world. We are all in the spirit world and we are all here and we may all be somewhere else as well. It's kind of like the way Nicki can talk to 6 people at once online. We multi-task multi-dimensionally. Dorothy sounds cool, but I could never be a vegan and I could really never be celibate. I understand all about raising the kundalini energy that begins in the lower root charkas and that celibacy can help do that but it's not my thing. I think God gave us bodies and sent us to earth school to enjoy and use our bodies. I think that sensual and sexual merging, with love, with another human being is what it's all about. I love making love. Not enough times have I felt truly loved though. I want to experience that. Your lack of experience may not be a lack after all because I feel you can bring love into our lovemaking. It's just a feeling, can't know for sure until our eyes meet, like you said, but it's a strong feeling.

Mary Ann sounds like a more loving experience than Chris. How long were you and Chris together? It sounds like 23 or 24 years. It makes me sad that you lived that long without a joyful life. Tell me how it was with your children. What were the family dynamics like?

I don't like the "class" stuff you talk about with Sue. I find you very classy and I respect you because you are self created, very creative and enterprising and not somebody's employee or just somebody born into the "right" family. That was a learning experience though, wasn't it; something else that has left an impression. I'm very self created as well; maybe that's why I respect that in you so much. Yes….if they could see you now……..

I think we'll be more like you and Angela, two young teens discovering their hormones and playing and kissing together. That sounds like a lovely memory and a time of joy of life.

You intrigue me and I want to know more. Tell me about schools, teachers, jobs, travel, what it was like growing up in your house. As you find the time over the weekend and beyond that tell me more. I'll tell you some of my story later tonight after you are in bed.

I just got back from taking Marley and Nicki to their private gymnastics lesson at the gym where their father picks them up and he has them all weekend. My roommate Terri is on a cruise with her boyfriend, so I can enjoy some complete solitude this weekend (when I'm home). I'll probably spend 6 hours at the office tomorrow and three on Sunday. There is an early booking discount expiring on Sunday and I want to be there for calls and to make follow up calls. I'll also spend a lot of time going through files, catching up on things and getting better organized. I need to do that at home too so this will be a working weekend. I'm going to eat and then take a nice relaxing bath by candlelight (you can peek). You might as well peek, I'll be thinking about you. After doing that I will sit down and write to you about me (maybe the first 20 years).

I'm looking forward to your call tomorrow. We should keep it short so you aren't broke when you get here, but I love talking to you, it's hard to say goodbye.

Love and kisses

Dianne

The miracle baby is born

To my King

I am now bathed (you were there with me) and not yet sleepy, so I shall talk to you about my beginnings. My parents are both Jewish by birth but not at all religious. My father came from an orthodox Jewish poor area in New Jersey where religion was pretty much beat into him. That and the fact that both of his parents died a painful death of cancer very young made him an atheist. His parents are of Eastern European (I believe Polish) descent and my mother's father was born in Russia. Have you seen "Fiddler on the Roof"? My grandfather said he lived that story. He came to the US at age 8 with 11 brothers and sisters and does not have a high school education. The man was very business oriented and very street smart though. I think I got my business sense and my risk taking from him. He said he used to stop streetcars and beg for money which he slowly invested even as a teenager. I think there was some sort of Jewish mafia and he was part of it. He was also a Mason, which really impresses me as they were very metaphysical. I went to a Masonic temple somewhere in your part of the world and was impressed with the symbology, ritual and mythology that was evident there. He bought and sold many businesses in New Jersey. I believe his biggest was a shoe store. I liked these things about him. I didn't like how he controlled everybody (especially the family) with money.

My mother has one sister who has always been a little on the schizophrenic side. I think my grandfather contributed to her low self esteem and although there is a biochemical basis to this type of mental illness, I also think there is an instability in the soul. I also think that some of it is as simple as food and environmental sensitivities. Anyway, my mother was born with a hole in her heart (a ventricular defect) and she was always weak and couldn't do much physically. Interesting that my controlling grandfather had a physically weak and a mentally weak daughter. Anyway, they did have money and my mother was raised by maids and cooks as her mother worked a lot in the store with her husband. Right after high school, she went to a teacher's college for a while, then went to work in a secretarial job having to do with the war. She wrote to a marine and a navy man and I told you how the marine was my father's brother and how she started to write to my father.

They fell in love at first sight and married pretty quickly after he returned from the war. He was a piano player in a band and stayed awhile in France after the war ended. He sowed his wild oats there. He was a very good looking man. My mother and father, grandparents and aunt moved to Miami very soon after the marriage because of my mother's health. The cold weather was hard for her. My grandfather again bought stores that my father worked in, the longest lasting one being a luggage store that my father worked in for about 20 years and eventually owned. My grandfather was very helpful to the Cuban immigrants and set a lot of them up in business. He also started buying land that was everglades (alligators and swamps) and very speculative as to whether development would ever reach there. He also invested in penny stocks. He did well, but he probably could have done a lot better had he been a little less speculative.

My mother was told not to get pregnant by 4 out of 5 doctors as she could die in childbirth due to her congenital heart defect. It wasn't without risk but my parents decided to do it anyway as they really wanted a baby. I was very wanted (then). My father used to take movies all the time and there are home movies of my mother making a trial run to the hospital and other corny things like that. You can tell by the movies though that I was very wanted and very loved. My mother labored for two days (it's amazing she didn't die), and I was born almost dead (the umbilical cord was wrapped around my neck). That is a bit of a metaphor for how they treated me most of my life. My mother lost a lot of blood, but we both survived. I was probably one of the most planned babies of the 50s. My parents tried once to get pregnant, on my mother's birthday on the 9th of May. I was born 9 months later on February 9th, 1954 at 4:04am. Little did I know of this baby boy in Scotland that would steal my heart 45 ½ years later. But I'm getting way ahead of the story...

I do subscribe to the spiritual belief that we choose our parents (as well as the rest of our cast of characters), in the inter-life before birth. I believe that they are part of helping us fulfil our soul's purpose. I resonate with the probability that I have been a rebel before in past lives, most probably burned at the stake more than once as I'm quite afraid of fire. Probably pushed or forced to jump from a high place as well as I'm deathly afraid of heights. I feel that in this life I'm taking the role of rebel again, but this time I will meet with success and happiness. In order to be a rebel, I needed something to rebel against. My parents played that part for me for a lot of my life.

I think I'm going to go read in bed now, I'm getting tired. I wish you were with me. Good night baby, come under the covers with me and hold me tight.
Love
Dianne

My parents when they first met

Re: The miracle baby is born

That is a very interesting story and beautiful story and so different from my own. It is also a miracle that two people from such diverse backgrounds could be so enchanted by both each other's differences and their similarities. I'm so glad your parents

139

took the chance and brought you into the world for me. I have some ideas of how I will present my story to you. I'm looking forward to doing it.

Here's some ideas for our Kingdom:

It could be an island – water has to figure in it (sea or ocean) to be seen and heard through the bedroom window. How about an enchanted forest where we could walk hand in hand through the soft bracken. Some hills, one of which is where the castle is situated. Mountains with snowy tops on the horizon for us to see from our dining room window and one dragon that I can protect you from.

The weather – always wonderful, no hurricanes or cold miserable rain. The senses – touch, smell, hearing, seeing, tasting and feeling. Heart, to include love, inner feelings, senses (mental telepathy and any others we can develop through being soul mates). Soul mates is a far better expression and more appropriate than boy/girl friends. We are different from that and that makes this so special.

I must lie down now as tiredness is taking over and both my head and arm are aching now.

With love from your tired King of the enchanted Kingdom of Florsex

David

xxxxxxx

Jupiter is lovely

To my King

Well, I'm just now at the computer since I went outside to look at the stars after we talked and I just couldn't resist sitting on the patio looking at the sky. My new little cat Krystal cuddled up on top of me. You are my preference but since you were in our bed in sex I had to settle for the cat in flor. I felt your presence with me though. I wouldn't have stayed there so long if I hadn't. It is incredibly powerful this pull I'm feeling toward you. Yes, our kingdom will have one dragon so you can protect me. I like that.

As strong and independent and confident as I may appear I still want my man to protect me.

That was another thing that didn't work out with my last boyfriend. He didn't think anybody should need anybody. He was very hung up on not being co-dependent. I have different feelings about that. Of course I want to be happy within myself and I feel that I am. I also want to be financially independent and not need a man for that. But the bottom line is I want to be needed and I want to need my man. Not in an unhealthy way but in a loving way. I want to nurture a man and be nurtured by him. I want to want my other half, my soul mate. He just saw that as being needy and not healthy. He lived a four hour drive away and I only saw him once every 6 to 8 weeks. He liked that we only saw each other that often because it would always be new and exciting. Although new and exciting is nice in the beginning, what I really long for is long lasting and comfortable. I suspect I'll see you just as often as I saw him and you are 7 or 8 hours away by plane! I don't think of you as my current boyfriend even though I described him as my last boyfriend. I think of you as my soul mate. It's just a knowing that I have.

Your goddess and lover
Dianne

Always with you in your heart
Oh my wonderful Goddess

You make me so happy; we have our kingdom, our joined spirit and love. Don't worry about dragons, I will protect you, you are part of me. I am here no matter what tricks or shapes the dragon may take on. You are so right; we are here for each other, but not to lean on. We must be strong for each other and ourselves. You will not find me trying to own you or dictate to you, but you will find me here longing to be with you, to talk to you, to listen to you, to laugh with you, to cry with you and to share our love in the most passionate ways we can find together. I think your last boyfriend will be your last. Time to move on, join the florsex kingdom, the King welcomes you, not as a girlfriend, but as a soul mate, sharing and caring, nurturing and loving, no matter what the distance, time zone, we will be together spiritually, comfortably and forever.

I must go now, I have to have my bath, clear up a little and pick up Rachel to look for a car… maybe I will see more of her then. Vickie is coming Monday night, so I will be off line, but on our florsex special hotline of spirituality.

Lots of love from my heart to yours sweet Goddess
David

xxxxxx

Re: **Always with you in your heart**
Dear sweet David

I woke up early and I'm going to start my day. What a wonderful start to my day receiving your mail. You are everything I've ever dreamed of. I feel like Cinderella or Sleeping Beauty whose Prince has just come. Leave it to me to manifest not just a prince but a king! I am a powerful creator. Plus, I have good karma. The fact that you come form the land of Kings and Dragons makes it all the more wonderful, but I'd love you even if you were American!

When I got off the phone with you still smiling and in a euphoric state I called my mother back and told her how happy I am. We actually had a nice conversation for about 15 minutes. My relationship with you is healing my relationship with my mother! Thank you for that.

Yes, Randall is my last boyfriend. I have found my soul mate. Our kingdom sounds wonderful. You are a wonderful architect (builder of dreams and structures). Yes, the senses, all of them. We will know each other so well. I want to be able to intuit your feelings and truly support them. Your feelings and mine will merge, I feel like they already have. As they say in Star Trek "Space the final Frontier…", I see this as a final frontier. In our kingdom we can go where no man and woman have gone before.

This will be the ultimate success in my life and it won't be difficult like past relationships have been. It will be pure bliss. I really believe that when you find the right person it is easy.

Enjoy Rachel today and Vickie tomorrow. If I don't hear from you Monday I'll know why and like you describe we are so connected anyway that we really aren't skipping a beat.

Lots of love from your goddess of florsex - Dianne

The Power of Love
Good morning great Goddess of Florsex

Just a short note as I am late as usual….

I could tell last night's phone call was doing much more than just drawing us closer. I am so pleased that you and your mother are a bit closer as the result of one phone call. Imagine what might happen by the time I fly home – high profits, world peace, happiness for all! An ambitious set of wishes, but I love you and anything can happen.

I will try to write much more this week – you are right about the phone bills, but I find the overwhelming urge to ring, like last night and it is magic. I must dash now, I am shivering in the hallway, and the bath is ready. Keep my hand close to your heart as yours is to mine.

Your loving King of Florsex, the first and last soul mate
David
xxxxx

Re: The Power of Love
Good morning my King

I can't seem to erase this smile from my face. I guess I won't even try. I'll make more sales this way, be a better mother and good grief even a better daughter! This is quite amazing. I'm not even afraid to ask you if you will meet my parents. My last boyfriend wouldn't. He saw no point in it. He said the relationship is us not them. I'd be grateful and honored if you would agree to meet them. I'm not even afraid they will scare you away as I don't think scaring you away is possible. That's a nice feeling, I feel really secure.

You know you have a physical effect on me as well as a soul effect. Last night, wow, in the silence between words I felt like you were making love to me.

I will try to write more of my story to you this week. It won't be tonight because Terri is home on Monday nights, but I can probably write a lot tomorrow night. I've never wanted a person to know me this well until you, and I've never wanted to know another person this well until you. Have we been enchanted by a powerful force? I think so. It's the power of Love, just like you titled this email.

This weekend is going to be hard to talk to me until Sunday night. In fact, I'll be pretty much offline for four days. Paloma and I are going to a cruise conference that is in Orlando Thursday through Sunday. It starts with breakfast at 7:30 and goes until 10 or 11pm at night with different things hosted by the cruise lines. Since we are local we don't have to stay in the hotel but that means getting up very early to drive there and getting home very late. A phone call on Sunday night will be wonderful though.

Your goddess of love forevermore

Dianne

No Way to Styrofoam cups in our castle!

Good evening my Goddess

Like you the smile is there, and still is now – you are like a magic potion to me.

I will be happy to meet your parents if that is your wish. I am not worried about that in any way. Actually I would like to meet them as people too; they sound very interesting and I always get on well with older people (being a listener helps). Anyway, as a soul mate, and someone who would love to learn more about you, I could not turn down the offer....so yes, I would love to.

I think we both know there was a lot more happening than just between our souls during last night's phone call. I long to hold you so much, and to transfer our energy back and forward between us. I love you, and I know we must go for a meal on that first night if I am to behave. My temptation would be to touch you, with a view to breaking the five date rule, and that ought to be aimed at (if not kept to the letter?). You have driven me wild with desire! My lust is to be with you, and to touch you and be touched in return. We are so close – I dread waking from this most wonderful dream. xxxx

I too want to know so much about you and will in turn write and give my story back. Yes we are in an enchanted land, and the spells are all good ones, and we will conquer all dragons. Talking of which, I did pretty well on the psyche tests you sent, until the table – I had nobody at it, you and I were out on a walk. The cup was china, and that was poor too, unless I secretly feel that our relationship is fragile. Maybe I do. Anyway, I said I would try and not say why again. But either way – I would never imagine a plastic or styrofoam cup in the grounds of our castle (with no fence). That was good fun! Plus your tarot card reading was excellent – long but excellent!

Don't worry about being away on work, I was and you coped… so shall I, my angel. Anyway, I will ring you at the usual time on Sunday if that is ok. Parts of me might burst if I ring you too often. xxxx

I owe you quite a lot of written words (my story) and I will attempt them between now and Sunday.

With the deepest love for the most wonderful Goddess
King David of Florsex

xxxxxxxxxxxxxxxxxx

Re: No way to styrofoam cups in our castle!

My dear sweet King

I fully agree, no styrofoam cups in our castle. Mine were china also. Any relationship can be fragile, even ours, unless it is nurtured. You fill my cup with nurturing like I have never received before from anybody. My promise to you is to always nurture you and honor this magical bond that we have. In that way our china cups will never break. They will last forever, just like we will.

Thank you from my heart to yours for meeting my parents. You have no idea how much that means to me. It is an incredible gift from you.

There is a new song out on the top 40. I don't know the name of it or who the singer is but the words in it include "I knew I loved you before I met you....". I'm going to find out who sings this song and buy the single cd so we can listen to it together. Maybe if we both like it, it can be "our" song.

Yes....you are right about this 5th date thing. It will be difficult. Is there really a point to it? I just wanted to make sure you didn't just love me for my body and I already know the answer to that. It's kind of like if I won the lottery I wouldn't tell you until after you are quite sure of me because I wouldn't want you to love me just because I became rich. I already know that isn't the case either. So, how about if we have no rules? I think even Suzin would understand. By the time we are both finished writing our history to each other we will know each other better than most people do after 6 months of dating. Plus it will be our five month anniversary; that should count for something. Do you like my idea of going to the hotel in Longwood instead of the expensive one at the airport and just going together in your rented car? Then we could at least have a two hour rule!

Will you try something for me? Marley wakes me in the morning at 6:30 so I'll be awake and ready to take her to school at 7:00. Will you think about me at 11:15 your time and pretend you are kissing me and caressing me. I want to see if that wakes me.

By the way, you will never waken from this most wonderful dream so don't worry about that. The powers that be who run the universe have deemed this to be so and nothing can break this enchantment.

One other thing I meant to tell you. I was looking at the description of a new book on intuition and it said "the soul has a non-linear sense of time". That is something similar to your friend's description of existing multi-dimensionally. But more importantly it says to me that when soul mates re-find each other the fact that they haven't "met" means nothing as in another time they knew each other well. Because the soul's sense of time is non-linear, there is no such thing as 5 dates. What do you make of this logic my King? Are you thinking what I'm thinking?

I love you soul mate David

Dianne

I'm not worried

Oh great Goddess

I am not worried. I know there is no waking from your spell. This sudden surge of passion flowing through me has to be the sort of magic only a true Goddess could produce. I love both you and the passion you raise in me, you make me feel wonderful! I totally agree on the non-linear thingy too!

I'm not going to do anymore responding tonight. I have a few ideas for you (for my story) that I want to do offline. They may take some time to do or they may come to nothing.

Talk again very soon...

Your ardent lover

King David of Florsex

xxxxxxxxxxxxxxxxxxxx

My childhood

Dear David

I can't wait to see what your ideas are that you are gathering offline. I also can't wait to wake up tomorrow morning to your caresses. Thank you for all the gifts you give me. I am the most fortunate Goddess in the universe! I have a lot of time to write today as I've left work at noontime to be home for the pool man and I have taken the rest of the day off. I'm in the mood to write my story so I will continue it now.

I think when I left off I was just born. Here's what my childhood was like. Although we weren't rich, I didn't lack anything. I had all the lessons (ballet, tap, acrobatics, dramatics, baton, guitar) that anybody could want. I didn't really like it though because of the way my parents were always following me around with their camera (movie and still) taking my picture and grinning at their wonderful miracle baby. It cramped my style a bit and I didn't really feel normal. I wasn't allowed to play outside alone much or get dirty like the other kids. I rode a tricycle until I looked like an idiot and then rode nothing until my parents would finally buy me a bicycle at a much later age than the other kids. I stopped celebrating Halloween because my parents wouldn't let me go trick or treating with other kids, I had to be with them. I was intelligent, shy, and amazingly, did have some friends in spite of all this. Until I was 12 though, it was always the friends that my parents approved of. My parents were (still are) the opposite of me in that they live in fear whereas I live in total trust and positive thinking. I was really shy though and had to get a doctor's note to get out of giving an oral report in a class because I was terrified. I've come a long way baby! Now I address a cruise crowd of 700!

I spent a good part of my early years with chronic bronchitis and had to stay in a room with a steam humidifier. My mother, having been born with a hole in her heart, was never allowed to participate in physical education at school and it was natural for her to find a way to get me excused from it quite a bit as well. She was never good at mathematics, so hence, neither was I. She and I were readers. In fact, I taught myself, with her help, to read at age three. My mother said I was reading encyclopedias before starting kindergarten. I missed half of kindergarten because of bronchitis, so it was a good thing I was ahead anyway. I did enjoy reading though and do owe my love of reading today to my mother.

My grandfather sort of controlled the family (like the Godfather). He opened a luggage store and gave it to my father with multiple controlling strings attached. The control got so bad at one point that my father went to night school to learn a trade so he could get out from under this control. He became a dental technician and made crowns, bridges and dentures. He liked it but the pay was low and his eyesight was strained. That lasted just a couple of years. My grandfather and my uncle ran the store for those years and then my father took it back. He is very creative with his hands and he did luggage repair including sewing and creating luggage covers. He wasn't as into the money making aspect as my grandfather was. I think I got my love of business more from my grandfather.

My mother was away when I finished elementary school and the summer before starting middle school. She was at Deborah Heart Hospital in New Jersey having the open-heart surgery that repaired the hole in her heart, with a Teflon kind of patch, and enabled her to live a long normal life. The entire trip was about three months as it included the pre-surgery tests and the post-surgery recuperation. This was a relatively new surgery and this was a teaching and a charitable hospital. My parents were both from New Jersey and my mother had a lot of relatives there supporting her including my father's sister.

I grew up that summer without my mother being there to witness it. I remember my breasts grew that summer. I must have already started my period because she was around for that happening and was really cool with it. My grandparents lived with us because my mother needed the help in the household in the years leading up to the surgery so it was natural for me to be taken care of and driven places by my grandmother. My relationship with my father began to deteriorate though as I became a woman and no longer his little girl, yet he trusted no boy with me.

I found it very odd that my father didn't go to the hospital to be with my mother at least for the days surrounding the surgery but he owned a business and had a very strong work ethic and never took a vacation. Practicality always won over sentiment. If I didn't know how much in love my parents were and are I might have doubted it because of things like that but I guess it is just a work ethic born of the depression. He didn't even go to New Jersey for his own mother's funeral. I believe I was angry at my father for this, and for changing his name as well. My father was born Jewish, with a very Jewish name, Abraham Joseph Kempinsky. When my parents married and moved to Miami in the post World War II years, my father found it difficult getting a job. He assumed it was anti-semitism and changed his name to Alex Kemp and did find work shortly thereafter. So I was born Dianne Michele Kemp and felt that a bit of my heritage had been stolen from me. Miami became a very Jewish place and I didn't experience anti-semitism there at all. Of course with a name like Kemp, who knew I was Jewish?

During the surgery my mother had a spiritual experience just like people who are speakers on my cruises who have had near death experiences. I distinctly remember her telling me that she saw a light and she saw God. They do have to stop people's hearts to put them on heart-lung machines for surgery. Now she will deny having that experience and is back to being very non-spiritual but I know I didn't imagine her telling me that. Once she came home after the surgery she could do things, like breathe and walk without turning blue. It was nice to not consider my mother an invalid anymore. She even learned how to drive shortly after that and went back to college. She doesn't drive now (she forgot again or got scared).

I'm going to sign off on this email so AOL doesn't lose it and also so I can take a break and do a few things in the house but I will be back to write more.

Your Goddess
Dianne

My adolescence and teen years
My wonderful King David of Florsex

Boys in my adolescence were not too many. I do remember a party in 7th grade where we played spin the bottle and I kissed a few boys. I had one boyfriend when I was 12 (Mickey) and I remember sneaking him in a window. We may have kissed but really didn't know how. Kids stuff really. No other boyfriends until Tony in 9th grade. I thought I was going to marry him and wanted to give his little sister my Barbie dolls. My mother wouldn't let me and said I had to save them for my daughters. More kids stuff in kissing, nothing more.

End of 9th grade, beginning of 10th – high school and real boys stuff began. I tried out to be one of the sponsor/sweethearts of one of the Jewish boys' clubs. I was in a Jewish girls' club. Three girls made it and I was one of them! The boys liked me. I had a nice personality, looked pretty good (weighed a lot less than I do now), and I didn't mind giving a few kisses. That's all I gave was kisses, not even a little feel of the boobs, I was basically a good girl.

I had three boyfriends during the course of high school and the third is the one I married. The first one was Mark. I was 15 and in 10th grade and he was 17 and in 12th grade. I was in love with him and he loved me too but was basically a high school jerky boy who did dumb things. He was way too appearance conscience and told me that I'd be beautiful if I got a nose job. Well, lots of Jewish girls were getting nose jobs at the time and I decided I wanted to do it too since Mark said I'd be beautiful. My parents got me a nose job for my 16th birthday. It isn't a cute little turned up nose or anything. It fits my face and my personality but it is much better than the one I had so I guess I'm thankful to Mark for that. Don't worry; I'm not the type who is into cosmetic surgery. My breasts are all mine, I'd never get a face lift or have liposuction. I believe in being natural and loving who you are. I just felt a little different at 16. Now I don't even wear much makeup. Some women look completely different with their makeup on. Me, I'm pretty much what you see is what you get. I'm very natural.

Mark and I used to get luggage that the airlines had damaged and my father couldn't repair. We took it to the flea market on Sundays and sold it. That's how we got date money. That was the first time my family supported my boyfriend. Stan became the second but that's getting ahead of the story. Mark and I got along really well. We fought a little but it was actually a very deep and strong relationship once he started growing up a little. We were together for over a year and maintained a friendship beyond that. Sexually, we made out hot and heavy and he did touch me waist up. I didn't touch him and he didn't touch me below the waist. He did lie on top of me when we kissed and I felt him and liked that feeling. I remember that well. Just this past year I wondered about Mark. I thought he had become a dentist and I did a search on the internet and found him in Syracuse New York. I wrote to his office address and sent him one of my cruise brochures and told him I was Dianne Kemp Silver Rillings. He was really glad to hear from me. He's married and has two little girls and is a dentist. We still email occasionally and I'll always have a warm spot in my heart for him.

After Mark, I started dating one of the boys in this club, Stuart. Stuart was fun and we had a lot of good times but there was no love and no sex of any kind, only kissing. One night we double dated with Stuart's best friend, Stan Silver and his date Gina. Within a week I was dating Stan and Gina was dating Stuart. Stan and I got very close. He was one year ahead of me in school and when I was 17 and he was 18 we had sex. My parents liked him. He was going to be a dentist and they thought that was wonderful, I'd be provided for if I married him. My parents had wanted me to be a dental hygienist because that's a good trade. That didn't interest me in the least so at least I found a dentist to marry. Since my parents liked him they let me go away to the University of Florida where he was and my mother even took me to a doctor to get on birth control pills. She figured I'd do this anyway and better I didn't get pregnant. I was Stan's first as well and the sex was pretty immature and not all that loving or satisfying until at least two years later when he learned how to satisfy me.

Did we love each other? I think so but in an immature way. I was infatuated and so was he. I did see him as a way to escape from my over-protective parents. Because of him I could go away to college and also after that leave Florida for wherever he went to Dental School (if we were married). He graduated from high school in 71 and I did in 72, so my last year of high school wasn't all that great. I went to Gainesville to visit him a few times. We did date other people, which was better for him than for me because I was feeling much too mature for high school boys. I had a few assorted dates but nothing special.

Back then you pretty much married the first man you slept with; it was expected. When I got to Gainesville we still dated other people for a little while. There was nothing serious and no sex or anything near it. We broke up a few times and got back together. My grandfather bought me a car when I went away to college and Stan used it more than I did. That was the next time my family sort of supported one of my boys. Stan wasn't really all that nice to me. He really wanted to be young and free and I really wanted to get married. I did college in 3 years to catch up with him. He spent the first semester in dental school without me and then we got married in December 1975. I think the second big reason I married him (first was to escape parents) was that we had had sex and I thought I had to marry the guy I had sex with. So when we married in 1975 he was the only guy I had ever had sex with.

In college I majored in psychology much to my parents' dismay since it wasn't anything you could get a job in with just a bachelor's degree but I was marrying the dental student I had had sex with so all was well with the world. Little did we all know that one day he'd have an affair with his hygienist (who happened to be my cousin's wife). That's a story for another day! Basically, I consider this all to be very adolescent. I really hadn't tasted adult relationships, sexual or otherwise. So that's my first 21 years. More tomorrow......

I love you....sleep well my love.

Your Goddess

Dianne

Your adolescent and teen years and the beginning of my story

Oh Goddess

It's so late. It was late when I came back online, but I have now spent an enthralling age reading your early life. I felt through yours, surely this time she would find the sort of love that made her abandon the only gift you could never replace. Not that my story is full of torrid love scenes either! I can't wait for the next part, you were lovely and innocent. xxxx

Let me know what you think of this tale.

*   *   *   *

My American readers may find this a bit more difficult to understand than my British readers as this is written in David's very own style of Old English. I have added in brackets a couple of interpretations in some of his writing to help but my best advice is to just enjoy it like I did and don't worry if you don't fully understand it!

*   *   *   *

The Road to Florsex part 1 "In the Beginning"

Once upon a time in a far off place named Celtland, there was a Scottish soldier named Hugh, who fought battles in a kilt of many woven dark fibres (whose pattern is known to the people of this land as "Black Watch") and to the sound of pipes and drum. He was coming home from distant battles in the jungle wilderness of Burma. He was of a family large of brothers, names unknown to my generation, only the younger and older ones have this sacred secret. He met his love, Ruby, a young angel of the nursing profession – used to tending the sick of fevers, which were numerous and virulent, in that international area of trading ships on the Clyde.

Their union produced a future king despite their lack of knowledge of these wonders. They named him David. He was very yellow at the time of his birth; he suffered from a common disease – jaundice of the liver. However, with the powers vested in his future he made a full recovery.

While the soldier was out toiling in the coal mines deep in the earth under the city, he should have kept better company, for he fell amongst those who sought to corrupt and destroy him. They introduced him to the ways of their sister….and alas he was a mere mortal. When there were signs of another fruit, the brothers bullied and persuaded the soldier to do the right thing by her. So it was that the king and the angel were cast out with nothing.

At this time in a land of foreign settlers, a Goddess was born against all odds, into a very special family, whose love was strong and with many capabilities. This wondrous child was nurtured and cherished, and allowed to grow into someone so important to this story, that she will have her own place in its history.

The angel had a mother living in that city, with the angel's sister named Gladys (the sister who must be obeyed). Gladys was the oldest sister of that brood of 14. The way was there for the king's development. At two years he was holding conversations with the natives of this land and could speak their unusual tongue like he was one of their own. This young developer soon discovered the ways of the flesh, and found himself an older female companion, the four year old daughter of the local corner shopkeeper. Many a day they could be seen, playing on the local swings until a bad wind swept through that land and the king was knocked forward by a swing onto a metal spike, left behind after railings had been removed in a bygone age to produce weapons of war to fight the Blitzkreiging Hun. The king now was marked with a blue dot on the forehead, distinguishing him from mortal men of that land.

The angel was having to work by night to feed and clothe her offspring and this was not a solution destined for many years. To produce a secure future for the king, she struck up an old relationship with a man she had previously met on the shores of Loch Lomond – his name was Vincent Blackshadow. Soon they married, and a big black metal train exited that city with three passengers, destined for a town on the outskirts of the noble city of London, in the county of Essex. The name of this town was Billericay. The king grew up there very alone for the next two years. He was so lonely that one day whilst playing alone in a field, he saw a boy Paul, of the same age, walking home from the shops with his mother, Rose. The king found it so difficult being alone, he asked the rose if he may be permitted to play with the boy Paul. They remained friends from that day until Paul's death, six years later.

Very soon it became time for him to have some contact with the people and so it was he started school. On his first day he met and became friends with many people, one especially is remembered now – he being Peter of the tree house. Many hours of fun were had playing as boys do. Peter too is among the knights of the king's table, still to be listed as a friend of the King.

To be continued.......

Warm thoughts and your story!
My darling King

Were you thinking those warm thoughts just a tad early? I woke up thinking of you at around 5:45. I lingered in bed, being there with you until 6:30 and it was very nice.

I love the way you write!! Your story is beautiful. It's kind of fun to write it, isn't it? I felt your mother's pain and her resolve to make a life for you. I felt you being a young boy and your friendships. How sad that one of them died. I had a close childhood friend who died also. I believe it was Hodgkin's Lymphoma or something like that, some type of cancer. Interesting that you have a friend named Peter who would still be considered one of the Knights of the Round Table. I also have a Peter in my life. He's the one I do the Inner Voyage with. You'll see his picture if you got the brochure. Did you get it yet? He lives in Greenwich Village.

I can't wait to hear more of your story. I want to know you so well. I can continue mine this evening before picking Nicki up from cheerleading practice.

Another thought that would be in favor of you going right to the hotel in Longwood is that I could have Paloma drop me off at the airport as she lives near there. Then my car wouldn't even be there it would be at home. After we spend several hours together at your hotel in Longwood you would take me home and you'd know your way back to the hotel and how to pick me up in the morning. If you want, just get the reservation there for four nights. If we need you to go back there for one night I'm sure they'll have a vacancy. But really, it will probably be fine for you to spend that last night at my house even though Terri and the girls will be there. First of all they will know you pretty well by then and if we want to be "proper" you can always sleep on the sofa. Really, that won't be necessary though since me and the girls are sort of like sisters and they can tell if I'm lying (which isn't easy to do with them). They'll ask me if we had sex and if I say no they will stare me down and smile at me until I say yes! I will explain to them that we didn't just have sex, we had conscious and sacred lovemaking, and I'll explain to them the difference and that that is what I wish for them. Anyway, we can play see how it goes but why don't you just reserve the hotel for four nights. The only benefit to the expensive airport Hyatt is that it is elegant and it would make our first time holding each other very befitting of a Goddess and her King. I'll leave it up to you but really I think my preference would be to drive with you to Longwood that first night so you'd get the rental car starting on the 29th. I don't need an expensive hotel room to enchant you. I'll pack a bag with some goddess magic inside of it (candles, nightgown, CD and CD player, etc) and you and I my King will be transported instantly to the Kingdom of Florsex no matter where we are. You have created such magic in my life. I want us to enter our world with nothing short of the proper magical ritual.

I love you David (always have and always will)
Your Goddess
Dianne

Dragon children?

Oh my Goddess

I am so sorry I woke you early, I had no idea I was that powerful. I have been thinking the same thoughts of you since I wrote first thing today. Every time my mind was free to wander, it and the hand of tantra tried very hard to get a sense of my being with you through the ether. It makes me feel really good if my effort can please you, I always want to do that.

More delight that the method of writing worked! I had the idea while talking on the phone, but kept it to myself in case it didn't work. It's fun to write to you. You appreciate the differences between me and the rest that I alluded to in my profile all those months ago.

I am using author's license in relation to my mother's pain as she has not confided that much in me, but it is about the only scenario that fits what she has said and the world before me.

Yes, it is very sad about Paul, he also died of cancer. His was of the bowel.

Re Peter, later he marries Kate who is a lovely person. One day you must meet them both, and their daughters Anna and Charlotte. Your Peter, which one is he? The brochure arrived this morning, very wet and stuck together a bit. I saw the lovely Ms Rillings, she does have a similarity to my Goddess don't you think?

I am speaking at an international conference on electronic obsolescence on Tuesday and have not done very much planning yet on my talk, so must do that. I will therefore not have much time to progress the story but I will. I want you to know my past as well as you know my future. xxxxxx

Going to the hotel in Longwood sounds great. I don't need fancy distractions while I get to know you face to face. I have to say, that we have moved our goal posts a long way in the last few days, from 5 dates to possibly first meeting! Who knows, by the 29th you will fly alongside, do a mid-air transfer and join the mile high club! Fun apart, the feet on the ground me knows how tiring travel can be, and really wouldn't want to ruin such lovely plans by still being human. Just remember, I want every second to be total magic for you. Keep the plans and hopes coming, they are lovely. The bag idea sounds wonderful too. We can rest awhile, enjoying each other as we do so. I LOVE YOU! Does Paloma have any idea what your plans are?

I like the thought that the three of you are all like sisters. That sounds very warm and cosy. Shame they can see through you. Telling them about us when challenged would be the smart option. All children know a lie, much more so than adults do. However, I have never faced a family in the morning after having stayed the night......go away dragons! xxxx Terri is another story too, she will understand exactly what is happening. I hope she will be happy for us. I long to be in your arms right now!

Must go for now – I will keep my hand on your belly a little longer. It is important not to lose you while I work.

Lots of love

David

xxxxx

Re: Dragon children?

Oh my King

You make me laugh so hard! Damn right you are powerful! If you are this powerful over the ethers I can only imagine what it will be like making love in person. Your energy is very powerful and your magic very potent my King. Did you train with the great Merlin? Don't worry about being human and being tired after travelling. We are simply loving each other; we'll see what happens naturally. Remember we have the rest of our lives to discover what each other likes sexually. I just want to be about loving each other that first night. You are right that we have moved our goal posts a bit. You really made me laugh about the mile high club! You have really transformed into a succulent wild man! I look forward to hearing your voice again, but let's not have phone sex before we have real sex!

I do have a few hopes and fears that I will share with you later as I share my history. I feel you have a capacity to understand me better than anybody I have ever met.

You may have used author's license in writing of your mother's pain, but I also used reader's license and intuition in interpreting it. You didn't even use the word pain, I did. I just followed your words and the feelings behind them, and yes my love, I do so appreciate the difference between you and the rest.

That is wonderful that you are speaking at that conference on Tuesday. Don't worry about writing your story while you are busy preparing for that. I won't be online anyway for the next four days because of the conference I'm going to. It will be difficult in a way not hearing from you, however, our connection is so strong that I believe we will both still feel it. This has gotten so much stronger since you went away for a week.

You asked if Paloma knows what my plans are. Keep in mind she is not just an employee, she is my best friend. I come in the office every morning and say "did I tell you how much I love David". Our secrets are our secrets, you don't have to worry about that, but to answer your question, yes, I think Paloma does have an idea what our plans are! She is very happy that I am so happy and that you have created such magic in my life. Terri is also very happy for us. Even my parents are happy for us! I'm telling you, you are a powerful magician. Ah yes….the dragon children….. they are happy for us too. They no longer ask why I'm smiling, they know. They are very cool. I told Nicki you felt bad that you couldn't instant message her and me at the same time. She said "it's all good". That's American teenage slang for no problem, it's cool. She does want to talk to you though.

The time is getting away from me. I'm going to sign off, have some dinner and if I still have time before leaving to get Nicki I'll start at age 21 and see how far I get.

Your lover and soul mate

Dianne

I LOVE YOU xxx

To my dearest love Dianne

Just the shortest of notes to say I LOVE YOU. Take care on your journey. Talk again on Sunday night.

Lots of caressing moments in our thoughts

David

xxxx

Re: I LOVE YOU xxxx

Dear wonderful David

I LOVE YOU TOO! It really sounds good to hear you say it though because I know those aren't words you take lightly. I don't take them lightly either.

When we got off the phone last night I went into the kitchen and Terri was saying I love you to her boyfriend. I went to Marley's room and she was saying I love you to her boyfriend. Luckily little Nicki wasn't saying I love you to anybody. I think I have a succulent household here.

You woke me again this morning early (4:30am). Maybe I was just dreaming about you. I'll be tired tonight so I doubt I'll be awake at 1am, but before I go to sleep I will travel to your bed and kiss you and maybe more....let me know if you awaken early tomorrow.

Take good care of yourself and stay warm and never forget how much I love you.

Your lover and soul mate

Dianne

Came home early

Dearest David

Hello my love. I've been thinking of you constantly. I came home early tonight from the conference because I was tired, had a stomach ache and a head ache. With a stomach ache I would much rather be in my own bathroom than a conference hotel with a long line of women waiting to use one of the 3 toilets. I'm a bit shy that way and don't like a person on either side of me and a whole bunch waiting outside the door. So I left and didn't stay for the dinner and the Caribbean entertainment hosted by Royal Caribbean.

Other than being tiring, the conference has been very nice. I've had some really good networking opportunities. The consortium I belong to has merged with others into vacation. com which will have a big internet presence. There will be an opportunity for me to wholesale to other travel agents maybe if they recognize my niche as worthy. Some people are just really ignorant of it and make stupid comments. Being a top producing agency I was invited to a private cocktail party last night in the penthouse which was fun. Also, Dreamtime won an award today from Princess Cruise Lines. We were the most improved travel agency in booking volume from 1997 to 1998. It is a really pretty glass piece. So all in all it has been a very good conference.

I'm going to get something to eat right now and then if Terri isn't home yet I'll get back on the computer and write to you more of my story. I can't wait to hear your voice on Sunday.
With love, hugs and kisses from your tired Goddess
Dianne

My Twenties
To my wonderful King
Stanley Silver, my high school sweetheart and I were married on December 21, 1975 at a hotel on Miami Beach. We had just a three-day honeymoon in Jamaica as it was high season and very expensive and also because he had to be back to dental school. We drove my car to Washington DC. He didn't have a car. He got my car and I took buses and subways to work. Even though I was working to support us when he was in dental school, what he did was always judged as more important than what I was doing so he got the car. We got a $10,000 wedding gift from my grandfather which we used for dental school, so my family and I really did support him. $10,000 was a lot of money in 1975! I remember

my car which as a new Toyota Celica in 1972 was only $3,000. So this gift was more than three times a nice car in value! They were all happy to see me married off to the nice dentist. Now I'd be provided for. What a joke that turned out to be, but that is getting ahead of the story.

We drove my car to Washington DC and set up our first apartment, a one bedroom in Arlington Virginia, just outside of Washington. Everything there was old and all of the apartments were pretty infested (at least in the kitchen) with these little German roaches that came out at night, and when you turned a light on they ran all over the place. This was not the style I wanted to live in but I had to do it for 3 ½ years. I was not yet a Goddess but I was a bit of a Princess.

I had four different jobs in Washington. First I had a government job at the Treasury Department as a typist. Since I had a degree I could have entered their training program to be a securities transactions analyst. I knew this was not a very creative job and not really my thing so I turned it down. I then went to the Smithsonian Institution and worked as a secretary at the Natural History Museum. On my lunch hours I slowly saw all of the museums really well and I loved that. I was there in the summer of 1976 which was the American Bi-Centennial and there were all sorts of exhibits for that. I worked as a volunteer information specialist in the museums on weekends because I liked it so much. Besides, Stanley was studying all the time anyway.

After that I got a job on Capitol Hill for Senator Daniel Patrick Moynihan from New York. That was very interesting and I got to attend some very high-powered Washington parties! I learned a lot about life and politics then. What angered me was that the people my age who graduated from Ivy League colleges like Harvard and Yale got to write the letters to the constituents while those like me who still had a degree but from a lesser university (their opinion, not mine) were only employed to type them.

As you can imagine, I was interacting with all sorts of dynamic people of all different ages. Stan, on the other hand was acting like a college kid, studying all the time when he wasn't getting high with his friends and listening to music that I didn't particularly like. He wouldn't associate with anybody over 30 and I had a lot of friends over 30 because of my jobs in the real world. This was creating a problem. We lived in separate worlds and really drifted apart.

The problem got much worse with my next job. I worked as a legal secretary for a big Washington law firm and the lawyer that I worked for really liked me. He was 40 and I was 25. Of course I was flattered that this older man liked me and everything with Stan was very boring at the time. He was always with his friends, either studying or partying so when my boss kept inviting me out for a drink after work I finally accepted. He was Irish Catholic and a bit of an alcoholic. There was an Irish pub right next door to our office and I entered that world with him. Being a Jewish girl I'm not much of a drinker, never have been. One drink is all it took to get me drunk. This was a world I had never lived in and frankly it seduced me. We did kiss and fool around a bit too which I wasn't proud of, but like I said Stan and I were in different worlds and I think a bit too young and selfish to know what it takes to make a relationship work. I certainly wouldn't have left Stan for this man but the allure of this different lifestyle did have a pull on me.

Stan and I left Washington in June of 1979 and moved to Orlando. Wow, I've been here over 20 years! Time sure does fly! In less than two months this millennium will be over. Just as well for our new life together. Anyway, Stan was an officer in the Navy for two years after graduating from dental school. We were told to make three choices of where we wanted to live. We knew we wanted to settle in Orlando, so we picked that as choice number three. If we got that we'd find where Stan would set up his practice after getting out of the Navy and get a head start on it. The other two places were San Francisco and San Diego California. We figured those would be interesting places to live for two years. Well, we got Orlando.

Needless to say, I'm way too different from the usual Navy Officer's wife, and I was a bit of an outcast. I found the whole thing silly and the women lacking in brains. Most of them didn't work and I did. Most of them had babies and I didn't. Stan didn't want to have a baby until he was set up in practice.

My first job in Orlando was as a marketing support rep for Lanier Business Products. This was before PCs and it was the beginning of word processors. We had a Lanier word processor in the law firm in Washington and I was quite good at it so in this job I taught secretaries how to use it. I would have taken a job as a legal secretary but salaries in Orlando were about half what they were in Washington, so it was an insult to me! I liked this job but got laid off after a year because they didn't have enough business.

It was then (1980) that I got a real estate license. Selling real estate was sort of fun. It was business, and it was self employment which I liked. Unfortunately, in the early 80s interest rates were about 17% so it was a tough market. I never made much money but I did enjoy it. I did it on and off the first half of the 80s even while helping Stan start his practice. I even got a broker's license which was a step above salesperson and meant I could go on to open my own office if I wanted to. We used my license to acquire some rental properties with creative financing (nothing down). We would assume a low interest rate first mortgage, get an institutional second mortgage to give the seller some cash and have the seller hold a third mortgage. These properties were not slum, but they were lower middle class and the tenants weren't all that great. Since Stan did the dentistry and I did everything else, I had to manage the properties as well as find them. I worked my ass off doing this and did begin to resent it.

I'm going to hit send now so this doesn't get too long and get lost like what happened to you. I'll be right back......
Love you very much
Dianne

My Twenties (part 2)
I'm back my King

Stan got out of the Navy in June of 1981. We had already found an office location and had it equipped and ready to go. He was going to partner with a friend from the Navy, Bert, who had another year to go and would work part-time in the practice that first year. He was a warm sensitive man with a wife and three kids and was about eight years older than us.

Well to get out of the Navy they do an exit physical which, among other things, includes a chest x-ray. The chest x-ray showed a large growth in Stan's chest cavity the size of a grapefruit. They flew him to the National Institute of Health in Bethesda Maryland for surgery at a large Naval hospital and I went with him. After the surgery the surgeon told me it is certainly a benign cyst all filled with fluid but they were sending it to the lab for a pathology report. The report came back with elements of seminoma, which is normally a testicular cancer. Very strange for this to be in the chest! There were a lot of possibilities (migration of fluid while he was in his mother's womb, a hernia when he was a child causing tissue to migrate, a serious cancer). He didn't seem to have any testicular problems so they decided to give him radiation treatment to his chest and neck area as the cyst was in the thymus gland area. They still weren't sure what they were treating but thought it best to treat it with radiation. He was able to go back to Orlando for that. He didn't feel very good, but he could function and continued to open his dental practice with my help. That was quite a summer, very scary for me but I can imagine much scarier for him. As usual, he kept most of his feelings inside.

The good thing was that they put him on temporary disability retirement leave (TDRL) rather than discharging him and he continued to get paid by the Navy for two years while he worked in his new practice. I was creative and he was money hungry so we did pretty well almost from the beginning. The problem was he was so materialistic, still waiting for the perfect time to have a baby (we weren't rich enough yet) and he wanted more and more and more. In addition to investing in real estate we did the Amway business and I worked my ass off in that too. That's a very hard business to do well in but we sure tried and put a lot of energy into it for two years (mostly my energy). I brought bookkeeping home from the office, and between the dental practice, Amway and the real estate and investments all I did was work. I get tired now just reliving those years in writing it to you.

I really wanted to get pregnant and I soon realized that Stan's delay could last a long time as he wanted to make money a lot more than he wanted to have a baby. Everybody we knew from both dental school and the Navy already had kids. So I finally convinced him and we started trying when I was 28 and he was 29. It took us over a year. Possibly the radiation treatments he had caused some problems in conceiving, but finally I was pregnant. I loved being pregnant and I loved eating for two! Marley was born February 26th 1984, two weeks after my 30th birthday. Nicole was a little over two years later on April 17th 1986. I really love my children and wanted them both so much.

Terri is home now and I have to go. I love you David from a deep place in my heart. I was doodling at the conference today.... Dianne and David now and forever. Paloma thinks I'm just like a 13 year old, you make me so happy!
With all my love now and forever
Dianne

Your Twenties (you need more love than that)
Good morning my Goddess

I was so sad to hear you were feeling off colour. I had a feeling something was wrong with me. I had pains in my lower belly, like I had food poisoning just for about an hour or two before reading of your problem. I had nothing wrong with me; am I getting sympathy pains? I hope you are well now. My pains left soon afterwards, I hope yours did too.

I will be very short this morning due to many things to do, but I just had to write to reassure you. Your story so far is very moving, real and not shocking. Your story is told with pain and desperation for Stan to love and nurture you, but that result appears to be totally missing. I hope you have had some love from him; he appears to be blind to the magic you possess.

I love you and I love the things you say. Is my name on your pencil case? I believe that what we have we have for a reason…I don't know the reason yet other than it is a very positive one and that major good is to come of it.

Do you find the whole thing of writing your past helps clear up some of its problems? I do and find it is helping me move forward. I have progressed a little more with my story and will send it in a few minutes.

Are you back from the cruise weekend? Some of the people there sound like they are lacking spirit and others perhaps know a good thing when they see it but lack the ability to carry it off. I know a star when I see one and you are a star, the brightest one in my heaven. xxx

I look forward every day to reading more of your past and present, and being a big part of your future.

Lots of love and care from your King

David of Florsex

xxxxxxxxxxxxxx

Another instalment

My dearest love

Here's another instalment of history – up to the marriage. Here goes…..Part 2

Peter figures very heavily in the long term future of the King. Peter and the King had a mutual friend Robert Sutton, another natural born fool, still close friends with Peter and whose news is still handed on to the king upon meeting with his faithful knight. Many years later the faithful knight was to marry the lovely Kate/Katherine/Kathy (the name changes with everyone who talks about the raven haired, pale skinned beauty) who was a close friend of the deposed queen, who had plotted against all the will of the universe to bring them together. Probably the most positive act in her whole existence.

In the same time (age 5 – 7 years) there were girls of the court. The king had always liked girls, Anne, Diane and Elaine were some of the aforementioned. The day came when playing with a group of others it came to pass the king's education had to begin. In the long grass amongst about 6 or 7 others a new game emerged, "I will show you mine if you show me yours". This was a great revelation to the hitherto ignorant king. However, that lasted but a few seconds, as Anne's mother was nearby and thought such was unworthy education for king and companions – a major negative to the king's development! This negativity was added to by a horrible tutor from the school attended by the king, the knights and Anne, Diane and Elaine. This is not a fitting subject for sending in this fashion but will eventually be told to the great goddess when a level of comfort is reached.

At this time the king and the king's mother only travelled when the black shadow decreed it possible. There was very little experience for the king to use for progression – so little that the king was offered a chance of going to a private school. The king thought this was the lesser of two evils and accepted the offer, but fate chose the destiny to be to stay at home – mother's choice.

At a similar time the king was also offered a chance to have a new brother/sister and again the answer was of the affirmative. However, it was obvious to the God of fate that the consequences of that act would upset the stability of the universe, so no sister or brother would be forthcoming. The king never truly recovered from this – he never wished to be alone. A spiritual sister one day would change his life, and he never expected such a change.

It came to pass that the black shadow was offered riches in a new land – Sussex, such a place that the new kingdom of Florsex is based loosely around it. So at age 10 the king is on the move yet again, this time by vehicle with just 3 wheels. A vehicle of 750cc and no rear side windows [three wheeled car].

At age 10 the king had already been judged by society (the eleven plus examination) and failed this test – destined to be a failure for the rest of his life. Success of this 11 plus is destined to give the winner a good chance of success in the academic world. Failures were destined (theoretically) to be failures. Shame the last Prime Minister of the land! Peter and the king had no idea of this. Peter is now one of the senior partners of a large firm of solicitors. In this group of outcasts from the academic land were Graham, who is another of the king's knights and Andrew, a lesser knight.

Andrew was uncovered by the black shadow as being of unsuitable character and an unworthy friend of the king, one who was destined to be cast into dungeons for treachery. This "unworthy" knight married the girl he met at age 13, is still married to her and is now a director of a Best Western hotel in a local town. Was the black shadow wrong? A short tale of Andrew. At the time of the fighter Cassius Clay, the young knights travelled to their place of education by Iron Horse [train]. (Did you spot the native American speak?) Whilst in transit, the king used to perform mathematical works due to be done in the knights own castles [he did their homework for them].

Andrew has one other task to perform whilst still a youth. He introduced the king to his first fair lady – Angela, a lovely tall leggy blond, with a future of many hours of kissing in the hayloft. The mode of transport for the weekly visits was a vehicle of mass transportation on the turnpike. The frequency of these vehicles was but twice per day, so accuracy of timekeeping was imperative. The king was sad that this wonderful relationship ended, the magic removed by a sickness.

A time of sickness soon followed for the king. He suffered two plagues simultaneously – tonsillitis and appendicitis, each of which cast doubts in the minds of the physicians, thus causing them to procrastinate. Eventually the physicians' procrastination caused a time of great fear in the nation. The king was rushed to the local nearest site of St John [hospital], by carriage with twin tones [ambulance]. The news around the land was that the king was saved and the evil appendix was vanquished from the land. This wonder then removed the physicians' paradox, and so the king was cured.

From that day forth, the king's academic ability was no longer stifled and so his progression began.

From age thirteen years the king was taught by a great philosopher and bender of metal, Bill Bedford. He told tales of making iron steeds (Scott Motorcycles) in the years known to bygone generations as "the thirties" in the county of Yorkshire. These steeds were well known to the king, as the black shadow brought the king into an empire of old iron, oil and noise. An affinity was made between the tutor, the family and the king.

The first iron steed was "given" to the king at about age 12. Few years have passed since he has been without such.

The king remembers many times when he was able to act parts in dramas, operettas, and success (of limited scales) were reached through this educational period.

At the age of ten and five, the king was set to move into the world of financial creation. An apprenticeship was sought and 5 were offered. The king's favourite was banned by the black shadow (to produce silver birds for the transportation of 4 to 5 kings/emperors). Eventually a decision was reached and a suitable company selected. This company produced a style of machine, destined to create the impossible – travel of objects at the speed of light, under the base of a mountain. Qualifications were part of this ordeal – the king was not a good student, he preferred to be relaxed and free, not entrapped by academia.

A time of hardship fell upon the land with strife and darkness. (Political upheaval with the miners of the black coal for creation of power.) Thus it was the country was plunged into darkness, cold and deprivation. So it was that many members of that company joined a great number of others seeking gainful employment. It was during this time that the king met the old queen, and a great darkness fell upon the land.

These sad days caused the king to want to move company. So it was that the king moved to the land nearest the sea, and started to produce drawings of items electronic. He discovered a liking for PCB layout, the challenge, the torment.

In the year 1975, the king was married to the old queen. From that day forth, she changed from the damsel with conversational effort, into the dragon queen of conflict and argument, only lapsing when the knights and their damsels were in close proximity, upon such times she was transformed into the perfect hostess/guest.

That's all for now folks......

A long joke...

A man goes into a bar. He has with him an ostrich and a cat. The barman says what would you like to drink? The man says... ...a beer please, the ostrich says.....an orange juice please, the cat says.....a large whiskey and I am not paying for it or them!

The barman serves them. Later when their glasses were empty he came back and offered them a drink. They said the same things. This went on another three times and the barman who was by now quite bemused said "what's your story mate?" The man said....I was digging in my garden one day, when I uncovered an old lamp. Being intrigued, I cleaned up the lamp, and whilst polishing it, a Genie came out of a puff of smoke and said "Thank you my new master for releasing me from this lamp...such goodness gets you one wish". The man who lived alone, but for a collection of old magazines, said....I would like a leggy bird with a tight pussy. Hoping you are well and thinking of you constantly...

Your soul mate

David

xxxxx

Re: Another instalment

My dear King

Wow! What a story. I have to read it a few more times to absorb it, then I can comment. I just got home and Terri isn't home yet so I was able to get on the computer and check my email and find your story. I printed it and I'm taking it to bed with me. What a day. I'll tell you about it tomorrow. It was wonderful to get your email this morning, which I was able to get before leaving at 7am as Terri was awake. I almost fell asleep driving home. I could have sworn your voice woke me. I think you really did have sympathy pains for me yesterday. I feel so connected to you and think about you constantly. Can't wait to hear your voice again tomorrow.

I love you so much and feel honored to be hearing your story.

Your soul mate
Dianne

I am with you

To my lovely Goddess

I am relieved that the story is decipherable (just). It sounds like you were having a very good day. I am so glad, you deserve it. I was beginning to wonder when you told me of those fools who couldn't see your power.

I can't believe the change in my life since we found our souls. I feel that there is half of me with you and half of you with me. Please drive very carefully, remember I am in the car with you. Maybe I better move my hand from your belly now. It was intended to be soothing but that will take your mind from your driving. It is now changing to your shoulder all the time you are driving, and you tell me where it ends up when you are not!

The tickets arrived yesterday, the car is booked, hotel hopefully Monday. Wow, I can't wait to see the purple goddess at the airport. I am grinning just thinking about it.

Look forward to ringing you sometime after 6:00 your time. Take extreme care of yourself and half of me.

Your loving soul mate and King of Florsex
David

xxxxx

Re: I am with you

My beloved King

Thank you for moving your hand to my shoulder while I drive. You have no idea how much I love your hand on my belly. It is the most sensual and soothing thing you could possibly do. How do you intuitively know that? All of my pain and hurt and anger from the past are stored there in my solar plexus chakra. As many transformational classes that I take, although some of it is released to the universe for healing, some still remains. When I visit psychics and healers they all see that and do a temporary chakra clearing and healing but there is still a level of self preservation that I maintain. Hence the weight on my belly that still isn't coming off. It's interesting that whether I stick to this diet or not, it isn't budging yet. I even have an affirmation "I release the wall I needed to protect me". I do have a belief that once you see me in person and unconditionally love and accept me as I look today (just like I do you), the pounds and inches will magically melt away like a spell has been broken.

You know just the right words to say that make me so happy and make me feel so close to you. "since we found our souls", I like that, and I feel the same way about carrying part of each other with us. It certainly seems that way, doesn't it? When we watch "What Dreams May Come" together you will see in that movie how that does work with soul mates. Because I feel I understand you on a very deep level (a level that doesn't even need words), I pick up on all the meaning and feelings in what you are writing (the story). From a left brain logical and intellectual point of view though I will need to ask you some questions to clarify some things. Your style of writing is magnificent. It goes beyond the Queen's English into a whole new realm, but some of it this American goddess will need a little help with. My desire is to be an even better listener to your soul's story when I am lying in your arms and that trust level is high enough. I've always wanted a man who could be my best friend and I could be his and I believe I've found him. This is a whole new world for both of us.

Yesterday, in between the afternoon session and the evening at Universal Studios, Paloma and I went to Downtown Disney to browse and walk around for an hour. I went into a really cool new ageish kind of store and bought us a sensual lovemaking kit. It will be in my bag Monday night and I will show it to you, but I'm not expecting to use it that soon. Well maybe we will use one thing from it. It is important to both of us that this be slow and gentle and all about love.

Well, I guess both of us should get some work done. I'm in my office right now but will be leaving in a ½ hour to go to yoga. When I get home I'm going to swim and enjoy the sun a little before it sets. It is about 65 or 70 degrees today and not a cloud in the sky. Days like this make me happy to live here. I hope you will like it here. I'm already enchanted by your land so I hope you'll feel the same way about mine. You know, a couple of psychics told me a while ago that someday I'd have two homes (live in two locations).

Concentrate on your speech now. Tell me what time you'll be giving it on Tuesday so I can send you appropriate energy. Don't worry, I'll behave. I'll try not to let my hand go below your belly!

I love you David and eagerly await your call tonight.

Dianne

I was in contact but not that much contact

Dearest Dianne my great goddess

At 11:00 this morning I was laying horizontal in a dental hygienist chair and thinking of you. Perhaps not as much as you received as I was with another woman! But I was thinking of you for strength to cope with the ordeal.

I notice our five dates has now dropped to two hours. Don't worry about the time scales my goddess, the spirits can make love at the drop of a hat, but I feel natural shyness will slow us physically down to safe limits, failing that, it should be dark at 8:00 in the Orlando airport car park! Like you I know that this is so special to us both that we won't let lust catch us unaware.

We are already both very aware and long to be together properly as soon as we can.

Thank you for your lovely words of support about tomorrow. I will have you with me there on the podium. I do trust you to keep your hands still and not distract me from the reason I am there. I will take great strength from your presence.

In all our other conversations I didn't tell you my itinerary for this week.

Monday, nearly over, just a lecture to prepare.

Tuesday go to London by train, give lecture, have stiff drink and return home.

Wednesday drive to the Midlands, stay overnight.

Thursday, give sales demo to a division of the army that repairs PCBs, drive home, pick up Rachel and Matt, take them over so she can collect the new car.

Friday, back to work. Friday night go to Vickie's to plumb in her washing machine.

Saturday, drive home.

Sunday I was keeping clear but Rachel tells me that the old queen insists that the king is to clear the loft. But the king will not be alone with the evil old bat and so most probably will not go.

Important Itinerary:

Leave London Heathrow 22/11/99 (date of doubles!) 11/22/99 in US speak

Arrive Boston late evening

Leave Boston for Miami 2:34 11/29/99

Arrive Miami 6:09

Leave Miami 7:15

Arrive Orlando 8:17

Blank space for each other to fill in with warmth and love.

Leave Orlando 2:01 via Chicago 12/5/99

Arrive London 6:20am next day

This will not do will it. I am talking to you and not cooking supper or preparing the lecture. I must go, but I don't want to. Lots of our special love, hand on belly for now.

Your lover and king
David
xxxxx

Desperately tired
To the most wonderful person in the world – my very own goddess of love

I have to admit being exhausted and drained – still have not completed my lecture but will do it in the morning as the plan is now there.

The army account would be excellent, and we are very close to it. They were at the very first exhibition, then visited us at the second, and now have invited us up to sell ourselves to the money people.

Thank you so much for your response to my cry for help. You are lovely and I too can't wait to hold you and be held in return. I wish I felt able to overpower the old queen's spells, but too many years of trying to please her have made me not wish to be near her ever again. But the court has agreed to me helping to clear the loft. I feel that she is deliberately waiting to do it until I get there. Vickie attempted to do it but Chris stopped her. She is very manipulative. It sounds so weak of me but we are heading on for three years from my leaving and she is still unreasonable and bitter, so I can't imagine this time will be any different.

It is always great to sign on and see a message or two from you, I actually feel quite lonely when there isn't one.

Exhaustion has a strangle hold on my eyes and brain, so I am off for a recharge of your wonderful energy – see you soon. Be very gentle with me for tonight I am too tired for anything but being cuddled. xxxx
Your loving King of Florsex
David xxxxx
p.s. – before signing off I will send you more of my story which I obviously wrote much earlier offline.

The years in the frozen wasteland

Once the King and the dragon queen were wed, (29th March 1975) they set off on a honeymoon planned by the King, who was still ignorant of the destiny that lay in the following plans. The marriage had taken place in a frozen wasteland near the dragon's parents' house, in howling gale and deep snow. The journey the king had to undergo to be at the chapel on time was a suitable Herculean trial!

The honeymoon plans were as follows:

The king had written to the tourist board of the country, and asked for a list of hotels that possessed four-poster beds, and set about a plan to travel to the south of the land, viewing scenic and interesting places whilst staying at hotels with said sleeping apparatus. The conclusion of the honeymoon was a cruise to Santander in the kingdom of Spain. The king and dragon enjoyed this greatly, dressing for dinner and wonderful food. This was not to be repeated whilst a couple due to costs. This was one of the reasons for the timing of the final decree from the king's courts. The dragon was making it known around the land that the couple were to go on a 25th anniversary cruise!

When they returned from this wondrous journey they rented a room in a castle by the sea, which was both small and uncomfortable, and an unease fell upon the land (bickering and nastiness). So a decision was reached by the couple, as that was what they were in those days of yore, that a suitable residence be sought. After many days of looking no such castle was found within the budget of the privy purse. And so it was that the king set off on his travels north, to a kingdom called Northumbria, where the dragon's parents lived. For a short while they stayed in the residence of the local authority dwelling known as "Council House" occupied by the dragon's parents. This was far from ideal. Both parents smoked, and the father was a very strange and unusual man for a northerner. He was both a strong Methodist and a teetotaller. His tastes in food were those suited to a simple man, very basic. Yet strangely contradictory, he liked a steak on a Thursday, but when the king has steak cooked on a Saturday (plain grilled) the father would say unusual words like "what the dinkin is that, it's too fancy" in a dialect that only the dragon could translate as she was from that cold windy part of the world. His preference for steak was boiled in gravy until it disintegrated. The dragon's mother was a lady of good heart, and not a true ancestor of the fiery beast. Her greatest sin was that of overcooking vegetables, and serving sherry/brandy etc as medicinal extracts, thinking them to be without alcoholic content.

Soon the King and the dragon moved to a brand new house, and all was peaceful again. The king tended to the garden, the decorating and working long hours to pay the mortgage and ever increasing food bills....the dragon believed the way to a man's heart is through his stomach, and also liked feeding herself too.

Decorating was one area of creativity in which the dragon was a notorious failure. Painting straight lines down straight edges was unheard of, and so she was forbidden to do such. This actually pleased the king, and he created a warm and suitable home for the couple. However, the dragon had a plot to give up work, something she had done with regularity, always having one excuse or another. Now she had a long term plan....babies! This plan was not made crystal clear to the king, who was (and still is) ignorant of the ways of devious dragons. A story was told that if the couple was to conceive in 1 – 2 years time, then the dragon must come off the pill of infertility in plenty of time. Being of 14 stones (198 lbs) and rising weight it was said she would be not likely to carry a child for many months. Most probably the next morning Vickie was well on her way.

A suitable nursery was created by the dragon, with the art and finance of the king. Nothing was too good for this first born. The king used to lie in bed explaining the world to the yet unborn Vickie through the dragon's smooth underbelly. And so it came to pass on 31st January 1977, after many hours of labour, that the King's first born arrived, in the presence of the King, the dragon, and a pair of metal sorcerer's tongues. This grabbing of Victoria

Amo Purdie (as she was known in those days) by the head, and dragging into the world, left her with a pointed head, and so affectionately she was known as Noddy (a fictional character from the land).

The finances of the royal family started a serious downturn, all expenses and little income. However, within months of the royal birth, and as soon as the king had improved the kitchen, the dragon insisted on moving to another house, with grand archways and stable for the carriage.

Yet again another baby was demanded. However, a resistance was raised against such a sudden move, but dragons being dragons, on 25th May 1979 Rachel Amo Purdie was born. Unlike her older sister, she was described by the king as arriving by express train. The king was, as usual, delighted with his creation.

By this time the king had new powers within a mighty computing corporation of American origin. And so his time for working in the house diminished and house and garden were handed over to the dragon with the exception of decorating, weeding, lawn cutting and doing the night shift with the children (the dragon had been busy all day). This was the only time the king earned more than the dragon would spend, for he was on good money, but told white lies about just how good.

But a famine swept through the land, and many businesses closed per week. The danger to the king's livelihood was great, and so it was that the king set about the search for a more suitable kingdom to occupy. The search took years of hard work, and many job offers were refused by the king for one reason or another – until one day the king met a senior Knight of the Grand Order – Douglas Lasseter. This knight interviewed the king, and an affinity was struck that lasts to this very day. However, this time was a tough time for the king as he has to live back with the black shadow and the angel. He spent his days working and evenings out looking for a suitable castle. For entertainment, occasionally he would take the company of the dragon's ex-workmate (Karen). He enjoyed her company, eating out, looking for castles, and generally chatting, and always going to the evil one's house before spiritual darkness fell.

This was an especially cold winter, and so the king used to take the overnight coach to Northumbria as a travelling plumber, fixing burst pipes – and seeing the two princesses.

Rachel, Scott & Vickie

Re: Desperately tired

Hello my King

I tried to call you after getting your voice mail message that your trip to London was horrible but I got your voice mail so you must have been on the computer. I left a message to call me back at work. I'd love to hear your voice today too.

Your story is incredible! You are such a good story teller and I feel your passion and your pain. It sounds you have something in common with Stan in not being ready for kids. Of course you were much younger and probably too young to be ready. He was already 31 when we had Marley. Also, I continued working and Chris didn't. It sounds like you did love them from the moment of conception though even though you did resent Chris.

Those northlands sound awfully cold! I'm so looking forward to warming you up in my Florida sunshine. If I don't get through to you this afternoon from work, please do call me at around 6:00 my time. Don't call me much later as I might be out shopping with Nicki.

Your loving goddess

Dianne

I LOVE YOU – repeated again, and again, and again

Hi my sexy super goddess of Florsex

What a tonic it is to hear your voice, to say I love you and hear your confirmation of the compatibility of that. I checked my voice mail, no tones, no messages. So a stage further found 16 messages unanswered! I have now reported the fault.

I owe so much to you, you are wonderful. We must be Mr Yin and Mrs Yang. I feel we fit with no gaps. xxxx

Agreed, I was not ready for kids, not for any reason other than being conned into it. No doubt I love them and wouldn't be without them, but it is important for such things to be agreed; otherwise it's easy to see it not far from rape. Less violent but against my wishes for that time.

Try not to compare beauty, sunshine and love to the old queen, you are so different.

I believe the Northeast wind blows continuously from Siberia to the northlands, and although beautiful in the countryside and beaches, they are people wildernesses. It is uninhabitable if you need warmth.

I love you so much, you have changed my life, my view on things, cleared up my opinions on my spirituality; you are so powerful. I worship you and honour your every thought.

Your most loving King of Florsex

David

xxxxxx

Re: I LOVE YOU – repeated again, and again, and again
My wonderful King

Hearing I love you from you means so much to me. I know what a surprise it was for you to feel that way before we met. I know you aren't just saying words either; you are speaking your heart. The intensity of where we are right now is surprising even me. I was looking back at some of our email and it was only two weeks ago that you were telling me what you don't like about yourself physically. Only 2 weeks ago! You felt our relationship fragile at that point. I hope you see now that although it is precious like fine china and must always be honored and sacred, it isn't fragile at all. I can't imagine my life without you in it. You understand me and I understand you. I think I told you before that several psychics told me that very few people in my life would really understand me. Thank God I finally found you, I was feeling very lonely. It's a good thing you planned this trip for November. I don't think I could have waited one day longer.

I truly mean it that you are really brilliant. Your English may have a different meaning than mine. In case of confusion to clarify, I mean that you are really intelligent, more so than some people with PhDs, really witty, a great personality, creative, an excellent writer, an excellent feeler, communicator and passion producer and the most worthy and powerful King Britain has ever seen. You even have what my father has and calls "American Ingenuity". We'll have to change that to "both sides of the pond ingenuity". I'm not sure where that term came from or if my father made it up but he's really good at electronics and at fixing things. He won't go near a computer though. I think you'll like my father, actually both of my parents. I can't wait to meet your aunty and I promise not to scare her.

I rented the movie "A Christmas Carol" for Nicki so she doesn't have to read it and I'm going to watch it with her in about a half hour. I love that movie. I'll be thinking of you constantly tomorrow as I do always. Good luck with the Army account. You can do it!! You could have done today too just by being your charming self but it's okay. Every day can't be a huge success or we wouldn't know success when we see it. As Thomas Edison said, he didn't fail 999 times, he was successful 999 times in finding the ways that were not the exact right one. I wish I had been there with you today. Sometimes it's better to walk away from dragons than to let them eat us alive. That's a bigger courage because the desire to survive is an important and brave one. The bottom line is you're fine; the real David is alive and well. I love you even more because you are so human and you share your humanness with me. There couldn't be a better fit for me than you. Can you imagine how good the physical part of our relationship is going to be?

Love from your goddess

Dianne

Healing from the Goddess saves souls

Dearest of lovely Goddesses

You were so special to me last night when I needed it – what a tonic you are. Soul scarred but recovering nicely thanks to the medication.

You are so right, I don't feel our relationship is fragile, I feel you will be able to stand most shocks there may be on meeting me. You are so special it takes my worries away.

I do hope that I understand you and you understand me. Don't forget that kings are mortals, not like gods and goddesses! I do look forward to meeting your parents. Will they object to me not being Jewish?

Lots of my warmest thoughts until we write again, talk again, make love again and again…

Your loving and longing soul mate

David

xxxxx

Re: Healing from the Goddess saves souls

My wonderful King

You say the most wonderful things as well. I also have faults just like mortal women and I'll tell you all of them. What isn't clear from my story I'll share with you in person.

My parents won't care at all that you aren't Jewish. Remember, they aren't particularly Jewish. They aren't spiritual either, they are pretty much doubters. If you are good to me and love me, they will love you; it's that simple. Oh yes, and laugh at my father's jokes. Throwing in that their grandchildren are wonderful of course adds big points. They live for those girls.

I long to see you at the airport. Remember to email me some more pictures so I'll know you. I only have that one picture from match.com and it is dark and unclear. I know you'll know me but I don't want to have to smile at every man who gets off the plane, or God forbid hug the wrong man!

It was really busy at work today. I have a feeling I'm really into my busy season now. Don't worry, Paloma and Janet and Gloria can handle it for me that week. We'll just stop in the office so you can meet everybody but no working for me.

You heal me too, my king. My belly feels so good with your hand there. I love you so much.

Your loving soul mate
Dianne

A little more of my story
Dear David

Terri isn't home yet and my girls aren't fighting me for the computer so I thought I'd write a little more.

When we left our heroine she had her beautiful babies but the marriage was failing. Stan did the dentistry but I did everything else and a housekeeper did a lot of the day-to-day things with my babies that I wanted to do. I want to backtrack a little and tell you of Marley's birth. I was in labor for 2 days and in a lot of pain. This was at the Navy hospital since Stan was on temporary disability retirement leave from the surgery he had, so I was able to have a baby for free. Since we don't have socialized medicine here, free is a very good price. However, since the Navy doesn't have to worry about being sued for malpractice they aren't too quick to do a caesarean section when a woman is having a tough labor. A private doctor would have cut me after just six hours. They sent Stan home after one day thinking that I couldn't be far enough along and I just have a low pain tolerance. I'm telling you I was in excruciating pain. The contractions were quick and didn't give me time to rest. What nobody realized is that I hadn't peed in a day. Who had time in between the pain! When they finally realized that they should put a catheter in me I felt an incredible amount of relief. At that point I could have kept laboring but they were ready to cut.

They called Stan back and the phone lines where we lived were down. So they called a friend of ours who woke Stan up in the middle of the night to go back to the hospital. By that time they had me sitting up and curved over to receive the spinal. The baby was very low in the birth canal and I felt like I was breaking her neck. She has back problems today and I think that caused it. I have slight scoliosis so my back isn't completely straight and it hurt to do the spinal. Finally I was numb and Stan was there and they cut me open and Marley was born.

When they saw my uterus up close and personal they saw that there was a defect in the muscle and I never could have pushed a baby out. The cut is a horizontal bikini cut only about three inches but the fat won't go away above it so that is another physical fault of mine. Nicole was an easy birth. She was a planned caesarean section and because of my scoliosis they put me to sleep rather than torture me with a big long needle.

Stan wasn't happy and he left me in December 1988. I told you, on one of our phone calls. about his relationship with Lisa who happened to be my cousin's wife. I'd rather not write that story again now. I was 34 years old. Marley was four and Nicki was two. I then embarked on a journey of finding myself. This journey that leads me to Florsex with my beloved is a long journey of 11 years. I truly wanted to love and be loved and that explains some of my behavior. Up until this point I had only had sex with Stan. As of today I've been with about 15 men (some of whose names I don't remember). I feel bad about this and pray that telling you isn't a big mistake. I have another single friend who says she has been with over 70 men and that my count is nothing for 11 years. What do you think?

I'm going to hit send now so I don't lose this and so I don't chicken out on sending it to you.

The goddess sets out to find herself............
I'm back my king....are you still with me?

In January of 1989, I was faced with first of all what to do career wise. Not working was not an option although I could afford to go back to school or go back to real estate if I sold the big house and moved to an apartment. I wanted to sell the house anyway because I just wanted to get rid of memories from the marriage and I wanted to live in town and not in a distant suburb where the dental practice is. I got the house as part of the legal separation agreement that later became the divorce. It was valued as having $50,000 worth of equity. Meanwhile I was paying $2,000 a month for the mortgage, the pool and lawn service and the high electric bill. The market was very bad. To fast forward to what happened to the house, I sat on it for two years and finally let it go for only $2,000 cash above the mortgage I owed. So much for the big equity. I made the big payments all that time too. I did get alimony for the first two years so that helped, but if I didn't have the expense of the house that money would have gone a lot further. I also got good child support until the girls are 18 and I got 50% of the value of Stan's practice as of December 1988. This was fair since I put him through dental school and worked in his office from the beginning. This 50% was paid to me over a 10-year period with no interest. The monthly amount I got was a little over $1,300. It has just recently ended. That money also enabled me to find myself, and for Tony to find himself as well. The Tony story is for another night.

My first thought was to go back to school for a business degree since I was very business oriented. I took accounting and business law and basically decided this was too much theory and bullshit that I didn't need. I just wanted to create a successful business on my own and didn't need all this silly coursework to do it. So that ended after one semester. Then I decided to try to go back into real estate. I did it for a few months and then realized that a single mother of then a 3 and a 5 year old would have a hard time doing real estate as that is largely a night and weekend occupation. Since I was doing all this part time (school and real estate), with my parent's help I could keep the girls in pre-school part time instead of full day care.

Sometime in the time period of the first 6 months that Stan and I were separated, I stopped by the office of his former partner and our friend from the Navy. Stan had basically divorced Bert the same way he did me. He just wasn't happy. I was lonely and wanted to talk to somebody. After work Bert and I went out for drinks and then dinner. My girls were sleeping at my parents that night so I brought Bert home with me and we ended up making love. It was making love and not just sex because we cared for each other in a very high way and had been friends for years. He was very tender and it was just what I needed. However, we didn't use a condom and guess what…yup, I got pregnant! Bert felt awful and of course we both knew I wasn't going to have his baby so he paid for me to have an abortion. A friend took me. It was horrible and it hurt very badly. This may account for my belly that I can't seem to release and the psychic pain I store there. So…are you now convinced that I am a poor mortal woman with many faults? Do you still love me?

I just thought of something to tell you about when I said that Stan divorced Bert pretty much the same way he divorced me. In 1987, Stan and I got involved with a medical and dental practice and financial management organization that charged big bucks to straighten out doctors' and dentists' lives which they tend to screw up. The practice management stuff was very good. I still use the philosophies today in my own business. Things like treat people like a guest in your home and create a feeling of ownership with the staff so that they aren't just employees. The financial stuff was very good too. We set up a pension plan and invested a lot of money in the last two years we were together. I resented how much money Stan insisted on saving because my lifestyle wasn't much better than it was when he was in dental school. All he cared about was saving enough money to retire by the time he was 45. (Now that he has a three year old he'll be working a long time). I handled all our finances and the dealings with the bank, the pension plan, loans, etc, but he controlled what we spent as far as going out and buying anything and he was really tight.

Anyway, this company also dealt with the philosophical and psychological aspects of life and taught that everything in your life should either be a 10 on a scale of 1 to 10 or add meaning to your life. I obviously wasn't a 10 and didn't add meaning to his life so I was pretty much let go. It really did happen like that. A lot of marriages ended around this management course. Dentists decided it was their God-given right to be happy. What Stan didn't realize then was that another person couldn't make him happy if he wasn't happy already. I doubt even Lisa was able to do that.

I have to close here, Terri is home. I love you so much and hope you still love me.

Your goddess

Dianne

Feeling insecure

Hello my love

Will you write me a short note if you can? I know you are with Rachel tonight getting her new car, but if you possibly can send me a note before you go to bed because I'm feeling insecure after writing my story yesterday.

How did it go with the Army today? I hope it went well. You deserve to get a good account easily. I've been working really hard.

I have to answer 100 email messages that are being forwarded to me by the astrologer on the cruise. She mentioned the cruise in her online newsletter and all these people want info. Most of them didn't leave a snail mail address so I have to ask them to leave one. I have tons of follow up calls to make. I'm staying here at work until 6:30 then I'm going to yoga from 7 to 8 tonight. I'm really hungry but I can't eat before yoga so when I get home I'll be famished!

I want to write more story to you but I'm not kidding when I say I'm feeling some fear right now. See, you aren't the only one who gets nervous.

Much love to the most wonderful King of all the lands…
Your mortal goddess
Dianne

Of course I still love you – don't be so silly!!
My dearest Goddess of Florsex

Nothing, and I mean nothing (almost) exceptions being genocide and driving a bright yellow car, would even make me think twice, as long as they were history. Your history has made the goddess I love, so why would I stop loving you for the ingredients that were used.

Will you be free to have a phone call on Sunday? I hope so, I think you need telling again – I love you. Do keep up your story and I will try to keep mine up when under less pressure. I have missed you and long to hear your voice again.

With the greatest of growing and deepening love.
Your King of Florsex
David

xxxxx

Re: Of course I still love you – don't be so silly!!!
My dearest King of Florsex

You are the best thing that has ever happened to me. You make me feel so good. You are right that our history really does make us what we are today. I have been through so much in the 11 years since Stan left me. Today I'm stronger, prouder, happier, and oh so ready to really love a man and let him really love me. And you my king are that lucky man! Sometimes I would doubt my ability to really love a man. Now I am sure that I am capable and not only capable but quite good at it. You, my love, are destined for some wonderful love.

That sounds really good about the government contract. I know those things take time, but can be very long lasting and lucrative. I'm so excited about your success! You are a really good businessman and I'm looking forward to having you look at my business.

Well, I'm going to get back to my Dreamtime email and then I'll write some more of my story.
Your feeling much better now goddess of Florsex
Dianne

It was quite a year!

When I last wrote it was somewhere around May of 1989. I turned 35 in February of that year and wasn't having a very easy time of being left by a man, finding a new career, and raising two young children on my own. Right around May of that year I started working for a builder who was a friend of mine. He was a very successful builder in the area near Stan's dental practice and he was trying to develop a new area. Since I had both real estate experience and experience running a business we both thought that I could be an asset to his business and he hired me to be pretty much his executive assistant. Parts of the job I really enjoyed. I enjoyed going to the city planning and zoning meetings, going to different parts of the state to look at ideas from other developments, writing letters, working with advertising and public relations and helping him with business stuff. The part of the job that I wasn't all that confident with was hiring and training sales reps. Although I had been in real estate sales and had even worked selling new homes for a builder as part of my real estate career, some of the people I was hiring were stronger sales people (more successful closers) than me. I didn't feel qualified to be their manager. I left him after a few months and got a similar job with another builder.

This time same title executive assistant, but the work was more in house office work and although I did write sales and training manuals I didn't actually manage anybody. I liked that better as my confidence level wasn't high enough for that. I did this job for a few months as well before burning out. This was an office that expected people to be at work at 7:00am and work until at least 7:00pm. Everybody was very career oriented and did whatever it took. A lot of them took some sort of speed to maintain the pace. I didn't like that. They weren't my kind of people and it was hard for me to have those hours with small children. I had the girls in full day care at that point but I relied on my parents to both drop them off and pick them up. I didn't like relying on my parents that much. So I left that job in October 1989.

Let me back up a little since all I talked about in the above info was my job history. I didn't know where else to go to meet single men and I really wanted to date, so I joined the Jewish Singles in Orlando. Not so much because I like Jewish guys. Really I don't; most of them are not my type at all. It's just that I'm not into the bar scene, the metaphysical stuff I attended was mostly women, and match.com wasn't invented yet! I really wanted to date to help me get over Stan and prove to myself that I'm desirable. The first man I dated from there was a judge. He was a typical neurotic Jewish man and quite full of himself. We met at a dance. I remember him liking me and saying "save the last dance for me" as he proceeded to meet other women. We did dance the last dance together and he took me out afterward to show me his judge's chambers. I was supposed to be impressed. I sort of felt like "Oh Stan, why did you do this to me!" but I forced myself to date and he was as good a candidate as any. I was pretty horny as well, as Stan and I really didn't have a sex life at all the last 6 months we were together. Other than that one night with

Bert in March it had been almost a year since I had sex. This was May. So when he got sexual with me on probably the third date he didn't have to work through any resistance to have sex. I was ready and willing. It was good as sex goes but it wasn't making love and although I was destined to repeat that (sex without love) another 10 or so times in the next 10 years I knew in my heart even then that lovemaking could be so much more than this.

I went away for a week in May to attend a really good personal growth course called Life Mastery (now called The Garden Company). One day I'll show you some of my notes from there. It was very good. It really got me far along the road of letting go, not trying to control things and feeling good about myself. It was very experiential. It took place in Mendocino California and a lot of the exercises we did were written assignments of self exploration that we did sitting at our "spot" which was an outdoor location that each of us picked on cliffs overlooking the Pacific Ocean. I remember that one of the writings was to use a metaphor for our life with either the ocean, the sky, the earth, etc. I choose the ocean (that was the beginning of me knowing I was a seagoddess). What I wrote was really powerful for me. I still have it and I'll read it to you on the phone. Anyway, it was quite a week. It was one of the things I treated myself to with the money I got from the marriage ending. I didn't get all the money until the divorce was final but I got enough to be able to do this.

When I returned from Life Mastery, the judge had already found another woman. He was a bit of a womanizer. Actually he ended up marrying that one. That wasn't the only time a man would meet the love of his life after meeting me! Some fear still remains in my cellular memory that that could happen again. What if I'm getting you happy and juicy for another woman? I know that's impossible. Excuse me for even thinking that but this is free floating writing as it enters my brain with nothing held back so I didn't think I should hold that back either. There is something about me that scares most men. But you aren't most men....you are my king of Florsex.

I dated once or twice a few other men that summer, nobody I liked enough to go out with more than twice or felt enough chemistry to have sex with so the summer had no sex. I don't like to date just to date. I'd rather stay home and read or be with my children.

Three weeks before I quit the job with the builder I was asked to find a computer consultant to evaluate some of our computer needs. The person they had used before had left town. That person referred me to Tony Rillings whom I called to come into the office to talk to my boss about computers. That began the Tony Rillings chapter of my life that lasted from September 1989 through December 1996 (one year after he left me).

To be continued..........

I'm going to go feed the cats and do the dishes. I'll be back. Thank you for listening to my story. I love you.

I feel that we love across time and space and multi-dimensionally as we make love seemingly before we've even met. What a strange concept that we have not met. How can that be....I feel so close to you......my beloved soul mate David.

Dianne....Goddess of Florsex

I LOVE YOU SO MUCH my sweet Goddess

Hi my wonderful Goddess. I have read through all you have sent tonight, and feel even deeper for you now – do not doubt our feelings, they are magical and special. I will so look forward to tonight's phone call.

I love you so much and long for the next two weeks to melt away so I can be in your arms. It does not feel like we have never met....it feels more like we have been apart far too long.

You say such wonderful things to me and I hope I am going to live up to this superhuman picture you paint of me. I am just an ordinary quiet, shy chap who loves a real goddess – and dreams of success against all odds.

I do have enough staff, currently too many, so this Army job will help greatly when it does kick in.

I love you so much my dreamtime goddess.

It is almost 1.30 am and I am very tired so will log off until tonight.

I love you.

Your king and lover

David

Re: I LOVE YOU

Dear David

Two cards in one evening! How lucky can I get. I love you so much. You are so perfect for me. I had just written you an entire page about the beginning of my relationship with Tony and the computer said default error and kicked me off AOL, so I lost it all! I'm not sure I have the energy to rewrite it tonight. This will probably be my last message tonight. Lisa (Stan's wife) just called and zapped some of my energy. That's probably why AOL went nutty on me. Marley is with her boyfriend and Nicki is with a friend spending the night. Lisa is mad because Stan's mother is in town and the girls don't care enough to be there. Marley will be there later tonight and Nicki will go there tomorrow. She was giving Nicki a big guilt trip on the phone (Nicki called me all upset) and then she tried to give it to me. I just blew her away and said "they are teenagers....this is to be expected....they don't spend that much time with me either." She didn't care for my answer and pretty much hung up on me!

I can relate about your staff situation. I've been so often overstaffed because I'm geared up for the busy times and don't want just seasonal employees. Now, because I'm making big payments to consumer credit counselling to get out of debt I can only keep me and Paloma full time. Gloria and Janet only work 12 hours a week and Amy 8. We are finally busy and I may be able to increase their hours. My being so nice over the years is a big part of why I'm in this financial mess now. But I, like you, am a success oriented positive thinker and I know Dreamtime will make it. Isn't it nice to have each other as a support system?

I'm going to go do some Dreamtime email now and then I'll check and see if you sent any pictures or anything. Don't worry, I know it's late there, I'm not expecting it. Sure would love to wake up to it though. Gotta run, I think my food is burning. Remember I can't cook!

Your office and bedroom (but not kitchen) goddess

Dianne

Too late for photos

Dear Dianne

I am so sorry those cyber demons are at it again. Tony has been lost for the night – but he will be back.

I spent last night sleeping on Vickie's floor when I went there to help her solve her plumbing problems. It was very uncomfortable and so I am very tired. I had to sleep on the floor because Vickie has a small two-seater settee, but will be getting a better one in the January sales I hope.

It is now even later than when I said I was going to bed – and I must, but at this rate you will be joining me very soon – please.

xxx

Loving and longing for you – your king of Florsex

David

xxxxx

Moi.....

Hi Goddess

I hope this turns out. The other software ran for a few seconds correctly then gave up, so here it is now using the poorer quality video phone camera. Please say if it works or not.

Lots of Love and Hugs

Your soul mate

David xxxxx

Re: Moi…..

Hello handsome! Well I'm at the office and I can see your picture from this computer! It is adorable. I like the unshaved look actually. It came through as a picture and not as a movie. And you call yourself shy! I don't think so. I see a nice hairy kissable chest. I shall not send you my chest by email. You will just have to wait for that. I love your looks David. Now I can feel the physical chemistry as well as the psychic kind. Send me more! By the way, please have your clothes on in at least one of them so I can show my friends at work.

I have to take Marley to her dad's now. She didn't win her competition today. Her team is "small coed" because they have only one boy. There were no other small coed teams so they had to compete against a team with 8 boys and there was no way they could win. My back hurts from sitting on stadium type seats all day. Or maybe it's sympathy pains for you from sleeping on the floor. I'm glad you had success with her plumbing. You're a genius!

Gotta do some work. Looking forward to your call later.
Love always from your lover and soul mate
Dianne

I love you so much
My wonderful King

Every time I hear your voice I get a big smile. I got you (us) a king size bed (what else would a king get) at the Ramada Inn in Longwood. The rate is $54 per night. They had no travel agent rate available for those nights.

I better get back to work. I may try to get to the health club tonight to work out a little. I really hate working out (I do like yoga though) but I want my body to look as good as possible for you. I bought a new dress at a discount store (it was only $13). I'm wearing it today. It is short and shows off my legs, which are one of my better features. As long as I'm not worried about my belly it's a fun dress. I'll try it on for you and you can tell me what you think. The purple dress I'll wear to the airport doesn't show much leg (it's a longer goddess type dress). I'll be a little shy at first with you. I love you so much.

Your lover and soul mate

Dianne Goddess of Florsex

Safe picture enclosed

Good evening my goddess

I am enclosing a safe picture today that you can show your friends. Please don't tire yourself out too much at the gym before I get there, or end up all muscles. I do want a feminine goddess to be soul mates with.

The picture you sent was really nice. You have lovely looking daughters – what a beautiful family you all are.

I will ring you at bed time, earlier than my usual, as I have still not fully recovered from the floor at Vickie's. I don't think I said that she has a kitten now.

Your King and soul mate, lover and friend

David

xxxxx

The Tony Rillings story 3rd try!

Dear David

I'm starting to wonder if I'm supposed to be telling you this story. For the second time I typed a page and then got bumped off AOL! I had gotten to about the same point as the first time. I refuse to believe that I'm supposed to hide anything from you so I am trying again to send this. I'll just write a little and then send it.

Tony and I talked to each other a lot when he was doing the computer consulting and training at Continental Development. We had a lot in common in our interests in personal growth, metaphysics and spirituality. He was involved in a personal growth course similar to Life Mastery (not as good though) and was in fact one of the facilitators. He also facilitated attitudinal healing groups which is a branch of thought taken from A Course in Miracles. He was very different from Stan with long blond hair and was basically a new age, sensitive man. We had a lot in common and I was surprised that he hadn't asked me out on a date in the three weeks we knew each other. I found out later that he had no money. He had a real problem in business and never billed people for what he did. I think he had a major self-worth issue hidden underneath all the personal growth stuff he spouted. He didn't like money. Stan loved money. I therefore had the misconception that money made relationships go bad. I guess the universe sent me Tony so I could experience the contrast and ultimately seek out a man who is right in the middle (a good businessman with a healthy relationship with money who is in touch with his feminine side but still very much a man who wants to do things for his woman). There's more to my description of you than that but that is just a little bit about how Stan and Tony are different. Stan was ruled by money. Tony wanted nothing to do with it.

I'm going to hit send now so I don't lose this. Be right back.
Love
Dianne

Tony seduces me

I invited Tony to my apartment after work one night when the girls were either with Stan or my parents. We talked for about three hours. We listened to music and he kissed me for the first time during "Perhaps Love" by Julio Inglesias. I asked him if he's ever been married. He said "I'm married now". I should have kicked his ass out the door and bolted it shut....but I didn't. I guess the universe had some lessons in store for me that only Tony could have taught me. He told me he was in an "open marriage". His wife Wendy was 10 years older than him. He had rescued her from an abusive marriage and was helping her raise her kids who were already 16 and 18 by the time we met. They had lived together for many years and decided to make it a marriage just for reasons of health insurance, taxes, etc. He didn't believe in marriage basically because he loves too many people to be exclusive and feels that marriage is exclusive. In his facilitation of people in personal growth classes and attitudinal healing, he tended to rescue people (mostly women-type people). Obviously I was giving off a rescue me type of energy or we wouldn't have connected.

Remember, I wasn't strong like I am today. I was stressed from raising two young girls by myself, working long hours and I wanted somebody to love me. Lisa was obviously with Stan by then and I wanted somebody to be with me. So the warning signs of him being both married and broke didn't phase me. I was ready to be seduced. After kissing for about a half hour he said to me "I would honor you either way...but would you like me to make love to you?" Yes, I said yes. There was definitely love between me and Tony and a high level of chemistry so it was making love and not just sex. It was very difficult when at 1:00am he walked out my door to go home to his wife.

I'm going to send this now and go work on dinner. I'm really looking forward to your call.

Your goddess

Dianne

Nicki and Marley age 5 and 7

Chapter Fourteen
A Major Confession!

When chapter 13 ended it was the 13th of November, two weeks before David was due to arrive. The relationship seemed very strong and both of us felt like we would feel the same way in person. His phone call to me that night was a bit short and he seemed stressed. I didn't say anything because I didn't want to read anything into the situation that wasn't there. However, at 10:00pm which was 3:00am his time he called again.

I used all my good listening skills to let him just talk as it was clear he was distressed and so afraid of how I would react to what he was about to tell me. What he told me was that from before he had started writing to me he was writing to a woman in Boston named Denise. His feelings for her never hit the level that his feelings for me did but he also never bothered to tell her about me (or me about her for that matter) or worse yet cancel the plans to see her. Turns out my "shy British lad" who had very few women in his entire life was planning to see two of us on this two week holiday!

As he had become closer and closer with me and realized that he loved me and didn't love her, this plan soon became obviously uncomfortable and unacceptable to him. Still only six or eight weeks ago he had made the flight reservations to spend one week in Boston and then one week in Orlando so he must not have been so sure at that point or he lacked the nerve to get out of it with her.

The bottom line was that he did not want to see her; in fact the thought of doing that was making him ill. Well I was certainly glad to hear that but must confess it was difficult to feel pity for him. He had certainly gotten himself into this mess. He was so sincere in his confession and sorrow though that I had to feel compassion for him. Besides, he hadn't cheated on me physically as he had met neither of us yet and he realized that he couldn't cheat on me and had to cancel the plans with Denise. Who was I to be judgmental? I had still seen Randall one more time in September before David and I talked on the phone for the first time and had sex with Randall while writing to David. He had forgiven that. In a way this was a big win for our relationship as he realized that there was no way he could be with anybody but me.

David would like to have a chance to tell this story and the story of finding me on match.com from his point of view, so here's David........

The dilemma – from the male perspective (we think differently you know!)

Well the book is almost done – before the man is allowed to speak, and then it's to justify his wrong doings.

Let me start by explaining the e-mail dating system (as it was for me).

- First you write a profile – in my case as honestly as possible (to get the same back).You sit patiently waiting for an answer – (the internet is very slow especially on dial up in the 90's).
- Eventually the replies start, and you correspond back and forth.
- Out of the blue, and without any notice, the replies stop… new ones start, and stop.
- During this process of continuous flux, you end up talking to several people at once.
- So miraculously Dianne was added to the pot… she was an interesting but not very attentive writer (until well into

the relationship) but there was something very special, and I never did the dropping of conversations thing.

- Time moves on, the relationship grows, and I was down to just three (not starting anything new, but not ditching the current conversations either – hindsight says it was a mistake).

- The other two e-mail relationships were with Denise and Pat.

- Denise was a single mother with a daughter aged about 14, living in Boston – a fun person to write to. She kept making the point she was a pagan, and a very active protester against injustice and war.

- Pat was a seaside landlady in Wales, whose conversations mainly consisted of asking for business advice (something I was always keen to give).

- The relationship with Dianne developed, and we grew closer. I was blissfully unaware of the major task ahead of me, as I expected the high rate of attrition to continue, leaving me with just Dianne... but it did not come.

- Pat was no issue, our relationship was purely business (so I thought).

- However Denise was not going away...

- Dianne's relationship was now developing and we knew each other very well (200 letters in each direction, many phone calls, etc).

- It was time to plan my holiday... so where better to take it than in the USA.

- However I was left with two destinations a very long distance apart. (This was the logic – not too much thought of the rest of the situation.)

- So logically it would only make sense to see them both (trust me – ask a truthful man, and he would confirm this). I have as you already know cancelled the Boston visit – due to stopping long enough to realise the consequences of the first plan.

- Therefore I hope history will not judge me as a philanderer, just someone who could have been. After all they say men are all potential rapists, and we do (I hope) accept that doesn't mean all men are rapists, just because they could be.
- Coming clean in that phone call was one of the hardest things I could do – as this meant owning up to being (potentially) another Tony, and risk losing the most important relationship I had ever experienced.
- I am so pleased to say Dianne took this so well, and reassured me that my honesty was a plus bigger than the potential dishonesty.
- During that night (it was already 3am at this point) I had to call Denise and explain myself for a second time; this time – suffer the wrath of a woman scorned! (But the pain has been so worth it.)
- After my visit to Dianne – I thought I should give my happy news to Pat, well that was amazing. Despite us not talking of anything but business, weather, and general news topics, she acted like a wife being told of the secretary having the boss' baby (and I had been the husband/boss). I did not hear from her again.
- I did hear repeatedly from Denise, who would not let it go (I must have been a better catch than I thought). During this barrage of abuse, promises of having me back, etc. I deleted all of her e-mails and mentally detached myself, and got back to being the guy Dianne deserved.

So let's go back to the "why?"

Why did I try the internet for dating in the first place – especially on unreliable systems and dial-up internet connections (very slow and continuously dropping out – taking everything with it as per Dianne's e-mails in this book). That was for the historians of you or those too young to remember.

Anyway – you may know I own and run my own business, and like so many others drive myself very hard to get the business to the elusive earning state I wish it would be at. This means that at that point in my life I had been on my own for over two years (and I had been very happy with that, but now I thought I wanted someone to share my life with). Being on my own suited me. I liked cooking… I had that cracked in that I would cook a couple of big meals, freeze them in single portions, and select one per night to oven bake as I chose the nationality or flavour I fancied. I like my cooking – Dianne and her friends say I cook very well – which is great as I really do not like washing up, and that is an equal work share.

There was no doubt at all I wanted to have a wife to share my life with, even though I knew I would have to give up my freedom. So with no time to go out and meet people, one night while working on my computer I discovered (maybe by pop up – maybe by fate) match.com. This had a massive advantage to going out; I could read women's profiles (like the initial drink in traditional dating) at midnight. Then I would write to them and go to sleep. Next morning I would be impatient to see if the fishing trip produced anything.

Sorry I got a little ahead of myself – once you find match.com you have to prepare a profile of who you are and who you wish to date. This is the most serious part of the whole exercise as in my view you need to be honest. This honesty needs lots of thought… not because dishonesty rules, but because we all have a view of ourselves that may be more of what we want it to be rather than what it is. However being a believer in "the law of attraction" real care is needed in the whom do I want section. You can draw to you, whatever you desire, plan for and take actions toward… which is exactly what this process does! I feel it's vital you leave no holes in your desire or you could get someone who fills all of your listed items but has a flaw you hadn't thought of. If you are someone who repeatedly gets the same problem person – this area is where you can change the habit… I did!

My main need was for an equal, in all areas, someone who could talk as a friend, confidant and lover. I was determined to have someone with a mix of independence and attentive – not needy.

Although I am very happy to teach, nurture and generally support, I did not want someone who wanted me to live their life for them.

The usual male requirements (leggy blond) – (busty brunette) etc were not on my list (even if they would have added a superficially good edge to the relationship – luckily I got those bonus features thrown in as part of the deal.

One of my hobbies is/was stained glass. Prior to match.com I had made 2 glass panels, one of a Greek water carrier, and one of a Turkish belly dancer. When I showed these to Dorothy, she looked at them and called them Goddesses and told me I would have three not two. In the month/years that followed I looked for inspiration, I had loads but none that became goddess number three. Much later on when Dianne was on the scene and family photos came out, I saw Dianne (with Marley as a baby, and it was the Greek water carrier. When I saw her photos from her cruises – there was my belly dancer. So now with Dianne, I got my third goddess! (Well she didn't say it was a glass panel.)

I was an only child brought up on my own. This makes people who meet me say "so you must have been spoiled by your parents". Well I was far from spoiled, being on my own for most of my first 5 years, and then not being near to any school friends meant that was not much better. Being single and communicating on match.com has allowed me to be on my own without cracking up, but I have been very keen to have a suitable partner to share with. I do have an ownership issue – I like my things to be mine…but emotionally I do share, so I could be a tricky person to get along with.

Using the internet is absolute proof of the Law of Attraction – well in my case anyway, by having an honest desire, with fully written out request, that is fed by working on the e-mails. The need was filled, and that was before I started reading/listening to Abraham-Hicks, The Secret, Napoleon Hill, and Tony Robbins. (They have all proved that I was doing the right thing long before I found out what to do).

Goddess Etched Glass Panels by David

Chapter Fifteen

Countdown 1 week till we meet!

Thank you for being so wonderful xxxxx
My most forgiving goddess
Well I have done two of the hardest things of my life tonight, telling you and telling her. I have now spoken to Denise, explained (well almost) and she is deeply hurt. I feel very bad that I have caused this.

Yes, I have done it – and I really do appreciate your help, and will always need your love, as I will be giving you mine in return. xxxx

I can't say upsetting her makes me feel good – but upsetting you would kill me, and I so want to be with you. Even one extra minute would be worth all the agonies I have been going through (and no doubt will be going through) worthwhile.

Also, I have tried to cancel and rebook my flight. This is not possible, so I am trying to get booked on a flight from Boston to Orlando that leaves at about noon on the 23rd (getting to you about 4:00pm).

Although I know I have done the right thing in the end, I wish I wasn't causing so much pain to do it.

I love you so much my goddess and I will ring you later tonight.
Your very humble and weak king
David
xxxxxx

Re: Thank you for being so wonderful xxxx

Dearest David

It is only 3.45am and I am awake. I couldn't sleep. It's a combination of your energy and emotions and my period, which I'll get either today, tomorrow or at the latest Wednesday. Judging by the cramps I'm having already it will be sooner than Wednesday. Perfect timing to be over it by the time you get here. Did you get the flight reservation yet? I want you here as soon as possible please. Everything will be well with the world when we can embrace.

Yes, what you told me was a bit of a shock, although a part of me suspected something like this. You notice I didn't ask you why when you told me you wouldn't be here Thanksgiving weekend. I wanted to give you dominion over your own decisions and thought then that it was either business or financial reasons or that there was somebody else you were visiting that you weren't telling me about. At the time, we hadn't discovered each other to the level we have now and I would have had no right to request exclusivity. When you told me you were going to Cape Cod I did consider that odd to be going alone and I had a small suspicion that you weren't. I also felt some tension in your first phone call of last night. I think that maybe what freaked you out and brought you to where you are now might have been what I wrote just a few emails ago that I hope I'm not making you juicy and happy for another woman and that it was a subtle fear of mine since it's happened before. I think that if I were to lose you before I even got to look into your eyes.....well I don't know.....I can't even end that sentence.

I am truly sorry you have to hurt somebody else, but maybe her Prince (you are the only King) will appear shortly. I really do believe that everything that happens in the universe, every meeting, every interaction, has a divine purpose. You stepped far enough into the relationship ring with somebody else to gain clarity about your feelings for me. You didn't mean to hurt anybody. This kind of stuff happens though in the adult dating world that you are in after being married most of your life. I'm glad we have found each other and don't need to be in that world anymore. I love you David. I'm glad you are a mortal king. That's quite enough proving it though. I couldn't bear a repeat of my relationship with Tony. In fact I now have the good sense that I wouldn't bear it. I'd have to turn you over to my friend the Wicked Witch! Going to check and see if you've written so I'll send this now. I love you David.

Your goddess of Florsex (don't tell me you also had a Bossex)
Dianne

2nd email now daylight

Dear mortal King David

I still believe that every hurt I've experienced in the past 11 years since Stan left me, every man including Stan that I have ever loved and lost, has all been my unique destiny that brought me to the point of meeting my soul mate…you.

Every relationship was important, every soul I touched unique and something was learned on a soul level. I believe we make agreements on a soul level with other spirits before coming here. I'm writing this to make you feel better about Denise. Her soul mate will come and she will be a little more ready to really meet him and keep parts of you in her heart always as all of us do with people whom we've loved.

As strong as I sometimes appear, please remember that I'm also mortal and as much as I trust our relationship this has brought up some hurt from my past. I'd barely gotten into my story with Tony. Maybe you intuited it. It took him forever to leave his wife. He never really left her completely. For the first year we were together (living together) he and his pillow left me twice a week and slept with her. I can't believe it in thinking about it today. He didn't want to hurt her, and although he loved me, he also still loved her. I was way too understanding. I was an idiot! I won't do that again. Do you love Denise? Sometimes

I get too understanding because I don't want to scare men away with my strong businesswoman empowered woman seagoddess energy. I want you to know of all my energies. I am a strong businesswoman, I'm also sometimes a weak businesswoman and a pushover because I'm way too generous. I'm a good mother and have a strong nurturing side that I can give my mate as well.

Sometimes I don't nurture myself very well at all and I treat myself like shit. I'm very honest and at the same time try not to hurt anybody but my honesty comes first. That statement was about me, not you. Besides your honesty ultimately did come first. It was only quite recently you were confident and sure about me. I don't blame you for having another choice. Although it does go against your philosophy that you can succeed at anything you really believe in enough. You see how powerful you are! You even succeeded while having a dual focus. Don't ever doubt yourself, you are powerful.

Back to me. I'm a very passionate lover and can be the aggressor and the seducer. My preference is to be the beloved and be seduced and have my man be in control. Writing both of those sentences felt odd actually. My real preference is to flow naturally with my soul mate in and out of the dominant/submissive, nurturer/nurturee, lover/beloved, intense passion/quiet relaxation ebb and flow of our lovemaking that will include a hand held and a hand placed on a belly or chest as well as hands everywhere on each other's bodies making our entire bodies erogenous zones. Hmmm, I'm getting carried away.

Actually, I'm also writing again to read to you my horoscope for Tuesday, November 23rd (I have a book that gives the entire year). Not only is it a wonderful day because it's a full moon but I think the universe is smiling on that day in general. Here's what it says. "The full moon forms in your fifth house of love, delight, joy and ecstasy. Celebrations, parties, entertainment, and all social involvements are favored. Your sense of unity with your beloved and children is especially strong and effective. Orchid and lavender are your colors." So you see my love, all is well in the universe and I'll eagerly await your arrival at 4pm on the 23rd. We can kiss under the full moon and begin our life together.

Thank you for your bravery my King. I pray that you feel you have made a wise decision and choice. I love you.

Your soul mate, Goddess and Lover of Florsex (the only kingdom)

Dianne

Bad day at the castle – until later

Hi Goddess

This has been a very rough day, maybe like the time around the eclipse was for you. I got a phone call on my voice mail while I was in the bath. She has since sent two emails.

In addition to that I had it pointed out to me in no uncertain terms that cash-flow is turning critical again. I must do something about it, but I feel dead today. I do love your support and hope you are there for me. I love you. xxxx

No, there was no Bossex – nor Sexton. But we did have a creative writing of our own called the v's.

I look forward so much to hearing your voice. Until then I will ache quietly to myself.

Lots of love and kisses

David

xxxxx

One more week!

My wonderful King

I can't believe that in only one week we will be holding hands and smiling at each other. I love you so much and send you all my energy and warmth to help get you through this week and all of its challenges. I am so happy you are going to be with me for two weeks. That gives us time to really feel close and get to know each other again after such a long time since our last life together.

I only have a few minutes right now. I dropped Nicki off at the gym at 6:30 (Marley drove), then we picked up Marley's boyfriend. They dropped me off at the mall while they went to the office supply store and Burger King, then they picked me up. I bought the CD that has the new song by Savage Garden "I knew I loved you before I met you". I can't wait to play it for you. I also went to Victoria's Secret and bought some new bras and panties. I want to be a beautiful goddess for you. Marley was a little spoiled brat and made the comment "Oh, you can get a massage today and shop at Victoria's Secret and I get nothing". This was the first time I had shopped for myself in about 6 months and it was important to me. The only reason I could do it was I have a Victoria's Secret credit card. I've been living without credit cards for four months now. This was a pick me up I needed and don't feel I have to justify to a 15 year old. The massage is therapeutic to me and without it every other month I get stress and tension backaches. With it I never have to spend money on a doctor. She and her boyfriend sat in the back seat all the way home while I drove and they made out. These kids think they are the only one allowed a life!

I hope I'm not scaring you away with this little story of my dragon child. She can be quite charming, just chose not to tonight. Well it's time to pick up Nicki and take Marley's boyfriend Mike home. I'm going straight to bed after that with thoughts of your body next to mine. Can't wait to get your new itinerary tomorrow. Wednesday would be a good day for you to visit your aunt in case you want to tell her. That way we can spend Tuesday together and I can work Wednesday, since it will probably be busy that day and to prepare the office to close for four days. I can tell you where you can go shopping for clothes also that day. It wouldn't hurt for you to sleep some that day too. I have a 5:00 nail appointment on Wednesday and that way I wouldn't have to cancel it. I could go to it and then we could have dinner and the evening together and not be apart anymore for the rest of the two weeks.

I love you my soul mate…..your soul mate

Dianne

Re: one more week!

Good morning soul mate Goddess

I had my early night, about 11ish, went straight to sleep and woke up at 4.30, got up at 5.30 with that desperate feeling of too many things to do and too little time to do it.

I feel very weak right now and appreciate your energy. It made me feel so much better after our phone call last night. I am sorry that Marley was bad to you last night. I hope she isn't upset at your happiness.

I can't make the final plans about days until after 8:00 when the travel agent is open, but I feel I ought to pick up the parts in Boston if I can. They are so important to the business and they need paying. That's a longer story and for tonight when the plans are fixed. Either way I expect to have a wonderful dedicated time with you (and Aunty for a day).

I long to be with you, and let our love blossom, at its proper pace, and not the explosive way that was necessary before. Please forgive me, but it makes me nervous to think we were going to be too fast – that really isn't news to you though is it!

I have to have my bath now. Am thinking of you, and long for our meeting, holding hands and looking into the blue and brown depths of each other's eyes. I will leave you sleeping soundly in bed this morning, 1:00am your time, with a peck on the back of your neck, and a gentle caress of your shoulder....sleep well my goddess...

Your lover and soul mate

David

xxxxx

Re: one more week!

Good morning soul mate King

I love you and you are so special. I feel the same way about us going a little slower and we do have time now so slow it shall be. I like that idea too. Besides, I haven't gotten my period yet so will probably still have it Monday night, so mother nature will force slow.

I'm really busy today. I pick Marley up at 5:30 and will be home with her a little before 6pm. How about calling me right then? I have to go out again to go food shopping so I won't go out until you call. Or, you could call me at work at 4.45 before I leave to pick Marley up. I love you David and I long to hold you.

Your goddess who adores you

Dianne

Until 4.45pm then

Hi my wonderful, understanding and sensuous goddess.

You are so good to me; I feel I will respond very well to you with or without your period having gone away. Could the delay be stress? I will try to call you while you are at work if that is still okay. That would suit me as tiredness and stress are still my concerns.

I am pleased you are busy today; that may help pay for yesterday! I have been busy today too, trying to sort out the cash-flow and getting people motivated to get the work in faster and arrange a proper visits programme for my return.

I have now been told that they have changed my booking to go direct to you via Chicago. My new itinerary is to arrive in Orlando at 18.36 from Chicago. So if the offer of reserving my room is still on then yes please. Return journey is the same as previous. They charged me a fee equivalent to the flight from Boston to you, but this saved a hotel room in the wrong town.

I am still unsure about the reactions and future actions of Denise, but I hope she recovers quickly. I am so looking forward to our time together; I feel we will be wonderful.

Talk to you very soon....your soul mate

David

xxxxx

Cruise special!!

Dear David

What do you think about this possibility? I got a fax last week from Carnival Cruise Line about a travel agent special they are offering on November 29th. It is a four night cruise on the Ecstasy sailing from Miami to Key West and Mexico for only $199 per person including all taxes. I didn't think of it for us before because you were only going to be here for a week but since you will be here for two weeks it actually isn't a bad idea. I know you will see those ports on the Inner Voyage in March but I'll be always a hostess on that cruise and I won't be able to really relax. I love taking cruises without one of my groups because I can really relax and enjoy them.

You don't have to pay for me; I can pay for myself and write it off as a business expense. You'd only have to pay $199 for yourself. If you took me out to dinner four times you would spend that much. We could do this and then not do anything expensive in Orlando. I don't want to spend money I just want to relax and enjoy you and you'd really enjoy me because I'd be a real seagoddess. What do you think? The deal could fill up and expire at any moment. If we do this I could also show you Miami, including the house I grew up in and the exciting south beach area I was telling you about. Let me know.....

Your adoring seagoddess

Dianne

You are so wonderful – my nerves have gone (for the moment)

Hi my super Goddess

Wow – us going on a cruise, seeing the sites, being soul mates, and getting to know each other. That sounds like real magic to me. How could I be so lucky!

Well I got my phone call, lots of interrogation, including asking if I would have the balls to ring her back if it doesn't work out. I lied and said yes (was I wrong?). However, although she was distressed, she wished me all the best, and I feel she has come to terms with it, even though she is a long way from healed.

I am so happy, I do hope you were successful with the cruise booking, that sounds too good to be true. xxxx

I love you Dianne, and long for our meeting and our first kiss, hug and eventually becoming one with each other. I must go to bed now. I will caress away your cramps, and return the strength you have leant me in the last few days. We are so good for each other. Our life together starts in less than 6 days!

Your loving soul mate David xxxxx

No mother frightens me – children maybe

Dearest cramped goddess

Do not worry about your period, my hand is on the cramps and your stress blockage will soon go. I am going to take care of you, hold you and give you energy to cope. Don't fret about not starting causing this to continue into my time with you. I am not of a religion that treats women as untouchable. In fact, I want to be there and reassure you that I love you always.

Your idea of us doing the Thanksgiving meal sounds exactly right, and I will look forward to that, and getting the provisions, etc, so don't do it without me please. We need to discuss this when we meet, but I love the idea and I can't wait! How will the girls feel if I am there in their family get together. Are they as lovely as their mother?

Tonight was the first time you said that your mother was judgmental. How will I cope? I am pleased that you said your mother will be okay about us, that is important. I don't think your mother will scare me away, not if we are together anyway. I will be paying special attention to her, as that could be you in 20 – 30 years! I would love it if your parents could see them in us.

I look forward to meeting your wonderful daughters, but do admit to fears about that. I will respect their personalities, but desperately need information as to what they are! Without that I will be wandering through the darkness and be bumping into the problems as I go, so info on everyone I am likely to meet would be a great reassurance to me.

This time with you is going to be so wonderful, I can tell that we are really ready for each other. I love you! I feel ready to meet your parents, daughters, friends, and the world. I wish I were with you right now, period or no period. I want to hold you so much. I want so much to be affectionate with you. My only failing is doubting that you will want to be with me. Forgive me that weakness, oh my wonderful goddess, please. I look forward with excitement to Monday evening (only 5 days now). I love you so much and want to make you happy too.

Your loving soul mate

David

xxxxx

With you in no time xxxx

Good morning lovely soul mate Dianne

These five days are not going slow here; every minute is jam packed with urgent jobs, some very good, some not. Sunday will be loft clearing day at the old queen's residence. That will not be a fun day, but I can smile to myself that I am coming to you and she will be unaware. Rachel will be there with me. She knows about the holiday, but never tells her mother things about me. That would end up in long self pitying lectures of how hard done by she is. So, I am going away on business next week.

I can't wait to come off the plane and look for my purple goddess – very soon now.

With regard to work, I do feel that they want to lean on me, but that is very bad for them. They can't grow personally that way. There is a mood sometimes from them that a job is impossible, because the customer has changed the rules mid-way through. I have started teaching them something very useful. When a customer opens his mouth, make money from it! It goes hand in hand with nothing is impossible. So find the answer and quote for it, don't give up.

Time for my bath…come and join me. I am longing for your touch, your soul and your body.

David

xxxxxx

Stressful day

Dear David

Wow, I'm glad today is almost over! My father called me and told me that the stress test went poorly and he definitely has a problem. He is having another test later and the heart doctor will need to do a catheterization. He said I hope I don't ruin your Thanksgiving plans by being in the hospital. I sure hope not too! It is really busy today and it's hard with Paloma being out. Janet doesn't work on Thursday so it's just me and Gloria. We're both leaving at 4:30. I have to pick Marley up at 5:00. Just wanted to say hi again and tell you about my dad. I can't wait till you are here. I need you.

Your lover

Dianne

I did it!

My King David

You are such a good influence on me! I told my parents I love them! I called my father back after his second appointment today to see how it went and he didn't know anything new. He said he probably won't know anything more or have any more appointments until after Thanksgiving, which is good. He isn't feeling very well, which is bad. When we ended the conversation I said "I love you guys." My father said "me too" and my mother said "that's nice to hear." I said that was good and we said goodbye. Are you proud of me? See you are melting ice from way over across the big lake. Just imagine how powerful you will be here with me. I love you so much. It's easy to say those words to you!

Okay, a little about the girls. Well, they are both competition cheerleaders. Until you see a competition you really won't know what that means but it's a big sport here involving dance, gymnastics and cheer. They have to have "attitude" to be good at this and they do! They are very athletic (unlike me) and have good muscle tone, but don't worry, they still look very much like soft women. Big bottoms run in the family and they already have that trait, Marley more than Nicki. When they stop cheerleading they'll have to stop eating as much as they do or they will have a weight problem. They are very cute and they know it. For the most part they are good people though and wouldn't do anything to hurt anybody even the usual teenage cruelty.

They are both smart but Marley is probably a little smarter. She gets all A grades in honors classes without even trying. She is very mechanically inclined (I call her my man around the house). She has two tool chests and also likes to watch the boy next door work on his car. She put together the desk in my home office pretty much all by herself. You'll be impressed when you see it. She wants to be an engineer. She understands the pool with all its inflows and outflows and I don't have a clue. She has a boyfriend of over two months that seems pretty serious. He's a nice enough guy. She is a flirt though so I'm not sure how long she'll be able to stay with one guy. She is a virgin and I believe she wants to stay that way at least through 10th grade. She'll be 16 in February and we'll be getting her a car with the money she inherited. I told you about that money, didn't I? She is a very sweet girl with a beautiful smile. A bit of a succulent wild woman though. Her profile on AOL says for her quote "Smile, it's the next best thing to do with your lips". Sometimes she can be selfish and only care about her own needs but usually she's really nice. She still calls me mommy, even in front of her friends. She wrote me a beautiful poem for mother's day.

Nicole is 13 and also a bit of a succulent wild woman. A lot of boys like her and fight over her. She's always on the phone usually with boys. I have four phone lines here, I have to! She does have high morals though and told me that she just tells the boys she's not interested in doing more than kissing. She's very sensitive and very intuitive. Nothing gets by her. She will probably want to get to know you more than Marley will, just my guess, I could be wrong. She will want to give me her seal of approval. Don't worry, you'll get it. She sometimes likes me to tuck her into bed and lie with her for a little while. That's her way of staying attached. She calls me mom now and not mommy. That's her way of growing up. She can be selfish regarding her needs just like Marley. She is smart too but getting A grades don't come quite as easily for her, she has to study more. She talks too much at school and chews gum too much so gets a lot of detention, but I don't get upset by that. If that's the worst she does it's no big deal. She may want to be a lawyer because she likes to argue and debate.

Both of the girls like rap music and sing it really well. What a talent! Basically they are well adjusted normal teenage girls. Any questions?

I'll sign off here so I can get some stuff done and go to bed early. I don't feel 100%. Still trying to get my period! My head aches too. In four days you will be in my arms and all will be well. I still can't believe it. Our story is quite amazing, all of it. I love you my King.

Your lover and soul mate
Dianne

Have extra energy

Dearest Dianne

I am so sorry to hear about your father! Is it really that serious that we may not have him at dinner? If he is in hospital, we can have new plans that take that into account. We can adapt to allow you time for him; he is very important to you.

You poor thing, you have so much going on, and are almost alone to deal with it. Remember that I am here offering you my love and support my soul mate. I feel wonderful that you need me in your times of stress and I hope never to let that part of our special relationship fail.

My day was more empowering than yours. I took the questions that one employee was asking, and built a rousing speech for the managers and staff and gave it to the whole workforce at 3:00 my time. I was getting them to think that they could answer anything by getting into small groups and brainstorming. Currently I am the only one who calls brainstorming meetings. They have been worried about redundancies, and so I explained my plans and actions, but added that this had to be a team effort; I couldn't do it alone, especially when I was in the USA for the next two weeks. I think they were listening. John says he has seen some actions already! Let's hope tomorrow and onwards they keep it up. You have given me so much extra strength. I love you! You allow the extra focus I need at times like this.

I came home with a bad headache, maybe sympathy with you again. Then I went around to Doug and Eileen's to hand over the New Years day walking menu – the day of walking in my kilt!

Every day you get closer, I long to see you, hold you and support you in this stressful time. I love you!

David

xxxxx

Well done I am so proud of you xxxxxx
Oh Goddess

I am so proud of you. I know from everything you have said that today has not been easy, but you will reap all kinds of rewards from it, both with them and me.

The girls sound much more human now, and truly daughters of a Goddess. You have done so well. From conception to young adults they have you to thank for their wonderful looks and their talents too. I found it a little odd previously when you said the girls were in a coed cheerleading group. So boys do it too?

Both girls sound wonderful. The selfishness will change as they look around and see how hard you have worked for them. No questions about the girls and it's far too late for questions about the others so do sleep well, rest and think of me like I think of you.

I love you so much and long to be with you.

Your soul mate and future lover

David

xxxxx

Password protection suggested

Good evening soul mate

I want you to switch off those stresses for the rest of the night. Relax, come sit beside me and let me put my arm around you. I want to kiss your ear, run my fingers through your hair, then give you the most passionate kiss I have ever given anyone in my life. I want your hair to stand on end, all your parts tingle, and the blood to race around your body like the internal fire alarm was sounding.

Then before you recover, I want you to stay totally relaxed while we each kiss and caress, slowly learning the areas that have the most effect on each other. I am undoing your blouse and slowly slipping my hand through the gap, nervously finding those warm and sensitive areas that have both of us quivering with desire. The kissing is continuous. I feel the changes through my fingertips and note the eyes and the breathing changing too. I stop the kiss and whisper in your ear "I love you my goddess and need you to be so close to me". You reply "Oh yes my King but only above the waist only tonight." I kiss you again and say "I love you, trust me...you are too important to me to do anything that will upset you, and anyway this is our first meeting, what kind of chap do you think I am, and all those people over there would be embarrassed. The airport is no place for that."

Later in the hotel after long silences full of hand holding and spiritual transactions throughout the journey, we are finally alone. Wow, I never thought the reality would come after many months of dreaming. We are alone together, tired, excited, and very much in love. We talk and get to understand some of each other's ways, so much more to learn, what excitement life has in store for us. I drive you home and we kiss in the car outside your house. Passion fills the car; the air is full of scents, all erotic and new. My head is in a real spin, longing to be asked in and also longing to get some sleep, not knowing which is more important. Passion rages on. We love each other so much, such ecstasy fills us. You break away with womanly cunning, knowing it is always better to leave the man hungry for more. I realise that this is perfect. We will progress next time and I get my sleep too. "I love you" I say as you leave my arms at your doorway. Now where was that hotel, my mind has gone all blank!

Good night my wonderful soul mate, sleep well, and I will be with you in spirit tonight and physically as soon as American Airlines gets me to you. I love you and long to be with you.
David of Florsex
xxxxxxxxxxxxxx

Good morning my love xxxx
Dearest Dianne

Well, just three days until I have to get up at 4am Monday….. no nerves yet, just a warm feeling. After signing off last night, I realised that I don't know your parents' names. That may be useful. Things look very busy in the next few hours to take off, and I expect that is true for you too.

Are you saving the rest of your life story for face to face? I have been very busy and feel confident that I can tell you anything, not that there is that much more to tell, mainly the positive of the children and the business. Time to leave the old queen's negativity behind.

Must go now, bath is waiting. How about a chat tonight – or Saturday night?
Take good care of yourself my goddess.
David of Florsex
xxxxxxx

Re: Password protection protected

Oh my King!!!

I didn't read this until this morning. I think you stayed up later than I did. My tummy was aching and I went to read in bed at 9:00 and fell asleep quickly. God I love your fantasy...but it isn't a fantasy....except that all that won't happen at the airport! In the car, that's another story. My skin is so eager for your touch. I want it now! The weather will be warm so I'll wear a sundress that buttons down the front. It will either be the purple and gold one I got at Findhorn in Scotland, or it will be a blue flowered one. Is that okay with you my king? Please touch me soon or I shall faint.

I know for sure that Suzin is involved in this matchmaking from heaven. She always said that there is to be no touching below the waist until at least the third date. It's interesting that you mentioned the above the waist only. She must have put that thought in your head. I also know that it is her doing that I don't have my period yet! Please Suzin, I want to make love with him on Thanksgiving. I have to get my period right now! No sign of it yet. At this rate you'll be easing my cramps.

You need your sleep so don't call me tonight. I won't be home until after 9:00pm as I have to take Terri to the airport after taking Nicki to the gym and picking up Marley after 6:00 at her practice. When I get home I'll write to you. Saturday would be wonderful to talk. I'll make sure I'm home by 6:00pm then or earlier if you need me to be. I better get to work, I have a lot to do and will work Saturday for a few hours too. The weather is going to be sunny and beautiful on Tuesday so I think we definitely should go to Epcot that day. You better get good rest this weekend as you aren't being given any time here to get over jet lag!

My parents' names are Anne and Alex. I'm glad you are proud of me for what I did. That means a lot to me.

Your longing soul mate

Dianne...Goddess of Florsex

Deep pools of love

You are so wonderful my goddess

I did stay up late, but that was because your email came in when I had just finished mine. I had to answer, you were so good. I really am so proud of you. So now you have said it once, it shouldn't be difficult to do it when the desire or need is there.

I love you saying those sexy things to me. But you must wait for the right time….airport, airport car park, hotel, your house, who knows when Suzin's magic will strike. I too ache to touch you, which is why I wrote that. You are right, it was not a fantasy, more of a forecast of desire that may or may not materialise. The airport building was meant light heartedly to make you smile. Your words do so much more to me than make me smile, and most of that is below the waist!

Stop fretting about your period. I love you with or without it and we can still be close with it if you are happy and that is what both of us want. It may sound strange to you, but I do wish to ease your pain, by being there, holding you, and showing you spiritual love and caresses.

There's no chance of rest this weekend. I have to work a little tonight, at home, and some of tomorrow at work. Sunday is loft day, and Monday is holiday! Wow it is so close!

Your parents Anne and Alex, is that what I should call them? Or should I call them Mr and Mrs Kemp?

There is still a small nagging problem, in that I have had another email from Denise, saying that it is still raining in her heart, and she is composing something else. Sorry but I feel you need to know, as I may still need the woman's touch not to hurt her, but to end this properly, which I thought the phone call did.

I love you so much, and have never felt like this about anybody, even when I have met them. This is most certainly magic – it is so powerful, spreading happiness in most places.

My goddess, how I long for you too, and am eager for that right moment to slip my hand in the warm space between dress

and breast and to look into the depths of the dark brown pools of love in your eyes and go swimming in the depths of our love.
Your loving soul mate
David, King of Florsex
xxxxxxxxx

Re: Deep pools of love
You are so wonderful my king

Oh David, I am getting a bit nervous, but it is nervous with a burning desire. I feel like we're already physically intimate and that is probably because our spirits and souls have already merged. Still, the thought of your touch from the first time you hold my hand to your lips meeting mine......your hand upon my breast....your hardness inside of my softness....your passionate love consumes me. Still no period. Suzin the seawitch has quite a sense of humor. Don't worry, I feel completely comfortable with you. Nothing will stand in the way of whatever we do, wherever we do it. You are my soul mate. I do understand when you say you want to ease my pain, because I feel the same about you. It feels so good to feel this way.

I wish I could ease your pain regarding Denise. I don't think I can though. I don't know enough about her to know where her head is and I don't want to jump to incorrect conclusions as that doesn't do anybody justice. It's hard to not tell you thoughts that come to my mind though, so I will. I'm wondering when you began writing to her. Was it a long time before you began writing to me? It seems that perhaps she has some traits similar to Chris in being a little bit manipulative and into guilt trips. We do tend to find people who can help us heal wounds of previous relationships whether the previous relationship is our first one (our parents) or a love relationship. In my case, I think one of your purposes is definitely to help me heal with my parents. Don't worry, when that is healed there will be many more purposes for you. I shall always need you. You give me such strength.

Since you can't stand to be around Chris anymore, perhaps a lesson or an opportunity the universe has given you with Denise is another try to say goodbye with dignity and strength to both people. Since you care so much for others' feelings it is easy to put yours aside. You put yours aside for way too long with Chris. It is David's turn now for a really good life with no guilt for anything. You didn't lead her on as you made no promises to her. You simply moment by moment shared a part of yourself with her and while it lasted it was good. Nothing can be promised to last forever. I wouldn't want you to promise me that. I'd rather you choose day by day to stay with me because there is no place or nobody you'd rather be with. I want to be your conscious choice, not an empty promise that must be fulfilled because of some silly sense of honor. It is far more honorable to tell the truth and to release someone to be able to love again with somebody who can better love them than you can. I'm very brave in saying this because I feel so secure in our love. I feel even more secure now knowing about Denise because you chose me and I felt the passion with which you chose me. I also know how honorable you are and how hard it was to tell her.

My intuition may be way off on this one. You hadn't gotten far enough in your story to tell me more about Scott. When we are together I want you to tell me about him and what happened. I remember it was a story similar to Suzin's but I don't remember all the details since we weren't nearly as close as we are now when you told me. You were probably closer with Denise at that time and you were testing the waters so to speak with me. I feel like in some way Scott was (is) a very evolved soul and had (has) a lot of love for you. Maybe even karma from another life where you did something to save him. I feel like he chose to go to help you release yourself from Chris as once he was gone there was no need for you to stay together. He is an old soul and an old friend of yours, I suspect of mine as well, maybe even of Suzin's. I think that year called a lot of wise ones home (Mother Theresa, Princess Diana,

Scott and Suzin), perhaps to help us struggling ones. I sure got off on a tangent, didn't I?

What all that has to do with Denise...I'm not sure. Her grief is human and real and she needs to feel it to work through it. She obviously felt more for you than you did for her. Some of her grief has to also have to do with the fact that she told a lot of people about you and she is embarrassed. From that point of view she wants you to feel misery too. That is a guilt trip and you don't need to own it. You are closing the door to that chapter. If it isn't closing as quickly as you had hoped that's okay too, sweetheart. I love you at whatever point you are at in your story. You have unconditional love and support from me. Chris will probably attack old wounds on Sunday and Denise is doing it now. Same wounds, different woman. That happened to me so many times with men. I can relate and feel. I want to heal your wounds and create happiness where there once was pain.

Boy am I rambling and I still don't think I've answered your question on how to end this properly. Maybe the phone call gave her a little false hope. You did tell her that if it didn't work with me you'd let her know. You may have to be a little more firm (in a loving way). Tell her you are sorry from the bottom of your heart and soul and being. You probably already did that. Beyond that apology, though, you are probably not the person to help her feel better. Perhaps a good friend can help her. Tell her you are so sure of what you have with me that you really don't want to continue even a platonic email relationship and feel it would be better at this point to go cold turkey and just let go. Tell her that knowing her has enriched your life, she's a very special woman and you know that she will make some man very happy some day. Destiny has pointed you in a different direction, though, and you must focus completely in that direction. You know she'd appreciate that from you if it were her you had chosen. If she feels strongly for you as a person she'd want to respect that. If she doesn't then she's at the stage of love that I was with many relationships of the past. What could that person do for me rather than the way I feel with you…what can I do for you.

I hope I said something that meant something. I'm getting tired now and you must be sleeping already. I hope you are because you need it. Yes our love is magic and it is spreading love in most places. Let's take the magical optimistic viewpoint which is so our style and assume that it is doing the same for Denise because it is freeing her to meet her true soul mate. Maybe not right away. Maybe who Denise needs to meet and establish a love relationship with right now is Denise….and for Chris it is Chris. It took me several years and being pretty much discarded by two husbands to come to that level of self love and my journey was worth it because it led me to the promised land….Florsex! So I have followed the heroine's quest for the holy grail and I have found it. Let's let Denise find it as well and sometimes we as women just have to go through the pain to come out the other end a real goddess.

I love you David…King of Florsex, and I believe I always will. Till I can touch you, I keep you safely in my heart and succulently at my breast with one hand on my tummy.
Your very eager lover
Dianne…Goddess of Florsex

Even goddesses…..
Dearest David
Even goddesses have nerves and insecurities. I woke up at this ungoddessly hour because I have so much to do this weekend, both at home and at the office, but I ran to my computer first… and you haven't written yet. Now it's my turn to feel insecure. You didn't like my last email, everything was way off base? Denise convinced you to go to Boston instead? I know, I'm losing it! I just can't wait to love you in person! You are probably at work now finishing what you need to finish so you can get to me with a clear head. Please excuse this minor interruption of craziness. I'll finish my coffee, read the paper, take a shower and go to the office. Is it okay if I buy the turkey today? I'm afraid if I wait there

won't be a good one left. We can buy the rest of the stuff when you are here. You are almost here my love. You have such a long journey ahead of you and I thank you for taking it. The fact of it is, though, the really long journey is now behind both of us. The quest is complete, heaven is smiling (okay, Suzin is laughing cause I still don't have my period), the road to Florsex is paved with gold (and purple) smiles, the Ecstasy (ship) awaits us and we have so much to be thankful for on Thanksgiving. I love you my king.
Your very eager and a bit nervous lover
Dianne

This might help
Dearest David

I'm in the office, supposed to be working. I found this little piece called "Letting Go" and I thought something in it might help you in your situation with Denise. I felt like last night I rambled and didn't say anything particularly helpful. But then of course the first thing that this piece says would apply to me helping you with this. Here it is.
Letting Go

To let go does not mean to stop caring, it means I can't do it for someone else.

To let go is not to cut myself off, it's the realization I can't control another.

To let go is not to enable, but to allow learning from natural consequences.

To let go is to admit powerlessness, which means the outcome is not in my hands.

To let go is not to try to change or blame another, it's to make the most of myself.

To let go is not to care for, but to care about.

To let go is not to fix, but to be supportive.

To let go is not to judge, but to allow another to be a human being.

To let go is not be in the middle arranging the outcomes, but to allow others to affect their own destinies.

To let go is not to be protective, it's to permit another to face reality.

To let go is not to deny, but to accept.

To let go is not to nag, scold or argue, but instead to search out my own shortcomings, and correct them.

To let go is not to adjust everything to my desires, but to take each day as it comes, and cherish myself in it.

To let go is not to criticize and regulate anybody but to try to become what I dream I can be.

To let go is not to regret the past, but to grow and live for the future.

To let go is to fear less, and love more.

Author unknown

I love you David, King of Florsex...my skin is tingling in anticipation....

Your goddess

Dianne

Silly Goddess!!

Hi oh you foolish goddess

I am here, and I am getting prepared for you, both mentally and physically. But you were right I went to work for an hour, and have just got home.

Life is never simple though. Denise is trying very hard, another long email and a vase of flowers on the doorstep. I will use some of the very useful info my goddess gave me, and try to put it nicely (again)...but she thinks there is always a chance it will not work out. No chance would be the correct way of putting it!

You don't ever need to worry about overstepping the mark; I value your opinion, and if I ever did feel it was not the thought for me, I would make up my own mind.

It has turned very cold here; my fingers and legs are frozen. I long to be warmed up, partly by your climate and partly in a more loving way. xxxxxx

I will sign off for now and say, do not worry, I am coming.... just a few more hours now. I love you and nothing is going to stop me from having my hand held at the airport. xxxx

Your loving and eager King

David of Florsex

xxxxxxxxxxxxxx

ps – Is 6:00 still okay for me to make my last phone call before looking into your eyes?

Re: Silly Goddess!!

Dear David

Yes, please 6:00 is wonderful. I have to run now to watch Marley's competition and then take her home as she is feeling sick. It is very warm here, will be 80 today. I pray that everything warms you my love.

Now I'm getting mad at this woman. Flowers! I'm about ready to ask for her email address to put an end to this myself! I love you and you are mine!

THE Goddess of Florsex

*   *   *   *

There must have been a very nice phone call at this point making us both feel really good........to say the least!

*   *   *   *

We are one and it feels so good

Dearest David, most worthy King

Nobody has ever made love to me like you do, how could they? We are soul mates. I haven't been with another soul mate in this life. I've been waiting all my life for you, and now it is only 45 more hours until you are in my arms. I want to make you so happy and I want you to feel ecstasy like you never have in your life. I want to feed your spirit and your soul with my love and your body with my body, mind, heart and soul. I want to touch you and feel you grow hard with my touch. I want to kiss you deeply and passionately, and I want to feel you deep inside of me.

I want to cook with you, cruise with you, dance with you, watch movies with you, go to Disney, Epcot and Universal with you, shop with you, go to cheerleading competition with you, hold your hand and not let go. I want to enchant you and be enchanted by you. You are my lover and I am your beloved. You are my beloved and I am your lover. I want to please you and be pleased by you. I want to learn your ways, your desires, your dreams. I want you to be mine.

Keep me with you on this last leg of our long journey to our Kingdom. Keep that bravery you had tonight. We were made for each other, so there is nothing to be nervous about. I love you and honor your with every bit of my heart and soul. I'll see you very soon my love.

Your goddess who adores you

Dianne

Countdown started engines on xxx

Good morning my sweet Dianne

Shhh, don't move, I just want to look at you laying there, warm and sexy, just as we fell asleep last night, interlocked and entwined. Your hair across the pillow in an array of dark rivulets. Your smile of happiness at mine. Last night was the sexiest of my entire life Dianne. You are so wonderful and I am yours to do with as pleases you, and I am here to please you in the best ways I can.

I do long to look at you, and caress every inch of you. I want you so much! I love you. xxxxx

I leave in 21 hours, and suddenly thought that my sleep apnea machine is not the one I took to Cuba (where they use low voltage US type electric) and I can't find how to switch it to 110v. So I have rung the hospital, and they will ring me back while I am out (I hope).

I am longing to be with you and tell you in person how much I love you. I want us to pass all previous boundaries of emotion and feeling, and we can. I say that not from any physical experience, but from the power within us at this range. I know this is supernatural, and it is ours. It is going to be really soon now.....

Please put on a warm woolly jumper [pullover, cardigan] to keep your love with you.....it's going to be really cold in the old queen's loft.

I must go now before I freeze my bits off and the bath goes cold.

Your soul mate, lover and aroused dreaming King of Florsex
David

Countdown started, engines on – as David Bowie once sang. Just packing, sleep and travel to go. I love you with all my heart and soul. Please relax, finish your work, and enjoy the next two weeks of passion, love and togetherness.

Re: Countdown started engines on xxxxxx

Good morning my love

Hmmmm 4:14am eastern time you wrote...no wonder I'm awake. I lay awake in the dark for about an hour hugging my body length pillow and knowing that soon it will really be you. It's now 5:45, the Sunday paper isn't here and I knew you had written which is much jucier than the paper anyway.

I'm glad I mentioned the US electric plug thing. I don't want you to have the wrong thing. I have a converter from US to foreign that I can travel with. That won't help you here. You have me confused with sockets and plugs. I'm sure that we are what worked for you in Cuba. Thank goodness our sockets and plugs work without a converter! The UK man and the US woman fit quite nicely I can tell.

That will be wonderful if you can send me a picture or two. If not don't worry, I'll know my King with the blue shirt and the glow around him. I'm with you now as we approach the old queen's house. She doesn't see me; I've put on my cloak of invisibility. It's a warm one since it is cold here. Let's work fast and leave; she doesn't look very friendly. I'll try to play with you as we work. Not enough to slow you down too much, just enough to help you remember that this is the past and I am the present and the future.

Longing to be with you in every way, to keep you aroused, happy, warm and loved. You are already the best lover I've ever had, could ever want. I am the most lucky of all women for you to have found and chosen me. Yes my love, the countdown is on. I love you…..come to me.
Your soul mate and lover
Dianne…Goddess of Florsex

Weird cramps
Dearest David

Would you believe I had to go back to bed after I wrote to you? I was having really bad cramps. This isn't like me. I usually don't have really bad periods. My intuition tells me that it is all the hurt and pain that is hidden in my cellular memory in my womb coming up for you to heal with your love. I massaged castor liver oil (an Edgar Cayce healing remedy) into my belly and pretended it was your hands doing it. I love you so much. I'm at the office now and a little panicked with everything I have to do so I better start doing. I'm in love with you David Hugh Purdie!
Your devoted goddess
Dianne

Go to sleep my love
My dearest soul mate David

I want to put you to bed early tonight so you can get some sleep before your long journey. I will kiss you gently, caress you softly and although I will sleep with you to keep you warm I shall not try to arouse you because I really want you to sleep. I will spoon you and softly kiss your neck and your back. Wake in the morning with a big smile on your face as I will have on mine because soon we will see each other. I love you David, I'll see you in my dreams and tomorrow in my airport.

Your devoted lover

Dianne

Off to sleep now

My dearest goddess Dianne of Florsex

This will be my last letter ever before we embrace....so I will say to you that I have never been so in love. xxxxxx

You are so incredible, I wish it was me putting on the oil and massaging your belly. It soon will be. I will be getting up in less than 6 hours from now so I will sign off and get some sleep alongside you, and gently longing to caress and be caressed. Not long now Dianne and I will be with you. I hope your cramps have receded by then or I will have to lay hands on you sooner rather than later.

I am enclosing three pictures. Me in tomorrow's shirt, a picture of Scott and a photo of Rachel and Vickie. If these work out I wouldn't mind a print for Aunty Margaret. Thanks in advance.

Today's visit was fine. The old queen was not too well and barely spoke to me directly. See, I was protected by my very own goddess. xxxxx

I love you Dianne and will see you so soon....

Your soul mate and lover

David of Florsex

xxxxxxxxxxxxxxxx

Good morning my love

Good morning sweetheart

Again I wish you a wonderful journey to me and I love you with all my heart like I've never loved anybody before. Yes, I got the pictures and am now printing them for your aunt. You look very handsome in your blue shirt. I can't wait to kiss you. Here's to us and our life together.

Your soul mate and lover

Dianne

Leaving on a jet plane (very soon now my goddess)

My dearest goddess

With all the excitement of the last few hours I didn't tell you which flight I am on.

London to Chicago AA87 then Chicago to Orlando AA669 arrival due 18.36 today. I haven't checked the status of my first flight yet so I'll do that on my mobile on the way.

Must dash now, I have packing to finish, bath to have, shirt to find, etc.

I love you.

See you very soon......

David KOF xxxxxx

Chapter Sixteen

We Meet!!

I am writing this as a 55 year old woman in 2009, almost 10 years after the meeting I am about to describe. David and I live in England, have been married over 8 years and are incredibly happy. But that's a preview of a future book! I must now channel my younger self to fully appreciate and be the experience I am about to describe. So I will leave you now and the 45 year old Dianne who is about to meet her soul mate will enter.....

It's Monday the 23rd of November 1999, a few days before Thanksgiving. I'm at my Dreamtime office and all my friends who work with me see me as a complete basket case as far as doing any work today. Tonight I'm going to meet David, the British man I believe to be my soul mate. My friends are a bit more open to this possibility than my daughters and my parents who are all a bit sceptical. After all, I met him on the internet. My teenage daughters have asked me what I would do and say if they had met a boy on the internet. I told them of course that I would be extremely cautious. But they are 13 and 15, I'm 45! When two spiritual and intuitive adults are intent on honest communication, they end up knowing each other quite well. David and I have shared about 200 letters each. True it has only been since the end of June, so basically 5 months, but we feel the internet is an incredible medium for knowing a person without the physical and other bits of dating getting in the way. Yes, I know, there is the Denise story, but nobody but me knew that so there was no reason for my friends or family to doubt him. My mother wants to know how I know he isn't an axe murderer. I turned that back to her and asked her how she knew my father wasn't as they met by writing letters during World War II. This is just that, set to the internet.

Most of my friends at work knew my second husband Tony and all I went through as well as most of my dating history including internet dating. They saw the sense of ease I had with David and how it wasn't always a big drama like it was with other men. While of course they didn't want me to get hurt they also wanted me to finally find happiness and they were very open to the possibility that he was the one.

That morning Paloma picked me up at home to take me to work so I wouldn't have my car. The plan was that she would drop me at the airport at 5:30. I would meet David, David would rent a car and we would drive together in his rental car to check him into the hotel in Longwood. He would then take me home and drive himself back to the hotel which was close to where I live in Winter Springs.

We leave for the airport at about 3:00, a bit early but like I said I am a complete basket case and I feel ready for the next stage which is waiting at the airport. I can imagine how David is feeling as he will already have gone through Customs in Chicago and be on the plane heading for Orlando. Paloma asks me if I'm sure I want to do this as she drops me off and also asks if I want her to wait with me. I thank her, smile and tell her thanks but I'll be fine. I don't buy a magazine or any other distraction; I'm just alone with my thoughts and my dreams.

I truly believe David and I have known each other in another lifetime and the recognition will be immediate and comfortable. I'm nervous, but in a very warm fuzzy kind of way.

This is, of course, pre 9/11 and there isn't the same level of airport security. People without boarding passes are allowed to go to the gate, so the gate is where I decide to go at about 5:30, approximately an hour before his arrival time. The board is showing his flight is on time. I watch as people greet passengers coming in at this and other gates. I wonder what their stories might be. When I see couples of all ages in love, I have a really good feeling. This is so different than the trip on the Holland America ship I took with Suzin while married to Tony. When I saw old couples dancing and holding hands then I knew without a shadow of a doubt that Tony and I would not be an old couple. Now I know that David and I will be.

6:20, okay, now my heart is starting to beat a bit fast. No, I'm not nervous, just very excited. 6:30, the plane has landed and is taxiing to this gate. I'm at the window looking into the plane with a big smile on my face. Of course I wouldn't know or see him but he might see me and know it is me. About 10 minutes later the passengers are disembarking into the gate area......now my heart is doing that double time again! Oh my God, the moment is actually arriving!

After about 20 passengers are off I see him and he sees me. We give each other a loving smile and he walks to me, our eyes locked the entire way. I have tears in my eyes. He puts down his carry-on bag and we give each other a really big bear hug and don't drop the embrace for some time. We may be blocking other passengers but we don't seem to care! We break the hug long enough to look at each other and then we kiss. It was a sort of "you can kiss the bride" kind of kiss. Long for a first kiss and very exciting yet gentle all in one. Then we look at each other, give each other a big smile and kiss again.

We realize we are blocking the gate so we find a somewhat discreet spot to sit down and we kiss like we are 16 years old. Perhaps we are being watched but it doesn't matter. When we come up for air we realize that yes, we are being watched! My daughters would probably be mortified if they were here. He then takes my hand and we hold hands leaving the gate area and walking to the monorail train that takes us to the main terminal. We don't say much, just hold hands tightly and keep glancing at each other and smiling. I think we may have stopped one time on the way for another kiss. Words would have been so inadequate. What was I to say, "how was your flight?" There would be time for words, right now holding hands very tightly was enough.

After the ride on the monorail to the main terminal, we finally start to talk a little while walking to the baggage claim area and waiting for his luggage to arrive. His flight was good, my day was surreal; mostly we express how thrilled we are to be together and keep looking at each other and smiling and holding hands. When we have the luggage we head for the car rental desk. Interesting how they speak British to him and tell him the car is in the "car park" rather than the parking lot. They ask if he needs a map and he informs them that his goddess lives here so he should be fine. I suggest that a map might be helpful on the day he is alone visiting his aunty. We get the car, he sits in the driver's seat, I sit next to him and again we look at each other with a big grins on our faces and then start kissing again. His hand touches my breast on the outside and I melt into him. Well I melt into him to the degree I can sitting in the front seat of a car!

David expresses that he is thirsty so we pull into a fast food drive through for a milkshake to share. He isn't keen on American fast food. However he has taken the position of when in America do as the Americans do. As is typical in a drive through, one person takes our order, another takes our money and a third person serves it. I see nothing unusual about that but David thinks it is a very overstaffed country if it takes three people to serve us a drink! I never thought of it that way and wonder how they get anything done in England if only one person has to do all that.

The ride after that to the hotel is a bit more normal as far as lots of talking instead of just looking at each other and smiling. We check him into the hotel and go to his room. Of course I still have my period and also we both want to take it slow but we really want to be close and undress each other down to our underpants and get into the bed for some wonderful cuddling and kissing. The chemistry is good, just like we knew it would be, but more than a purely sexual charge there is real love, which feels so good to both of us. We have both been waiting for this for a long time.

It is, of course, five hours later to David and he is very tired so we don't stay in bed longer than about an hour and then get up. If we stayed there any longer I don't think we would make it to my house (or not have sex). We have a quick dinner en-route to my house and he takes me home. He doesn't come in as he wants to be a bit less tired when he meets my girls so we kiss in the car and he promises he knows his way back to the hotel. He will come back for me at about 8am after the girls have left for school and we will spend the day at Epcot. I have a big smile on my face when I walk in the house. Marley and Nicki are very suspicious but curious to meet this British man who has their mother so charmed. They will meet him tomorrow after we get back from Epcot.

We have a great time at Epcot, the weather is beautiful and we of course hold hands the entire time. We both have the same level of amusement park tolerance. Neither of us likes fast or scary rides. Luckily, Epcot is quite tame and he did agree nice for adults. His favorite Epcot event was the parade at night as he doesn't see anything like this in the UK. This is definitely working, we feel really good together. I've never been with a man who wants to hold my hand so much. Randall probably came the closest but he only wanted me once every 6 weeks. I feel like David and I will want each other 24/7. Of course that isn't possible right now but it will give us something to look forward to.

Meeting Marley and Nicki Isn't too bad. They are both curious, Nicki more than Marley as I suspected. They both find his accent interesting but at some point lose interest and leave us alone. If memory serves me, we all go out for something to eat and then to the food store to shop for Thanksgiving. David goes back to his hotel around 9 or 10pm that night still a bit jet lagged but a lot of the scary bit is over as he and the girls have now met. My parents aren't nearly as scary as the girls are.

Wednesday I work and David visits his Aunty in Kissimmee. I tell my friends at work how wonderful I feel with David and that he really is the man for me. My friends can tell that this does seem to be true. My manner is comfortable and confident and doesn't carry the drama that other possible soul mates I have told them about have had. I'm no longer a basket case, I'm just really happy.

Thursday David checks out of the hotel as he's moving in with me this weekend when the girls go to their dad's house. We are having dinner at about 1pm and they will have it again with their father, Lisa and their brother Andy at dinner time. Then after spending Thanksgiving weekend with Stan and Lisa they will be spending four nights at my parent's house as we are leaving on our 4-night cruise on Sunday. The girls are still sleeping when he arrives to start cooking Thanksgiving dinner. I help as I know the menu but he does most of the cooking. He is a bit overdressed as he is wearing a white shirt and a tie. I guess the British are much more formal than we are. I explain to him that this is Florida and a very casual place but he doesn't yet own that type of casual. We will have to go shopping for him. The girls will just have to think he is weird. They eventually wake up, do find him a bit weird but are polite enough thankfully. In between cooking, David hangs all my framed photos that needed hanging, mostly pictures of Marley and Nicki.

My parents arrive around 12:30 and are very nice. They notice the pictures instantly so they like David immediately when they realize that he did it. They are really into family pictures. My mother thinks his last name is McDonald but she has him confused with Marley's boyfriend. We explain that David's last name is Purdie. We talk a little about what David does and we also talk a little about how my parents met. David holds my hand in front of them and I think my mother likes that, as she hadn't seen that with either of my husbands. My mother also likes the big hug he gives her at the end of their visit. They all of course love his cooking and so do I. All in all the meal is a great success. I even used my good china! I think my parents actually did like him in spite of the fact that we met on the internet. Their other suspicion was that he was meeting me to get a green card to be American. They probably were still suspicious of that, even though they seemed reasonably convinced that he wasn't an axe murderer. David was very cute the way he said to me "Why would I want a green card? I'm British." An American wouldn't understand that comment unless they were very used to the British culture. At the time I wasn't used to the British culture so it still sounded weird to me. But I wanted a different, non-ordinary, man and different he was!

Later that afternoon we drop the girls off at Stan and Lisa's house and then go back to my house to really get to know each other. I don't have my period anymore so we are likely to make love. I think even Suzin would have agreed that the three dates of kissing and hand holding since Monday night are now over.

I must draw the private curtain now on our lovemaking. I can tell you it was good, I can tell you it was making love and not just sex and I can tell you we both are very happy and know this relationship is working on all levels. I don't think I've ever smiled at somebody so much other than my babies when holding them.

We have a really glorious few days together in my house. We swim in the pool and relax in the hot tub a lot. The weather is beautiful and we are both so grateful for this gift of this wonderful time together. David cooks for me, meets some of my friends and visits my parents at their house. Needless to say, we talk, hold hands and look at each other and smile all the time.

David is getting a real American education and we both laugh at how different things are here from the UK. For example, we went to the food store, which is in a strip shopping center. I also needed the bank, which was on a diagonal opposite corner of the parking lot. We walked to the car and he wondered why in the world we were getting in the car when the bank was just over there. He said "next you are going to tell me it's a drive through" and he was amazed when I said "yes". There are no drive through banks in England!

We now really know each other and feel very comfortable, like we have been together forever, so it's time to take a cruise!

Sunday we drive down to Miami to leave on the 4-day cruise to Mexico and Key West. I will show him some of Miami when the cruise returns. Today we will board the ship as soon as we arrive at the Port of Miami. David is very excited about the cruise ship as it is the first real modern cruise ship he has been on. I am thrilled to show him my world of cruising.

The first stop is Key West and we both enjoy it a lot. We take the trolley tour of the town and just walk around. We both really appreciate the laid-back atmosphere, especially since we work so hard in our businesses and life. Maybe one day we can have a laid-back life together somewhere.

In Mexico we do the tour of the Tulum ruins. I have been there before but this is David's first time in Mexico. I chose that trip as it gives a good feel for the Mayan culture but also is in a beautiful location overlooking the Caribbean Sea. I suffer from IBS (irritable bowel syndrome) unfortunately. And very unfortunately I desperately need the ladies room while at the Mayan ruins. The ladies room is a bit of a trek back to the entrance. I quickly leave David where he is, briefly explained my problem and run. David feels a bit uncomfortable being left in a place he has no idea about, without a guide and not knowing the language and with armed police all around (something he had never seen in England, especially the machine guns). Luckily for both of us I return about 30 minutes later!

David really enjoys it, particularly the cliff overlooking the bright blue Caribbean Sea with its palm trees and white sand beach. It seems we both have an affinity for the Mayan culture, a past life together perhaps. We both feel very good in Mexico other than it is a surprisingly cold day. The Yucatan peninsula of Mexico has some cold spells, a bit unusual for late November/ early December, but I tell David it would be colder than this in Orlando right now and hopefully it will warm up again by the time we get back. This man really loves warm weather so I assume one day our relationship will take him to Florida rather than me moving to England.

Speaking of our relationship, it is obviously as good in person as we imagined, even better actually. On the second day of the cruise while we are lying in bed cuddling, David says to me "When the time is right will you marry me?" Wow. Believe it or not, this was actually the first man who asked me to marry him! I did the asking with both Stan and Tony. I am thrilled that he has a strong enough feeling about our relationship after only one week of being together to ask me to marry him. I smile at him and say "Yes I will; I would love to be your wife." We are both incredibly happy! I can only describe it as a full heart experience. Other than my children whom I am obviously connected with in a very strong way, I don't believe I have ever felt this way about another person.

There is obviously no ring at this time, as he had no idea he would be asking this question on this trip. This is just an example, though, of how well this relationship works on all levels and there is no struggle or drama as in my past; it just flows really nicely.

David says he needs to ask my father for my hand in marriage. Now that is even stranger to me than a man asking me to marry him! How old fashioned and sweet! I said okay, so we spend a lot of money, as ship to shore isn't cheap and call my parents from our stateroom. My mother answers the phone; my father isn't there so David asks her. She has a very strange reaction and says that Dianne never asks their permission for anything. So rather than think this was old fashioned, proper and sweet like I did, she sort of blows the moment. We don't spend long on the phone and decide we are happy even if other people aren't happy for us.

The rest of the cruise is really good. We tell the waiters at dinner that we are engaged and they bring us a cake and sing to us as waiters do. We truly enjoy each other's company and it is so rare for both of us to just relax and not have any obligations. Neither of us wants to leave the ship. If we could stop time and just prolong the cruise forever we would be happy.

When we get back to Miami I show David South Beach, which is very art deco and a bit wild even in the daytime. Then we drive into Coral Gables and West Miami so he can see where I grew up, where my father's store was and the house I lived in until leaving for college. It is nice taking a trip down memory lane with him, very nice actually. He seems so interested in me as a person.

Thursday night we come back, pick up the girls from my parents' house and tell all of them in person that when the time is right we will get married. My daughters are really shocked but I assure them the time won't be right until they are out of High School. David has a 5 year plan to build up his business and sell it and move to Florida and then we will get married. My daughters act like I have lost my mind, Marley more than Nicki. I guess that is to be expected. After all this is a big shock. My parents don't say much but seem a bit more accepting as I think they actually like David. I think I have probably cried wolf too many times though for any of my family or friends to be totally convinced that I really have met my soul mate. Still, I know it and that's what is important.

As we are engaged there is no reason to pretend we aren't sleeping together so David stays the last few days of his trip in my house with Nicki and Marley there. Actually on Saturday we bring the girls to Stan's house and he experiences them acting out in the car and me getting fed up and asking him to stop the car so I can get out. There he is in the car with two crazy teenage girls and me outside of the car walking who knows where. He actually handles it quite well although he does tell me later that he wasn't at all thrilled with that situation!

We go to the mall and the movies those last few days. On Saturday we return the rental car. The last day is very difficult, as we are getting ready to say goodbye. We enjoyed being together 24/7 for almost two weeks and we are going to miss each other a lot. We have already decided that I will come to England for a long weekend (5 days) in February to see where he lives and meet his family and friends. This is two months away and we are already feeling like husband and wife, so a two month separation will be a very long time.

Taking him to the airport is difficult as is waiting for his plane to be ready to board. Saying goodbye, even though we know we will see each other in two months is very hard. We have become so close in this first meeting and we really are going to miss each other. It's like parting with half of you. Besides that the end of this two weeks means going back to our everyday reality that involves a lot of work for us to both make our businesses work. We really don't want this time to end. This was a wonderful beginning to the rest of our lives. The last hug, kiss and wave are emotional yet powerfully loving. This visit has been everything I knew it could be.

The first public engagement

Chapter Seventeen
Back to (Un)reality

This chapter represents the first two weeks after David left to go home. Both of us had to get back to work full force. David broke the news about us to his friends and family although he did leave out the part that we are already engaged. He'll let that happen on a later visit as he prefers to go slowly with his people. For both of us though, we are going through daily life with a glow of happiness about us. There is still stress but always happiness behind it.

I love you very very much
Dearest David

I love you with all of my heart and soul and will forever. This has been the best two weeks of my entire life, probably all of my lives. I've never felt so close to somebody before. I still feel like we are holding hands even now so I know we can maintain this feeling forever. It was weird saying goodbye but I know we both have a lot of work to do. I miss you already but I'll try not to dwell on that. I'm part British now you know so I do have a stiff upper lip. I'll be happy when I know you've read this and you are safely home. You must be exhausted! I think that our very strong love and focus kept us awake sometimes when we should have been napping.

Good news about my parents! They are very weird and didn't really understand this asking them thing, but they do like you.

There was a voice mail message on my phone that came in at 10:30 that said they were wondering if David was going to stop by to say goodbye to them. They were dressed and weren't going anywhere. Paloma said they also called at the office looking for us. So I left a message on Marley's voice mail telling her that when Anne and Poppi took her home to have them look at the pictures on the dining room table and that there is one wrapped in tissue paper for them. They took it and Marley said they liked it.

I spoke to them on the phone and apparently they were waiting for us to call them. They didn't understand that we were engaged. My father said "I didn't know". I said "didn't mom tell you?" He said she said something about David asking her which they both thought was the strangest thing they'd ever heard of since I have been doing whatever I wanted since I was a kid. They didn't realize that you had asked me and that I had said yes! I explained to them that it was just a nice old fashioned thing you were doing in asking them and that the question was entirely between me and him. And had I not said yes why would I have allowed him to spend $60 to call them? I explained that that was our way of breaking the news to them and we were hurt by the response. I said that we were hurt that they didn't mention it Friday night and that my father didn't even get on the phone. They said that I was in a hurry to get off the phone and I said that was because they were draining my energy with negativity and I didn't want that especially at this happy time for me.

Anyway, bottom line is they do like you and did want to see you today. I told them that you liked them as well and that we both said we want to be married 50 years and have a marriage just like theirs. That warmed their hearts quite a bit. I also told them that you not only paid for the phone call but the picture and the frame as well. I wanted them to know that you aren't like Tony, who lived off my income. You are, in fact, a very successful businessman; but you've been temporarily wiped out by your ex wife and are now in the process of rebuilding so you can come here with good assets from the sale of a good business. They still can't understand why you didn't find a woman in England and they also can't believe that we both will be faithful for 5 years but we know we can so that is all that really matters.

Please send me a little note telling me you are home before you go to sleep and then have a blissful sleep. I am there with you in your bed and always will be. While it will take a little getting used to writing instead of being in person, I really do feel the bond to be every bit as strong. I look forward to our life together in every aspect.

Your adoring soul mate, lover, goddess, queen and devoted wife
Dianne

Honey I'm Home!!

My dearest Dianne

Well it's 10:30am UK time and I have just arrived home. Chicago left late and London made us wait. I eventually found my third love (the other purring female) [meaning his Jaguar] only 10 rows from where I thought. Very slow driving home; do try Gatwick rather than Heathrow for your visit.

Excellent news about Anne and Poppi (tell them I am so pleased). Another good reason for not having an English wife is I had one already, and didn't like it so want a more regal one (Princess, Queen, Goddess and Angel). Very much more exotic and exciting and lovely and sexy and perfect!

The electric blanket is on (a substitute for my dearest love until January).

My answer phone had many messages on it – including one from Denise asking if I was going to Boston to meet her for a cup of tea as I owed her that much! (What would I have been able to say to someone I had ditched at the 11th hour in favour of another woman?) Well as you know, I didn't!

I too have had the best two weeks of my life and I know without doubt you are the one for me. I love you! xxxx Did you see me waving from the plane in Orlando? I had to explain most of the story to the old lady sitting next to me. She liked it!

Must sign off now to unpack, put washing on and sleep. I love you now and always and yes without others! I don't feel I am missing you as you are with me as I thought you would be.
Love you and will ring later on
David
xxxxx

Re: Honey I'm Home!!
Dearest David
I love you and I'm so glad you made it home safely. Sleep well my king, I'm there with you always. I am now about to have a very busy day just catching up on phone calls, emails, bank stuff and bills and just getting oriented to what is happening here. Looking forward to hearing your voice later today.
Your lover
Dianne

Your voice soothes and excites me....
My King
Hearing your voice gives me all sorts of warm fuzzys. It's a little different now that we have been together. It's even more comfortable and right but no less sexy. I only have a second because I have to answer some business email and then go shopping and food shopping with Nicki. Just wanted you to have a little note from me when you wake up tomorrow. Sleep peacefully my love and I send you warmth and courage to face business challenges tomorrow. I'll remember your strength as I make business contacts to grow my business this week at the Cruiseathon. You never leave me even for an instant.
Your devoted lover
Dianne

A King's strength for my wonderful SeaGoddess
Dearest Dianne

Your words and voice mean so much to me too – I love you so much. xxx

I too am pushed for time so I will be brief. Good luck with your new business ideas, and look on everyone as a potential source of recovery for your business. I will be there with you, standing very close behind you to whisper helpful thoughts in your ears and to nibble your neck.

       I love you now and always.

Your King

David

xxxxx

Dear Diary what a day it's been ....Wednesday

My dearest of dear seagoddesses

Wednesday, 8th December 1999 – my first full day back at work.

I told Shirley about us. Not the best news I could have given her. She was very upset and mixed up. She was happy for me/us, but felt that any minute I would be leaving to be with you, and I had not even told her about our engagement (that will follow when she is ready, after the March cruise). She asked to see the photos and I agreed to take them in tomorrow. I wanted to tell everybody today, but have to do it in a suitable order, priorities first!

I told Doug and Eileen tonight, (they are my alternative parents as they chose me) and showed them the photos. They were delighted and invited us to dinner. I agreed on our behalf as they already think you are wonderful!

That's the news apart from the bad news about our position at work when I returned home (not being able to pay the 3 tax bills that are due right now).

I love you for now and always

Your King of Florsex

David

xxxxx

Dear Diary – Thursday evening

My dearest love

Today I travelled to Kent and saw a customer who had to be convinced that we had the answer to his problem and that we know what we are talking about. I took Daniel with me as head of development. We persuaded them that they should have the best quality job available and not compromise due to logistical problems as they had felt was the answer. I felt we did a very good job. When we got back Daniel told me that he thought the way I played them was masterful, then I overhead him tell Reg the same thing. This is praise indeed, but I do feel so strong with you in my life. I hope very deeply that you have been having similar successes at the Cruiseathon.

We had a valuable rush job due to leave today and some of the staff had worked very hard to get things done for the others to complete. They just left and went home leaving the work undone, so Daniel, John and I stayed to complete it and Reg drove it to Brighton to the customer's home ready for the morning. People will be spoken to on Monday morning!

I will be working in the morning, then picking mum up for a drive out to tell her what a lucky son she has.

I do miss holding and touching you, and can't wait to hear your lovely voice again. I love you so much and miss you deeply physically, but spiritually I know you are right here with me, and it is so wonderful I could yell I love you; but people would think me mad and lock me up. I'm not mad, just madly in love with the most wonderful woman I have ever known.

Your strong king of florsex

David the great

xxxxxxxxxxxx

Dear Diary – Saturday

Dearest Dianne

How I miss you, life is very quiet without you. I can see your image as I relax my eyes, feel our warmth as I go to sleep, hear your giggle when I smile, but I miss your presence in my life.

It was made much worse today, when telling mum and you were not there to hug as I did it. She seemed pleased, but also worried that I would up and leave her alone with him! I reassured her that it was a longer term plan, to build up and sell the business first. This should generate money and maybe she could have use of my flat, or come to the US too (staying somewhere else nearby but not with us – she does not want to be a burden and I don't wish that either). She was happy though. So tomorrow it's Rachel's turn and I expect happiness there too. I brought mum over to the flat for the afternoon/evening to talk alone to her and show her the photos. I also took her shopping for food so that we could have tea (roast pousin with honey and ginger, baked potato and gravy, with sprouts and butter). Not too bad even if I do say so myself. I think I will have great fun cooking for you.

Part of the discussion with mum was related to the conversation with Aunty Margaret (from Kissimmee) where she told me that she didn't understand why mum stayed with dad. That progressed to her saying she was too tired to leave and me telling her that that was how I was, my energy being drained by Chris, but now I am with you and so full of happiness. Wow! She also felt her income was too low to move away, but she was trying not to loose her capital so she could leave it to me. I explained that although £40,000 was good, from my point of view, it was a bad burden, if I received it as a result of her suffering. Her entire demeanour changed and I could see her re-thinking the position. I explained that if she didn't go too silly with the money it could last 10 years. (I know she isn't expecting to be here in 10 years time). Then she could go into a home, paid for by the government, as a worst position, and hopefully, I would have the money to make the last few years as comfy as possible, no matter where that may be. It's down to her to make the next move.

Goodnight my love, my angel, my lover, my soul mate,

my wife.
Your loyal and strong King
David of Florsex
xxxxxxxxxxxxxx

Dear Diary – Sunday
My dearest Dianne

More news, Rachel is very happy for us and that is pleasing. No mention from her about me leaving her alone, so instead I told her that one day she would have somewhere warm for holidays. She was happy. I asked Rachel for a prediction of Vickie's reaction. She said she didn't know but knew it would be much warmer than a few years back. So I rang her just now and asked when she was working this week, with a view to going down to see her and tell her my wonderful news. We will be making the date tomorrow night after I have checked my diary at work.

I have been sleeping much longer since I returned. Today I awoke after 11 hours and then spent an hour lazing in the bath thinking of you. I know you are working hard this week on your business and I also know you can make a big success of it and I am so proud of you!

Looking forward to your phone call tonight!
Lots of love and devotion
David of Florsex
xxxxxxxxxxxxxx

I adore you!
Dearest David

It was so good to hear your voice last night. I was really missing it. You make me feel wonderful. Ours is truly an enchanted relationship. I think you are the greatest and I know that you did a wonderful job this morning with the army. You face dragons with the grandest bravery, cross oceans to find your beloved, so what's an army! Really, I'm truly impressed with your business

258

abilities. You can do absolutely anything. I'm looking forward to hearing your good news tonight.

Remember our song "You Can Relax Now". Don't ever doubt my devotion to you. We will always be aware of the necessity to keep our love sacred and not ordinary and to always honor each other and our relationship. But you truly can relax now. You've found me and there is no chance you'll ever lose me. You are everything to me.

Well my love, I have a lot to do here at Dreamtime, a very lot. I remember what I was going to tell you about Wednesday. I had a nice talk with the person putting together some of the Inner Voyage land journeys. She and I have an excellent working relationship as well as personal and she may want to use Dreamtime to sell some other things she creates. She understands how I've built Dreamtime and she wants a retail travel agency like that behind her. She is a wholesaler, not a retail travel agency.

I love you my king and I'll write to you later.
Your devoted queen
Dianne

More from Dreamtime
Hi my love

I am swamped here! We have tons of people to send brochures to. Islands Magazine just sent us about 80 leads. They send us mailing labels but we still have to stuff the brochures with price list and deck plan, close them with little sticky dots and put a stamp on them. Lots of busy work. I'm going to see if my daughters will work at all during their Christmas break that starts soon and get them to do some of the busy work. Gloria just told me that she is taking the last two weeks of the year off to go with her daughter and son-in-law (my cousin) to California and Lake Tahoe and Las Vegas. I can't really tell her no as she is just part time. Janet is off next week so that week will be just me and Paloma.

I have to run now so I can get home and then get Nicki to cheerleading. Then I pick up Marley's boyfriend and take them both to the mall so we can all do a little holiday shopping. Then I pick up Nicki at 9:00, go home and fall asleep soon thereafter. I won't be able to write again tonight. I hope all went well for you today. I thought of you constantly.

Love from your devoted goddess

Dianne of Florsex

What a day!

My dearest Dianne

I am very pleased to hear about your networking with the land journeys woman, that's very good. Every extra product you can sell in your own market is very welcome. Great news, well done! It is also great news that you have lots of mailings to do. Hopefully it will end up with a percentage turning into paying passengers.

Well over to my day, the Army:

The first person to turn up came in a wheel chair, with no advanced warning to me, others had been told but nobody told me, and didn't think of checking the loos, [restrooms] etc. So I made that the first thing on the agenda, he was so pleased. The rest of the visit was great. All five of them were totally in awe of the company and the services offered, leaving to tell the relevant people in the MOD and Army about us. This is down to the strength you gave me. I did feel powerful, and all of their worries were dealt with in the first few minutes.

At the end of the meeting they told me that companies like British Aeorospace would be after buying us up, once we got involved properly because we would upset their plans and systems. They strongly advised against it, as they would lose out. Wow, does the purchasing battle for PRS begin sooner than forecast?

After work I drove to Southampton to see Vickie. Well, it took a long time to bring myself to tell her; she always has so much to say about her life and I thought that ought to be allowed to happen first. So then I told her about the internet, meeting you, and how well we were getting on, showed her the photos, answered the ever-present question (am I going to the USA) with a maybe but not this year! She wasn't like Rachel, but she too is happy for us, and would like to meet you. I asked her if it was a shock that I should now be in love with someone other than her mother, and she said that she had sort of expected it to happen sooner or later. I love you so much, and long to be with you soon. She was fine about her birthday and everything. I almost can't believe it. I really was expecting jealousy, even if only limited amounts. I am so happy!

I love you and long for you, to have and to hold from this day forward...

Your loving King and devoted soul mate

David of Florsex

xxxxxxxxxxxxx

You are amazing!!!

Dearest David

You are the greatest! I am so proud of you and I'm so proud and happy that you are mine! Wow, the Army and Vickie all in one day. You can do anything. I'm so pleased that Vickie was positive about us. I can't wait to meet both of your daughters and hope they like me in person. That is very cool that there may be many wanting your company. Just keep on building it, you can do it. I'll bet you went to bed smiling tonight. I'll write tomorrow morning from work.

Your devoted lover

Dianne

Re: You are amazing!!I

Dear Dianne

I am over the moon with your comments re yesterday, and my daughters will love you in person because you are you, not because you appear in photos after my holiday along with smiles and a new story.

Now that I am up, I will get on. It's going to be busy at work and home needs me to clear up my papers that I have started sorting out as I told you last night. Plus I have the first Christmas lunch today. It is five of us from the last company, when I had to actually work for a living (when Doug was my boss). Doug is one of the five and we have been doing this for about 20 years now. I do the arranging, I'll tell you more tonight when we talk.

I love you, worship the ground you walk on and the bed you sleep in and I want to sleep curled up with you....all the time I am not fighting the dragons of life for our future.
Your soul mate and lover
David the King of Florsex
xxxxxxxxxxxx

You are doing so well
My dearest Dianne

How is Dragon Daughter progressing? Or were you saying that she had made a full recovery on your return? So as not to forget those who are not too much against us, how is Nicki? I shall not forget that goodbye from her; it did make me feel much better.

My Dragon Daughter rang while I was at work to say that she felt that she had not reacted very well to my news. It was a bit of a shock, but that was better than I had expected, so maybe she will get even better? That would be good. I will ring her later to see how she is and ask her for an explanation. Rachel also rang and said she would visit me for tea here with Matt on Sunday. She was sad that Vickie wasn't as happy as she was, but we agreed that I had done very well to get as much acceptance as I had.

The lunch went well, and everyone was pleased for us. Not many people have any concept of the internet and what power for good there is in it. They just hear the stories of evil that it also carries so this is a pleasant revelation to those who are not too sceptical of people who advertise to find their soul mate. I am very happy with this system anyway; it has worked so amazingly well for us, and I would be happy for my daughters to use it. It is a very good way to test the other person's personality and staying power prior to meeting.

A suggestion:

Why don't we have two regular calls a week, one from each of us, say Wednesday and Sunday. Please do say if this is beyond your current means and I will do them until you can afford it. So if you agree, I will ring you at 6:00 your time tomorrow.

I will go now and do some of my desperate work sorting things out.

Your totally devoted King for now and always, hoping you will keep me warm even when I'm old and gray and we have seen all there is to see and done all there is to do! We will still be together and still in love.

David of Florsex

xxxxxxxxxxxxxx

Re: You are doing so well

Oh David of Florsex you are so wonderful!

You are the love of my life; we are quite a team. Of course I will keep you warm when you are old and gray, don't worry. Interesting thought when we have seen all there is to see and done all there is to do. What a wonderful life we have.

The magazine is being slow about deciding about their land journeys. They have already told me they don't think they'll be ready to have the first one be in the spring. They are thinking more like summer. This could mean a dry spell for a couple of months unless I get some other business quickly like the reunion cruises idea I had. They would be summer cruises but I'd start selling them in March. The magazine has given me an interesting proposition for being their conference registration company for land based weekend conferences they do. They faxed me the details and Paloma took it home with her tonight to read and evaluate. I'll look at it tomorrow. I'm not sure it would be a good thing, as I don't think they would pay enough. I'll tell you more about it when we talk on the phone and you can give me your opinion.

Dragon daughter is pretty much all better. Today was her last day of school. She doesn't have to take exams the rest of the week since she has straight A grades. She worked in my office for two hours after school today. If I don't pay her $6 an hour she'll work someplace else and I really need the help. Actually that is market rate for her age and experience. Even babysitters earn that now. Marley may work for Stan on Thursday; he pays her more. Nicki is good. I'm really happy you liked her hug and I'm happy she did that. Let me know what Vickie has to say. She may not be a dragon after all. Did you tell her that I'm also an Aquarian?

Glad to hear your lunch went so well today. That's cool that you also told all of them. Their initial impression of meeting a woman on the internet is probably that it is just a sex thing.

Two phone calls a week sounds really good to me. I think 6:00 tomorrow will be good but if I'm not there don't be mad. I have to drop Marley off at a cheerleading party that starts at 6:00 so make that 6:15. I have to pick Nicki up from cheerleading at 7:00 so I'll only have about 25 minutes.

Well my love, I am going out now with the girls again for some more holiday shopping. Hopefully I'll catch up on my rest this weekend in between working a lot. Sleep well my king.
Your adoring goddess
Dianne

Re: You are doing so well
To my wonderful warm and sexy queen of Florsex

Our three quarters of an hour took no time at all last night, being with you is so terrific.

Your conference deals…sound good, and could be calculated out to see if they are economic so you have a reasonably clear idea of what your costs are and what you will earn. There may be a problem though if there isn't enough in it. You said that the mailing list belongs to the magazine, and the cruises belong to

Peter, but the cruises are also the magazine, isn't that right, and they are the same audience, so they will cross over. Peter will only gain from this and they would gain too, so isn't it worth asking to use each list together?

I didn't tell Vickie about you both being Aquarians as my worry is jealousy and that is making comparisons. People over here don't actually say that the internet is a sex thing; they just show signs of worry, so I tell them about general chat for months first.

It's so good to now have the date of January 27th to focus on for your visit. I gave Reg a two week period to keep clear of selling trips but now I can reduce it. I'm so pleased you have booked the flights!

I wish you were coming with me tonight to the office Christmas party. That would be perfect, a night out, and then to come home in each other's arms. I'm looking forward to a more relaxed conversation on Sunday night with my angel. I may have news of Vickie by then.

Talk again soon, I love you so much, now and forever
Your King
David of Florsex
xxxxxxxxxxxxxx

The Christmas party
Hello my love

I wish I were with you tonight too. Soon I will be. I just finished the last of my holiday shopping. I did it with Marley who worked with me this afternoon. It was actually quite nice; she had me to herself and liked it. The pool is costing me a total of about $200 to finally fix it. Marley is going to clean it and shock it with the chemicals tomorrow. Being broken for over a week caused it to get algae. The pool guy explained everything to her and she understands it. She even let him use her tool kit to tighten things up. She told him that she's the man of the house. I think she likes that role. Interesting dragon. I do love her so much, in spite of her tendency to be a dragon at times.

Well, I have gifts to wrap that I'm giving to staff tomorrow (Gloria is then out the rest of the year and Janet is off next week). Also, I have some work to finish. I have to clean up the house tonight too since the cleaning person is coming tomorrow and it's too much of a mess for her to clean. I haven't even unpacked yet from the cruise conference! I did go food shopping yesterday and Terri and the girls were very happy.

I don't have to make any decision on the conference registration business for at least another week. I have to have a long talk with Linda at the magazine hopefully tomorrow. The entire thing may be put on hold until January as she leaves on the 26th for Hawaii for the millennium event there and is really busy for the next week.

Better run...I'm swamped, exhausted and have PMS!
Your loving goddess
Dianne of Florsex

Re: The Christmas Party
Good morning my glorious goddess

I woke up rather late from last night which went very well! A great selection of people including partners.

It looks like Marley would be best tackled by assuring her that I am less of a man than her!

More people are aware of the vague idea I had re quantum links than I imagined.

Must go, regrettably.
I love you
David of Florsex – King of our spiritual empire, lover of the queen, soul mate of the goddess, and luster after the woman xxxxxxxx

Re: The Christmas Party
Good morning my love

I just love your words, you are so cool and I am so pleased. How's that for half American and half British! I am the luckiest woman in the universe to be your queen. The queen got in trouble this morning. I got a speeding ticket on my way to work. I tried everything to talk the officer out of it. (I'm really stressed, single mom, business understaffed, holiday season, his supervisor lives in my neighborhood, his kid plays with my kid, verge of nervous breakdown, can't afford the insurance if they raise my premium again, pppllleeeeaaassee (that was a whine)). I should have said I'm the Queen of Florsex! Nothing I said worked. I got a $155 ticket. Now I am really stressed.

Well, I better get to the work that I speeded here for. I will write you a better letter tonight. I'm glad your party went well, you deserve good times.

Your devoted and slightly stressed goddess
Dianne

My goddess....I LOVE YOU xxxxx
Oh dear my speedy goddess

What sort of speed were you doing to get a fine so high? Our standard fine is $60, which is what I got for doing 93mph in a 70mph area. I only did it once, didn't like it and so won't do it again – getting fined, not going fast!

I barely believe, even now, that I could be so lucky as to have such a perfect wife (other than the speeding ticket). I was talking to Reg today and he was very interested in us and how we could be so compatible from the beginning. While talking to him, I came to a greater realisation of just how lucky I am. He told me tales of meeting great women he got on so well with, but there was nothing great elsewhere (he means in bed – he is British too). Or women who were keen in bed but lacked personality. He was amazed that I should be able to meet you, via the internet, and know within less than a second that I would allow my reserve to vanish. That is what happened, when you were still 20 yards away, I knew I was going to kiss you, and that the phone calls were for real…and wow! What a wonderful fortnight we had…looking forward so much to January. Only 40 days to go!

Reg and I went to school together from age 11 to 16 and he is exactly the same now as he was then, but he looks a bit older. He spent 4 ½ years unemployed before we took him on and we think he should do very well. He arranges our visits out, and there is going to be an increasing number of those due to our low turnover. The next is Tuesday/Wednesday, so there will be no communication Tuesday night. Then in the New Year, he has already got lots of them up to your visit and already one in February.

Today at about 11:00, I had a phone call from a customer in Scotland who told me he was flying down on Monday with a serious problem for us to fix urgently. That will keep me busy until lunch when I have Paul the non executive director here to discuss business and do our annual appraisals. He is due to come back to the flat after that for a meal and a general chat about life, etc. I have told him about you and how happy I am. I seem to be telling everybody, and that is not like me. He knows that Shirley is not too sure of what I am going to do, but he knows like me that the business will do well while I am so happy, and I know the same will be true for you too. Isn't life great?

Tomorrow night has come around quickly. Graham and Moira are coming around for dinner, and although they don't know it, they are also due to be told. I'm a little peckish [hungry] now, so I will prepare some tea, and maybe start on the dinner for tomorrow night.

Sorry again about your ticket – but please take some of my strength, and become as ultra happy as I am.

Your lover, friend and king

David of Florsex

I need you…….

Dearest David

Wow, I'm not usually this needy, but I sure do need you right now. I got my period early this morning (right on time) and I have really bad cramps. Please put your hand on my belly and keep it there. Your hand is so healing to me. I'll write you that longer letter I promised you now. I'm all alone in the house now until 11:00 when Marley and Mike return and I have to take them back to Lake Mary.

I was going 17 miles over the speed limit, which I guess was only 35 on Tuskawilla Road. That means I was going 52. That's the road where they are cutting down the trees and making four lanes. We have high speeding tickets here. He actually did me a favor as the sign said speeding fines doubled in construction zone. He told me he wasn't going to write it up as a construction zone even though he could. So it could have been over $300! Now I have to go to traffic school to avoid points on my license. Do you have traffic school there? It is four hours and really boring and I have better things to do with my time. That hurts worse than the fine, believe me! My time is money and I hate wasting my time. I guess I see the world rather black and white. I want to be either working or playing (or working and playing at the same time). Traffic school is right up there with cleaning house as not fitting the description of either working or playing and not what a goddess should be doing! I do think though that even the most mundane task would be in the playing category if you were with me. You make everything fun.

Reg sounds nice. Will I meet him? I love the way you describe telling people about us. The wonderful thing is I feel totally the same way. You couldn't be a more perfect husband either. We are incredibly compatible. I also knew from 20 yards away that I was going to kiss you!

That's great that he is arranging all those visits out for you. Does Shirley go with you on all of them? You are doing such a good proactive job business wise. I'm bogged down with so many details and busywork right now that I should have staff do, that I can't create new business right now. I'm going to work most of tomorrow to try to get caught up and organized so that maybe next week can include some outreach. You inspire me! I want to be just like you!

That is very cool that you also told Paul. I knew that with you I finally found a man capable of sharing his feelings (not just with me but with other people too). You may have needed my magic and inspiration, and I need to be able to give that to somebody who can receive it and run with it! Tell me again about Graham and Moira (the next people who will be told about us). I don't remember their story.

I will definitely accept taking some of your strength and don't worry; my happiness hasn't skipped a beat. I'm just tired and stressed and have cramps but that doesn't stop my happiness.

Love forever

Dianne of Florsex

Good morning my goddess

My special angel, soul mate and lover

I am so incredibly lucky to have you! You are amazing , sexy, lovely, beautiful, fun, creative and understanding. I hope you have had a good night's sleep after your busy evening. I am very tired after mine, and so happy, and it's all down to this miracle of our incredible relationship.

When you arrive at Gatwick, there will be hundreds of people waiting at the barriers at customs, all waiting to make love to their loved ones. But nobody will be as happy to see anyone arrive as I will ......I long for your arrival!

I hope today at work will be successful, it's bound to be good with so many brochures going out, just through the maths of quantity.

I must dash, bath, work etc. I will read/write again later. Don't worry if your work means you have too little time, I do understand.

I love you so much now and always

David

xxxx

I ADORE YOU!!

Oh my King

   If you make me any happier I shall explode! It feels so good to be desired by you and to desire you. I'm slowly but surely getting organized. This will take all weekend to do. I'm trying to put about 10 hours of in office work in and another 5 at home catching up on trade magazines and the rest of the piles of reading material in my room. I also have to catch up on bills and other paperwork at home. I plan to catch up on sleep and yoga too in the next couple of days. I want to be healthy, wealthy and wise when I land in London! I'm already happy. I'll write to you later tonight and let you know how I did today. I want to be disciplined at work first. Just know that you never leave my mind and everything is easier and more fun because of you.

Your soul mate

Dianne of Florsex

Chapter Eighteen
The End of the 20ᵗʰ Century

Your magic and my happiness
My wonderful soul mate David
Wow! I'm really in the flow today. I just had two good incoming phone calls. I bonded with both of the people. Both women 60 years old. One going through a divorce. I really got the magic of the cruise through to them and they are both excited and feel it will change their lives. Although they both want to receive the brochure in the mail before making a final commitment, I told them I'd pencil them into their requested cabin category and they both said thank you, I know I'm coming. They both are so glad I'll be on the cruise and can't wait to meet me. When I feel good I can really do this. Thank you for making me feel so good. Okay, I have to go back to work, just had to tell you this and say thank you.
Your soul mate forever
Dianne
p.s. – Do you feel this is getting stronger by the day? I do.

My soul mate David

Where did you come from it happened so fast
Out of my dreams my soul mate at last.
Your touch it is gentle, your heart is sincere.
You even understand me, I have nothing to fear.

With you I'm a woman, with passion and desire.
With you I'm alive, you light my fire.
I totally receive you, a goddess in love.
You're a king of all men, a gift from above.

We've been lovers before, what took you so long.
I've known too many men who for me were all wrong.
Your touch is electric, your words hypnotize.
Your mind it is brilliant, you are very wise.

You see I adore you, you're the light of my life.
And I'm honored and pleased to be your chosen wife.
I need you and want you to have and to hold.
I want to see the world with you before we get too old.

You soothe me, you excite me, you heal me too.
The nice thing is I do the same for you.
You're my soul mate, my lover, my very best friend.
I'll love you forever, our story has no end.

So hold me dear David and never let me go.
I give you my heart and I want you to know
I find our love sacred, enchanted and real.
My spirit entwines yours my body loves to feel.
Your embrace keeps me warm on a cool winter night.
My soul is rejoicing, with my world all is right.

My Soul mate Dianne

Oh Dianne

Is there no end to this, you write so amazingly; that poem was so special. I feel even more special than I did yesterday. You too have such power, we are going to be ecstatic for the next thousand years, and others everywhere will benefit from this power.

Like you I know that in a future life we will have children. Just think how wonderful they will be with the combinations of our genes, giving intuition, poetry, mathematics, love of travel, love of life, love to give others, no fear of dragons….we will be so happy!

Last night we had snow and this morning it is still here! Maybe it will do that when you are here and we could take a stroll to the sea through the snow and then warm up nicely on our return.

I have a lot of clearing up to do from last night, plus prepare for tonight's tea (Rachel and Matt). I will write again soon but first I have to say two things. 1) Your poem was the loveliest I have ever read, let alone had written for me – that was so special. xxxx 2) I love you so much! You are incredible and I honour our magic relationship and always will.

Your lover and king

David of Florsex

You ARE special

My David

I'm glad my words made you feel special, you are special. You are the most wonderful thing that has ever happened to me and I honor our magic relationship just like you do.

You write the most wonderful things to me. You have since the very first day you wrote to me. You did when I didn't. Your heart was with me a long time before you even realized it. Suzin the seawitch must have put an enchantment on you. I only pray it never disappears. The problem with other lives is we have to be kids with parents again, go to school, be adolescents, have our hearts broken, etc. It's highly unlikely that we will meet and never separate from age 5 on. We should probably go for meeting at 25 when we have "been there done that" enough to recognize love when we see it.

Now at 45/46 we are mature (well sort of), financially stable (well sort of), free to travel and enjoy life (well almost). Okay, so we are madly in love, still have lots of obligations, but it doesn't matter, not even the 4,000 miles that separate us, because we've found each other and our lives are enchanted!

Snow! How romantic! I hope that we get snow when I'm there. A stroll to the sea and warming up on our return sounds wonderful even if it doesn't snow.

I'm going to read the Sunday paper now and go to work around 11. Have a nice evening with Rachel and Matt and I'll look forward to talking with you on Monday.

Your devoted lover

Dianne of Florsex

Re: You ARE special

My most lovely cuddly one

I spoke to Vickie and she has said that she would like the four of us to go out for dinner on her birthday. No doubt somewhere expensive, but this will be good as you will meet Rachel and Vickie and socialise. I have left the venue to Vickie; I hope she will be staying with Rachel that night.

If we meet at 5 years old (and people do), that will be very romantic and it would cut down the heartbreaks. Let's not have another life like the early part of these. Let's start the way we mean to carry on – very happy.

I love you Dianne, and long to be in the same 3-dimensional world as you. But I am quietly content to wait the next 39 days knowing we are together in spirit. I am an eager learner of all things spiritual and look forward to learning with you.

I better go read more of the business emails you sent me yesterday before you ask me questions and I appear ignorant of their contents.

I love you so much my super goddess

David

xxxxxx

Re: You ARE special

My most handsome cuddly one

Okay, this is the last letter. I really have to get more work done, but I just love your words and your spirit and have to respond.

Very cool (I am so pleased) about Vickie. I can't wait for that dinner! I hope they like me. I'm just going to be natural and be myself and be very loving to you. That's okay, right? Wow, the four of us, I feel like a family. I love you!

Regarding learning about spiritual things, you intuitively know everything; you just don't realize it yet. If you want a book suggestion that is really good for beginners to this stuff, it is "The Celestine Prophecy" by James Redfield. You can get it on Amazon. com or I can bring you my copy when I visit. It is actually fiction, but it is a story about how the world will be when we all recognize our true spiritual identity. It's about synchronicity, the human energy field and that of plants, etc, intuition and insights that mankind will discover as we evolve spiritually. It is written as an adventure taking place in Peru. I know you'd like it.

Thank you for your support of me business wise. It means the world to me. I'm going to work on the business plan as soon as I get out from under this clutter. I'm so in awe of you and the great success you had with the Army. I know that is only the beginning for you. It's easier for you to learn my business than it is for me to learn yours, but I know an excellent salesperson, relationship builder and businessman when I see one. You are so perfect…spiritually oriented and a business person just like me. No wonder I don't scare you….you are my equal. Remember I told you I scare most men.

You are more than a soul mate, you are a twin flame. I love you!

Dianne in awe of her wonderful husband

They will love you almost as much as I do when they see us together
Dianne

Twice now I have spotted your insecurity regarding Vickie. She will love you if you are yourself. It was just a shock, me saying I love you without having mentioned you before. Rachel confirmed that too. Maybe I was wrong to keep quiet until I was sure, but that is me!

You are wonderful, and they will see how I feel about you, in case they just think it was sex on holiday making me see you through rose coloured glasses. Anyone who meets us together will know how we feel, or they are blind to real emotion. Rachel is not, and I hope Vickie isn't either, but if she is, then Rachel will be able to explain.

Please don't think of Vickie as a dragon. She can be, but she isn't breathing smoke about you, she wouldn't have said the four of us if she was. So please smile and be relaxed.

I have so much to say to you from my heart and soul, but time will make me sleep very soon.
Your lover and greatest admirer.
David xxxxx

Forward: My letter to the magazine

This is what I wrote to Linda at the magazine about my current thoughts on the conference business. Please give me your opinion.

Hi Linda

It's Saturday and I'm spending a good part of today and tomorrow here. I have tons of catch-up paperwork to do and I'm also answering the phone and talking to some really nice people. I like the people who subscribe to Andrew Weil's newsletter. We should have used that mailing list a long time ago! I predict a lot of sales from it. I have two already who want to see the brochure first but I think I did a good enough job talking to them today that I am positive they are booking. I told them I'd pencil their names into their desired cabin category until Thursday and they asked me to do that. This is a nice group of people to talk to, just like the Red Rose clientele were. Get me more of those people!

I'm really devoted to this niche so I hope there is some way we can make the conference business work. The numbers still don't look so good to me and there are a few things that scare me. One of them is depending on your accountant to pay me on time. I'm sorry but I find her really difficult. I'll need an assurance on how that system will work.

Can you send me examples of the reports you are asking for and what "marketing data" means exactly? Also, do you anticipate four of these conferences a year which means I would multiply the anticipated payment by four? I have a lot of other questions that are too long to write here. I know you are going to be really busy next week getting ready for the Hawaii millennium event so if you could just answer the above and fax me examples of reports we can cover the rest next year/century/millennium.

While I'm in the flow and really connecting with people today, I guess I should try to express my feelings about "selling" vs "registering". This concept of registering is foreign to me as I'm used to relationship selling, getting into the client and answering their fears and concerns. I can't believe that just because the product is just a weekend conference the client is any different. This may be why we close more sales than your current conference registration company registers people. Is there any way you could change your paradigm of the process a little and find a way for us to be able to do it our way, which would include building a relationship and cross selling in all directions – cruise/land based journey/weekend conference? I'd be willing to bet we could do a good sales job on this. You have nothing to lose, I pay the phone bill. Let me know your thoughts.

Dianne

Re: Fwd: My letter to the Magazine
Hi Dianne

This is very good. You know how to mix buttering up with pushing your requirements, and that is going to be necessary as you spread the work load amongst other suppliers. Well done! I only have a minute now but we can discuss this more on the phone.
I love you my great seagoddess
David
xxxxx

Fwd: Re: I like your cruise offers
David

This forwarded email from a previous client is one reason I keep doing this even though with the overhead we've talked about me having I'm not making any money.

Hello Dianne

How sweet of you to remember me. Strange as it may seem, that cruise adventure made me very happy! Would you believe that I still keep my cruise guest card from the Costa Romantica. If somehow, one of your cheapest cabins became available at the last minute, do let me know. I enjoyed working with you. You're an excellent businesswoman and an all around important people-person. I still have a yin/yang Bermuda insignia on my key chain that always reminds me of that terrific Inner Voyage. Today, I meditate daily and also listen to nature/ocean sound CDs while on my computer. The trip made that much of an impact on me. I do dream of taking one again, not only for the journey, but to visit the peace and tranquillity of the various islands. Hey, you aren't called Dreamtime for nothing! Do keep in touch.
Camille

Re: I like your cruise offers
Oh Dreamy cruise arranger

Your lips are so sweet, your body so wonderful. Your cruises are a dream – even being on other people's cruises with you is heaven. Roll on March, when I can taste your work first hand and sleep with the boss too!

Other people do love you and the service you provide. I will be very honoured to join your team one day in our future together. Lots more love
David

Re: Offering of a free newsletter

"Everything we ever want /need will be ours, if we are wise about what we want". I agree totally. What a wonderful life we have created!

I've already received another one of these newsletters. Do you want me to forward it to you or will it bog you down with more than you want to read? It's very new millennium oriented regarding the next 1000 year cycle.

You know, somebody said to me that they can't believe you and I aren't finding a way to be together for New Years Eve. I said why, it's only a day. She said it's a day that won't come again for 1,000 years. But really, 27 days after the turn of the millennium won't happen again for another 1,000 years either! It's only a day. Collective consciousness has placed an awful lot of importance on that day, and besides, we will be together. We'll be on the phone and in bed together. What do other people know anyway?

I love you and must get back to work now.
Your devoted soul mate
Dianne

Re: Offering of a free newsletter
Hello again

Yes, I would appreciate the copy, even if I just read the highlights ….I ought to read more anyway.

Your friend is right, we should be together, and we are, they just don't have our level of love to see it.

I welled up with emotion from your words. I love you so much, only we know our love, and the rest of the universe is missing the point. Although I do long for the 3D contact, I can wait another 27 days for you. You are worth waiting another 1000 years for!

Lots more true love
David
xxxxx

Re: Good bookings coming

Darling David

It is probably true that not enough people have said good things to me. Not enough people have told you how wonderful you are either. (Except for the recent fan club of Denise and the Queen (who said you were quite a dish). For me, I've had compliments, but not from the people who "should" be giving them (my parents, my husbands, Peter, the magazine). So yes, you make me feel really good. Especially since what you say is from the heart and you aren't trying to get something from me.

Wow, we are almost instant messaging each other today with our back and forth comments!

I adore you now and always
Dianne

Re: Good bookings coming

Darling

I do want something from you – I am just like everyone else in your life. The only difference is that I am prepared to give you everything for one of your smiles, and to borrow to pay for a kiss, work hard for a touch, and die to be in your arms.

The reply from the magazine reads very well but for the bit where she says she is only going to do one or two in the coming year. She was very good about cross selling, and genuinely sounds like she liked receiving your email – ten out of ten. I now have to ask the old question. Where is year 2000's income coming from? This was not meant to stress you, as you have had plenty today, but from a deep sense of love, which is sent to protect you from the grief of no income.

This is about the coldest I have ever been in this flat so I will close now and go to bed and eagerly await Wednesday night when I can call you again. I love you and miss you physically.
Your lover, soul mate and frozen King
David

What a day!
My wonderful David

I think today has certainly been an all time record of writing emails to each other. I really enjoyed it (and our talk) and I even got a lot of work done today besides. I'm running on extra energy right now. You gave it to me! Everything we talk about is meaningful. I loved spending the day with you today. Yes, it has been 13 days since we had physical 3rd dimension contact. In some ways it feels like only yesterday since we are so close spiritually. In other ways it seems like it has been much longer as I really do long for you.

I'm looking forward to meeting both of your daughters. I picked Marley up from her dad's tonight (Nicki was at a friend's house) and I was chatting with her and I told her that I'm going out to dinner with David and his two daughters. She looked kind of surprised or sort of had a faraway look in her eyes. I said "I hope they are nicer to me than you were to him." She didn't say anything, just remained quiet. I think the idea of me as part of another family is weird to her. I had to adjust to her and Nicki being part of another family. At Stan's house I see pictures on his wall of the four of them and it feels strange to me, at least it used to. I'm used to it now. I don't own my children; they are spiritual beings on their own accord. Maybe me telling her this has made it sink in how serious I am about you.

Stan bought Marley a model car (the same model that Mike may get in a real car) a 1964 Chevy Impala. She is putting it together and painting it now. Mike doesn't think she can do it without him. Of course she is proving that she can. She is one determined girl!

Well, bed is calling me so until tomorrow.

Your enchanted lover and soul mate

Dianne

Re: What a day/weekend/life!

Darling Dianne

You make the sun shine in my life and always will. This weekend was so special with us writing and talking so much. I am more rested than further forward, but that is further forward in itself. Interesting to see Marley's reaction to you meeting V & R. Nicki's would be interesting too.

Don't worry about the 5 year plan. It may take longer, but like you I am already aching to be together and will do everything I can to speed it up, and the Army may just do that. Please be sure the 5 years was not a way of holding you off, it was just a best guess figure from back then. So be sure I will not be here any longer than necessary for my staff and us.

Love from your bewitched King and Soul mate

David

xxxxx

Life is so confusing

Dearest David

I almost called you and woke you up since you are up late anyway, but I decided to put some of my thoughts in writing since I honestly don't know the answers to some of your questions in our last wonderful phone call. You ask good questions and make me think. I love you so much.

Some of my feelings are different now than they were ten years ago when I was having major problems getting along with my parents. I was trying to be an empowered superwoman then and I had a lot to prove. Now I've proved it and what I want more than anything else is a loving relationship with somebody who I can give and receive total love with. That's you! The whole consciousness of the new millennium, in my opinion, is a softer spoken more loving dynamic between men and women. I am woman hear me roar has become how can I serve you my beloved. More of a return to the 50s in some ways. We've already burned our bras, demanded orgasms, started our own businesses, raised children on our own, travelled alone, bought homes on our own, done our male bashing, etc. Now we want to curl up in a warm bed with our man. We want him to receive pleasure as that gives us a deep psychological pleasure, see the world with our man and even ask for help from our man. Wow, I used to think I was too proud to admit that one. But I like asking for help from you, whether it is hanging pictures, starting a business plan, reading my business correspondence, helping to heal my relationship with my parents. It is good to ask for your help and to see you provide it so willingly. That alone is healing for me.

I'm also not so quick to go into debt (been there done that). I wouldn't say I'm cycling back to a 50s mentality as some debt isn't all bad. I just want to be able to live on my pay check (prefer by making my pay check larger than by making my needs fewer). It's not so much us against them mentality. There certainly isn't the generation gap between our kids and us as there is between us and our parents. That's because in many ways we are still adolescents. We didn't suffer through a war and a depression like they did which caused them to grow up fast.

The thing is, my parents aren't going to change. They will most likely remain fear based and judgmental. I can heal by knowing this and unconditionally loving them anyway. I think I've already come far with them just in the past couple of months and you have been a major factor in that.

Thanks for your comments on the magazine's response to me. It is really helpful. Regarding your question of where is income coming from in 2000, the good news is that they have decided to do land journeys starting with one in the spring to Sedona. I have to review the journeys and put my desired time line on them. We are talking about Sedona, Mexico, Peru, Egypt, Tibet and Nepal and Damanhur with an Italy tour or with a Greece tour. Speaking of Damanhur, now that you are almost a quantum physicist you may be more interested in spending some time at that site and reading about time travel and the other interesting things they are doing there. Anyway, hopefully we will do four land journeys in 2000. I won't always accompany them like I do the cruises but I definitely want to go to Damanhur and I want you to go with me.

We haven't bottom-lined the money that Dreamtime makes yet. I asked for $300 a sale rather than a commission since Tibet is high priced at $5,000 and Sedona is only $1,000, yet the same amount of work goes into a $1,000 sale as a $5,000 sale. I suspect they are going to take me down to $250 a sale. I make an average of $225 a sale now on the cruises. If 200 people do a land journey in 2000 and Dreamtime makes $250 that is $50,000. Yes, I still need more but that is a start. I need to find a fall cruise for them. I'm looking at Boston to Bermuda in October, but haven't had time to work on it.

I'm also trying to figure out how to work with the high school reunion business guy to offer reunion cruises. The problem is the cruise line's required deposit to hold group space. I don't have it and neither does he. I may just have to offer cruises 'space available' and share the commission with him. It's new business in my door but not necessarily high profit. Of course volume is good too. I have to work on that as soon as I can. The Dream Network wants to work on a Dream cruise but again the same problem of no money. The vacation.com website will be doing something for me by February and I can also buy leads from CLIA (Cruise Lines International Association). I can also try buying mailing lists (just to try to sell regular cruises, not Inner Voyages).

I have two investors who have agreed to take a lesser amount as a payoff this month. Unfortunately, I had to tell both of them I won't have it this month. I'd like to try to get it to them over the next 6 months so that I can pay them off with a lesser amount. I'm going to suggest that to them. So see, I am spending a lot of time thinking about year 2000 income and expenses. Don't worry, even though I no longer describe myself as "I am woman hear me roar", I am still very determined to make this business a success. You obviously feel the same way about your business. I'm not the Suzie homemaker type. I like having a business although I'd like it to produce a little less stress and take up a few less hours and produce a lot more money!

Poor Shirley, she is worried, isn't she. Tell her that I'm convinced that you aren't going anywhere until the business is built to the point where you can get a good price. She needs to be convinced as well. So when do you go after the Navy and the Air Force? I hope you are able to have a nice heart-to-heart talk with her in the car tomorrow. I want her to like me too.

I do need to get back to my stuff that needs doing. Writing to you just helps me balance my thoughts though. It's like a diary or journal. There is something else that I wrote that I want to share with you when I find it. It isn't on the computer because I wrote it right on AOL and that disappears after a month, but I think I have a hard copy somewhere. It is something I wrote to Randall and it's about the 3 sides of me (and all women), Maiden, Mother and Crone. He only wanted to love my Maiden. I know that you love all three parts so I want you to read what I wrote. It's quite creative even if I do say so myself.

So until Wednesday night my love, I wish you safe driving, good sales calls, nice time with Shirley, health, wealth, happiness and above all love.

Your goddess of everything (that's a better term than superwoman)

Dianne of Florsex

Time to share life's confusions and sort them out xxxx
Good morning sweetheart

You were even more stressed than you sounded, and I think of you as very naughty....you were so stressed but you didn't ring me back!

Please do ring – as your husband I do expect to share your stress, as well as your love. I do tell you that being woken by you would be the kind of pleasure I long for, either to say you love me or to say you need my help to resolve something. That is so 50s, isn't it, but I long to be needed by my lover in every way. Yes, I do want to have the Maiden, Mother and Crone (but can she be sexy too!) for I shall be old one day too and wish to be wanted also. You are my chosen one, and that means all of you. I do not have any plans to change you, but to assist you change yourself (remove stress, etc) and to assist in changing your parents' perceptions of you, which can be done. I love you so much, and anything you want can be yours if you want it enough and are prepared to play chess to get it. Trust me I know... I have got you, my business and my freedom from my old queen.

You have many plans for your business, and that is excellent and essential for its success. I long to assist in any way I can, and I do feel that the future holds good opportunities for both of us together and currently separate too.

Yesterday through talking to Paul and Shirley, I realised that the engineer in me treats staff like machines. I expect that when I have oiled the machine it would run smoothly (when I have solved someone's problem they would do the job), but unfortunately, they don't do that; well not often enough anyway. There were many things I have to do as a result of my appraisal, but one of the smaller ones is removing the clutter I have collected on and around my desk (but I will try and do it to the rest of my life too).

You have answered my questions very well, especially considering you say I didn't make it clear quite what I was saying. We must be very in tune! I will no doubt upset you one day, and do hope the magic temper you possess will forgive me, as I love you. It may mean one day telling you things that are important, but you do not wish to hear, as you must do with me. Honesty is the only way for us to do our 1000 years plus. I do really wish to assist the stress in your life from your parents through modified approaches to them. It may not work, but I am optimistic that it will, with me being new to them and as they are not too against me; it may be enough to get things moving. I want to be a part of you in every way so let's make those parts wonderful together.

Wow, that is excellent news about the land journeys! They all sound wonderful and I would love to go with you on some of them. Hopefully this will reduce our worries about your finances, and empower you (as I will) to go onwards and upwards from here. Well done, I am ever so proud of you.

News flash – my radio alarm has just switched on and is playing "I knew I loved you before I met you" by Savage Garden. I will love you forever and through all parallel universes. You are so special.

I must stop now as I have to pack, have my bath, go to work and then pick up Shirley at 8:00 (so I will be rushed).

I love you – looking forward to Wednesday night.

Your King and lover

David of Florsex

Re: Time to share life's confusions and sort them out xxxx

Hello my love

I'll write to you more tomorrow. Today is another really busy day and you aren't home anyway to receive this. Just wanted to tell you I was gazing at the big full moon and thought of you gazing at the same moon. I long for the time when we will gaze at it together. Your letter that I got this morning is really special. You know exactly what to say to me. I love you now and forever.

Your devoted wife

Dianne

I'm so proud of you!!!
Darling David

It was wonderful talking to you and hearing of your recent successes with your business. You can sell to anybody! I'll be looking forward to you being my partner in Dreamtime. Wow! You inspire me with your discipline and dedication to get the job done. As soon as I can get out from under all the busy work I'll have to do for the rest of the year, I'm going to be the best salesperson for Dreamtime and make sure I dedicate a high percentage of each week to looking for new business. Even though things look good for both the conference and the land journeys business, I still want at least 25% of my business to have nothing to do with the magazine or Peter. Then I'll know Dreamtime is going to make it.

You sounded so tired. Not just sleepy but really tired. Please include rest in your plans for the holiday week. Your body, mind, spirit and soul want that. In 5 short weeks I'll be with you and I want you to be rested.
Your soul mate and lover
Dianne

The moon
Good morning my Dream Angel

When I got in last night the special moon was hiding behind the rain clouds so no signs of it. But I awoke very early with it coming through my window and lighting the whole room – wow, then I went to sleep safely knowing it was watching over you too.
xxx

Despite a good night's sleep, I am still very tired, and with Vickie here tonight, and her cat Poppy, and a plan to see Doug and Eileen, after rearranging the furniture in the flat, I will no doubt be tired tomorrow too. But I will have long lay-ins before working in the flat and factory over the break.

It was wonderful to hear that things are taking shape at Dreamtime, and you are right to keep pushing for other business.

It will only help your strength, personally, business wise and in negations with the magazine.

I love you and miss you. 5 weeks will be here very quickly, especially with the amount of work we both have to do before then. I hope not to be too tired, but that will be real (just like PMS) and we should appreciate everything about each other. I long to live with you and see all your moods, reactions etc, and fully experience living as one with you my wonderful wife.

As you may see, I am a little late for work. I'll read/write again later. I love you sweetheart. xxxx

Your king now and always

David

xxxxx

Re: The moon

Dearest David

I'm so glad you got to see the big special full moon. I didn't! We had a big cloud covering. In spite of the clouds it was very light outside but I didn't see the moon. You are so sensitive and wonderful and I can't wait to live all the time with you as well. When we are together full time I'll never experience the tired from working so hard David, because you will be done working so hard. So please ring me when you are tired and need some soft words of encouragement always during these years.

At risk of sounding insecure, I have to tell you that I spent many hours thinking about what you said last night that it could have gone the other way and you could have gone to Boston instead of Orlando. I have to organize all the email of ours that I printed out and see where my head was at different times and how our energy was flowing. I find it a complete miracle (with definite help from Suzin and Scott) that you chose me. I guess that should make me feel secure rather than insecure but you know I'm a silly woman with raging hormones sometimes, no matter how powerful I may appear as the seagoddess and President of Dreamtime. I may even feel a little insecure regarding Shirley.

Since her marriage isn't perfect, is it possible that she was looking at you with more than one retirement plan in mind?

I better get to work. Today it's just me and Paloma and I'm staying late and going to yoga tonight. I'll write again at the end of the day if all goes as planned.

I love you now and forever

The Seagoddess

Bigger answers

To my insecure soul mate

Please don't let Shirley make you feel insecure, she is in a terrible state about Steve, but her state is in trying to get him to respond to her. He is very cold in discussions about the state of their marriage and just says that she is going to leave so what is the point. I am sure she finds me wonderful, etc, but also very irritating. She is not a romantic like us. xxxxx

I long to collect you from the airport and bring you home. It will be wonderful to be together again. I have so much to do here to make it habitable for a queen.

I will look forward to reading/writing later but like you have to go to work.

Your fiancé, husband, lover, king, soul mate and knicker remover (very soon)

David

xxxxx

Re: Bigger Answers

Hello my love

Don't worry, I'm not insecure about your love for me. It wasn't easy for you to realize you did love me and you made a major and difficult exclusive decision when you did decide it was only me. I have complete faith and trust in you and your love for me. Don't stop telling me though. I do love to hear it.

I still believe that Shirley had plans on the back burner for you. Otherwise your news about me wouldn't be such a shock and so upsetting to her. She may not be a romantic like we are (and always will be) but she does fit the pattern of the stereotype of a wife. Husbands and wives do sometimes irritate each other and push each other's buttons you know. I find you perfect, but who knows, maybe in 20 years something about you will irritate me as well and even stranger to imagine something about me may irritate you! I hope you will still be my romantic soul mate when that happens.

Well, as you can see, I'm up early. I took Terri to the airport so I could hang out in heaven with you. I suspect I would have been granted entrance anyway, but what the heck. I'm already at the office and ready to finish this mailing project so it will all get picked up by the mailman when he gets here.

You don't have to call me tonight, I'm fine really, just write back. I'll call you early my time tomorrow. I have to pick up Nicki Christmas day in Lake Helen. She's spending the night with a friend's grandmother and attending their Christmas Eve party. Lake Helen is right next door to Cassadaga, the spiritualist community I told you about, so I'll probably go to the Christmas service at the Church in Cassadaga and see my friends and tell them all about you.

Hope you closed early today. Happy Christmas Eve. I adore you and send you a big hug.

Your lover who is longing for you
Dianne

Are you home yet? It's Christmas Eve!
Hi baby

You should be home by now. Are you being scrooge? I'll be at work all day. I can't seem to get the mailing finished because the phone rings and you've trained me to answer it. Also, about thirty other requests have come by mail or phone or internet just in the past 24 hours and I want to get brochures in the mail today. I can't afford to not make sales next week. I love you. Write to me

so I can check my mail and smile and not feel sorry for myself that I'm sitting here all by myself.
Love you always
Dianne
xxxxxx

Re: Are you home yet? YES
Honey I'm home.....
　　We did finish early – so tiny Tim could have a Christmas
xxxxx
　　On my way home I stopped off to get some food for the next few days. I was short of two items to do tomorrow's meal properly, sausage meat and something else. Well $100 later, I have bought the meat and plenty of things that could have been the something. I brought them in through the torrential rain, brought them upstairs, started unpacking and realised that the butter was the missing item (still)....so walked (yes, walked in the rain) to the local shop and bought bacon and butter. Now that's it, no more shopping for the next few days. It's now siege time, just Poppy and I until Vickie returns or I walk on the 27th.
　　You are getting very good now, both at the idea your customers may ring and be interested even at weekends and holidays. These could be some of your warmest leads, and they will remember the lovely person who answered on Xmas eve!
　　I will be in all day tomorrow and will look forward to your call so much. I will do a few small jobs and then ring you despite you saying not to – but I want to - I love you, and maybe I am a rebel!
Lots of love, hugs and kisses
Your King David

Flood warnings
My wife and wonderful one
　　The TV has just put out a flood warning for the South coast (me). There is the highest tide for over 100 years tonight at about

midnight, and the current storm has got the sea stirred up badly and there are 20 foot waves at the moment. I will hope that the Jaguar is only washed by rain and not sea water!

I have done two types of lottery for tonight, and they are guaranteeing to make at least 25 millionaires within the next half an hour, so by the time you read this we may be rich in money as well as love. I'll go now and see how we do – fingers crossed!

My deepest love

David

xxxxx

Re: Flood warnings

Hello my wonderful husband

That is weird that you are having a high tide tonight. That was supposed to happen with the big full moon. Delayed reaction perhaps? Please don't let it be the Y2K end of the world stuff. I would feel very cheated if the world were to end now. I'll surround your third love [the Jaguar] with lots of white light to protect her from the storm. Don't forget you can call me at any time of the day or night if you need me or want to talk. (Hmmm that sounds familiar).

Did we win the lottery? Thanks for reminding me to play here. I'll buy tickets on my way home.

I love you!

Dianne Queen of Florsex

I would rather be King Midas

My most wonderful of loves

I can't explain the reason for the high tides tonight not the 22nd, nor can I stop the waves. Thank you for the white light of protection – maybe I should go down and sleep curled up on the backseat for my safety. xxxxx

I forgot to say, John came in to work today with the copy of the book (the Celestine Prophecy) at about $7.50 which is half the original amazon.com price and a quarter of the final bill price.

Does the US tax books, or does amazon.com make the sort of profits we should be aiming at? I hope to start reading the book tonight or tomorrow.

Unfortunately we didn't win the lottery here, but the one I discussed with 25 millionaires is actually New Years Eve, not tonight. Good luck with your lottery, but we don't really need any more good fortune – or do we?

Have a wonderful night, and I will ring you with tears in my eyes if the Jaguar can't swim.

Lots of love and extra bits

David, King of your heart and soul

xxxxxxxxxxxxxxxxxxxxxxxxxxxxxxxx

King of my heart and soul

My dear King

You are all that and more. I like that King of your heart and soul. Do you feel it would be greedy of us to win the lottery since the universe already gave us each other? Maybe. We really do have all the riches in the world. I don't need to win millions but a few hundred thousand would do nicely to pay off debts and let us travel. I think for both of us our businesses are more than just the money we hope to make. They so represent who we are and we are driven to be a success for many intrinsic reasons.

I'm glad you got the book and I hope you like it. I worry about recommending something (what if you hate it?). If you get a few chapters into it we can talk about it tomorrow. In the beginning, if I remember correctly, it is a lot about synchronicity and nothing being an accident. All meetings have a purpose. Yes, we charge tax on books, don't you?

You don't have to be sitting in the car to receive my white light of protection; I always surround you with my psychic energy. I'm very sleepy and I'm going to read in bed very soon. I'll probably fall asleep before you tonight! I love you so much.

Your soul mate

Dianne, Queen/Goddess of your heart and soul

Re: King of my heart and soul

Happy Christmas my Goddess

I think that we could not win the lottery if we wished it just for ourselves; the universe would see that as greedy. But if we wanted to share our happiness, love and care...then maybe, just maybe......

You are so right that our businesses are not just financial, although my pension fund would be very useful. But there is so much waste in the world, and I feel we help in our small way to redress the waste, and could do so much more with open-minded customers. Your business has less to do with money, but that does need to be maintained now you have started to focus a little harder on it. Keep it up my love, you are doing so well.

I took the book to bed last night, read the intro, back page and the first paragraph before nodding off. I hope to read today, between cooking, eating, clearing up and playing with Poppy [Vickie's cat]. She got me up at 8:00 by crying in the kitchen, so I brought her to our bed, but she wouldn't curl up like you do. She just wanted to run around, lick my face and show me her bottom!

The storm has passed here safely, thanks to your protection. We have gone from red alert down to amber. Other areas were not so lucky. Thank you my protecting angel.

You are so wonderful, I long to hear your sexy voice again very soon.

Lots of love from your soul mate

David

xxxxxx

Merry Christmas my love

Hi honey

I just got out of bed 20 minutes ago after 13 hours in bed! I think I needed that. A couple of times I woke up and was going to get out of bed but was in such a dreamlike state that I didn't get up and I fell asleep again. I'd love to spend 13 hours in bed with you!

I just tried to call you and got the expected "We're sorry but all circuits are busy, please try your call again later". So Merry Christmas by email. I hope you are having a lovely day cooking, eating and reading. After I finish writing to you I'm going to read the paper, have a little breakfast and then try calling you again.

I hope you are enjoying the book. I have two of the sequels, *The 10th Insight* and *The Celestine Vision*.

I'm so glad your third love is fine. Vickie's little kitten is doing what they like to do. The only way you will get to sleep late this week is if you leave lots of food out for her overnight so she won't have to wake you for food. This will be a nice week for you, being mostly alone and able to just do your thing at your leisure. I'm just like you in very much enjoying my own company. We will be wonderful in that way too when we've been married awhile. Most of the time we'll be in the same house doing our own thing and can check back with each other for strokes and kisses at regular intervals. It is helpful that we are so alike. I also agree that you and I will continue to help make the world a better place.

Signing off for now, I'll try to ring again later.

Your goddess

Dianne

Re: Merry Christmas my love

Hi Gorgeous

I am sorry you didn't get through, I will be trying to make it work from here. I love you and want to hear your lovely sexy voice again.

Your desperate soul mate

David

xxxxx

After the phone call......
Merry Christmas my lover

Wow my love! What a wonderful day you have given me – I just thought I would write and say it again, you are so wonderful.

Your three stages of women, the poem you wrote me, and many more things you have written and should write will make a wonderful book of spiritual feeling from within relationships. You are very talented and I am so lucky to be your chosen one – I love you.

All this activity today has me tired out, but not tiring out Poppy who is having a mad half-hour of running, biting and chewing, so I will have an early night. Please do wish Nicki, Marley, Anne and Alex a happy Christmas from me.

Good night my angel – I love you so much.
Your ardent husband
David
xxxxx

The perfect soul mate
Darling David

I had a wonderful day today too thanks to you. I just finished organizing and reading all of our letters that I had printed out and now I'm going to finish printing out so it is caught up to today. Maybe this will be a book someday! The whole thing still has me quite amazed even though you are exactly what I asked the universe for. In fact, you do have to be careful what you ask for because when you are worthy you do get what you ask for. I remember thinking (about a year ago) that it would be nice to know my true soul mate is coming even though I'm way too busy now with children and business to be able to devote the time to a relationship. Randall was a part time relationship so he didn't interfere with the girls but he never had long term soul mate potential because what he wanted and what I wanted were so different. I longed for somebody who wanted the same things as me. I just wasn't sure I was ready for him to come yet. I knew my daughters liked not sharing me and I knew my time with them now is important and can never be relived. I also knew that if I didn't dedicate myself to my business it would fail and I would never find something else to do career wise that would make me happy.

So….I wanted to know that He was on his way and that He would be perfect for me but I wasn't ready for it to happen yet because of the business and the kids. So, when you think about it, our current situation is exactly what I asked the universe for, only better. Not only do I know you will be here, but you are here. You make me incredibly happy which I think makes me a better mother and businesswoman and since I don't have to waste my time dating and being on the internet I can devote even more time to my daughters and my business. The girls don't need a lot of time; they just need quality time. I should take them to the movies or out to dinner more. As long as they feel they are important to me (and they are) they shouldn't resent the time I will spend with you over the next few years. If time and money allow, it would be perfect if we could see each other at least once every 12 weeks. I can't imagine going longer than that. These next two times are shorter than that which is good. I think we really need that in the beginning. Maybe next year we can spend Christmas and New Years together. Next year is considered by some to be the new millennium anyway.

Anyway, reading over our email was interesting. I think the energy got stronger after we talked on the phone. I'm so glad we did that when we did or I could have lost you to Boston. Wow, that almost happened. I know a higher power was in control here, in spite of me and the difficult time I had around the eclipse. It's amazing you kept writing to me, especially since you had a stronger relationship with somebody else at that time. All I can say is Thank God!

Today was really lovely. I so enjoyed connecting with you in every way. I hope tomorrow is a nice day for you also. I'll be going to yoga, reading the Sunday paper and going through my piles of stuff. My back hurts right now so I'm going to do some yoga here. I walked twice around the neighborhood today. I would have walked further but it is cold!

I love you with all my heart and soul

Dianne

Togetherness

Darling warm Dianne

That was a lovely letter "the perfect soul mate", thank you so much. You make me feel so good to be just what you want. Like you, I have never been perfect before. It's a wonderful feeling, isn't it?

There's an old saying if you don't ask you don't get. So you asked, and have now got...and I asked and have now got... woooppeeee. There was always something warm and different about your letters, maybe the warm hugs, maybe the fact I could see areas of the universe in your spirituality that my friend Dorothy had awakened in me and were missing in everyone else's letters. They (well some of them anyway) met the words I had asked for but not the thoughts I asked for, which is why Denise made it so far down the tracks. The strange thing is that I was resistant to talking on the phone to women I hadn't met because I thought it may end up with long awkward silences and be off-putting. But Denise convinced me to do it and that showed me that we should be doing it. I do still feel very guilty for getting so far down the road with her and then abruptly ditching her, but it was the only option for me. I was so certain that you were the one for me – odd for a 3D man to have that knowledge already.

You are so right the time you spend with Nicki and Marley is critical, and so is telling them and showing them that you love them, equally, but differently from me. They are still too young to understand that your love will go in many directions simultaneously. Our distance apart physically will help them see you do love in both directions provided some of what we say is communicated to them. Please do understand that although I used to talk about your Dragons, I actually feel mentally close to Nicki, thanks to her hug, and will feel very happy the day I hear Marley's first loving words (just like a father with a baby). The loving words are not meant for me, but for you. That will be my acceptance into her world.

Next Christmas sounds great, and that gives me a year to get Vickie and Rachel to plan an early xmas with me. Good thinking my wonderful wife. Twelve weeks sounds a long time, but money doesn't grow on trees. If it did I would plant us an orchard. xxxx

We have been discussing the millennium at work, but nobody appears to have spotted the reason for the two dates. This year is 2000 years from his birth, and next year he would be 2000 years old. It's normal to celebrate Christmas as a celebration of his birth, so I don't quite see why next year is significant to people. But next Christmas and New Year we will be celebrating because we are us, because we will have been together for 18 months, and it is the end of our first whole year and because I love you now and forever.

My day is planned to be starting putting up the kitchen cupboards, which I will make a start on after my bath. I am concerned that Poppy will not like the drilling and sawing I will have to do. Still I will let you know how I get on.

Lots of love and hugs while you read the paper. Don't let my noise disturb your quiet time.

David

xxxxx

Re: Togetherness

Good morning my love

Your beautiful letter just made my morning! I'm thinking about going to church in Cassadaga this morning. Lou is giving the sermon and I really want to see him and Marie and my other friend Patti. I'd have to leave here at 9:30 but I am up early enough to do that. I'm going to get the paper, read just the comics and travel section (and the lottery numbers) while I drink my coffee. Then I'll take a shower and see what time it is and decide then. I'll write again either after going to Cassadaga or sooner if I decide not to go. Poppy will get over the noise of the kitchen work, but you do have to be careful with sawdust or other debris. Why don't you put her in the bathroom for a few hours? Have a wonderful day.

Your devoted lover

Dianne

p.s. – If the money is good enough on either of our ends I do want to see you more often than every 12 weeks. I just can't imagine going more than 12.

Re: Christmas together

Hello my love

Just a short message right now since I stopped at the office. I'll write more later tonight from home. I went to Cassadaga and it was wonderful. I'll tell you more tonight but both Lou and Marie confirmed who you are after looking at the picture. In fact Marie got major chills. I ordered an angel for you from them. I had a really nice time there. I enjoy that church. I hope you'll visit it with me on one of your trips here. I'm listening to a set of 8 CDs that belong to Terri on Financial Freedom. It is very good about the psychology and spirituality of money and what holds us back. I'm on the third one and already have some good insights to share with you tonight. I stopped at the office to pick up more envelopes that need to be stuffed. I figured that since I'm listening to these CDs, I might as well do some envelope stuffing at the same time. I bought myself some lunch/dinner from a barbeque place and I'm sitting at my desk at work now. I'll eat here. It's my holiday treat to myself! I love you so much and I'll write to you more tonight.

Your lover and soul mate

Dianne

Love and money

Dearest David

You must be having a busy day. I haven't heard from you since this morning. The kitchen cabinets must be nearly finished. Or maybe you took a nap and slept all the way through. Well, I had a grand day. I'm so glad I went to Cassadaga. I find a lot of inner peace there. Even though I'm not one for organized religion, spiritualism is right up my alley. Plus, my good friend Lou was giving the sermon and it was on love and commitment. They were selling the tape of the sermon and the healing meditation for only $5 so I bought it so I could send it to you. I was wishing you were there with me so this way you can experience it. When Lou looked at our picture he put on his glasses to see better and he said "very definitely a big connection here". He didn't use the word soul mate and I didn't ask. It was evident I wasn't looking for his approval, just sharing with a friend. I told him you had blue eyes and he just gave me a big smile. (I think he had told me before that my soul mate was likely to have blue eyes.) I told you his wife Marie got chills when she looked at us. That's a good thing in case you were wondering!

After the service they have a "message service" in the fellowship hall. There mediums and student mediums "come to people" in the room and give them a message from spirit. It lasts an hour. Everybody doesn't get a message. Well the hour only had 10 minutes left and the last reader was at the microphone. He said how many people didn't get a message yet? Me and about 20 others raised our hands. What he did was a one line mini for all of us. He said to have a question in our heads. At first my question in my head was "will David and I be together forever?" Then I thought that's a dumb question, I already know the answer to that. Plus, thoughts of Dreamtime were coming through my head. So my question became "What can I do to make Dreamtime successful?" When he came to me he said "She says you must stop being a pussy cat and become a lion." It was obvious it was Suzin he was connecting with as she always told me to stand up to Peter and the magazine. Great message isn't it! So that was a nice time.

In the 45 minute drive to and back from Cassadaga I was listening to the Financial Freedom CDs of Terri's I was telling you about. There are actually 9 of them and they are 1 hour long each. I was getting a lot out of them so I decided to stop by the office and pick up the rest of the envelopes and things that needed to be stuffed in them and some other busywork filing that I'd have to pay somebody to do and bought all this stuff home. Well, I have about one more hour worth of stuff I brought home but I'm really enjoying it because I'm listening to the CDs. I'm on the sixth one already.

One of the things it talked about in the beginning was our earliest memory of money. Mine is my grandfather controlling people with it. Another thing we were to get in touch with is a fear we have regarding money and to see if it is at all related to our earliest memory. Well, my fear is very much related to my earliest memory. I don't want anybody controlling me with money, but even more important than that I don't want to do what my grandfather did (and now my parents are doing). I don't want to control anybody with money. In listening to some of the things she was saying to other people (the tape is of a live seminar), I realized that I scare money away or sabotage it coming to me because I don't want the possibility to be there that I could control somebody with money; that trait runs so strongly in my family. Do you understand the great psychological depth of that issue for me? This is something I want to share with you because I think you can help me with it. Don't feel like writing a lot right now but I'll want to talk about this on the phone and in person. Think about your earliest memory and your fear so we can talk about that too. I don't want to be the only one we are analyzing.

Also, the seminar discusses a healthy relationship and respect for money. The fact that I have a little wallet and my money is in little balls, not organized and not facing in the same direction shows a disrespect for money. Money is an energy and it can be attracted to you or you can repel it. Some of my actions do repel it. I want to be more aware of that. Also, knowing that we are worthy of receiving is very important. We are both good people and we are doing God's work. We are very worthy of receiving it. Just because we've received each other and are very grateful for that doesn't mean we should consider ourselves greedy if we also want money. Let's be careful of that or we will repel it. It was suggested to create an affirmation that assumes what you want has already happened. Then the universe can get to work manifesting it. Mine is "I am creative, powerful and successful and Dreamtime is making in excess of $20,000 a month every month". Why is that so different than "My perfect soul mate is here", even though you are really 4,000 miles away. What is so different? You really are here and so is our prosperity. You make one of those affirmations too, okay. We deserve a really good life and money is an energy that will help us get it. And we will do a lot of good things for people. That's just the kind of people who we are. What do you think of all this? I'm eager to listen to CD number 6, so I'll close here and really look forward to talking to you tomorrow after your walk. Remember, I'll be at the office until 6:30 when I'll leave for yoga. Have a wonderful walk. I hope the weather favors it. I love you so much and it is wonderful to have you to share all of my thoughts with.

Your happy goddess
Dianne

Until tonight my Angel
Dearest Dianne

Thank you for yesterday's mail. It makes me so proud of you. I am so sorry I didn't write last night, but I was very tired, not feeling too well and very depressed. Not a good combination for letter writing to the standard we have achieved; please forgive me my angel.

As for money, my earliest recollections are of being given coins by Mum and Dad's friends as little gifts. My biggest fear is of it running out completely (running very low I know I can deal with, and have had to so often in the 24 years of marriage including 15 years of the business). My aspiration is, as you already know, to sell the business in the future with sufficient funds to be financially secure and allow the freedom to be creative.

It sounds like you had a really spiritual day, full of positive energy. I wish I had been there with you to share it.

The cupboards are now ready to put up, but although I did have the strength to lift the large cupboard above my head, I couldn't control the positioning and need someone's help, so it is sitting in my kitchen. The whole place is such a mess, tools, cupboards, errrr.

Sorry that this is going to be short, but I still feel low and need to get myself ready to pick up Doug and Eileen. This low feeling has not been helped by Poppy waking me at 4.00 and not sleeping on the bed like I told her, but play-fighting me, biting my hands and boxing my face with her paws until I told her to get off. Then she ran around the floor, clawing everything, moving my shoes, until 5 minutes before I was due to get up. Then she comes and purrs (like you) and cuddles in close. I would so much rather it were you (the cuddles not the clawing of the carpet, etc).

Looking forward to hearing your lovely voice this evening at work.

Re: Until tonight my Angel

My wonderful husband

I do recall you telling me that you want to be part of all my moods both positive and negative and to never hold anything back from you. Why should that be any different from what I would want for you? Remember you are half American now so stiff upper lip will not be tolerated. My desire for our relationship is total communication. It scares me because of my past history when a man gets quiet on me. Please don't do that to me. Also, don't worry about wanting to see me in a different hairstyle. I want to see you in some different clothes. Your pants are too big and it hides your cute tushy. That doesn't mean at all that we are trying to change each other, at least not in my way of looking at it. However, if your list is actually longer than that then we need to talk!

It also scared me that you didn't sign your letter. It just sort of ended. Honestly, before getting your email my mind went to fear. I thought that you had fallen asleep in a nap without your breathing machine and you had died! Either that or you had gotten electrocuted drilling your cabinets. Please don't scare me like that. Even if all you write is I'm feeling down and not up to a long letter, please understand, that would have been better. Sorry, I don't mean to jump on you but you really scared me. The good thing about this is confirmation that my intuition is good and I am very connected to you because I knew you weren't feeling 100%. I'm looking forward to talking with you today. Hopefully the walk has cleared the fog from your body/mind/spirit. But you know what? It's okay to be down. Please let me see all of you.

Second topic. I'm excited about these financial tapes. They are psychological and spiritual and I'm finding them meaningful. In fact, I'm going to buy them myself as I'd like to be able to listen again and have you listen. It would be nice if we were on the same page related to the issue of money. If needed, I can help you with your affirmation based on what I have already learned in the tape. Besides making it in the present tense, it must also be short and "sufficient" is a limiting word. How does this feel? "I have sold my business in the UK for a good price allowing financial freedom and creativity in the US." You can change the words to feel better for you but something like that. Also, I want you to know that you are not your money. You are you and I love you whether you have 2 cents or 2 million.

Back to work for me. Talk to you soon.
Your soul mate who adores you
Dianne

You are so wonderful
My wonderful wife

Talking to you has improved how I feel immensely. It has not removed my logical problem, nor could you because it is mine to resolve, but you untied my spirit to allow it to fight back. I felt spirit had gone when logic had arrived. You really help me, but one day I will not need that, it's just so new to me, I will need you so we can go to new heights together. xxxxxx

Your fears keep coming true; I keep falling asleep on the settee, either reading or watching TV (yes watching TV). I was too tired to do anything and after talking to you it was too early for bed I thought – but I was wrong, I should have done so.

I will be going to work for the afternoon tomorrow, when I hope to clear the decks a little ready for a new start on the 4th of January 2000. It sure seems odd writing that! I have also got work to do on the fish tank at the office that has been badly neglected – not completely but badly since Scott died. We used to do it together. Shirley thinks I should abandon it, but I just need to get my head around it and there is so much to do to it!

I love you so much. Good night my wonderful wife.

David, lover of Dianne in all her many forms

xxxxxxxxxxxxxxxxxxxxxxxxxxxxxxxxxxxxxxxxx

Re: You are so wonderful

My wonderful husband

I could not be such a wonderful wife if you were not such a special husband. It's an equal exchange of energy. I brought home my Celestine Prophecy book so I could review it and follow along with you. There's a lot in it about exchange of energy and there is also a lot about control dramas dating back from the first ones we saw which was our parents interacting. I'm going to re-read this stuff. I remember getting a lot out of it. One thing the book says towards the end is first that we can clear our old repeated dramas and find our true selves. Secondly, we can set in motion the evolution of these true selves through question, intuition of what to do, and answer. Staying in this magic flow is the true secret of happiness. I do try to do that and so I seldom engage my logical side anymore. I try to live in intuition, magic and mystery and I try not to question miracles when they appear. Notice I say try. I'm not telling you I'm there yet. I'm just a little bit ahead of you, just like you are little bit ahead of me in business. We are so good for each other. I like that I can help you with this, although I do realize that you need to do the real work yourself. I can give you bits of insights, recommend good books and tapes and listen to you with my heart. But you are the one who has to integrate all of this so deeply into a cellular level of your body mind and spirit/ soul that a strong sense of inner peace surrounds you.

As much as I believe in miracles, intuition and magic, I'm as taken with what is going on with us as you are. It happened very quickly. I agree that it definitely defies logic. I don't like logic like you do though so that's okay with me. You don't have to believe everything I do, you know. You will create your own unique belief system once you have sorted through all of this a little more. Your path and mine may not be identical although it certainly appears that we are merging and becoming one. I want to support you to be all that you can be and that certainly permits you to disagree with me. I know, you think I'm perfect and you aren't sure you deserve such a perfect wife.

Let me relate that to the $20,000 I got from Merrifran. I think I told you the story of how I tried to talk her out of it. I didn't think I was worthy of receiving it. I'm a much better giver than I am receiver – so are you. But many people whose advice I value who are further along a spiritual path than I am said to me "until you learn to receive, you will block the universal energy flow that is supposed to come to you with love, money, happiness, etc." So that was a big step for me and I learned to receive. I'd have to look in my checkbook and see when that was. I believe it was the beginning of August. Then the eclipse came and I had what I told you that you may be having, a healing crisis and I really went within. When I emerged from it you were there. Had I not received from Merrifran you might be with Denise right now; it's possible.

I am worthy of somebody saving my business by giving me $20,000 without any expectation of being paid back. I am worthy of finding the most wonderful man in the universe and accepting his love. You are worthy of the love of me, a goddess. Accept it in faith and with an open heart and the money will flow into your business. That's how energy works. Also, be grateful, the universe appreciates being appreciated.

Do you enjoy doing the fish tank or did you enjoy doing it with Scott? I'm sure it produces a major memory but it isn't Scott and Scott wouldn't mind if you abandoned it if that is what you choose to do. You need to do anything you can to nurture yourself and simplify your life. If the fish tank adds meaning to your life then by all means keep it. If it provides a good way to think about Scott then keep it. If you just aren't sure how you feel then keep it up for awhile. Just try to shift your mind a little out of logic and operate out of your heart and your true sense of what is right for you. That is what you did when you chose me. You can do that more often now that you know how. I know you'll be thinking of Scott when you walk on New Year's day. I feel you are missing him a lot right now in this holiday season. The only person who can come close to you in missing him is his mother and she isn't somebody you can reach out to. I'm here for you to reach out to me. I want to tell Scott how happy we are and thank him for his role in bringing us together. I want to tell him how much I love his wonderful father. I want to tell him how I wish I were meeting him next month. I feel he would like me. It's times like this I wish I had developed my psychic abilities better. All I can do is imagine I am communicating with him. In the dimension that he is in (that all of us are in) that may be all it takes.

I'm going to close here since this is very long and I fear AOL will take it from me at any moment now. Plus I have some work to do before leaving for the airport to get Terri.
Sleep well my love. You can relax now....I am really here.
Dianne, Queen/Goddess of King David

Re: You are so wonderful

To my wonderful wife

I was too tired to read last night so you need not race away and get too far with the book. Remember I said I read very little, mainly due to tiredness and lifestyle.

I will find it very difficult (not impossible) to let go of my logical side. My intuition had not always been as good as it was in choosing you, but I will aim for it. Business is generally run on the left side of the brain, with the exception of ideas which can cross over to play with non-spiritual people – you need your intuition to guide you and the logic to play them at their game (just like chess). Between us we can develop this properly, as we have both of these sides. I long for your assistance with the spiritual side of my life. It is an area I long to be deeper into and you are my idea teacher.

I actually want the fish tank for me, at least until I get the one for here set up in the bedroom. It's working on the tank that Scott and I did together, buying fish, etc. But it's the work I find hardest to do, and I am not sure really whether that is Scott related or just being "too busy" with other priorities. If you had those psychic abilities I am not sure whether to disturb Scott or leave him in peace. Just thinking about it makes a lump come to my throat, but maybe it's because your letter did that when I read it. I love you so much.

I am getting quite cool sitting here in my wet towels. I will look forward to reading and writing again at bed time. I love you and miss you xxxx

Your King and lover now and always

David

xxxxx

Wow! Flowers!!

Darling David

I got to the office at 9:45 (a little late since I didn't get home from the airport until 1:30am) and Federal Express was delivering something here. Wow, It was for me and it was from you and it was beautiful long stem roses. That was such a wonderful surprise. You are the most wonderful soul mate lover husband in the world and I am so lucky. Thank you so much! It would be nice if you got my gift today too. I have never had a romantic husband before. You are so incredible! I love you!

So much to say but I do have to get to work. I'll write again later this afternoon.

Your lover forever

Dianne

You make my day

Dear wonderful David

You make my day when you call. You are so wonderful to me. I can't wait to go home and tend my roses. I'm writing to you from the office because as soon as I go home I have to pick up Nicki and Marley at Stan's house and then I'll have to fight them for the computer and then Teri will be home. Plus I really should go food shopping tonight.

Just a few more thoughts on intuition vs logic. At least in this country they are teaching some very spiritual concepts in the business world these days. Spirit in business and intuition in business are real buzzwords here. Did you ever look at those papers you brought home with you that were ideas I had for a brochure? The brochure that would be used for getting corporate seminar at sea business has lots of those things listed. For instance, don't you think you could "play chess" better when selling if you could intuit what your customer is thinking or feeling? Even corporate souls are being fed these days and people want to "feel" good, not think good. It's actually a very handy device.

You'll read about the old paradigm control dramas in Celestine Prophecy. This new way of being is a different way of interacting where energy flows and is shared in a win-win for everybody. I don't like to think of anybody as a non-spiritual person. Some people just don't know they are spiritual beings but we all are. To further my cause, all great ideas, artwork, music, inventions, etc come from the right side of the brain. That's where inspiration originates. I'd also like to say that I don't think you used intuition when you chose Chris. I think that was more a logical practical decision. Just some thoughts...not well written and in a bit of a rush right now since I told the girls I'd pick them up at 6:00.

Be good to yourself and go to bed early. That is what your body wants right now. Go to bed at 9:00 and I'll bet you'll sleep through the night.

Thank you again for the roses. They are beautiful and you are wonderful!

Your soul mate and lover forever
Dianne

Busy day

Hi honey

I have been talking to Vickie, and we have agreed Sunday the 30th of January at a place called the Parsonage for her birthday meal. It's a very old building, as old as America. The food is consistently good and you will love it.

Why didn't Mike get his car? It appeared a certainty, and I was looking forward to seeing the Impala or whatever it was called. Was it too rare to find? Or did he get found out doing what his father was so convinced he would do?

I am very pleased that you have been active in selling. You will definitely do much better as an organisation with you talking to the customers.

Vickie is due to stay until the 31st when she goes back to work. The hospital forecast a busy time from then onwards, and she is on nights. She does like the extra money (who wouldn't), but I couldn't imagine staying awake all night.

Bad news today – my aunty with cancer (another of Mum's sisters) died today. She is the one who gave mum and I a home when my father ran off with another woman when I was a baby. I only found out because dad wanted Aunty Margaret's phone number. I don't think he would have rung me to tell me otherwise. It's odd though; although I liked her, I do not feel upset by the news. I asked how mum was and dad couldn't answer; he didn't know. That's what I dislike about him, his lack of care for her. She has just lost her older sister who cared for her, and he doesn't know how she feels.

I do think you will be wonderful curled up in my bed. This morning I had Poppy sitting on my head purring very loudly in my ear, which was just about okay until she started to slide off and used her claws on my neck to assist her stability. I need you to protect me from these wild animals at night please. xxxxx

Tomorrow is the girls' Christmas and Rachel has said she will join us between 3 and 6 – she is so helpful on timing. Generally she is late so Vickie forecasts 7.00.

My bed it too cold without you. Less than four weeks now and you will be here. I love you so much.

Over and out for tonight my angel.

Your king and lover of all of you

David of Florsex

xxxxxxxxxxxxxx

My car got "slightly hit"

Hi sweetheart

Well, I got a phone call from Mike from the car saying it got slightly hit. I'll see when they pick me up how slightly it is. They are fine and that's the most important thing and he said he'd pay for the damage but it's frustrating. My next door neighbor will do it for me again cheaply I'm sure but this will leave me without my car for a few days. I guess I shouldn't loan out my car. I'll be really glad when Marley has her own car. I hope your busy day is going well. Mine is, I'm getting a lot done here in the office. I love you.

Your goddess

Dianne

Re: My car got "slightly hit"

Hi Goddess

I am sorry to hear about the car but delighted no one was hurt. You are right about lending it though, and I would never have mentioned it unless you did. I hope the damage was small to insignificant. Don't let it spoil your run of successful energy.

I love you – take good care of yourself.

Your loving husband David of Florsex

xxxxxxxxxxxxxxxxxxxxxxxxxxxxxxxxxxxxxx

Good night my love

My wonderful husband

I won't expect much email from you since you now have Vickie for a couple of days. Enjoy her and Rachel when she arrives. You are so funny the way you describe Poppy clawing your neck. My poor baby!

You could have expressed your opinion to me that I shouldn't loan my car to Mike. I wouldn't have taken it as bossy or poorly. You can always express your opinion to me.

I didn't answer your question about why didn't Mike get his car. I don't know, but I think it was never a sure thing. Probably his father didn't have that much money to spend for Christmas. I don't think he did anything wrong, but what do I know?

I also got so caught up regarding the car that I forgot to respond about your aunty. I feel bad for your mother who must need somebody to understand how she feels. That's so sad that your dad doesn't give her that. I feel bad for her. Don't you think that it is doubtful she'll leave him at this age though?

I almost forgot to tell you, the flowers look beautiful! That was so nice of you to send them to me. I'm going to buy more flower food so they will live a long time.

Now I'm really signing off for the evening.

Goodnight David, King of my Soul, I adore you.

Dianne

Good morning soul mate

To the most wonderful wife a king could ever have – you xxxxx

I wasn't expecting any mail this morning that was so lovely. Those sound great roses. It's rare to get ones with scent, as they are usually force grown and also don't last long – this is just the magic of the internet again!

Regarding mum, I had explained previously that dad wouldn't show her any kind of love or affection and that goes for care too; it's so sad. But it is down to her to do something. I will support her, but do believe I shouldn't lead her until she actually says that is truly what she wants.

Since Vickie has been home Poppy has kept all of her play-fights for her. Currently she is curled up asleep on my lap on the towel. She is fascinated by the bath and the scented aromatherapy water.

Today is making the Christmas work day while Vickie is visiting her friend Tina. I still have yesterday's jobs to do. Maybe if I am lucky I'll get the time. I have to prepare the meal, put up the tree, clear more of the spare room so Rachel can sleep tonight, and all before 3:00 or 6:00. You haven't seen the spare room (junk room). I have already collected loads of cardboard boxes to burn and they are in the summer house in the garden.

Do have another wonderful day at work. I am so proud of you. You are my favourite travel agent. I will only travel with you, both physically and spiritually. You are my angel.

Latest news – George Harrison and his wife have been stabbed – but neither of them appear badly hurt. Plus there are small stories of Millennium bug problems over here already, but have no fear; I am a man of steel (so far).

Lots of love

David, soul mate, lover and biggest admirer of the Goddess Dianne

Re: Good morning soul mate

Good morning my love

Mike's father found out that Mike and Marley went to Universal Studios yesterday and he has grounded Mike from seeing Marley. He yelled at me on the phone and I could barely get a word in edgewise to defend myself and them. I feel they are basically very good kids. I don't know where my powerful businesswoman persona was. She was obviously hiding from this mean man. Talk about a man using his power to intimidate a woman. This interaction brought womankind back to the 50s! I feel awful that I didn't defend myself. He had no business talking to me like that.

I went right to Marley's room to warn her of what happened. She was on the phone with Mike and his father walked in and demanded that he hang up. I had a nice talk with Marley. She understood that there was nothing I could do and I did my best to protect Mike. If he knew Mike also got hundreds of dollars of damage on my car he probably would have felt like killing him (and me as well)!

I went to bed at 10:30 completely mentally exhausted from Mike, Marley and Mike's dad. Then Marley came bouncing into my room to tell me that Dave is on his way over. Dave is a boy she liked before Mike. I liked him too. He's like a reincarnated hippy (doesn't do drugs though). He's just very much like we were 30 years ago. He likes the Beatles, Moody Blues, Peter Paul and Mary, etc. He plays the guitar and sings our kind of stuff. How could I not like him? He's 18 and a senior and has a car. She remained friends but didn't see him during this three or four months she's been with Mike. All of a sudden Dave is on his way over! I said "what about Mike?" She said that she and Dave are just friends. Okay, I told her to give Dave my love and I wasn't getting up because I'm too tired and to please lock the door when he leaves. I can tell that if Mike is grounded long term, Marley will be seeing Dave. She sure isn't very loyal! I do like Dave much better though. When she came into my room to tell me about Dave she gave me a nice kiss on my forehead. That was really special.

The other thing that happened last night is Nicki had her friend Sara spend the night and they went outside for "a little while" at 8:30. Well at 9:45 I had to go outside looking for them. They were on the corner talking to two boys. You know I'm a cool mom but these next few years are not going to be all that easy being a single mom with two teenage girls. The fact that I am cool is a bit dangerous. I don't want to be overprotective since my parents were that way with me and it was awful. Still I can see that my permissiveness can get all of us in lots of trouble. I need your advice here.

I agree you shouldn't lead your mother in any direction. You are a lot younger than her and definitely should have left your situation. Sometimes older people can't change and trying only makes them unhappier. However, maybe I'll feel stronger that she should leave after I meet both of them.

Poppy sounds cute on your lap, but that is my spot so I'm a bit jealous. I guess I can share you with a cat though. I can't believe you are putting up a tree 5 days after Christmas. You are just like me, unique and a rebel! What is the summer house? You didn't tell me you have two castles, or is that a British word for an outdoor tool shed or something? I have so much to learn.

I don't see how you can accomplish what you said by 3:00. I don't expect you to write until it's all over. My thoughts are with you and I wish I were there too. Enjoy your December 30th Christmas with both of your girls. I'm only working in the afternoon today. Janet has the morning. I'm taking Marley and Nicki to a waxing appointment at 10:00. Then we are meeting my parents for lunch at The Olive Garden (an Italian restaurant) for our New Year's dinner. Then my parents will take the girls back to Stan's house and I'll go to work. I won't be making any more follow up calls today; it's too close to a holiday. I have plenty to do, though, and I may go to yoga tonight.

That's terrible about George Harrison and his wife! I pray the world doesn't go crazy. Well, by this time in two days at least we'll know what has happened. It's the not knowing what to expect that is nerve racking. I never watch TV but I am going to watch it pretty much all day and all night tomorrow. It should be quite interesting. I pray we still have a 3rd dimensional world for us to make love in. Hopefully in this millennium the world will get its collective act together and we can have the spiritual heaven on earth that some of us do know is possible. If the world should end, I know I'll find you on the other side and we can continue our soul mate journey there. I love you sweetheart, always have and always will.

Gotta run, looking forward to hearing from you much later tonight. I know you'll have the girls so don't write a lot; be with them. I'll tell my parents you said Happy New Year. Did I tell you they asked if the storms in Europe affected you? I told them about your high tides and big waves.

Your meek (today) goddess
Dianne

*   *   *   *

Rather than write back to this email David called me and we had a good talk about these issues in my life. He made me feel both loved and powerful and told me what a good mother I am and I'm actually overprotective by British standards where kids grow up at a much younger age.

*   *   *   *

I love you – now and always
My dearest Goddess

Well it is peaceful and quiet in the castle now; all three of them have gone home. The first cupboard has now got a shelf and two doors, is sealed into the plaster work and only needs cleaning prior to using.

319

I am in the process of trying to remove the creases from the Gilley shirt that I wear with my kilt that I will be walking in tomorrow. It is cotton and had the new fold marks from being new, so I washed it and the result was not to lose the few creases it had but to create a thousand new ones. I hate ironing and this is the most difficult shirt because of its linen-type appearance and the style is puffy sleeves and so has lots of intended creases to keep and others to lose.

Additionally, I said I would pick Rachel up and drive her to a party at 9:00, and Doug and Eileen asked me to go over for a drink. I told them it has to be a small one and they know why. So I will ring you when I return from Doug and Eileen's, hopefully no later than 11.00.

I am glad to see that you have switched off for the day. You need that type of rest too. It will be wonderful to be together, where I can look after you on one of those types of days, so you can just rest, and have drinks, food and whatever your heart desires delivered to you by your adoring husband. xxxx

Must get back to my ironing, and get my bath etc, or I will be late ringing my soul mate and that will not do.

Lots of love and warm hugs for my wonderful wife
From her loving husband
David
xxxxx

My wonderful King

I'm glad to hear there is peace in our castle. There is peace in our castle on this side of the pond as well. Nicki called three times whining that she wants to go to Jackie's house and nobody there will take her and won't I come pick her up. I warned her from the beginning of the week that Friday was my day all day for peace and quiet and not leaving the house. I would not give in to her. My parents stopped by because my mother wanted to do the little princess (Nicki) a favor and put away all her clothes that were in the dryer. (Nicki and Marley do their own laundry, I don't do it). My parents were very nice. My father showed me how to program the new satellite TV for my 30 favorites. I put BBC on there as one of them. I watched it for some time today and it was nice to get the British perspective. They had something cool regarding the Age of Aquarius. Did you see it? My mother said to tell you that she watched something on the travel channel about Scotland. She said she wants to learn all about her son in law. I thought you would like that. They both said Happy New Year to you.

Sorry I couldn't help you iron your shirt even if I were there. I'd probably make it worse. I'm not an iron goddess. You will look wonderful tomorrow even if there are a few creases. Maybe Eileen can help you if it's really bad. Enjoy your drink with them and tell them I can't wait to meet them and Happy New Year from me.

I am trying to switch off for the day but have to monitor the messages at the office and there have been 13, including two calls I do have to return.

It will be wonderful to be together on a lazy day like today. I'm eagerly awaiting that. I'm already glued to the TV and it is very awe inspiring. I watched on CNN the fireworks display in Sidney Harbour. It is now half past midnight there and so far no Y2K glitches. Y2K headquarters in Washington DC said no news is good news but they knew that Australia and New Zealand were prepared so they weren't expecting anything from there. I'm all showered and in my comfy clothes (no bra) and I'm going to read and watch TV all day. I adore you and I'm so happy that you are the love of my lives and I have found you. I thank God for you every day. Have a wonderful day. I'll let you call me before it is midnight there since I called you on Christmas but if I don't hear from you I'll assume you are having a hard time getting through and I'll call you.

Your soul mate for eternity. Dianne

*   *   *   *

We had a wonderful phone conversation and toasted in the New Year together at midnight his time, 7:00pm my time.

*   *   *   *

Love from the 20th century

Hello my love

I know I said I wasn't going to write again tonight. I just couldn't resist sending a love message from the 20th century into the 21st century. You represent my future and this is certainly a metaphor for it. I just spoke with my mother. She called and said "Can't you and David get married sooner? I want to be alive for your wedding." I told her we wouldn't wait any longer than we had to and that we'd know when the time is absolutely right. I told her you were happy that she watched a show about Scotland. Such an interesting energy is taking place here. Our enchantment is melting ice. Hopefully the power of love will move things along quickly for your business as well. I really do long to be with you. It seems much longer than 3 ½ weeks since we were together.

I'm going back to the TV now for the rest of the 20th century here. Nobody has ever captivated my body mind and spirit soul like you have David. I love you no matter the millennium, the country, the planet, the time or the space. You and I were created from another dimension. This is the most powerful feeling in the universe.

Your loving wife, soul mate and lover

Dianne

Joining you in the 21st century

Good morning my love

I'm very tired and going to bed. This is just a test to see if your computer says 1/1/2000. All is well with the world. No Y2K problems and no terrorism. We created a great world for our Millennium. I love you!

Your goddess

Dianne

*   *   *   *

Although we don't know what challenges lay ahead for us both individually and as a couple, we feel very much a couple although 4000 miles apart. We are both looking optimistically at both the present and the future. It is only 6 months since our first email and we know each other as well as we know ourselves (or better!) and love each other very deeply. Some will still say that we've only been together once and it was a holiday romance and we might not feel the same with day-to-day living but we know from a very deep level of intuition that we will feel the same and that no two people could be better for each other than we are. I'm afraid you'll have to read Book Two to see what happens next. For now Happy New Year from the 20th Century to the 21st and my Prince who happens to be a King truly has .com!

*   *   *   *

5th Wedding anniversary at Amberley Castle

Conclusion

I've heard it said that our daughters are our karma. I must have very good karma as I received the letter below by email after sending my younger daughter Nicki (seventeen years old at the time, now twenty-three), the introduction and first two chapters of this book. She's always been there for me but what she's written here means that I really have made a difference in her life. Wow! Sometimes it is so hard for me to accept that. I've had a life full of lessons and I've had so many people come into my life, many on a very deep soul level. Nicki is truly a soul mate of mine as we really do support each other and are there unconditionally for each other.

My older daughter Marley (nineteen years old at the time I started writing this, now twenty-five) is a soul mate of mine too though. Her comment when I sent her the beginning of the book was "I wouldn't buy it". Marley and I are opposites in a lot of ways, but very much the same in others; in fact she has been one of my biggest mirrors. I released her to be who she is at a very young age (I had no choice, she'd do it anyway). Marley has kept me on my toes, shown me my shadow side and has been a fun player in this game of life. I admire her audacity and her power.

In conclusion, I must have done something right. I have two wonderful daughters, and the most incredible husband in the universe. The next book, which will hopefully be written a bit quicker than this one was, will take you through the time until I made the move to England, and my feelings and choices. It will also be about life as an American in England and the unique set of challenges that poses. You won't be surprised to read that the marriage is everything we both thought it would be. You may be surprised at where we have chosen to retire. A hint, it isn't the UK or the US. After all we are rebels! We are looking forward to being ex-pats together in our new chosen country.

I am also very happy to report in 2009 that my relationship with my parents has completely transformed. The truth is, in calling them judgmental, I was judging them, therefore I was judgmental! We still have different philosophies of life. They think that when they die it is all over. I told them I expect to talk to them through mediums and that I expect them to admit that I was right! So, we agree to disagree about some things but there is real love there. I know the love was always there from all three of us; we are all quite stubborn. Getting older also gives me a whole new compassion for them. One day I know there will be a last time I will see them in this life and I will miss them terribly when they are gone. They have been a constant in my life and there is no replacing them. So when they read this book and see themselves described as challenges, I ask that they please come back to this page and see my love.

Letter from Nicki:
Mom

I just wanted to take some time and let you know how much I love you! I think the beginning of your book is great and that it will be an amazing book. I think you should put your heart into it and let your mind speak what feels right. Let people know who you are and the things you have experienced.

I want you to know that I look up to you. You have taught me so much and I have listened to the things you have told me since I was little. You have not only been who you are and lived your life with everything you have, but you have taught me to do the same. You have taught me to love unconditionally, to forgive, to trust, and to experience. I don't look at people's flaws; I look at the best in them and what really matters. I think of myself as a little you, and that makes me proud. You have given me strength to take risks, to love and not be scared to lose, to know that there is more to life than money and power, and that there will be hard times but that's what life is about. It's about learning and growing. You have grown and you have learned and you have made mistakes as we all do. But you don't let them hold you back, you keep living and you keep learning through it all.

I look up to you Mom. You are a perfect person in my eyes. You love with your heart and nothing will hold you back. God puts obstacles in our way, but you jump over them. You have let me live my life and make my own decisions. I thank you for that, and I thank you that you are always there for me to see the affects of my decisions, whether good or bad. You give me your advice but don't force your opinion on me. When you moved to England you told me, "My love for you is unshakable, undeniable, and unending - in every circumstance." I want you to know that I feel the same. You inspire me Mom, and I hope I inspire you too! You are my mother, the one who brought me into this world, my role model, and more importantly, my best friend! You don't judge me because of who I love. You accept him and love him too. You know when I'm happy and you know when something's wrong. You are everything I want to be as a mother.

I just wanted to take a few moments from my day to let you know that! I love you and I think you are amazing. Tell the world your story, and tell it with pride. Don't give up!
I love you forever!
Your Little Girl
Nicki
XOXOXO
Now go wipe your eyes because I'm sure you are crying by now, print this up, hang it up, and follow your dreams!

Dianne and David Purdie – cruising on the Sapphire Princess
2009

In *Some Day My Prince Will .com*, Dianne Purdie has written her true story of "kissing a lot of frogs" before finding her prince. After two failed marriages and with young children, Dianne enters the arena of internet dating where she begins writing to a man by the name of David in England. E-mail communication gives the opportunity for deep discussions about metaphysical concepts as well as sharing the humdrum activities of life with someone who listens and cares. Readers will discover the blatant honesty that both Dianne and David express before they meet.... preparing the way for truth that few couples attain. A delightful and magical story.

Janet Cunningham, Ph.D., internationally-known specialist in regression therapy and author of 10 books, including *Caution: Soul Mate Ahead!* and *The Upward Spiral: Breakthroughs to Joy* www.JanetCunningham.com and www.HeritageAuthors.com

About the Author

Although Dianne has a psychology degree, she was destined to be more a rebel and trendsetter. She is a builder of dreams and hope. In her former business Dreamtime Cruises & Tours and now in her book she offers inspiration to change, grow, love and live with passion.

"Of all the achievements I have had in my life, I have to say that succeeding in a loving relationship is the biggest one. I wish this success for everybody. If I can do it so can you!"

Cover artwork "The Enchanted Frog" by Jaimé Christina Wren